Untold

ALSO BY SHANNON RICHARD

Undone
Undeniable
Unstoppable
Unforgettable
Undressed
Unsung
Uncontrollable

Untold

SHANNON RICHARD

New York   Boston

Copyright © 2017 by Shannon Richard
Excerpt from *Undone* copyright © 2013 by Shannon Richard
Cover design by Elizabeth Turner
Cover photograph by Katie Lamb
Cover copyright © 2017 by Hachette Book Group, Inc.

Forever Yours
Hachette Book Group
1290 Avenue of the Americas
New York, NY 10104
forever-romance.com
twitter.com/foreverromance

First published as an ebook and print on demand edition: September 2017

Forever Yours is an imprint of Grand Central Publishing. The Forever Yours name and logo are trademarks of Hachette Book Group, Inc.

The publisher is not responsible for websites (or their content) that are not owned by the publisher.

The Hachette Speakers Bureau provides a wide range of authors for speaking events. To find out more, go to www.hachettespeakersbureau.com or call (866) 376-6591.

ISBNs: 978-1-4555-6509-2 (ebook), 978-1-4555-6512-2 (print on demand)

To Nikki Rushbrook
What you've done for this series
goes above and beyond.
I'd even go so far as to say you know these books
second only to me.
You are an invaluable reader,
brainstormer, and friend.
Also, thank you for bringing Julie Garwood,
and a love of historicals, into my life.
You've been a saving grace to me in so many ways.

Untold

Chapter One

A Girl Walks into a Bar

Bethelda Grimshaw was dead.

And there was no one to mourn her. She was the only child of only children. She'd never married. She'd never had kids. She didn't have friends.

She was survived by her cat.

The woman wasn't exactly what anyone in Mirabelle, Florida, would call well liked…or liked at all, really. She was more like a vulture, quick to swoop in and pick at someone's misfortune. In life she thrived on causing misery to anyone and everyone.

So no, she wasn't missed in death. Not even the least little bit.

The thing was, no one really knew *why* Bethelda was the way she was. She hadn't always been a horrible human being, but somewhere in those forty-seven years of her life, things had changed.

At one point she'd been a writer for the town newspaper. She mostly did local interest pieces, her stories focusing on the people of Mirabelle. They had the tendency to lean a little on the gossipy side, and when they turned downright defamatory, she'd been fired. It was only a few years later that she found another outlet to spew her hatred.

The Grim Truth was Bethelda's blog, and it had been around for about a decade now. No one would outright admit to reading it, yet everyone knew when a new story was up. One of those small-town mysteries. She changed the names of the people in her posts, giving them a new moniker that was insulting more times than not. It was always clear who she was dragging through the mud. There was never any doubt.

The night before Bethelda's funeral, there was some sort of weird memorial service going on at the Sleepy Sheep. It was Mirabelle's most popular watering hole, a bar built by Owen Shepherd just after World War II. The building had survived many a hurricane and a number of bar fights, but for the most part it wasn't a rowdy place.

The inside and outside were made of the same darkly stained mahogany, the rich brown walls giving off that Scottish pub feel. Well, what parts of the wall that could be seen. Some of the space was taken up with cartoons of sleeping sheep, and there were signed dollar bills attached to the walls and ceiling.

Over a dozen tables were scattered around the floor with chairs surrounding them, while booths lined much of the walls. Over the years there had been a number of additions to the place: pool tables, a dartboard, a jukebox, and a stage in the far corner where live bands would sometimes play. And those weren't the only things that had been added on. A couple of years back a small—but exceptionally efficient—brewery had been built.

The founder might have passed away over five years ago, but the business was still in the family and going strong. There was usually some member of the Shepherd family working behind the counter and serving up alcohol to everyone who wanted a drink. That night it was both of Owen's grandsons: Nathanial "Shep" Shepherd and Finn Shepherd.

It was clear they were brothers, with just a few variations here and there. They had the same wavy black hair, though Finn's was cut just a little bit shorter than Shep's. There was a slight gap in their heights, Finn standing at about six-feet-two to Shep's six-feet-three. The younger Shepherd made up for that inch by being just a tad bit more muscular. The biggest differences in their appearance were that Shep's arms were covered in tattoos and Finn was sporting a pair of black-framed glasses. But behind those lenses were the same startlingly blue eyes as his brother's.

And their eyes paired with those sexy smiles? Well, the Shepherd boys were a force to be reckoned with for sure. Though only one of them was still using his good looks and easygoing nature to charm the female patrons. Shep was a happily married man now. He and his wife, Hannah, had a fifteen-month-old son, Nathanial Owen Shepherd III, otherwise known as baby Nate or Nate junior.

Finn on the other hand? Well, he wasn't settling down anytime soon. Or ever. He had absolutely no interest in that path. None at all.

That hadn't always been the case, but after one particular woman had taken his heart and shoved it through a meat grinder, he was better off alone. Though that didn't mean he didn't enjoy the company of a lady here or there.

But Finn had a strict set of rules that he never broke: no locals, no staying the night, and no repeats.

Mirabelle wasn't the biggest of towns, either in population or size. It could be a bit jarring to run into someone he'd walked out on in the middle of the night. So nonlocals it was, and there were plenty.

The summer was the busiest season for tourists, but even in the winter people were still coming and going. The water was that stunning emerald green year-round, and a room right on the beach always offered a good getaway.

Though on that particular evening, Finn wasn't focused on finding someone to let him into her bed. He was too distracted by what was going on at the bar.

It wasn't a wake for Bethelda so much as a roast. If there was a mean thing to be said about the woman, someone said it.

"Good riddance," Cynthia Bowers hiccupped as she took a sip of her whiskey sour. "That *horrible* woman was full of hate."

"She was vile with a capital 'V.'" Mindy Trist lifted her glass of cranberry and vodka, clinking it to the rim of Cynthia's.

It was no wonder neither woman had any love lost when it came to Bethelda. They'd both been targeted in many a *Grim Truth* article. Cynthia's husband Rodney had a tendency to end up in other women's beds, while Mindy had the habit of letting any man into hers. She'd even tried to come after Finn a number of times.

The only reason Mindy and Cynthia were friends was because Mindy had never let Rodney into her bed.

"Hear! Hear!" Shelby and Herald Wiggins lifted their glasses in the air from their seats over in a booth.

It had been awhile since Finn had seen the couple not

screaming at each other. They had a tendency to get into rather *heated* altercations. *Heated* being the operative word. Just a few months ago Shelby had set Herald's truck on fire. Bethelda had a field day with that story.

Finn hadn't exactly been the woman's biggest fan, either. *Far* from it. Not only had she tried to destroy his brother's relationship with Hannah, but Finn himself had been the subject of more than a couple of the woman's stories. They'd mostly involved his ex-girlfriend Becky Wright...now Rebecca (because it was more mature sounding) Milton. It was fine with him. Becky had been his girl. Rebecca? Well, she was the one who'd shoved his heart into that meat grinder.

THE GRIM TRUTH

OLD LOVERS NEW LAST NAMES

Dr. Do Everyone a Little has been back in our small town for over a year now. He returned from his time away getting himself an actual education, unlike his useless older brother Wild Ram. A full-time bartender, I ask you, what kind of a job is that?

But that isn't today's story. No, today's story is about the younger miscreant. Now don't get me wrong, he is a fairly decent veterinarian. Though, there isn't a very high bar to compare him to considering the only other man capable of the job isn't the world's best, either. And again, that is a different story for a different day.

Years ago, Dr. Do Everyone a Little used to be seen

around town holding the hand of Gold Digger. There were more than a few times when the childhood sweethearts were caught with their pants down. They were like animals in heat. But in those years that Dr. Do Everyone a Little was away, Goldie moved on to better and richer pastures.

Tomorrow, Goldie will be walking down the aisle to marry Dr. Smarmy Smile. Apparently, she has a thing for men sporting that Dr. title, even if they are in a lesser field of said title. But Dr. Smarmy comes with much more than a fancy name. He comes with a whole-hell-of-a-lot of money. That family has been in the green for longer than I've been alive. And now Dr. Smarmy has a bit of a monopoly on the dentist business in this town. So as he is the one getting everyone's money, I'm sure that smarmy grin he's sporting is one of the shit-eating variety.

The breakup between Dr. Do Everyone a Little and Gold Digger might've happened years ago, but it doesn't mean that certain people are over it. I'm sure that a lot of my readers will remember that the two doctors have had a bit of rivalry going. They've always tried to one-up each other in all aspects of their lives, since way back when they were children. It appears now that Dr. Smarmy has won.

He got the girl.

Dr. Do Everyone a Little has apparently set himself out on a mission: screw every woman he meets. And he's doing a pretty good job of it, too. It helps that he regularly works at his family's bar, the Den of Iniquity. There are plenty of willing women who would be more than happy to drop their panties when it comes to Dr. Do Everyone a Little.

And drop them they do.

That particular article was old. Rebecca and Brett Milton had gotten married well over a year ago, but Bethelda had still liked to write about that particular story every once in a while. There were a couple of stories that were tried and true, and she apparently thought it was her part to keep everyone up to date with the saga. He didn't give a fuck about it, and he could say that in all honesty now.

These days he might live by the once-burned-twice-shy philosophy, but he was over Rebecca. Really and truly.

Finn pulled his focus from the people cheering Bethelda's death and moved to the other end of the bar toward his friends. Brendan and Paige King were sitting on one side of the corner, while Jax and Grace Anderson were on the other side.

"You want another?" Finn asked, nodding to Paige's nearly empty beer glass.

"*Please.*" She nodded, lifting the glass to her mouth and finishing off the last of the amber liquid.

There was no doubt his friend needed a drink…or five. Paige worked at Adams and Family Funeral Home, had since she moved to Mirabelle five and half years ago. Her job there entailed writing obituaries and putting together the photo tributes for the recently deceased. But it was just one of many jobs she held. She was also a pretty successful artist; her pieces were displayed and sold in many businesses all over town. And then there was the fact that she was raising three children.

Paige only worked at the funeral home three days a week, and that Tuesday had been one of them. She'd been the one putting together the program, prayer cards, and tribute for Bethelda's funeral. She looked like she'd had the day from hell because of it, too. The freckles on her nose and cheeks were standing out in stark contrast on her skin, and wisps of her long brown hair had fallen out from the messy bun on the top of her head.

When Paige had first come to town, Bethelda had set her sights on making Paige's life as miserable as possible. For whatever reason, Bethelda had a real problem with people who weren't from Mirabelle. And she let them know it. Regularly.

It was just too bad for Bethelda that Paige had met Brendan. Once the two had started dating, there wasn't a chance in hell Paige was going anywhere without him.

But it wasn't just Paige who Bethelda had gone after. Brendan and Grace were brother and sister, with two different fathers, and a mother who'd died of breast cancer years ago. That story had been written about enough times to be the length of a novel at this point. Jax's relationship with Grace—and the fact that his parents weren't the best of human beings and causing drama in their own right—probably made for two books by now.

Hell, Bethelda had written about all of Finn's close friends at one point or another.

"Today was that bad, huh?" Grace took a pull on the straw floating in the pomegranate-blueberry concoction Shep had mixed up for her.

"It was awful. Going through every year of Bethelda's life? Putting it in order? Seeing it all laid out? I don't know. It's just…" She tried to formulate the words. "She wasn't a nice woman. Not to any of us. Not ever. But to see her, from when she was a baby to now…" She trailed off again, shaking her head.

"It humanizes her," Brendan finished for his wife, reaching over and running his hand across her shoulder blades. "Which makes it harder because none of us ever really looked at her like she was one."

"I think this is just her reaching out from beyond the grave to make our lives more miserable."

"What do you mean?" Finn asked as he slid another glass of beer in front of Paige, taking the now empty one away.

"How many other funeral homes are in Mirabelle? And she picks Adams and Family. She came in last year and planned out the whole thing. Brought in the pictures she wanted me to use and everything. *Me*. She hated me. I mean, a case could be made that she hated everyone, but I feel like her vendetta toward me was stronger than, say, Stephanie Freck who works at Lawson and Sons. Or Kendra Barrington over at Sheffield's. And not only did she pick Adams and Family to have her funeral, she specifically chose the café to cater it. There were five other options and she wants Café Lula. A place that she liked to say on *many* occasions had the worst coffee in town."

"Which is such a ridiculous thing to say because everyone knows it's the *best* in town." The frown on Jax's face was more intense than usual, and rightly so.

Grace and her grandmother Lula Mae owned and ran the café, Lula Mae making more of the savory dishes while Grace was usually in the back baking sweets all day. And it was no wonder Jax was defending the coffee. The man went there every single morning that he was on duty; he'd get a cup before he started his patrol. It was something he'd done well before he and Grace had ever become a thing. He'd used it as his excuse to see her every day.

"Thank you, baby." Grace patted her husband's hand, giving him a small smile.

"And it isn't just that," Paige continued. "Writing that freaking obituary was one of the hardest things I've ever written. How do you honor the dead when you didn't respect them in life?"

"That is a question I do not know the answer to." Finn rested his palms on the bar as he leaned forward.

"I thought you were supposed to be the all wise bartender." Brendan raised his eyebrows as he brought his glass to his lips and took a sip of his beer.

"I don't work here full-time, so I'm only wise half of the time." Finn might be a veterinarian for his day job, but he still liked to pull shifts at the bar every once in a while. Kept him close to his roots. "It's my brother who is full-time wise."

"What do you need wisdom on?" Shep asked as he sidled up next to Finn, sliding a fresh mixed drink in front of Grace.

Finn grabbed all of the empty glasses and headed over to the bin in the corner, placing them with all of the other dirty dishes before he turned around. His eyes caught on the front door as it opened and someone walked inside. The second he was fully able to take her in, his step faltered before he stopped moving and just looked at her.

She had brown hair. *Long, rich* brown hair. It fell over her shoulders in soft, thick waves. The desire to sink his fingers into it came automatically; his palms itched to act on it, too. Instead he moved his focus to her face, taking in her golden brown skin, almond-shaped eyes, and a full mouth with the prettiest lips he'd ever seen.

It was the last day of January and that night promised to be a chilly one, already dropping down to the low thirties. She wore a formfitting, black leather jacket. It was zipped up the front, and she rubbed her palms against her arms in an attempt to warm up. The blue jeans she wore were skin-tight, the dark denim wrapping around each and every one of her soft curves. From her hips, to her thighs, and on down. He wasn't exactly sure how tall she was as she was wearing high-heeled boots—the black leather going up to about mid-calf—but if he had to guess he'd say she was probably five-feet-seven or so when she was barefoot.

This woman wasn't from Mirabelle. Finn would know if he'd seen her before, and he most definitely had not.

She hesitated for only a moment before she looked to the bar and headed that way, the heels of her boots clipping against the hardwood floors. It was a Tuesday, so even though there was a good crowd, it wasn't full. There were a number of empty spots at the bar, and the beautiful brunette headed for one a few seats away from Paige.

As Shep was standing closer, it would've made the most sense for him to get her a drink, but Finn stepped in and blocked his brother as he took the space in front of her. Out of the corner of his eye he could just make out the raised eyebrow Shep gave him before moving off down to another patron at the bar.

"What can I get you?" Finn asked.

The woman's gaze moved to his as she settled in her seat, and golden brown eyes focused on him. Seeing her up close, he realized she was tired. Not so much in a physical way, but more in an emotional way, and it was only in her eyes. But the weariness faded away when she looked at him. Her mouth fell open as she breathed in, and it stayed open for just a second, no words coming out.

It was clear she was slightly taken aback by him. Well, she could just join the club, because she wasn't the only one who was surprised by what—or more accurately *who*—was in front of them.

She was stunning.

"I-I'd like a beer. What do you guys have on tap?" Her eyes darted to the left and to the line of taps. There were a few brands on there, but what they served these days was mostly what the bar brewed.

"What do you like?"

"Something strong. Do you have a stout?" She had a very slight southern accent that was accompanied with just the right amount of husk. Sexy. *Super* sexy. The kind of voice he knew he'd really like whispering things into his ear, or moaning his name.

"Yeah." He nodded, grabbing one of the short glasses they used for tasters. He was more than slightly impressed that she requested a stout straight off the bat. "Here. This one has chocolate undertones," he said as he slid the little glass in front of her. "It's one of our own brews."

"Beer and chocolate?" she asked as she lifted it to her mouth. "That's how you kill two birds with one stone."

Finn wasn't going to lie, he was fascinated with the way her lips touched the glass. And he couldn't stop watching as her eyes closed in satisfaction as she drank. Her eyelashes were just long enough that they rested on her skin when her eyes were closed. She also had the lightest dusting of freckles across the bridge of her nose. And her cheeks were pink. He wondered if the coloring was from the cold outside.

It was probably only a moment—just a handful of seconds—

that she sat in front of him tasting that beer, but for him it could've been a lifetime that he watched her. And he wouldn't stop watching her if he had any choice in the matter.

When she opened her eyes he forgot himself. They were changing, becoming even more golden. It was the clink of the glass hitting the bar that brought him back to the moment.

"That's amazing. I would like one of those, please."

"Coming right up." Finn grabbed a bigger glass and pulled down the lever, the rich brown liquid filling it up.

"Thank you." She gave him a genuine smile as he set it down in front of her.

The woman's smile was killer. *Killer*. "You visiting?"

"Yeah." She nodded before she took a sip of her beer and swallowed. "Just in town until Thursday."

Two nights. He could totally work with that. Though for a fleeting second he wished he had longer to work with. He pushed the thought away; it went against some of his rules. "Business or pleasure?"

"Unwanted business. Unwanted, unpleasant business."

"Well, if you need it, you now know where to find good beer while you're here. And if you need any other recommendations on what to drink, I'd be more than happy to be at your service."

"Is that so?" That smile of hers quirked to the side.

"It is." He grinned.

"Well, how very chivalrous of you. So who is it exactly that is at my service?"

The way she said *service* put so many other ideas in his head of just how he'd like to spend a few hours with her. He could show her some service all right. "Finn."

"Well, you're very accommodating, Finn." And there was that smile playing on her lips again. He wondered what they tasted like. The beer most likely, but what else?

"We aim to please."

"Clearly."

"So who is it that I'm being so accommodating to?" He flipped the question she'd used to get his name.

"Brie." She stuck her hand out to him and he immediately grabbed it, their palms sliding across each other's. Her hand was soft, still slightly cooled from the weather outside, and it fit perfectly in his.

"It's nice to meet you, Brie." He didn't want to let go, but he forced himself to. Mainly because it would be a little odd to hold hands with a stranger from across the bar.

A roar of laughter filled the air, and Brie's golden brown eyes left his, looking over to the people in the corner. "Someone is having a good time."

Finn glanced at the group before returning his focus to Brie. Her head was still turned, her long hair brushed back and over her shoulder so that he could clearly see her neck. He wondered what the hollow of her throat tasted like, and he wanted to trace the delicate silver chain of the necklace she wore with his fingertips.

"They're placing bets," he told her.

She looked back to him, her eyebrows raised high in question. "On what?"

"Tomorrow's funeral."

Something flickered in her eyes, something he thought looked a lot like unease as she set her glass on the bar and leaned forward. "They're placing bets on a funeral?"

"The woman in question wasn't exactly…uh…popular with many people here in Mirabelle."

"That's the understatement of the century," Shep said as he came up on the other side of Finn.

"Brie, this is my brother, Shep. Shep, this is Brie…she's visiting Mirabelle for a couple of days."

"Shep…" she trailed off, her eyebrows scrunched together slightly as she studied him. "As in Shepherd?"

"Indeed. Have we met before?" Shep's eyes narrowed on Brie's face.

For just a second something hot and possessive burned deep in Finn's stomach. Yes, Shep was more than taken when it came to his wife, and there was no chance in hell he'd ever do anything to mess that up. But before Shep had gotten married, he hadn't exactly been celibate, and this might not have been Brie's first time in town.

"No, we haven't met." Brie shook her head. At her words Finn's knot of tension eased up. "I'm staying at the Seaside Escape Inn."

Shep and Hannah owned a giant inn right on Mirabelle Beach. It was three stories tall, not including the giant ten-foot-tall pylons it stood on. They'd remodeled the whole thing, keeping the first floor for their house, while the second and third floors had been converted into six individual condos that they rented out.

"Well, in that case your first beer is on the house." Shep nodded to her glass on the counter.

"It's delicious, by the way," she said as she reached for it, taking a sip.

"Thank you." Shep grinned. "Brewed it myself."

"Be careful how many compliments you give the guy." Brendan looked down the bar to Brie. "He already has a big head."

"That's a bit of the pot calling the kettle black," Jax said as he looked between his friends.

Finn smiled. It wouldn't be a typical time spent with Brendan, Shep, and Jax without a few insults getting thrown around. The guys had been best friends since they were five years old. Finn had looked at Brendan and Jax like they were his older brothers, and they'd always treated him like a little brother.

"Guys, this is Brie. She's renting a room at the inn." Shep introduced her to the group. "Brie, meet Brendan, Paige, Grace, and Jax. So if you need a mechanic, an artist/photographer, a baker, or a deputy sheriff during your time spent in Mirabelle, you know who to talk to."

"Well hopefully the first and last on that list won't be needed." Grace smiled at Brie. "But if you need something to eat for breakfast or lunch, Café Lula is just down the road from here."

"Best coffee in town, too," Jax added, making Grace's grin grow.

Everyone introduced themselves, saying "*Hi*" to Brie, and she returned the greetings. Another round of raucous laughter filled the bar. Brie glanced over to the group of people causing the commotion before she looked back to them.

"Who was she? This lady who died." She moved her beer to her lips, hiding her mouth with the glass as she took another sip.

"Her name was Bethelda Grimshaw," Finn answered.

He thought he saw that unease flicker in her eyes again, but it disappeared a second later. Must've been a trick of the lights.

"Why didn't people like her?" She lowered the glass and set it on the bar.

"Well, let me start by saying I don't think what's going on over there is OK." Grace frowned, glancing to the corner before looking back to Brie. "Bethelda wasn't exactly what you could ever call kind to me, but that over there is just perpetuating hate with hate."

"Agreed." Paige nodded.

"What did she do?"

"She had this blog called *The Grim Truth*." Brendan ran one of his fingers across the frosted glass of his mug. "And she liked to write about everyone's dirty laundry."

"The dirtier the better," Shep added.

"Even if she was the one making it dirtier." This from Jax, who took a sip of beer after he said it.

"She sounds delightful." Brie didn't hide an ounce of sarcasm in her words.

"Yeah." Paige tipped her head to the side. "The woman thrived on creating misery, and though I'd say a lot of the people in this bar were touched by that meanness—all of us included in that group—not everyone is celebrating her death."

"It just means you all are better people than she was." Brie's voice had gone very small as she spoke. She looked away from all of them, lifting her beer to her mouth and taking a long drink of it.

* * *

Bethelda Grimshaw was dead.

That sentence should've had more meaning to Brie Davis. It should've made her sad. It should've done a lot of things.

It should've, but it didn't.

Bethelda was a stranger. A stranger who'd given her daughter up for adoption twenty-eight years ago.

Brie had been eighteen when she found out who her mother was. Well, who her *biological* mother was. Because Brie's mother was Anastasia "Ana" Davis, the woman who—along with Brie's father, Marcus Davis—had adopted her when she was two days old. Those were her parents. The people who had raised her. The people who had taken care of her. The people who loved her.

This little venture into Mirabelle wasn't Brie's first time. She'd come down ten years ago, right after she'd found out who Bethelda was. It was something she'd been beyond intimidated about, and as it turned out, she was right to have been.

At the time, Brie hadn't told her parents about the search. Though they did know about it now. Her not telling them hadn't been because they wouldn't have been supportive, because they would have. No, she didn't tell them because she'd wanted to do it on her own.

Bethelda's name had been the only one Brie had gotten in her search. Her biological father hadn't been documented on anything. She'd thought she might be able to find out who he was from the meeting with Bethelda.

She'd thought wrong.

Looking back, she wasn't quite sure what she'd been hoping for when she met Bethelda. Happiness at being reunited? A bittersweet moment filled with the time lost but hopeful for the relationship they could have? Tears of joy?

Yeah, none of those things had happened. To say that Bethelda had been less than thrilled to see Brie would be a huge understatement. She'd been vicious. Told Brie she wanted absolutely nothing to do with her.

The whole encounter was probably a total of two minutes. That was all the time Brie had gotten of Bethelda. It had been the most painful, miserable moments of her life. She'd never felt more unwanted.

Yeah, there weren't any tears of joy, but Brie sure had cried. She'd driven to the closest gas station and sat in her car for an hour, sobbing like an idiot. Those were the last tears she'd cried for Bethelda, and she'd vowed the woman wouldn't get any more from her.

Brie hadn't broken that vow, either. Not even when she'd gotten the phone call from Bethelda's lawyer five days ago. There hadn't been any tears shed when she'd found out that her biological mother had passed away.

It was a brain aneurysm that had done it. Bethelda was driving back from the store when it happened. Her car had veered off the road and hit a tree. She'd been dead before the crash. The first thought Brie had at the information was that she was thankful Bethelda hadn't taken anyone else out with her. The lawyer had kept talking, trying to sound sympathetic for Brie's loss.

Yeah, he must not have known the woman very well.

She didn't understand why she was getting that particular phone call until he got to the crux of the conversation. Imagine her surprise when she found out her name was in Bethelda's will.

Brie's first thought on that? She didn't give a flying fuck what the woman had left to her. It could be burned for all she cared. There wasn't a single thing she wanted.

At least, that was what she told herself for the next few days. But that very morning Brie had woken up and she knew that wasn't true.

Maybe it was because she'd been given up for adoption that she was so obsessed with history. She hadn't known her own, so she wanted to know everybody else's. It was always her favorite subject. All through grade school and college, so much so that she'd gone on and gotten her master's. Now she was working on her PhD at the University of North Carolina at Chapel Hill.

She'd finished her years of course work and was now working on her dissertation. The focus? Post–World War II America. She was fascinated with how the country, and its people, where changed by such a significant event.

She'd settled into her life in Chapel Hill, found the balance between teaching and research. Though, she wasn't teaching that semester, taking the time to focus more heavily on her dissertation. Well, that had been the plan before that phone call.

So yeah, she had a thing for history, and this was an opportunity for her to learn some of her own. It was the only reason she was in Mirabelle. The drive there hadn't been the easiest thing. In the eleven hours it had taken her to get down there, she'd told herself to turn around a dozen times. What if that history she was going to discover was something she didn't want to know?

Now one night in town, she knew without a doubt there was going to be a whole hell of a lot of history she didn't want to know. Bethelda was so much worse than what she already knew—two beers and an hour at the Sleepy Sheep had confirmed that.

There was so much hatred. *Soooo much hatred.*

The hard part wasn't that it sucked seeing how much people hated the woman. No, the hard part was knowing that she came from the woman whom people hated.

She'd liked the people she met at the bar that night. Shep, Paige and Brendan, Grace and Jax…and Finn. God, she'd *really* liked Finn. She could stare into that man's sapphire-blue eyes for days. He'd had a good amount of five-o'clock shadow dusting his jaw, and the desire to know what it would feel like beneath her palm had burned her brain every time she'd looked at him.

He was all sorts of sexy, from his southern accent to the way his smile made his eyes even bluer. And his glasses that framed those eyes? Good Lord, she'd never known how glasses could make a man sexier until she'd met him.

When she'd looked into his face for the first time, she'd forgotten about Bethelda. It had been the first time her mind had been blissfully clear since she'd gotten that freaking phone call five days ago.

Once he found out who she was, he wasn't going to want a single thing to do with her. None of them would. She didn't blame them, either. How could she? She shared the same DNA as the woman who'd caused all of them so much misery.

When she'd gotten back to the inn she'd immediately opened up her computer and pulled up the blog she'd been told about. *The Grim Truth* hadn't been around ten years ago. If it had been, Brie would've found it when she'd done her research. And it wasn't like she would've come across it in the years since.

After that day, she hadn't wasted any time looking into the woman. She'd shut that door…or at least she thought she had.

Brie rolled over in bed for what was probably the seventy-ninth time and stared up at the ceiling. She hadn't gotten a full night's sleep in days, and tonight looked like it would be a re-peat performance.

She just needed to get through tomorrow, find out what was in that will, and then be on her way.

Then she could move on. Put all of this behind her.

Bethelda Grimshaw was dead. And it didn't bother her one bit.

Chapter Two

Freak-Outs, Flightless Birds, and Fortune Cookies

Adams and Family Funeral Home was in downtown Mirabelle. Like a lot of the businesses in the area, it was an old Victorian house. The building was two stories tall, had a wrap-around porch, and was painted a cheerful buttercream yellow.

It stood out in stark contrast to the overcast gray sky. The weather was pretty gloomy, and beyond appropriate for the day.

There were a dozen or so cars parked in the lot off to the side of the building, and Brie pulled her white and blue MINI Cooper into one of many empty spots. She shut the engine off before leaning forward, looking out the windshield and over to the funeral home.

"Just get it over with," she muttered to herself before un-buckling her seat belt and getting out of the car.

Clutch in hand, she made her way to the building.

She was wearing her leather boots, the heels clicking against the brick path and echoing in her ears with each step. A blast of cold wind blew in from behind her, plastering the back of her sweater dress to her thighs.

Her entire outfit was black. Her boots, her tights, her dress, her jacket, her scarf. She'd stood in front of the full-length mirror that morning totally aware of the irony of the situation. Black was a color for mourning, but Brie wasn't *in* mourning.

The front door of the funeral home was painted a dark green, the same color as all of the shutters. She wrapped her hand around the brass knob, taking a deep breath to steady her nerves. She had to do what she could to help ease those nerves; they weren't going anywhere. How could they? She felt like a lamb walking into a lion's den.

Letting out her breath in a foggy rush, she twisted the handle and pushed the door open. Once inside, she realized that the hallway was empty, and so was the front room just off to the right. No one was sitting behind the receptionist desk.

She took a few more steadying breaths, and the sweet scent of apples and cinnamon filled her nose. Someone had made cider, and the warmth of it seemed to sink into her bones, heating her up from the inside.

Calming slightly, she looked around the space, taking in the dark mahogany wood floors and railing on the banister. The furniture was all beautifully maintained antiques, and the photos on the walls were stunning. Even though she'd just had a short drive through town late yesterday and early that morning, she knew they were taken locally.

"Hello. How can I help you?" a thickly southern feminine voice said from behind Brie, making her spin around.

The woman in front of Brie was rather striking. Her face all angles, with a sharp chin and cheekbones. Her reddish brown hair was pulled up into an elegant twist at the back of her head, and dangling gold and emerald earrings hung from her ears.

She had a cup of something steamy in her hands, her fingers wrapped around the porcelain. When she walked by, Brie got an even stronger hit of the cider scent.

"I'm here for the Grimshaw memorial."

Surprise flickered in the woman's eyes. "Oh, it's just in there." She pointed down the hallway. "There are refreshments that you can help yourself to. The kitchen is just off the end of the hallway to the right."

"Thank you." Brie gave the woman a small smile before she headed off down the hall.

There was the soft sound of someone playing the piano coming from the room that the woman had indicated. When Brie stepped over the threshold, her eyes panned over the fifty or so seats. There were seven people in the room in total, including herself and the piano player in the corner.

Wow. Well, this was a promising turnout.

There wasn't a casket as Bethelda had been cremated. Instead, a hot pink urn sat in front of a poster-size photo of her. Brie barely glanced at it before she took a seat a few rows back from the front. The seat was at an angle behind an elderly lady in a thick, wool sweater. The gray material looked like it would be soft to the touch. She was rubbing her fingers against rosary beads in her tiny, weathered hands, the words of the Hail Mary just barely audible as she whispered them in a low chant.

Brie pulled her focus from the woman in front of her and looked up, her eyes landing on the photo of Bethelda a few feet away. It was the same photo that was on *The Grim Truth* blog. As Brie had only met Bethelda once, she wasn't exactly sure how old the woman was in the photo. Late thirties maybe. She looked like what Brie remembered from that day. Same expertly cropped hair. Same perfectly sculpted eyebrows. Very similar cat's-eye glasses. The ones in the picture were blue, but when Brie had met her she'd been wearing purple ones.

One thing Brie remembered so clearly from that day—before any harsh words were said…or before Brie had been rejected—was when she'd first looked at Bethelda. Growing up Brie had always wondered who she'd gotten her features from. There hadn't been very much time to figure it out then, but she sat there now, staring at the picture. Studying it.

Well, she hadn't gotten her eyes from Bethelda. Brie's were golden brown, Bethelda's were hazel. They didn't have the same nose, or mouth, or ears. Yeah, ears. Brie's earlobes weren't attached at the base, while Bethelda's had been. It was an odd thing to notice, but Brie had.

They did have the same jawline though. It was just slightly squared, shaping their faces and giving them the same cheekbones, too. Then there was their hair. Bethelda's was bright red, and Brie's was more of a mahogany, the reddish tints made even more noticeable in the sunlight.

They didn't have the same skin tone. Brie was tan year-round with no added help from the sun. That was probably from her father's Cuban side, something she found out from a DNA test she'd taken years ago. A DNA test that hadn't helped her find out who her father was. Another door shut.

Bethelda had pretty fair skin, fair skin that sported a good amount of freckles. Another small thing Beth had gotten from Bethelda, a slight band of freckles across the bridge of her nose.

That was it. They had nothing else in common.

"How did you know Bethelda?"

Brie pulled her gaze from the picture and looked in the direction the question had come from. It was the little old lady sitting in front of her. She had a pretty clear voice—steady but on the soft side—and blue eyes.

"I—" Brie was more than slightly taken off guard. How was she supposed to answer that question. "I actually didn't really know her. Did you?"

The woman looked Brie over for another second, her eyebrows bunching together. Brie knew the question the woman wanted to ask. If Brie didn't know Bethelda, why was she at the funeral?

Instead the woman's eyebrows relaxed and she nodded. "Yes," she said, giving a sad smile. "I'm Ella, by the way."

"Brie," she responded, relieved, feeling like she'd somehow escaped a firing squad.

"Well, Brie. I knew Bethelda from the day she was born. I was very good friends with her mother, Petunia."

Petunia…Brie's grandmother. Her grandfather had been named Harold. She hadn't been able to find out too much on them in her research, because there hadn't been a lot. Just a few archived articles from the *Mirabelle Newspaper* and what could be learned from public records.

They were both products of the Great Depression. They seemed like the kind of hardworking, God-fearing people who were formed by being raised in the south. Harold fought in WWII for two years before he came back to Mirabelle and got a job at the power plant. Petunia had been the secretary at what was still the only Catholic church in Mirabelle.

Brie's parents were Catholic, and they'd raised her in the faith. When she'd found out the Grimshaws were Catholic, too, it was one of those similarities that was pretty interesting to her. A tie she had in both lives.

Petunia and Harold had both passed away. Harold from a stroke seventeen years ago and Petunia from pneumonia thirteen years ago. Their deaths might've happened before Brie had found out who Bethelda was, but she still felt like she missed out on a relationship with them.

Maybe they would've wanted to know her…she'd never know. She wondered if they were kind people. But that was the sort of information she couldn't get from a computer.

"You were friends with Petunia Grimshaw?" Brie couldn't stop herself from asking.

"Oh yes. She was one of the first people I met when my Owen brought me to Mirabelle. She came over to the little place Owen and I were staying with the most heavenly peach cobbler. Their family was famous for that thing, made it for every single pot luck, and you were lucky if you even got a bite let alone a full helping of it."

Ella leaned closer like she was imparting the greatest secret to Brie. "When Petunia gave me that recipe she made me swear I'd never share it with a soul unless they were family. She didn't want it to die with her…and by that point she and Bethelda weren't on the best of terms. So four women have gotten it from me. My daughter, my granddaughter, my daughter-in-law, and my granddaughter-in-law, who bless her heart, can't cook at all, really."

"So you were close with Petunia."

"Very. It's the reason I'm here today, to show respect to my friend." Ella's eyes narrowed on Brie's face. "Have we met before? You look awfully familiar, and these days I don't remember as well as I used to."

"No, ma'am, we haven't met before." Brie shook her head.

"Well, next time I run into you, that won't be the case. Are you just in town for this?"

"I am. I'll be going home tomorrow."

"And where is home?"

"Chapel Hill, North Carolina."

"Oh, I've been there." Ella beamed. "It's a beautiful place."

"It is."

"Well, I hope you get back safely. Now, if you'll excuse me," Ella said as she slowly stood. "I need to use the powder room. It was nice meeting you, Brie." She offered her a departing smile. "And like I said, next time we run into each other we won't be strangers."

"It was nice meeting you, too, Ella." Brie smiled, saying good-bye to the woman as she slowly walked away.

Turning back to look at the front, Brie's eyes landed on the hot pink urn. Such a bizarre choice in color. But as Brie learned more and more about Bethelda, she was discovering that there really was no understanding the woman.

The thought kind of ticked her off. If Bethelda had given Brie the chance, maybe she would've understood the woman who'd given birth to her. Now? Now there wasn't much of an opportunity for that.

The longer Brie stared at that pink urn the angrier she got. She stood up abruptly, needing desperately to get out of the room. The back of her neck was hot and itchy and her heart was racing. She needed fresh, cold air. Needed to take deep, steadying breaths.

Once she got to the hallway, she turned to head back out the way she'd come in. She froze in her tracks instead. Finn was standing by the front door, Ella on one arm while they talked to Paige and Grace.

Fuck.

He was wearing a fitted navy-blue suit that more than showed off the impressive size of his biceps, and his black hair was slightly tousled, like he'd run his fingers through it multiple times.

No. No. Noooooooo. He couldn't see her here. None of them could. None of them could know who she was. She turned around and headed in the opposite direction, passing the door to the kitchen. Her eyes landed on a back door and she headed through the space, the scent of cider even stronger as she passed the pot of it steaming on the stove.

The lock was just a dead bolt and she flipped it, thanking God it wasn't one that needed a key on both sides. The second she was outside the cold air slapped her in the face, but fresh air or not she still couldn't breathe properly.

She needed to get out of there now.

* * *

The office of Schmidt & Whitley wasn't in Mirabelle. It was actually over an hour north in Tallahassee. And all during that sixty-plus-minute drive, Brie couldn't stop going over everything that had happened that morning.

Walking into that room, talking to Ella, seeing Grace, Paige, and Finn.

God, seeing Finn. That had been the most unexpected part of the entire morning. Because really, when she'd walked into that place there'd been no doubt in her mind she was going to have some sort of bad reaction.

Her bad reaction wasn't about being sad, though, because she wasn't sad. But shouldn't she be sad?

The woman who gave birth to her was dead. Not only that, but very few people had actually cared about that fact. Not that she'd been at the funeral home very long, but she had a pretty strong feeling there hadn't been many more people who'd come to pay their respects to Bethelda Grimshaw.

When she pulled into the lot of the law firm she found a spot close to the door and parked her car. It was still beyond gray outside, and as she walked up to the brick building she felt a few drops of rain hit her nose.

The car ride up to Tallahassee hadn't completely calmed her down. How could it when for the second time that day she had no clue what she was walking into. At least she was breathing regularly now though. She had one thing going for her.

She walked into the building and turned to the right. A woman sat behind a glass and steel desk, her platinum blond hair in a straight bob. She was typing away at her computer and glanced up looking bored when Brie walked in.

"How can I help you?"

"I'm Brie Davis. I have a one-o'clock appointment with Mr. Whitley."

"Have a seat. He'll be right with you." She gestured to the waiting room behind Brie.

It was kind of cold inside the room with its modern furniture and sparse decor. Everything was black and white. A very square leather sofa sat in the corner accompanied by matching chairs. There was a huge picture of an eight ball on one wall and a rusted bolt on the other.

Brie sat there for about five minutes or so, flipping through an entertainment magazine. She wasn't much for celebrity gossip, but there was an article about the newest season of *Sherlock* and as Brie was a pretty big fan—of both the show and Benedict Cumberbatch—her interest was piqued.

"Ms. Davis?"

She looked up to the man who'd just called her name. Their two conversations on the phone had been long enough for her to recognize the voice of Lincoln Whitley with just those few syllables of her name.

His voice matched how he looked. Late thirties, relatively attractive, fit. He had thick blond hair and blue eyes. Though his eyes paled in comparison to Finn's. *Everything* paled in comparison to Finn.

OK, she had no idea where that line of thinking had come from. She was probably just still losing it. Hadn't gotten over seeing him at the funeral home. Yeah, that was it.

"Mr. Whitley." Brie stood, brushing the sides of her dress down. She took a step forward, holding out her hand.

"Please, call me Lincoln," he said as he grabbed her outstretched hand and shook it. He didn't tighten his grip, one of those weak handshakes that men reserved for women.

It was like holding a limp fish. Nothing like when Finn shook her hand the night before. He'd had a firm steady grip. And good hands. Good Lord he had good hands.

Strong hands. Masculine hands.

"Right this way." Lincoln's voice brought Brie back to the moment, and he let go of her before gesturing to the hallway behind them.

There was more of the same coldness in the rest of the office. Not a single touch of color. Just white walls and more black-and-white photos. There was a close-up of the stem of an apple, old tires stacked on top of each other, a patch of mushrooms in the grass, a fuzzy caterpillar crawling along a fence.

Lincoln had a corner office, two glass walls separating his space from everyone else. Brie took a seat in the boxy gray chair across from his desk, a desk that was made of more steel and glass.

"I was surprised you called me yesterday," he said as he settled in his seat. "You sounded pretty adamant about not coming when I talked to you the first time."

"You weren't the only one who was surprised." She gave him a half smile that was fully forced. She didn't like being here and she wasn't impressed by this guy. Maybe it was the small talk he started with. Asking about her drive down, how the funeral was that morning, where she was staying in Mirabelle. She didn't want small talk, she just wanted to get out of there.

"Well, it's all pretty straightforward," he said as he opened the folder on his desk. "Ms. Grimshaw left you everything."

Brie was pretty sure she'd blacked out for a second. "I'm sorry, what was that?"

"Your mother left you everything."

The response came out before she could stop herself. "Bethelda wasn't my mother."

Lincoln's head moved back on a flinch. "I'm sorry, I didn't mean—"

"It's fine." She waved off his apology. "But if we could just refer to her as Bethelda or Ms. Grimshaw, I would appreciate that."

"All right." He nodded his head slowly. "Well, it's all yours, everything from the house to its contents and the cat."

"I'm sorry, there's a cat?" She sounded slightly hysterical

when she asked the question. And why Brie chose to focus on the cat at that moment she had no earthly idea.

"Yes." He looked down at the folder. "Her name is Delores. She was brought to the local shelter in Mirabelle after Ms. Grimshaw's passing. They've been taking care of her for the last week. If you don't claim her, she will be given up for adoption."

"Why?"

"Well, if you don't take it someone will—"

"No." Brie shook her head. "I didn't mean the cat. Why did Bethelda leave *me* everything?"

"Of that I have no idea." He shrugged his shoulders. "She contacted our law firm about a year ago and we drafted up the paperwork. All she said was everything was yours."

"You've got to be kidding me. This has to be some sort of joke." Brie sat back in the chair, staring at Lincoln in disbelief. This wasn't happening. This was *not* happening. The back of her neck started to get hot and itchy again.

"I assure you, it isn't a joke. It's all laid out here quite clearly." He placed one of his hands down on top of the papers.

Yeah, she didn't care what those papers said, because this *was* a joke all right. Brie just wasn't sure if it was one Bethelda was playing on her or if it was a cosmic joke the universe was in on.

Maybe it was a little bit of both.

* * *

Brie went to Target.

There was one just down the road from the law firm. She'd passed it on the way in, spotting the red and white sign like her own personal beacon. The second she stepped inside she made a beeline to Starbucks.

Shopping and caffeine. Two birds. One stone.

So now she was pushing her cart around the clothing section sipping on a venti green tea latte with soy milk—soy because it tasted better, not because she had a troubled relationship with dairy.

She really didn't need the fuzzy fox slippers she threw into her cart, or the blue and black flannel pajama pants, or the thick white sweater that would look awesome with her red pants, or the oversized floral T-shirt, or the pair of yoga pants with the bright blue stripe down the side. They all went into her cart anyway, along with the fourth book in a historical romance series she was reading and the first in one she hadn't read before.

When she got to the grocery section, all hell broke loose. Three different kinds of potato chips (sea salt, barbecue, and spicy jalapeño), two bags of Dove chocolate (both dark and milk), a bag of mini KitKats, and a box of wine.

Yup, boxed wine. Desperate times and all.

She might not have had any answers when she walked out of the store over an hour later, but at least she wasn't right on the verge of freaking the fuck out anymore.

On a scale of one to ten, she'd been over an eight when she'd left the law firm with the keys to Bethelda's house in her hand. Now? She was probably at a five, five and a half.

The woman had left her everything. E-V-E-R-Y-T-H-I-N-G.

Why?

Why?!?

WHY?!?!?

It just didn't make any sense. Ten years ago, Bethelda had

made it perfectly clear she didn't want anything to do with
Brie. Wanted *nothing* to do with the daughter she'd given up
all of those years ago. Yet, now Brie was the owner of all of the
woman's possessions...including a cat named Delores.

Brie hadn't ever really been a cat person. She liked dogs.
That was all she'd ever had growing up. They'd gotten Arnold
the pug when she was seven, and when she was twelve they'd
rescued Esmeralda, a Lab mix. They'd overlapped a little in the
middle, but when her parents had to put Esme to sleep a few
years back they hadn't gotten another dog, and for good reason.

Two years ago both of her parents had taken on profes-
sorships at the American University of Rome. They'd sold the
house Brie had grown up in, put most of their belongings in
storage, and moved across the Atlantic.

Brie hadn't told her parents about the recent development
with Bethelda. Ana and Marcus weren't coddlers by any means;
it was just that they knew exactly how bad it had been for Brie
when everything had happened before. She didn't want them
to worry.

So self-medicating with shopping and wine it was.

When she got back to Mirabelle it was close to five. She'd
stopped and picked up some sushi for dinner. It was one of her
favorite meals, and she was going to enjoy every last bite. Luckily for her, she wasn't the type to lose her appetite when she was
upset or anxious. Clearly from her food-purchasing binge, she
was quite the opposite.

She was probably going to gain a couple of pounds by the
end of this trip, but no one was looking at her ass anyway. What
did she care?

So there she sat at the dining room table of the room she

was renting at the inn, alternating between dipping her shrimp tempura and her California roll in the soy sauce mixed with a little wasabi. Her eyes kept darting to the other side of the table and to the set of keys she'd put down by her purse…the set of keys to Bethelda's house.

Once the sushi was finished, Brie sat back in her seat, grabbing the fortune cookie and ripping open the plastic. Growing up, it was the rule of fortune cookie in her household that the whole cookie had to be eaten before the fortune could be read. She cracked the cookie in half, popped a piece into her mouth, and slowly chewed.

What would she find in that house? Would she get the answers to the questions she'd been wondering for most of her life? Did she even want to know those answers?

She popped the rest of the cookie into her mouth, her fingers rubbing against the piece of paper in her hand.

Of course she wanted answers. She wanted the answers to those questions she'd been denied. And that house might have them.

Brie looked down at the white slip in her hands, reading the tiny print.

The penguin, ostrich, and kiwi have wings but cannot fly. Don't be a flightless bird.

And with that Brie stood up, snatching the keys and her purse from the table before heading for the door.

Chapter Three

Unwanted, Unpleasant Business vs. Pleasant Business... *Very* Pleasant Business

Bethelda Grimshaw was a hoarder.

Well, OK, maybe not a *hoarder* hoarder. There weren't dead animals in the freezer. Nor did the woman have bags of old hair or years of garbage piled up. Actually, her house was surprisingly clean—everything had a place and there was a place for everything. It was just that it was *filled* with stuff.

Brie had had no clue what she was going to walk into when she pulled up in front of the lime-green bungalow, with its robin's egg–blue steps and matching front door. It was about a fifteen-hundred-square-foot house, raised three feet off the ground on a concrete slab, and complete with an A-frame roof over the porch. The trim and shutters were all painted white. Somehow the whole look worked even if it was eye popping.

The inside, however, was about twenty times more overwhelming.

The front door opened up to a foyer, and down the hall was the living room, a living room with almost no wall space visible. What wasn't taken up by furniture was hidden with framed photos or paintings. The four windows in the room were covered with thick brocade curtains, the pattern a mix of magenta and baby pink. There was a turquoise sofa on one side and red chairs on the other.

Both of the hall closets were packed with Christmas. Each bin was made of clear plastic so that Brie could look in, but besides that, they were clearly labeled. In one closet she found garland galore, ornaments in every color, glittery snowflakes, snowmen, a Mr. and Mrs. Claus, and a box filled with stockings. The other closet held three trees in varying sizes, two massive plastic bins filled with lights, and a full North Pole setup, complete with an elf village and a reindeer forest.

Clearly the woman loved Christmas.

The spare bedroom had been turned into an office. A stunning cedar desk sat against the one mostly visible blue wall, while bookshelves took up a majority of the rest of the space (with more trinkets and knickknacks filling the shelves). A printer, scanner, and fax machine were all set up on a row of filing cabinets. Then there was the closet that was filled with neatly stacked plastic bins. There were a few labels on the ones at the front that Brie could read: "Mom's," "Delores," "Extra Lightbulbs," "Tablecloths," "Candles," and so on.

The room at the back of the house was Bethelda's bedroom. It held a mahogany antique bed set, the four posters stretching up high to the ceiling. The bed was covered with a rather elaborate quilt made of rich red, purple, and gold silks. The walls were painted a soft sherbet orange and the one and only thing hung up was a painting above the bed. It was of the beach at sunset. The rest of the space was taken up with furniture.

There was an armoire in front of the bed that held a flat

screen TV, the four long drawers underneath filled with movies. On either side of the armoire were solid mahogany cabinets. They were both filled with scarves. Silk, cotton, wool, knitted, woven, fringed, no-fringed, and on and on. There were hundreds and hundreds of them, all neatly folded and color coordinated.

Two dressers stood on the wall to the left of the bed, both of them covered with antique jewelry boxes of varying shapes and sizes, and all of them filled with rings, earrings, necklaces, and pins. The walk-in closet was packed to the brim, boxes and boxes of shoes on one side, clothes taking up the rest of the space, and more boxes stacked on the shelf that ran around the top, these filled with hats.

The den at the front of the house was a library, bookshelves taking up the entirety of the available wall space. Floor to ceiling was covered in books, magazines, and newspapers. An over-stuffed, emerald-green, velvet sofa sat in the center of the room facing a brick fireplace.

The fireplace was kind of cool, too. As it was on a wall in the center of the house, there was a hearth in both the den and the living room. Both had been fitted with gas, the ever-present fake logs always ready to go.

The kitchen wasn't as overwhelming…comparatively. The space between the ceilings and the tops of the cabinets was lined with an assortment of glass pitchers. There was one with lilacs, another with limes, one that was covered in cherries, while another was a shockingly deep purple. There were fifty-two in total. Brie knew as she'd stood there and counted them all.

The counters were a different story. They were tiled in a

pretty sage green and almost completely devoid of clutter. A purple Keurig machine was on one side of the sink, a sky-blue utensil holder sat by the stove, and three egg yolk–yellow canisters were next to the bright blue KitchenAid mixer next to the refrigerator. The appliances weren't brand new, but they were all in relatively good condition and shining white and clean. It all worked pretty well with the bright yellow walls.

When Brie walked into the bathroom, she thought she was in a safari. The shower curtain was a mix of tiger stripes, cheetah spots, and zebra. The walls were wallpapered in a shimmering gold. On either side of the mirror, tall green palm fronds shot up from ivory white vases. And the fuzziest of black bath mats covered the white tile floor.

And then there were the china cabinets scattered throughout the house. She'd counted seven in total. *Seven*. And each one was devoted to something special. There were three in the living room.

The first was filled with figurines and good Lord, there were figurines galore. Little porcelain cats, hand-carved wooden elephants, Russian nesting dolls, and soooo many other random things. The second held colorful glass-blown bottles of every shape, color, and size.

The third was all teddy bears, each wearing its own costume. There were some in biker outfits, others in steampunk; one was dressed as Scarlett O'Hara, another as Rhett Butler. There were debutant dresses and tuxedos, bikinis and swim trunks, superheroes and every Disney princess created. There had to be over a hundred of those little dressed-up bears.

The two cabinets in the dining room had an assortment of glass on their shelves, the largest one displaying seven different dish sets. The slightly smaller one was showing off probably close to thirty tea sets.

The cabinet in the hallway held a gnome village. An *entire* gnome village. There was a gnome post office, a gnome school-house, a gnome city hall, a gnome grocery store, gnome houses ranging from little cabins to rather large mansions, and so on, and so on.

Brie had never seen anything like it. Well, that was until she got to the last cabinet in the spare bedroom/office. It was the pièce de résistance when it came to everything in the house.

Bethelda had apparently been a George Michael fan…a *big* fan if the shrine to the man was anything to go by. There was stuff from his time in Wham! all the way through his solo career. Over a dozen collector's plates—with this face on them—were all prominently displayed. A shelf was completely taken up with books about him along with magazines, all with him on the cover. Bethelda had also collected every single one of his albums in every format that was available.

There were watches with his face as the face, framed photographs with his signature, coffee mugs, ornaments, key chains, postcards, concert ticket stubs, T-shirts, sweatshirts, bracelets, necklaces, and a stuffed bear. The bear was probably Brie's favorite part. It was wearing a black leather jacket with fringe, big sunglasses, and a cross earring dangled from its ear.

She had to laugh because it was the only thing keeping her from losing it. Walking through that house would've made Brie out of sorts even if it hadn't been bursting to overflow. And how could it not? These were the belongings of the woman who'd given birth to her. This was where Bethelda had lived…alone…with her cat.

And that was the moment Brie reached her threshold for the day.

* * *

Finn hadn't been on the schedule to work at the Sheep on Wednesday night. But he'd shown up around seven, hoping that a certain beautiful brunette would be needing a drink.

She was only in town for two nights, so if he was going to see her again it was now or never.

As there was a pretty good crowd at the Sheep that evening—a Jacksonville Stampede hockey game was playing on the screens behind the bar—Shep didn't give his younger brother more than a raised eyebrow as he went to help a group of guys at the opposite end of the bar.

For the next hour Finn's eyes moved to the front door every time it opened. Every time someone besides Brie walked in, he found himself getting more and more disappointed.

OK, so he had a little infatuation with her. No big deal. It wasn't *that* weird. He'd liked talking to her the night before, liked her smile and her eyes. She was beautiful, *beyond* beautiful, and he'd thought about her a couple of times throughout the day.

Well, maybe more than a *couple* of times. He'd had to take his mind off being at the funeral home earlier. It wasn't like it was even close to his favorite location to be in the first place, but being there for Bethelda's funeral had made the experience that much worse. If he could dislike the woman any more than he already did he'd be surprised. But when his eighty-nine-year-old grandmother had asked him to take her, he'd said yes. Because he *never* said no to Grandma El.

Ever since Grandpa Owen had died, his grandmother hadn't exactly been the same. Ella Shepherd loved fiercely and without end, and for her, Owen's death had been debilitating. Her mind had started to go over the last few years, and her lucid days were getting to be fewer and fewer. The worst were those times when she thought Owen was still alive. But Ella had been pretty with it on that particular Wednesday morning.

Good or bad days, Finn didn't take his time with Ella for granted. So he'd sucked it up and gone, and when he'd needed a distraction, he'd replayed Brie's soft laugh in his head.

Damn but did he want to see her again. Wanted to hear her voice again. Wanted to feel her under his palms again. Just that one touch of shaking her hand and he'd known it wasn't nearly enough. He wanted more. *So* much more. He wanted to know what her lips felt like beneath his, what she tasted like.

There was no doubt in his mind that actually kissing her would be leaps and bounds better than anything he could ever imagine.

"Who are you looking for?"

Finn turned to find his brother at his side, both of them at the beer tap filling up glasses.

"What makes you think I'm looking for someone?" Finn turned back, watching as the thin line of foam floating on top of the amber liquid moved up the glass.

"Because your eyes have been on the front door since you got here. It's the girl from last night, isn't it? The one you almost bulldozed me down to get to. What was her name again? Brittany? Brook? Brandy?"

"Brie," Finn answered without looking up. He so didn't want to see the expression on his brother's face.

"Oh, I remembered it." Shep's voice had taken on that smirking tone he was so good at. "And she just walked in the door."

"What?" Finn pulled his hand back so quickly that beer sloshed over the rim of the glass and splashed his hand and arm. "Shit." He turned as Brie made her way to the bar, her eyes on him as she pulled herself up on one of the few empty stools. Her hair was pulled up on top of her head, loose strands framing her face. She was wearing those black leather boots again, along with the sexiest red pants he'd ever seen and a white sweater that looked soft to the touch. His fingers itched to feel it.

"Here." Finn handed the now mostly filled beer to Shep before he crossed the space to Brie, wiping his hand on his jeans. It wasn't until he was standing in front of her that the look on her face registered. Her eyes held a slightly overwhelmed look, the corners of her mouth pinched with strain, and her shoulders were tense.

"You OK?" he asked, forcing himself to keep his hands to himself and not reach out to her.

She pulled her bottom lip between her teeth, shaking her head. He watched as that lip fell from her teeth a moment later. "No. Not even close."

Finn reached over and grabbed three bottles of alcohol, setting them on the counter. "Pick your poison." He waved his hand over them: Jose Cuervo, Bacardi, and Jack Daniel's.

She reached forward, tapping the bottle of rum.

Finn grabbed the other two bottles, putting them back before he snatched two shot glasses from the stack, setting them on the counter between them. And then he was twisting off the cap of the rum. In turn, he tipped the bottle over each glass, the amber liquid splashing at the bases before moving up and coloring them to the rims. He set the bottle down, grabbing one glass and lifting it as he put his forefinger and middle finger down on the bar and pushed the other shot toward her.

"Ready?" He raised his eyebrows.

Brie's answer was to reach forward, grabbing the glass and downing the rum. He copied her movement, the alcohol making its way down his throat, a slow burn to his stomach. It had been awhile since he'd done shots of rum, but he was ready for it.

Brie on the other hand was not. She coughed, her hand coming to her mouth and her eyes watering. "Another one please." Her voice was slightly choked as she set the glass down on the counter and pushed it forward.

Finn put his empty glass next to hers, only filling hers up this time. Brie reached for it the second it was filled, tipping it back into her mouth. The second shot she'd been ready for, and she closed her eyes, taking a deep breath and letting the alcohol set in.

"That bad?"

"Worse," she whispered, opening her eyes.

"That doesn't sound good." He grabbed a glass and filled it with water before setting it down on the counter in front of her.

"Thank you." She grabbed it, lifting it to her lips and drinking.

He watched her, waiting for her to finish half of it before she set the glass back down. "Does this have to do with the unpleasant business you came into town to deal with?"

"Unwanted, unpleasant business."

"Yes, the *unwanted*, unpleasant business," he amended.

"It does, indeed." Her eyes closed as she took a deep breath and let it out.

Finn had the sudden and unexpected urge to fix it; he wanted to take that tension and worry away from her. It didn't matter that she was a stranger…the need to help her was overwhelming. "You want to talk about it?"

"Not even a little bit." She opened her eyes again as she shook her head.

"You want another one?" Finn held up the bottle of rum.

"I should probably slow down. How about a beer? Anything. Surprise me."

"Coming right up," he said as he grabbed a clean glass and went over to the tap.

* * *

It had been almost two hours since Brie had gotten to the Sleepy Sheep. She was now nursing her second beer—the first had been an apricot wheat, the second a huckleberry blond ale—in between sipping on the ice cold water Finn kept refilling for her.

Every time he grabbed her glass, she'd get distracted by his hands. She'd pictured them on her more than once. Had thought about one at the small of her back as he guided her through a room, any room. She'd imagined both of his hands at her waist as he held her steady, leaning in close, his lips hovering over hers. And then she had a vision of those hands sliding down her bare body, Finn moving between her naked thighs as he kissed her over and over again.

Good grief, she needed to get a grip on herself. She was in the midst of an almost-breakdown (or she had been when she'd walked into the bar), and here she was imagining sex with an almost-stranger. Yeah, it was safe to say that she was losing it all right.

But being there in that bar filled with people felt normal, and she needed normal. And talking to Finn? Well, it felt right. *Really* right.

It wasn't like he'd only been standing in front of her for the last two hours. He'd gone back and forth between helping other patrons, but he'd always come back to her to talk. The topics of conversation weren't anything important or terribly personal. She'd said she didn't want to talk about what had happened, and he didn't pry. Instead he explained the hockey game playing behind them—she knew nothing about the sport—in between talking about movies, music, and TV shows. He liked *Sherlock*, too.

The more they talked, the better she felt. And it was because as they talked, she forgot about everything else. This wasn't the first time it had happened, either. It had happened the night before, too.

He somehow just made her forget.

Made her forget everything she was going through. Made her forget as his deep, steady voice filled her ears. Made her forget as she looked into his eyes. Those blue, blue eyes.

Good Lord she needed to cool her jets. She wasn't drunk—the glasses upon glasses of water had seen to that—but she wasn't thinking clearly.

She was still thinking about his hands. And his mouth. Whenever he'd come back to her, elbows on the bar as he leaned in close, her gaze would move to his mouth, and she imagined it on hers. Imagined his lips trailing down her throat.

He made her not think about why she was in Mirabelle, not think about anything besides him and whatever they were talking about. She wanted a whole night of not thinking with this man. Wanted to know what it was like to have him press her against something solid. Anything solid. A wall, a table, a mattress, the floor. She didn't care.

Brie wasn't what anyone would call impulsive. She was a planner. Knew what she was going into when she started something. That was probably why everything that had happened in the last week was throwing her off so much.

It had been a last-minute decision to drive down to Mirabelle the day before…she'd already decided against coming to the funeral. Yet, she'd changed her mind. Now another wrench was getting thrown into her plans with the reading of that damn will.

And that damn house.

But she didn't want to think about any of that at the moment. She didn't want to think about anything except for Finn and what it might be like to be a little impulsive with him.

"How you doing over here?" he asked as he slid in front of her again.

"Better and better by the minute."

"That's always good to hear. You want another one?" He nodded to her almost empty beer on the counter.

"No." She shook her head as she picked up her glass and finished off her drink. "I need to be able to drive back to the inn."

"Are you leaving soon?"

"In a bit. I want to see the end of the game."

"Really now?" He leaned in close to her again. And for what was probably the fiftieth time that night she could smell the clean masculine scent that clung to him. Soap and maybe a little aftershave combined with him. He smelled incredible.

So. Damn. Good.

"Yeah, I'm a Stampede fan now. I'm in it to win it." She couldn't stop herself from leaning in a bit closer herself.

"Commitment…I like it."

"Yeah?"

"Yeah." His smile grew and his eyes got more intense, the blue getting deeper. "It's not the only thing I like, either."

"What else do you like?" Her voice dropped low as she spoke. Oh God, the more time she spent with him, the more he affected her. The closer he got to her, the more he affected her. The more he looked at her, the more he affected her.

He just affected her.

"About you? The list keeps growing, and growing. Give me twenty minutes and I'd be happy to tell you about it. In great detail."

Her stomach flipped and the air in her lungs caught. This time her inability to breathe had nothing to do with suffocating pressure. "What happens in twenty minutes?" she somehow managed to ask.

"The game is over." He turned just a little bit so he could incline his head toward the TV, not taking his eyes off of her while he did it.

"You don't need to stay here? Until closing?"

"Nope, just came in to help with the rush during the game. I'm free after that."

"Right." She nodded slowly, her stomach doing another flip. "And if I said yes? What happens then?"

He moved back so that he was standing directly in front of her again, leaning in close. The nearness of him combined with the way he was looking at her and the topic of conversation— that she was 99.9 percent sure was one about them having sex— was making her pulse race. And that wasn't the only thing he was doing to her. It was taking everything in her not to squirm in her seat. She somehow managed to subtly press her thighs together. It was all she could do to combat the swelling ache.

"You said your bad night had to do with the unwanted, unpleasant business you were dealing with while you're in town." He reached over, pushing a strand of her hair back and out of her face before his finger traced the shell of her ear. Goose bumps spread out and across her body. "Brie, if you say yes, I swear to you, I can make the rest of your night *really* pleasant."

She didn't even wait a second to respond. "Yes."

* * *

It had been a few months since Brie had had sex. Seven to be exact. It wasn't her longest dry spell, not by any means. No, her longest dry spell had lasted a year and half and had been right after her last serious relationship.

It hadn't broken her heart when she and Aaron had ended things three years ago. The breakup had happened because he'd believed she'd been far *too* focused on school. He'd gotten tired of playing second fiddle. She hadn't blamed him when he'd ended it, either, mainly because she'd known he hadn't played second fiddle because of her focus on school.

After the breakup, she'd gone full tilt into her studies and hadn't come up for air, or a date. Which wasn't all that shocking when it came to Brie's social life. Thus, her current seven-month dry spell.

Besides her parents, it wasn't an easy thing for her to let people in. Her parents had always been honest with her that she'd been adopted. Though she'd heard that word a lot as a toddler, she hadn't really understood it until she was around six. But even before then, she'd always been more content to be on her own.

Sure she had friends, and there were a handful from her childhood she was still close with as well as a few here and there she'd made and kept along the way. But boyfriend relationships were a different story. What did it say about her that she'd always been slightly relieved when they ended?

Probably nothing good. Relationships were dangerous. Just another way to get your heart broken. She didn't need any more heartbreak in her life. That was why this whole thing with Finn was beyond perfect. There was no doubt in her mind that he was just offering a night of mindless pleasure.

No strings. She didn't want strings.

Once the game had ended—the Stampede beating the Nashville Predators four to two—Brie had excused herself to go to the bathroom while Finn finished up a few things behind the bar.

She was a little nervous, but it was an excited nervous. Her hands shook just slightly as she rubbed them under the cold water. Once the soap was washed away, she kept them in the steady spray, moving so that her wrists were now taking the direct hit, hoping to cool herself down.

But cooling down didn't look to be a reality, a fact made perfectly clear the second she walked out of the bathroom. Finn was coming out of a door at the end of the hall, just a few feet away.

His mouth quirked to the side when he saw her. "Come here."

He reached forward, grabbing her hand and pulling her back the way he'd just come. There was no resistance from her, she followed willingly, the warmth of his hand melting into hers and moving up her arm and through her body.

The light was flipped on, illuminating the room, and the door closed behind them. Brie didn't see anymore than a desk on the back wall and a black leather sofa off to the side. The next second she was pushed back against the wall and Finn's hands were on either side of her face, his thumbs moving across her cheeks. It was the only place he touched her, and yet she could feel it everywhere.

"I believe I'm supposed to give you a list of the things I like about you, and describe them in great detail."

"Th-that was the agreement." Brie nodded, her hands going flat behind her, palms to the wall. She was trying to pace herself, trying to keep her control. She wanted Finn to make the next move, and if she touched him she knew she wouldn't be able to wait for that.

"Where to start." He leaned in closer to her, his lips just grazing her cheek.

Brie closed her eyes, breathing in deep and filling her lungs with Finn's clean, warm scent. It had been months and months since she'd been touched like this. Too long. *Way* too long. She savored the simple, light press of his mouth as he moved down. And then his lips were brushing over hers.

"Look at me, Brie."

His breath mingled with hers as she opened her eyes, looking straight into his. God, they were so freaking blue, and she had a front-row seat to the intense desire that was solely for her. But it was more than desire…it was carnal. Raw.

His eyes dipped to her mouth and he moved one of his hands down, his thumb tracing over her slightly parted lips. "I think we should start here." The pad of his thumb was gentle as he brushed it back and forth. And he didn't stop with the movement as he brought his gaze back to hers. "What do you think?"

"I think that's an excellent idea." She spoke against his thumb that was still touching her lips.

"Good." He moved his hand to her jaw, pressing up at the same moment that his mouth moved down, closing over hers.

Brie opened for Finn on a sigh, her hands leaving the wall as she reached for him, grabbing on to his sides and pulling him closer. He was flush up against her as he slid his tongue past her lips and into her mouth.

It was sensory overload, feeling the hardness of every part of his body that touched hers. Her breasts were pressed against his firm chest, her thighs aligned with his oh-so-very-solid ones, his erection pressing into her belly.

Yeah, *hard* was the operative word, and Brie experienced all of that hardness as Finn completely and totally took possession of her mouth. He tilted her head back just slightly more as he sucked on her bottom lip. She couldn't stop the moan that rumbled from her throat when he twisted his tongue with hers.

God, the way this man kissed was exquisite. She'd never known it was possible to be that exquisite, either. Because if she had known, she probably wouldn't have gone seven months without it.

Finn's mouth slanted over hers as one of his hands dropped down to her lower back. His fingers spread wide at the base of her spine as he held her to him.

Scratch the *probably* in her earlier statement. If she'd known this was what kissing had to offer she wouldn't have gone a month…or a week…or a day. And this was just the kissing part of the evening. If Finn delivered on his promise of making the rest of the evening *pleasant*, she was in for something spectacular all right.

Brie was just a smidge breathless by the time Finn's mouth left hers. He trailed his lips down to her throat, pushing the material of her sweater away as he sucked and nipped at her skin, kissing his way across her collarbone. His lips landed on the tiny diamond pendant that hung from her necklace. He moved his mouth back up and over the silver chain, pressing more kisses along her throat and to her ear.

"So number one on the list of things I like about you is your mouth. I like the way you smile, and how your lips quirk to the side when you're thinking, the sound of your laugh, and how you kiss." His teeth grazed her earlobe and she shivered against him. His hand stayed firm on her back, his fingers tightening fractionally. "Second, I like the way you taste. Your lips, your mouth, your tongue, your neck."

He moved back just enough so that he could look into her eyes. For just a second she couldn't pull any air into her lungs.

"And I bet I'm going to like the taste of you everywhere, Brie."

This time when his mouth came down over hers it was at a

slant, and he deepened the kiss as his tongue found hers. It was then that she realized her hands, which just moments before had been holding on to his sides, were working up and under the soft fabric of his navy-blue flannel shirt. His skin was hot under her palms, and he groaned into her mouth as she lightly raked her nails across his sides and to his abs.

"*Fuck.*" He pulled back from her, resting his forehead against her.

"W-what's wrong?"

"Nothing's wrong." He was breathing unevenly now. "I just need us to not be here, in this office."

"Why?"

"Because if we keep going I won't be able to stop until you're naked and underneath me. And as I have every intention of not only keeping you there for a while, but making you beg for more over"—he nipped at the underside of her jaw—"and over"—he nipped again—"and over again, this office just won't do."

"Then let's get out of here."

He pressed his mouth to hers in another quick kiss before he pulled back, grabbing one of her hands from his stomach. Their fingers linked together as he led her from the office, turning the light off before the door snapped shut behind them.

Chapter Four

A Long List of Likes

It took a total of three minutes and forty-seven seconds to drive from the Sleepy Sheep to the Seaside Escape Inn. Finn knew because he counted every single one of those seconds. He'd visualized each one of those numbers, taking deep steadying breaths. In through his nose, out through his mouth.

It was the only thing that kept him sane. The only thing that kept him from replaying Brie's throaty moans as he'd touched her…as he'd kissed her.

She was in the car in front of him, and he couldn't help but grin as he looked at the back of her MINI Cooper. It was so tiny compared to his black Chevy Silverado. Her plates said she was from North Carolina, but he had no other insight on her…or what she was doing in Mirabelle.

He didn't really care, either.

When they pulled into the lot of the inn, Finn parked his truck next to her car and was out the door in a flash. Brie was standing next to the wooden staircase, the outside lights from the inn illuminating her face and clearly showing that she was chewing on her lower lip.

"What's this?" he asked as he reached for her mouth, pulling her lip free. "Are you having second thoughts?"

She shook her head as she stretched up, her hands landing on his chest as she leaned in, her lips hovering just above his. "Not even close."

The warmth of her breath touched his lips before she closed the remaining distance and kissed him. It was the kind of kiss that completely obliterated every ounce of composure he'd managed to attain since they'd left the bar.

"Brie." It was a struggle just to say her name between kissing her.

"Hmmm."

Just that fast, it became even more of a struggle when she hummed against his mouth. He felt those vibrations move through every part of his body. And to think, he hadn't imagined it was possible for his dick to get any harder.

He'd been wrong. Oh, so very wrong.

"Brie," he tried again. "Which room are you staying in?"

"Three-oh-two."

"Let's go." He grabbed on to her waist, spinning her around and lightly smacking her on the ass. "Before I fuck you on the stairs."

Room three-oh-two was on the top floor and to the right. So for three flights of stairs he had a perfect view of Brie's ass in those tight red pants, and the higher up they climbed, the more painful his hard-on became.

By the time they were at the door he was ready to knock the stupid thing down. Luckily for him, Brie was quick with the keys. And doubly lucky for him he'd been in these rooms enough times over the last couple of years to know the layout. Though, he hadn't been in the rooms because of a one-night stand. Tonight was actually a first.

Once the front door was closed and locked, Brie was in his arms again, and they picked up where they'd left off downstairs.

He walked her backward through the dimly lit living room, the little lamp in the corner guiding his path. She was already working on the front of his shirt while he was focused on getting them through the room. He pulled his glasses from his face, tossing them on the coffee table as they passed by it. When all of the buttons on his shirt were undone, she slipped her hands inside and pushed the fabric down. He dropped his hands from her body before letting the shirt slide the rest of the way off his arms and down to the floor.

Next, she was pulling up the fabric of his navy-blue T-shirt, her palms on his abs and then his chest as she worked it up. He was forced to break the kiss as he helped her pull the shirt over his head and they both tossed it to the floor.

"Good Lord," she whispered almost reverently as she laid one palm flat on his abdomen. The other went to the center of his chest, her fingers brushing over his nipple and making him groan as she moved out.

He knew her intended destination was his one and only tattoo, a tattoo that wasn't small by any means. It started at his left pecs, dog tags that were designed after the ones his grandfather Owen had worn when he'd fought in WWII. The chain stretched up and to his shoulder where it was grasped in the talons of an eagle.

His brother had an identical one in the exact same place.

She traced the chain with the very tip of her finger, and that little light touch was killing him. Well, that combined with how her other hand was currently exploring his abs, her thumb moving over every ridge as she moved down to the front of his jeans.

Finn moved quickly, grabbing her hands as he pushed her back against the threshold of the bedroom.

"Hey, I wasn't finished."

He grinned, lifting her arms up and pinning them above her head. "I don't doubt that. But it's my turn. You're still wearing entirely too many clothes. And once I take care of that, I'm going to need a second to look at you without your roaming hands."

"What? You don't like my roaming hands?"

"Brie, I like them way too much. That's the problem. I need to focus, and *you* are distracting me." He leaned in close to her mouth, the soft fabric of her sweater moving across his chest. It felt nice, but he definitely wanted to feel something else on his skin, like her bare breasts. "You going to be a good girl?" he asked before he nipped at her bottom lip.

"Not even a little bit."

"Perfect." He grinned as he let go of her wrists, but she didn't move her arms down. Instead she kept them in place up and over her head. Apparently she wanted a few minutes with his roaming hands on her body. Well, that made two of them.

Finn let his fingers trail down the front of her sweater and to the hem. He lifted the material, his hands moving underneath and his palms going flat on her warm skin. As he slid his hands up her sides the material bunched at his wrists, until he was pulling the sweater over her head and off her arms.

Taking the tiniest of steps back, he looked down the length of her body. There was the perfect amount of light to just see the blush on her golden skin. It extended beyond her cheeks, down her neck, and to her chest.

She had a good rack. A C-cup…or maybe even bordering a D. The bra she wore wasn't anything extravagant, just a thin covering of nude lace over the lined nude cup and the smallest of pink bows in the middle. Even through the slight padding, he could clearly see the outline of her erect nipples. The whole look was erotic as anything he'd ever seen, probably *because* of its simplicity.

Finn reached up, touching the diamond pendant that hung a few inches above the dip of her cleavage, before moving down and tracing the swell of her breasts. His fingers went from one side to the other, dipping down to the valley in between. "God, you're so soft. That's another thing I like about you."

Brie didn't say anything, just watched him as she licked her lips. Her breathing was slightly erratic, and it was made more so when he palmed one of her breasts and lightly pinched her nipple through the material.

"Finn." She gasped his name, eyes closing and back arching, pushing her breast into his hand.

"Do you like it when I do this?" he asked as he did it again. "Do you like how I touch you?"

"Yes."

"Then you're going to love this." He dropped down to his knees as he pulled the cup of her bra aside and covered her now exposed nipple with his mouth, sucking deep and tasting her breast. A throaty moan filled the air, the sound of Brie's pleasure making his dick twitch in his pants.

He wanted to be inside of her like he needed to breathe, but he had to take his time. They had one night together, and he wanted to make it really good for both of them. Really, *really* good. First stop was showing equal admiration to both breasts. He hooked his fingers in the other cup of her bra, pulling it down before he moved his mouth to the other side.

Bringing his hand up to her now freed nipple, he rasped his thumb across the peak. Brie writhed against him as he explored with his mouth and hands, sucking and licking, palming and pinching.

Brie's hands were no longer stretched up above her head. He hadn't seen her bring them down, but he had felt the slight movement before her fingers speared into his hair. Currents of pleasure shot down his spine as her nails raked against his scalp. Her nipple popped free of his mouth, and he took another long taste of it with his tongue.

Now it was time to taste other fine attributes. He placed open-mouthed kisses down to her belly. As much as he wanted to get the front of her pants open, he knew he needed to take care of her boots first.

The zippers ran up the inside of her calves, and he pulled the right one down, her hands landing on his shoulder for balance as she lifted her foot and he tugged at her boot, sliding it off. They repeated the process for the other foot, getting rid of her socks, too.

That was one obstacle down. Now for another. His focus went to the front of her pants, and he popped the top button free. The zipper was next and he hooked his fingers in the sides, pulling them down her thighs and freeing her legs.

"Oh, I like these." He ran a finger down the front of the

black lace thong she wore, the sheer fabric not leaving much—if anything—to the imagination.

His gaze moved back up the length of her body and over her breasts. They were still exposed and pushed up by the cups of her bra bunched under them. And then his eyes finally met her dazed ones.

"Take off your bra."

Brie's mouth quirked to the side as she arched away from the threshold of the door and slipped her hands behind her back. The bra fell down her arms, the straps getting caught at her elbows. She pulled it off, dropping it onto the floor next to the rest of her clothes.

For just a moment Finn forced himself to stop and just look, to admire the sight in front of him. And God, what a sight. Brie was fucking stunning as she stood there in nothing except her tiny black thong and that little diamond necklace. Her hair was still pulled up on top of her head, a few loose strands falling down around her face.

"Take your hair down."

She didn't say a word as she lifted her hands again, pulling a few clips from her hair. Each one echoed against the floor in a tiny *ting* as she dropped them. With a light shake of her head, all of that brown hair came tumbling down around her shoulders.

She was the most beautiful woman he'd ever seen in his life.

Fuck. He didn't need that kind of thought in his head. Beautiful, yes, that was fine. But *the* most beautiful? That was a whole different animal…and an entirely different story. Something he needed to not be thinking about now or *ever.*

So he chose to think about something else, like being inside of her.

"What do you think, Brie?" he asked as he traced over the very top of her panties, the pads of his fingers moving over the delicate lace. "Do you think I'm going to like what I find here?" His hand moved down lower and he touched her through the thin material, pressing in just enough to feel the heat of her. She was wet, something that the little barrier couldn't hide.

"No." She reached down and pulled her panties aside, revealing the small patch of neatly trimmed brown curls above an otherwise bare pussy. "I think you're going to fucking love it."

With an invitation like that, it would've taken a much stronger man than him to wait a moment longer. He leaned forward, and she gasped as he opened his mouth over her. He slowly licked over her folds, finding her even wetter than he'd felt just moments before. She was slick with her desire, and she tasted better than he could've ever imagined. Sweet and salty on his tongue.

She was right, he did fucking love it.

"Perfect," he whispered before rasping his tongue over her again and again. He reached for her knee, pulling her leg up and over his shoulder, spreading her wider. When he got to her clit, Brie's hands were in his hair again, her fingers tightening and pulling him closer.

"That's good, *so* good. Finn, your mouth—"

But exactly what his mouth was, he'd never know. It was then that he slid a finger inside of her, and instead of finishing her sentence she moaned as she started to move her hips, seeking more pressure. He gave her what she wanted, pulling his finger out before sliding two back in. He licked and sucked, her body writhing and her cries of pleasure filling the air. He didn't stop, didn't let up, just kept moving his tongue over her in slow, lazy circles.

"Oh God! Oh! Ohhh!" she cried out as her body went taut, the core of her pulsing around his fingers as she came against his tongue.

There was no stopping until she was finished, her hands loosening in his hair as she relaxed back against the wall, letting it take most of her weight. He turned his head, nipping gently at the inside of her thigh.

"Finn." She gasped his name.

The desperate edge to her voice made him smile, and he kissed the spot he'd just bit. He gently pulled her leg from his shoulder, lowering her foot to the floor before he stood and got a good look at her face. Her eyes were at half-mast, and she gave him a slow sated smile.

It was so sexy he was pretty sure it blew a few of his brain cells.

Brie reached out, her fingers hooking in the top of his jeans as she pulled him closer, his body flush against hers. He groaned as her bare breasts touched his naked chest.

"So." She looked up at him, reaching her hand to his mouth and swiping her thumb across his bottom lip. "Did you *love* it?"

"I did." He nipped at the pad of her thumb before he pulled it into his mouth and had her sweet taste on his tongue again. Her breathing became even more unsteady, her heavy-lidded gaze on his mouth as he sucked her. Letting go of her thumb, he leaned forward, bringing his lips to her ear. "But not as much as I'm going to enjoy fucking you."

"Oh, I'm sure we're both going to enjoy that, *a lot*. But first"—her hands landed on his chest and she pushed lightly, getting him to take a step back and into the bedroom—"I do believe your turn was *way* longer than mine." She continued to push, Finn walking backward as she guided him. There wasn't much light in the room, just what was trickling in from the living room, but she clearly knew where she was going. "And your roaming hands, and mouth, were *way* more distracting. So it's my turn." His legs hit the bed and she pushed, this time harder. "Sit down, Finn."

He did as he was told, his ass coming down on the mattress.

"Take your boots off." She stepped back from him at this command and crossed the room.

He did as he was told and started working at the laces of his boots. There was a small clicking sound in the corner before a little lamp was turned on and the room filled with a soft, warm light.

She didn't want to have sex in the dark. Well, damn. That was new and different.

He only had one boot off before she was standing in front of him again. There was no doubt he'd get distracted if he looked up, so he kept his head down and made quick work of his other boot and his socks. It was a good thing he'd waited to look up at her, too. Because the second he did she hooked her fingers in the sides of her thong and pulled it down, shimmying the lace down her legs.

Even though he wasn't wearing his glasses, he was still close enough to clearly see her. His bad eyesight was more of a distance thing.

"Holy shit." He swallowed hard, his eyes moving up and down her now entirely naked body. He was never more thankful for the invention of the lightbulb than in that moment.

* * *

Brie had absolutely no idea what in the world had gotten into her. Yes, she liked sex. Well, she liked it when it was *good* sex. Even better if it was great sex. She'd had fantastic sex a handful of times, the kind where she felt it the day after and used the memories to help her out when she was flying solo.

There was no doubt in her mind that Finn was going to qualify in that last category. Not only that, but he'd probably one up all of her past experiences. She'd feel him for *days* after, and he'd probably play the lead in her fantasies for months to come. And that was just with the memories of him going down on her.

They weren't even close to being finished with the evening, so there were even more memories to be made. Her panties slid down her legs, the lace skimming her skin on the way. She stepped free of the material, moving forward and putting herself between Finn's thighs.

"Lay down." The command came from her mouth like she was used to doing this sort of thing in the bedroom.

She was not. So, so, so, so, so not. Everything about this night was entirely out of character for her and she didn't care in the least little bit. She was going for it. Everything else was spiraling out of control around her, except for this. She could control this night. She could control what happened in that room.

"Yes, ma'am." Finn grinned as he lay back on the bed, his feet still planted on the floor.

Brie moved even closer between his legs, his jeans brushing across the outside of her thighs. She reached forward, her hands landing on the buckle of his belt. Her fingers were steady as she pulled the metal and leather free. Once the button was undone and the zipper down, she grabbed on to the sides of his jeans.

"Lift," she said as she tugged.

He lifted his hips from the bed, helping her get rid of his jeans. They slid down his thighs, revealing black boxer briefs that very clearly showed the outline of his erection. She'd felt him pressed up against her belly earlier, but seeing was believing. The man wasn't what anyone would call small, *anywhere*, and he definitely wasn't small there.

Once the jeans were free of his feet, she dropped them to the floor before she moved back between his thighs. This time it was the black hairs on his legs that brushed over her skin. She reached down on both sides, her fingers landing on his knees before she slowly moved them up and over his thighs. Just that slight touch made his cock twitch against the black fabric of his boxer briefs.

A smile turned up her mouth as she walked her fingers up and over to his rather impressive bulge. "This is nice," she said as she traced over him.

Finn's nostrils flared as he took a deep breath through his nose. "Sweetheart, you are going to have a way different word for it than *nice* when we're finished."

"I'm sure I will." Her hands went flat on his chest as she leaned over him, one knee sinking into the mattress next to his hip as she swung her other leg over his body to land on the other side.

He groaned as she settled over him, pressing into his erection. His hands moved to her hips as his back arched off the bed and he pressed himself to her. The pressure was exquisite, but if he kept at it she was going to get sidetracked, and she had a mission of her own.

"Oh no, you got your turn without distractions." She pulled

his hands from her body, shaking her head. "Put your hands behind your head."

Surprise and lust flickered in his eyes, probably a thirty-seventy ratio. "Yes, ma'am." He grinned as he lifted his head, folding his arms before lowering it into his palms. His muscles bunched and rippled as he moved into his new position, showing off impressive new angles.

God, this man's body was a work of art. And it was her turn to explore, so exploring she went.

She started at the top of his boxer briefs, brushing over the light dusting of hair that dipped down beneath the fabric. He had a pretty impressive "V" that she wanted to trace with her mouth, wanted to lick and bite.

Maybe later.

Her attention went up to his abs where she outlined each ridge with her fingertips. "One," she whispered as she moved to the other side. "Two." Both hands were on him now, all of her fingers on his skin as she continued north. "Three and four."

Finn shifted underneath her, rubbing up against her.

"Five and six." Her next inhale was unsteady and she looked up to his face. "You keep doing that, I'm going to lose count and we will have to start all over."

"Promise?"

"No distracting, remember?" She put her palms flat on his abdomen, her nails gently biting into his skin.

Finn pushed up again, this time circling his hips.

"Seven and eight," she finished before she leaned forward, hands skimming up his body, and captured his mouth with hers.

Her breasts were pressed against his chest, the light dusting of hair on his pecs tickling her nipples as she slid over him. Her tongue moved against his, licking and tasting. He rocked his hips underneath her, pressing his cock against her clit. To say that he was driving her crazy would be an understatement, but two could play at that game.

Pulling her mouth from his she started to kiss her way down his throat and to his chest. The second she swirled her tongue over his nipple, he stopped moving his hips as his back arched off the bed and he groaned, long and low and filled with pleasure. Brie treated his other nipple to the same swirl before she continued on moving south, kissing across those abs she'd counted earlier. She was straddling his knees when she got to his rather stellar "V," and she did do a little biting and licking…or a lot.

"Do you like this, Finn?" she asked as she nibbled around his belly button.

"So damn much." His words came out strained, like he was barely holding it together.

"Then you're going to really like this." She hooked her fingers in the sides of his boxer briefs and pulled down.

For just a second Brie stilled and just looked. Oh, seeing was *definitely* believing. Finn's cock sprung free and the man was gloriously long, hard, and thick. She wrapped her fingers around his shaft, her thumb swiping across the tip before she started to pump her hand up and down the length of him.

"Holy shit, that feels good."

"You know what's going to feel even better?" She squeezed his balls and he groaned, his hips coming off the bed.

"Me inside of you."

"Exactly." Brie let go of him as she slid off of his lap, her feet landing on the floor. "Condom?"

"In my wallet." He gestured to his jeans on the floor as his hands came out from behind his head and he pulled his boxer briefs the rest of the way down and off of his legs.

Brie grabbed the dark brown leather wallet from his back pocket and tossed it to him. He opened it, his fingers pulling out two.

"Well, aren't you confident?"

"You have no idea." He grinned before he tossed the extra one on the nightstand.

Brie snatched the other one from his hand and tore the foil open. "Lie back down, Finn. We're going to do this my way the first time."

"So you agree, there will be a round two?" he asked as he lay back down.

Brie straddled his thighs again before rolling the latex down his cock. "If you can get it back up"—she stroked her hand over him for good measure before lining him up to her entrance—"absolutely."

"Oh, sweetheart, that isn't going to be a problem." Finn grabbed on to her waist as he thrust up into her, while Brie pushed herself down onto him.

Neither of them moved for a second, both of them adjusting to the incredible feel of the other. Well, she at least thought he felt incredible inside of her, filling her up in every delicious way. And what with how his eyes were focused on her like he was right on the edge, she'd wager he was enjoying himself, too.

"Fuck, you're tight," he growled, his fingers digging into her skin.

"Does that go on the *like* column, too?" Brie leaned forward, her hands landing on his chest, using him for leverage as she pulled herself up, slowly dragging along every inch of him.

"It goes on much more than the like column," he ground out through clenched teeth as he moved up again while she came back down.

They were slow at first, getting a feel for each other before they picked up the rhythm. Finn clearly wasn't the type of man to just lie there while she worked. Not that she would've expected that for a second. He'd proven himself to be pretty dedicated to the task at hand early on in the evening.

And speaking of hands, one of his made its way between her legs, his fingers moving over her folds until he got to her clit.

"Finn!" As Brie's head had fallen back, she moaned his name to the ceiling.

Her back arched and she reached back, her hands on his knees as they continued to move. Up and down. In and out. Over and over again. She could feel it, could feel her orgasm building at the very core of her. Her hips rolled as he thrust into her, his fingers between her legs getting more insistent, his hand at her waist tightening.

"Come on, Brie, come for me."

And come she did, her body pulsing around Finn's cock as he continued to move. The orgasm wasn't a slow or sweet one. It slammed into her, taking her breath away for just a moment, and it was another moment before she got her voice back. When she did, she quite audibly showed him just how much she liked what he was doing to her.

Finn was right behind her, thrusting in a few more times before his body stilled. He was buried deep inside of her when he let go of his release, her name on his lips.

"Come here." He tugged on her hip, pulling her forward and onto his chest. His mouth covered hers as the hand at her hip moved up, his fingers delving into her hair.

The kiss was slow and languid, like he had all the time in the world. It was nothing like he'd kissed her so far that night, but it was perfect. She wanted more of it.

Luckily for her, there was another condom.

"Thank you," she whispered against his mouth.

He pulled back just enough to look into her face, the smile on his lips lighting up his eyes. "Did you seriously just *thank me* for sex?" There was a laugh in the question.

"No, not exactly." She shook her head, her teeth sinking into her bottom lip in an attempt to bite back her own smile. She let her lip fall from her teeth a second later. "I was thanking you for making me forget."

"Brie, we aren't finished yet. There's more forgetting in store for you."

"Oh thank God." And with that, she covered his mouth with hers again.

Chapter Five

A Rather Harsh Reality Check

It was just after two o'clock in the morning when Finn quietly shut the door to room three-oh-two behind him. He'd left a thoroughly satisfied and sleeping Brie behind in bed, snuggled up in the rumpled sheets and blankets.

They'd probably finished their second go-round well over an hour ago. That time Finn had been on top, Brie's legs wrapped around his waist as he'd taken her. It had been even better the second time around—something he hadn't thought possible—probably because they'd gotten a sense of what the other liked. She wasn't exactly shy about it, either…he knew what pleased her just by how her body responded to him.

It had been awhile since Finn had been that satisfied himself—neither of them had held anything back. She'd fallen asleep against his chest. Her mouth at his neck and her hand at his side, fingers stretched out against his ribs. He'd stayed there a little bit longer than he normally would've; it had just felt so fucking good to have her up against him. And he'd really liked touching her, having her under his hands.

When he'd gotten a little too comfortable, and had started to doze off, he'd forced himself to pull away from her. Before he'd gathered all of his clothes and left, he'd pulled the covers over her and kissed her on the forehead. He had absolutely no idea what had possessed him to do that last thing, but he had.

Now he was heading down to his truck, but he didn't make it past the first-floor landing before coming up short. Shep was making his way up the stairs. When his eyes landed on Finn he hesitated for just a second, shaking his head before he continued up.

"What?" Finn asked as Shep walked by.

"Just wondering when you're going to get tired of it."

And just that quickly, Finn's good mood disappeared. He glared at his brother's back. "Be careful, Shep, your hypocrisy is showing."

The thud of Shep's boots echoing across the wooden deck stopped as he turned around. "I'm a hypocrite?" His eyebrows rose high on his forehead, his frown pulling down the corners of his mouth.

"Correct me if I'm wrong, but you spent how many years working behind that bar picking up as many women as possible?"

"You're right, Finn, I did sleep around. Fucked more women than I can remember. And that's the point. I. Don't. Remember. You know what I do remember, though, *everything* about Hannah. That woman—and our son—is my world, and I would do absolutely anything for them. *Anything.* And all of that other stuff? Well, that's stuff I can't take back."

"Look, I'm not you. OK? Your life isn't mine."

"Really? 'Cause it sure looks like you're making some of the exact same choices I made. Can you tell me anything about the last girl you were with? Before tonight's rendezvous? Do you even remember her name?"

Finn racked his brain for a second…that had been a few weeks ago. "Margie." Or was her name Miriam…Marianne? *Shit.*

"It was Alicia, but nice try."

"How the hell do you remember that?" he asked, unable to keep the incredulousness out of his tone.

"Because *I've* been paying attention, Finn." Shep's voice rose, and he closed his eyes as he reached up, pinching the bridge of his nose. It was a second before he dropped his hand and opened his eyes. "If this is what you want to do for the rest of your life, sneaking out before the sun comes up"—he waved his hand at the floors above him—"and going home to an empty house, then that's your choice, and I can't stop you. But you want to know one of the last things Grandpa said to me?"

Finn was pretty sure he wasn't going to like the next words that came out of Shep's mouth, but as his brother didn't really even give him a second to respond, he was going to hear it anyway.

"He asked me when I was going to stop messing around with my life and settle down. He said I was twenty-eight years old and I needed to start acting like it. That was when I stopped fucking around. Three years before Hannah came back into my life. You're twenty-nine now, Finn."

They just looked at each other for a moment, Shep slightly blurry as he was a few feet away from Finn, who still wasn't wearing his glasses. *Shit.* He'd forgotten them in Brie's room. It wasn't the first time he'd left behind a pair of glasses, which was why he had a spare set in the glove compartment of his truck.

"Go fuck yourself, Shep. As much as I've enjoyed this little chat, I'm going home." And with that Finn turned around and headed for the steps, feeling like he'd just been punched in the gut.

* * *

The sensor light at the front of Finn's house turned on as he pulled into the driveway. He put his truck in Park and turned the engine off, looking at the building in front of him.

It wasn't just the Sleepy Sheep that Owen had built with his own two hands. He'd built this house, too. A two-story A-frame that sat on ten-foot pylons, the Gulf of Mexico stretching out behind it. Not that Finn could see the water at this hour, but it was a pretty spectacular view in the daylight.

When Owen had died and Ella had moved in with his parents, Shep had taken over the house. But when Hannah had moved down, Shep had given the house to Finn. He'd already moved back to Mirabelle at that point, actually he'd been living *with* Shep at that point.

Thinking about his brother pissed him off. Shep could have his opinions. Didn't mean they related to Finn. The circumstances weren't the same…not entirely anyway. They'd both gone down their respective paths because of failed relationships. Though, in Shep's case, the woman he'd lost came back to him. And for Finn, well, Rebecca had left because she hadn't supported what he wanted to be.

He wasn't enough for her to wait for. And what the hell did that say about him?

Shep could stand there and give his little Sermon on the Mount all he wanted. He got the girl in the end. Got *his* girl.

Finn hadn't. She'd been the only woman he'd ever been in love with, and she left. Left *him*.

Next to losing Owen, it was the most painful thing he'd ever gone through. He had absolutely no interest in experiencing that again.

None.

Finn got out of his truck and headed up the stairs to his house, keys jangling in his hands with every step. The second he opened the door the clip-clip-clip of nails on the hardwood floor echoed through the hall. His puppy was bounding around him, beyond excited to see him.

Well, maybe *puppy* was a loose term these days. Frankie was more than one and a half now, and a good ninety pounds. She was mostly white with a few light brown spots on her head and back.

"Hey, pretty girl." He dropped his keys on the side table before he bent down and started to rub her head. "Want to go outside?"

Her answer was to do two laps around his legs just in the time it took him to straighten and turn around. He pulled the door open and she bounded out of the house and down the stairs.

Frankie was yet another reason that Finn didn't stay the night places; he wasn't leaving her alone all night. The evenings he worked at the bar were the longest she spent by herself because he didn't leave her alone during the day. She came with him to work every morning, spending her time at St. Francis Veterinary greeting everyone who walked in the door in between her naps on the overstuffed doggie bed in the corner of his office.

His hands gripped the wooden rail of the deck as he leaned forward, looking out to where Frankie circled the patch of grass, sniffing around.

Finn was happy with his life. Happy with his job, his house, his dog, his friends and family. Well, usually with his family. His brother wasn't his favorite at the moment.

Finn was happy with the stability he had in those areas. He didn't need it in other places. He didn't need it in his love life. Scratch that, his *sex* life. He wasn't doing the whole love thing again. He wasn't interested. Not in the least little bit.

Shep's words replayed in his head: *I did sleep around. Fucked more women than I can remember. And that's the point. I. Don't. Remember.*

Finn didn't, either. Not everything. Snippets here and there, but nothing big picture. And as he thought about that, a flood of images played through his mind.

Brie walking into the bar for the first time. Brie walking into the bar the second time. Pulling her into the office, pushing her up against the wall, tasting her mouth. And then he got to the image of her as she stood in front of him, naked except for that black lace thong.

He'd known it then, right there in that moment as she shook all of that long beautiful hair down from her head and around her shoulders. He knew beyond a shadow of a doubt he'd forever remember what Brie looked like in that moment. He'd have that image in his head until his dying day.

That fact should've been unsettling, maybe even a little bit terrifying. Instead it was oddly comforting. He wouldn't forget any of that night. He wouldn't forget *her*.

* * *

It was close to eight o'clock in the morning when Brie woke up to find herself sleeping alone. She'd known immediately, opening her eyes to the empty side of the bed.

Brie didn't do regrets. Life was too short. Her choices were her own, and she always learned from them, good or bad. There was a reason for every single part of a person's past, for every single part of their history.

When it came to bringing Finn back to her room and sleeping with him, she'd do it all again. It still sucked to see that he'd left. That he hadn't even said good-bye.

It is what it is, and it ain't what it ain't. She repeated her father's saying in her head. It had been a one-night stand and it wasn't going to be anything else but that.

She rolled over in bed, feeling the slight ache in her muscles and between her thighs. Yeah, she definitely didn't regret the night before. Not even a little bit. He'd made her feel good—*really* good—and he'd made her forget. Yesterday, forgetting had been priority number one, so that had been a success. And so had the four orgasms he'd given her—those had been a *huge* success.

But there wouldn't be any more forgetting…or any more Finn-made orgasms. Today, Brie was going to face the reality of the situation. Face the reality of *her* situation.

Her eyes focused on the French doors that led out to the deck. The blinds on the windows were cracked—not enough to look into the room from the outside—and she could just see the glow from the rising sun peeking through.

The plan had been to leave by sunup that morning. Clearly

that hadn't happened. Besides, by this point in her trip she knew better with her "plans."

She was staying.

There really wasn't any other option. Her whole life she'd wanted to know her history, wanted to know more than the scraps she'd found with her research. This was her chance. A chance delivered to her by the one person who'd been the biggest roadblock before.

She had no idea what she was going to find in that house. Had no idea how long it was going to take her to go through it. There was just so much stuff. Everywhere. At least she had time to go through all of it. It was the second of February, and she didn't need to be back at UNC until classes started for the summer. That was over three full months from now.

Three months.

Well, one thing was for sure, she was going to need to figure out where she was going to stay. The inn wasn't an option, not for that amount of time, and not if she didn't want to be broke by the end of this little adventure. That left Bethelda's house.

There was no chance in hell she was going to sleep in the woman's bed. Just the thought didn't sit well. It was a recipe for getting even less sleep than she'd been getting. Though, she had slept pretty well the night before. She hadn't woken up once, not even when Finn had left. Clearly he had thoroughly exhausted her. Multiple orgasms could do that to a girl.

For just a second, she wondered how long he'd stayed. But then she shook the thought from her head. It didn't matter. She needed to focus on her current situation. No more distractions.

But, oh how she wanted one.

What she needed to do was come up with a new plan—

even if it did change, she had to have one—and she wasn't going to figure it out in that bed.

Brie grabbed the edge of the blanket and threw it off before getting up. First thing was first, she needed coffee and a shower. Once she got both of those, she could figure out what to do next.

* * *

St. Francis Veterinary Clinic was located almost right in the center of downtown Mirabelle. It was another one of the small-town businesses that was run out of an old Victorian house. This one was three-stories tall and painted a dark blue. There was an identical sage-green house sitting right next to it. That was where the owner of the clinic, Dr. Paul Laurence, lived with his wife, Delilah.

For fourteen years, Dr. Laurence had been the only vet in Mirabelle. There were a few other veterinarians in Atticus County, and some of the residents did take their business else-where, but the rest of the town had kept the man very busy.

And it was more than just the practice. St. Francis had started a foster/adoption program years ago. They'd done it be-cause the only other shelter in Atticus County was a kill shelter. The program at St. Francis had done a lot over the years in sav-ing animals from being euthanized.

Finn had begun volunteering when the program started. He'd been sixteen years old and he ended up cultivating a strong relationship with Paul. The man had become his mentor. Still was, as a matter of fact.

As soon as Finn graduated and moved back to Mirabelle,

Paul had offered him a job. That had been almost three years ago now. He loved working there, genuinely enjoyed coming in every day. Even if he was tired, or in that day's case, exhausted.

It was just before nine in the morning when Finn and Frankie walked in the empty waiting room. They both headed directly for the kitchen, Finn needing another cup of coffee to help with the grogginess that still lingered.

If he'd fallen asleep as soon as he'd gotten home the night before, he would've gotten five hours before having to get up for work. He could live off five hours. Even four would've been welcomed. He was working off of about two.

He blamed his brother.

Finn usually slept like a baby after he'd screwed his brains out. Yet that wasn't the case. Instead of sleeping he'd had his own personal slide show, the last couple of years playing out in his brain. After becoming a veterinarian, the significant things in *his* life were few and far between. Getting his job…getting the house…getting Frankie…that was about it. Everything else that was significant belonged to his friends and family.

Engagements, weddings, births. He'd sat in that hospital waiting room the night his nephew had been born, and he'd been so beyond excited for his brother and Hannah. Their joy had been his joy.

But that was the point…it was *their* joy. It had been awhile since he'd had his own joy.

The smell of coffee got stronger and stronger as Finn moved down the hallway, and when he walked into the kitchen he understood why the waiting room was empty.

For the last twelve or thirteen years, Gabby, a white and yellow cockatoo, had become a permanent fixture at the clinic.

When her owner had died, there hadn't been anyone to claim her so the practice had adopted her. The bird had settled in nicely to her new life and home, and she greeted everyone and everything that walked in the front door.

Well, when she was on her perch she did. She was currently on the shoulder of Janet Peterson—the official receptionist of the clinic, a job she'd held for about thirty-five years now—and being fed grapes.

"Hey, Janet. Hi, Gabby." Finn reached up and rubbed his hand across the bird's back.

"Hi." Janet smiled. Gabby lightly nipped at Finn's finger in affection before she squawked a *hello*.

"Coffee is fresh," Janet said before she slipped Gabby another grape.

"Thank God." The woman's coffee was usually strong enough to stand a spoon up in. It was exactly what he needed. He opened a cabinet door and pulled down a mug.

"Bad night?"

How to answer that, he thought as he poured the rich brown liquid into the mug. It made him think of the color of Brie's hair.

"No, not a bad night." Well, not bad until he ran into his brother. Before then it had been glorious. "Just long." Everything after he'd left Brie felt like it had taken an eternity.

There must've been something more to his tone, something that inspired concern, because Janet reached out and touched his arm. "You OK, honey?"

"Yeah." He looked at her and nodded, giving one of his smiles before he turned back to his coffee and added a little sugar and half-and-half. "I'm OK."

At least his words sounded a lot more genuine than they felt.

* * *

Checking out of the inn was the first thing on Brie's new agenda. Neither Shep nor Hannah were there when she left, so she'd put the keys—along with Finn's glasses—in the drop box by the front door.

Those had been a fun discovery that morning.

Then it was back to Bethelda's to take stock of everything, the kitchen being priority number one. She tossed the few spoiled items in the fridge and then went through the walk-in pantry that was grocery store organized. It had to be as it was packed to the brim with cans and dried goods. If the zombie apocalypse happened, this would be a pretty good place to hole up for a good two or three years.

She decided that for now she'd just use the overstuffed sofa in the den/library for a bed, which would mean she could sleep fireside if it got cold. Bethelda had enough linens to keep a small hotel going, so Brie threw some sheets and towels into the washing machine before she headed out the door.

The first stop was the Piggly Wiggly where Brie grabbed a few of her own grocery staples. Well, the staples she needed beyond the chips, chocolate, and wine she'd gotten at Target…like cheese, olives, and crackers. She'd also bought some cream for coffee, milk, eggs, bacon, bread, chicken, fresh fruits and veggies, and so forth.

After unloading her MINI—which had been filled to the brim—she headed over to St. Francis Veterinary. While taking stock of the supplies she needed, she checked to make sure she was Delores ready. And oh was she. There was an entire section devoted to cat supplies in the pantry.

Brie had no clue what to expect, but she did know that for as long as she was in Mirabelle she could at least take care of the animal. Once everything else was taken care of, she'd figure out what to do next. Her only hope was that the cat had a better disposition than the owner.

Well, the previous owner, because Brie was the owner now.

There was a strip of parallel parking in front of the old Victorian building, so she pulled her Cooper into one of the spots. She got out of her car and headed up the path to the wrap-around porch. The second she opened up the front door a loud squawk greeted her ears. Her eyes immediately landed on the white and yellow cockatoo perched a few feet away.

"Hello." The bird tilted its head to the side, looking at Brie at an angle.

"Hello," Brie said to the bird.

There was a woman working behind the front desk. She was probably in her sixties with steely gray hair and a thick southern accent. A very tall, muscular man stood in front of the desk, a leash in his hands and a large chocolate Lab on the other end of it. He'd glanced over when the door had opened, Brie getting a pretty good look at his handsome face. The dog looked at Brie, too, lightly panting as it sat on its back haunches at its master's side.

"I'll be right with you," the receptionist said to Brie.

She smiled and nodded before taking a step toward the waiting area and looking around. It was a warm space. Homey and rustic. The floors were all hardwood, the walls painted a deep red with black crown molding. Sage-green curtains hung from the windows that looked out onto the street.

A mismatch of wooden chairs lined the walls, all of them sporting a different fabric for the seat cushion. There were solids, flannels, florals, and stripes. A redheaded woman sat in the corner, a cat carrier at her feet. She had one leg crossed over the other as she flipped through a magazine. She was in her late thirties and looked vaguely familiar, but Brie couldn't place her. A man in his late fifties or early sixties sat a few seats away, his head bent over his phone as he scrolled his thumb down the screen.

Brie moved her gaze over to one of the walls that was covered with a black bookcase, though there wasn't a single book on it. Instead it was filled with products: collars, leashes, brushes, pet shampoo, treats, specialty dog food. A corkboard was off to the side, covered in pictures of people and animals.

Brie crossed the space to get a closer look, her eyes landing on a picture of a man standing with a bay horse. The horse, brown-bodied with a black mane and tail, was nuzzling its nose into the man's neck, while the man laughed, his eyes crinkling up behind his glasses.

He wasn't looking at the camera, but just one glance at the picture and Brie knew it was Finn. Recognition hit her like she'd just missed a step while walking down the stairs, that odd swooping sensation moving low in her belly.

"How can I help you?" The question brought Brie back to the moment and she turned around.

"Come on, Teddy," the guy said as he and his dog moved off to the side and away from the desk, heading toward the waiting area.

It took Brie a second to remember why she was there. Seeing the picture of Finn had thrown her for a loop. She lightly shook her head as she took a step forward. "My name is Brie Davis and I came here for a cat that you guys have been sheltering. The owner passed away and she was left to me."

"Oh, I'm sorry for your loss."

It was on the tip of Brie's tongue to tell the woman she hadn't lost anything. It was Bethelda who'd lost out. Instead, she just gave a slight nod of her head.

A clip, clip, clip echoed through the room and Brie looked over as a massive dog emerged from the back hallway. It was mostly white with a few light spots on its fur. The new dog made a beeline for Teddy. The chocolate Lab was dancing next to the man's legs in excitement.

"Wow. That dog is enormous," Brie whispered in amazement as she looked back to the receptionist.

"You should see her brother. Frankie is about twenty pounds smaller than Duke."

Brie's attention swiveled back to the dog. "Holy cow."

Frankie and Teddy were now nuzzling up to each other, licking the other's face and playfully barking.

"Brie?"

This time she froze at the voice that spoke behind her. She knew from just that one syllable who it was. That little swoop she'd felt in her belly at seeing Finn's picture was nothing compared to hearing his voice. It was a plunge now, like she'd just been pushed off of a cliff.

She closed her eyes, taking a deep steadying breath through her nose. Exhaling slowly, she turned around.

Finn was standing a few feet away, his eyebrows raised high

over his glasses in surprise. Apparently he had more than one pair. He was wearing jeans and a long-sleeved, hunter-green Henley. The material of his shirt clung to his chest and biceps.

God, he looked good.

"Hello, Finn." Those two words came out surprisingly steady considering her heart was beating out of her chest. What was wrong with her? Why was she so nervous? The man had seen her naked. He'd been inside of her for God's sake.

A loud bark rent the air as Frankie stopped playing with Teddy and bounded over to Finn. He didn't take his focus from Brie as he reached down, his hand landing on the dog's head.

"What are you doing here?" they asked in unison.

She would've smiled if she could've found even an ounce of humor in the situation.

"I work here," Finn answered first.

"I thought you worked at the bar."

"It's my family's bar. I work there every once in a while, but I'm a veterinarian full-time."

"Oh." She nodded. What did it really matter that he'd left that little piece of information out? A one-night stand with a local bartender was really no different from a one-night stand with a local veterinarian.

She, on the other hand, had left out a little bit more. Or *a lot* bit more.

Uneasiness settled in and she shifted on her feet. It wasn't so much that she'd set out to keep her connection with Bethelda a secret…well, except for that whole hiding and running away thing back at the funeral. It was just that once Finn knew, she had a pretty good feeling it wasn't going to go over very well.

Though, she wasn't sure why she cared about that fact anymore. Clearly nothing else was going to happen between the two of them. Him walking out had solidified that. So really, it didn't matter if he knew the truth.

It didn't matter at all.

Chapter Six

Secrets

Finn's initial thought at seeing Brie was *she's still here.* The hope that flared up in his chest was entirely unexpected, and he tried to shove it down.

Didn't work.

The hope was buoyant, expanding like a fucking balloon.

Shit.

He didn't need this. When he'd walked away the night before he'd been done. And yet, looking at her now, he didn't want it to be done. He wanted to taste her lips again. Wanted to bury himself inside of her. Wanted to feel her warmth. Hear her moans.

Fuck.

Fuck, fuck, fuckity, fuck.

"I came here to get a cat in the shelter," Brie told him...and everyone else in the room. Both Janet and Bennett Hart—one of Finn's close friends—were paying close attention to the whole interaction. Just what he needed while he talked to Brie, an audience. A captive audience at that. There was absolutely no doubt in his mind that they were both taking notes.

And that wasn't the only audience they were going to get, either. It was at that moment that Dr. Laurence and Annette Wharton (one of the sweetest but *loudest* ladies Finn had ever met in his life) walked out of an exam room. Mrs. Wharton's little toy poodle Chester was leading her on a leash in one hand while she gripped her cane in the other.

"What cat?" he asked, the question coming from his mouth automatically. Audience or not, he wanted to know what was going on.

"Delores."

"Bethelda's cat?" Finn's confusion only got worse. *Why was she getting Bethelda's cat?*

"Yes."

"Bethelda left you her cat?"

"Yes." Brie repeated like that one word was supposed to make perfect sense.

Too bad it made absolutely no sense. Not a lick. "Why?"

"My guess is because there was no one else for her to leave it to."

It was then that something clicked. "Bethelda was the unwanted, unpleasant business." Not a question.

"*Was?*" A scoffing sort of huff escaped her lips. "Try *is*. If only this whole thing with her was over."

"Did that young lady just say Bethelda left her a cat?" Mrs. Wharton shouted from the other side of the room.

Brie pulled her gaze from Finn and looked around. Finn did the same, seeing that they'd gotten the attention of the people in the waiting room, too.

Great. Just what he needed. Mindy Trist was sitting in there. The woman had a mouth made for gossip. She might've not liked to be in Bethelda's headlines for her own exploits, but it hadn't stopped her from repeating anything and everything. She was currently looking at Brie like a spider who'd spotted a juicy fly.

This was not the place for this conversation. Not even close.

"Do you have a minute to talk in my office?" he asked her, pointing behind him.

She nodded.

"Janet"—Finn looked to the receptionist—"would you please get everything together for Delores? Paperwork and supplies? I need to have a word with Brie."

"I can do that," Janet agreed.

Finn moved to the side as Brie turned, both of them heading toward the door off to the right. He had every instinct to reach up and place his hand at the small of her back, but he forced himself to keep it at his side.

Frankie had moved in front of them, leading the way as her long fluffy tail wagged back and forth. She pushed at the partially opened door with her nose, making it swing wider before disappearing inside.

Both Brie and Finn followed, stepping over the threshold. She moved farther into the room while Finn closed the door behind them and flipped the light switch. As the sun had decided to make an appearance that day, there was a decent amount of light streaming in from the back window, illuminating the space along with the overhead light. Finn's mahogany desk was off to the side, a bookshelf behind it and two leather armchairs sitting across from it.

"I'm guessing she belongs to you?" Brie asked as Frankie started to circle her legs, sniffing around her shoes.

"She does belong to me. She might be massive, but she's harmless. If you're scared of dogs or anything—"

"No, she's fine." Brie reached down, letting Frankie sniff the back of her hand. Frankie showed her approval by licking Brie across the knuckles. "Hello, pretty girl," she said as she leaned forward, her fingers delving into the dog's soft, thick fur as she started to pet her.

Such a small thing, but Brie greeted Frankie with the same *pretty girl* that he always did. That stupid balloon was still expanding. He needed to pop it.

"So you're here for Delores?" he asked as he leaned his hip against his desk. "After our conversation the first night you got here, I was under the impression you didn't know Bethelda."

She gave the dog another good scratch before she straightened. As soon as the petting stopped, Frankie went off to the other side of the room and plopped down on her doggie bed.

Brie's focus moved to his, something guarded in her eyes that he hadn't seen before. "I didn't know Bethelda." She shook her head. "Not really."

"But she left you her cat?"

"You ask that like it's odd." A small sarcastic smile turned up the corner of her mouth.

Finn's eyebrows climbed up his forehead. "Well, I've never been bequeathed a cat by someone I've never met."

"I never said I hadn't met her. I said I didn't know her. Two different things."

"Yeah, well either way, you left a couple of things out."

"So did you, *Doctor* Shepherd, like a good-bye." There was something biting in her words, and he felt them sink into his skin with a sharp sting.

"Look, Brie, I don't know what you expected from last night, but—"

"You don't need to explain yourself." She waved her hand in the air. "I know *exactly* what last night was. And don't worry, once I get the cat I will be out of your hair. I promise you, I won't darken your doorstep here or at the bar for the rest of the time that I'm in town."

"You're staying in Mirabelle?"

"By that ever-growing frown on your face, I see how happy that makes you."

Except she didn't really understand why he was frowning. It was because of that damn balloon. *She was staying. But for how long?*

He didn't get the chance to ask. The next few sentences that came out of her mouth completely sidetracked him from asking that particular question.

"I'm sorry to disappoint you, but as previously stated my unwanted, unpleasant business here isn't finished." She took a deep breath, like she was resigned to her fate. "Bethelda was my biological mother."

And just like that the balloon in his chest popped with an echoing burst. The sound rang in his ears while the shredded latex snapped across his skin. He had to force himself not to flinch.

"W-what?" He pushed his hip off of his desk and straightened. "You're Bethelda's daughter?" Why wasn't this fact computing in his brain?

Out of all of the things he could've imagined Brie saying, that was the very last. Bethelda Grimshaw had a daughter? No. No, that couldn't be right. Maybe because he just couldn't fathom someone actually sleeping with the woman. Procreation and Bethelda made absolutely no sense. He couldn't merge Brie with Bethelda. Brie, the beautiful, passionate woman standing in front of him. The woman he'd spent the night with.

Good Lord, he'd fucked Bethelda Grimshaw's daughter.

"Are you kidding me?"

Brie's eyes narrowed on his face before she shook her head. "No. I'm not. She gave me up for adoption twenty-eight years ago. I found out yesterday that she left me everything." She waved her hand in the air as if to indicate *everything*. "Delores included. So just as soon as I get my cat, I can leave. Are we done here?"

"Oh, we're done all right." The words came out a little harsher than he intended.

Brie flinched, taking a step back. "I was so beyond wrong about you." That was all she said before she turned around and walked out the door.

Well, she wasn't the only one who'd been totally wrong.

* * *

Brie wasn't sure if it was possible to feel worse when she walked out of Finn's office. Never in her life had someone looked at her like she was something slimy that had just slithered out from under a rock. Well, until about twenty seconds ago.

That being said, it wasn't the first time she'd been unwanted. His rejection hadn't even compared to what she'd been dealt at the hands of Bethelda ten years ago.

Not even close. Didn't mean it hadn't sucked. But wrong about him or not, she still wasn't going to play the regret game.

She just wasn't going to do it. What was the point? There was no use dwelling. None. It would get her absolutely nowhere.

Learn and move on, Brie. Just learn and move on.

When she walked out into the waiting room, it was a lot less crowded. The lady with the toy poodle was gone, along with both of the people who'd been sitting. The only people left were Janet, the receptionist, and the man with the Lab.

The man was leaning against the back wall, and his attention immediately moved to her. His gaze was entirely too assessing, and she had to fight not to squirm. Getting analyzed at that moment was the very last thing she needed.

God, she wanted to get out of there. But she still needed to get the damn cat.

Brie walked over to the receptionist's desk, putting space between her and the asshole she'd just left in the office. As she got closer, she noticed the hot pink pet carrier sitting next to the desk. She assumed it was the carrier for Delores, what with the loud color and all.

Bethelda was about as subtle as a gun.

The size of it had her coming up short, though. It looked like it would be more appropriate for two cats, not one.

"What do I need to do?" Brie asked.

"Just read this and sign." Janet handed her a pen as she pointed to the piece of paper on the desk.

Brie read over the paper. It said that Bethelda had left her the cat, that she was now taking full responsibility for the cat, and if for some reason she could no longer care for the cat, she had to bring it back to the shelter.

She signed on the dotted line before she handed the paper back. "That it?"

"Well, that and we need to get her down." Janet pointed to a spot over Brie's shoulder, and she turned, her eyes slowly moving up the bookcase.

Her eyes widened in surprise when she got to the top, focusing on the creature that was stretched out in the warm sunlight streaming in through the window.

It was the biggest, fluffiest feline Brie had ever seen outside of a zoo. It had gray fur covered in black spots and a thick mane around its head that looked almost white. Its long, black tail hung over the side, swinging back and forth like a fuzzy pendulum.

"Oh. My. God. That's Delores?" The question came out slightly strangled. "I was told I was left a cat. Not a snow leopard."

"Delores is a Maine coon cat. Though she is a little bigger than most females of this breed."

"What does she weigh? Twenty pounds?"

"Nineteen and a half," a voice answered from behind her. *Finn.*

Brie tensed and the back of her neck started to prickle, that uncomfortable itchy heat spreading over her skin. She was going to be lucky if she didn't break out into hives before she left this stupid town.

"Anything else I should know about her?" She balled her hands up into fists at her sides as she turned to look at him.

Frankie had followed him out of the office, leaning heavily against his leg. What was it with massive animals and this vet?

"Well." Finn frowned as he folded his arms across his chest. "She hates being confined, which is why we let her roam freely around here. She attacks any and all paper bags, sleeps on anything that's warm, loves to play in water, and won't eat her food if her dish is on the floor."

"Where am I supposed to put it?"

"We've been pushing two chairs together so she can sit on one while her food sits on the other," Janet answered.

"So she sits at the table?"

"Yup." Finn nodded, still frowning. "And she won't eat unless you're sitting at the table with her, too."

"Good to know." She nodded, unclenching her fists before she moved her arm and pointed up to Delores. "Any idea on how to get her down?"

Finn looked over to the man with the Lab as he dropped his arms. "Bennett, can you take Teddy into the exam room. Delores is skittish around most dogs, and she probably won't come down."

"Yeah, Teddy likes to make a big front with cats, but as soon as he gets a claw in the face he's cowering in the corner. Come on," Bennett said as he gently pulled on Teddy's leash. "Let's go." Man and dog walked across the room, disappearing through a door at the end of the hallway.

As soon as the door closed, Finn moved to the desk.

"What about her?" Brie nodded to Frankie.

"Frankie and Delores have become the best of friends in the last week. It's the strangest odd couple I've ever seen in my life. But to each their own." He shrugged before he looked to Janet. "Delores didn't see the carrier, did she?"

"No." The woman shook her head.

"Good." His hand disappeared into a fuzzy purple bag on the desk. When he pulled it out he held a plastic container. "Another thing to know is that she will do almost anything for a treat. I say almost"—his eyes moved to Brie for just a second before he looked away again, like he couldn't bring himself to linger on her for too long—"because going back to that whole she hates confined spaces, if she'd seen the carrier she wouldn't come down." He shook the container, making the little bits inside rattle around.

Delores's head came up, her eyes fixing on Finn. When he shook the container a second time her whole body moved. The bookcases were up against the wall that was connected to the staircase, the rungs of the railing stretching up behind them. She quickly walked across the top until she got to the bars, slipping through them and landing on the stairs. She was down the steps and across the room in a flash. As she passed by Frankie she rubbed her body against the dog's and then hopped up onto the desk.

Brie couldn't stop staring. The cat was even bigger up close. Bigger and beautiful. She had jade-green eyes, eyes that were focused on Finn.

"*Mrowww*." Delores tilted her head to the side, watching and waiting.

Finn unscrewed the cap, not moving his focus from the cat as he pulled out a little fish-shaped bit. He tossed the treat into the air and Delores moved her head back, opening her mouth and catching it. He repeated the process two more times before screwing the lid back on the container and tossing it back in the bag.

Reaching forward, Finn started to scratch Delores on the neck. The cat's eyes closed as a deep purring started to rumble from the animal's chest. He reached forward, lifting the cat into his arms. He continued to pet her, the cat's eyes closing in pleasure as the purring intensified.

It just freaking figured. The stupid jerk had the magic touch with more than just women.

Finn turned so that Delores was facing the opposite direction of the desk, nodding to Janet while he moved. She picked up the carrier, setting it down on the desk and opening the metal door. Before Delores even knew what had happened, she was in the carrier and the door was shut and locked behind her.

The purring stopped and a god-awful mewling started up. Not only that, but Frankie started to whine pitifully, circling around Finn's legs.

"Delores also does that"—Finn pointed to the carrier—"when she's pissed off. But she'll stop as soon as you let her out. She's actually a pretty good cat considering…" He trailed off.

"Considering who her owner was?" Brie finished for him.

"Yeah." His eyes narrowed on her, the frown on his mouth intensifying. He looked like he wanted to say something else to her, but she didn't want to hear it. Just because Bethelda was a shitty human being did not mean that Brie was.

But to Finn, they were one and the same. Whatever. He could have his idiotic wrong opinions.

She grabbed the fuzzy purple bag, pulling the strap over her shoulder. "Thanks for getting her down for me."

They both made a move to grab the carrier, but when their skin touched he pulled back.

He took a deep steadying breath, a muscle flexing in his jaw. "I can help you carry that outside."

"That's all right"—she shook her head—"I got it." She grabbed the handle, hefting the carrier and turning around.

She had to get out of there. Had to get away from him. And as she walked across the room and out the door, Delores kept up her mournful crying while Frankie howled behind her.

Chapter Seven

How to Eat Your Feelings
(Cover Them with Butter and Syrup)

Finn opened the front door of his parents' house, Frankie leading as they stepped over the threshold, and walked down the hallway. After a nod from him, she broke off when they got to the living room, heading for Ella who'd fallen asleep while watching *Jeopardy!* The dog lay down across his grandmother's feet, warming them.

He continued on to the kitchen, doing his damnedest to get over the lingering aftereffects of his afternoon. He hadn't exactly been in the best of moods since Brie had walked out of the office. Though that was putting it lightly. *Very* lightly. He was actually pretty pissed off and for many reasons.

One, Brie was Bethelda Grimshaw's daughter.

Two, she'd lied to him. And true, it was a lie of omission, but it was still a lie. Also true, he'd left out a few things himself, but the things she'd left out were much, *much* bigger.

Three, she wasn't leaving.

Four, she was Bethelda's daughter. *Clearly* this fact was bugging him.

He needed to put it all away for now, though. Especially as the evening was going to be spent surrounded by his family. The Shepherds weren't what anyone could call unobservant. Not a single one of them. Shep was probably the worst as he and Finn were the closest. The guy missed nothing. And really, being around his brother for an extended amount of time was the very last thing Finn wanted at that moment.

But he didn't exactly have any other choice because it was his father's birthday. They were having Nate senior's favorite meal: roasted chicken with garlic mashed potatoes and gravy. The chicken was already cooking in the oven, the mouthwatering scent of it filling up the house and Finn's lungs. His mother was famous for this particular meal.

Someone else who was entirely too observant for her own good was Faye Shepherd. He needed to not show weakness in front of his mother. If he did, she'd pounce.

He had to give her a lot of credit, though. She'd raised two beyond rowdy sons, and not only had she survived, but she'd thrived. She didn't back down from anything or anyone and would be the first to say exactly what was on her mind. Which was another Shepherd trait, one that Finn and Shep had gotten from both sides of the family.

What Faye Shepherd wanted more than anything was for her sons to be happy and settled down with a family. A few years ago, their mother's focus had been predominately on Shep. But that had been before Hannah had come back to Mirabelle and Finn had still been away at school. Now that Shep was happily married, and had already popped out the first grandkid, she'd moved all of that "settling down" focus to Finn.

It was exhausting.

When Finn walked into the kitchen it was to his surprise that he found Hannah was the only person in the room, standing at the stove and adding salt to a pot. Her strawberry-blond hair was pulled up into a ponytail and the sleeves of her deep blue sweater were pushed up to the elbows.

"You cooking tonight?" Finn joked.

His sister-in-law was a notoriously terrible cook and baker. There'd been one Christmas where she'd attempted to make Shep a cherry pie. The crust had been burned, the whip cream churned into butter, and the fruit filling had been sweetened with salt instead of sugar.

Yeah, she had the ability to be a disaster in the kitchen.

Hannah turned around, her sea glass–green eyes focusing on Finn as she adjusted her black-framed glasses on her nose. "The only way I'd be cooking tonight is if your father's favorite meal was heartburn with a side of nausea. No, baby Nate decided he wanted to wear his dinner instead of eating it. So your mom is giving him a quick bath while your father supervises. I on the other hand am boiling water"—she pointed to the pot—"for the potatoes. Something I am actually capable of doing."

"You sure about that?" He crossed over to her, bringing her into a side hug and pressing a kiss to her temple. "I feel like we should get the fire department on standby."

"You're hilarious. Not." She poked him hard in the side as she turned to look up at him.

"Hey, I'm just concerned about everyone's well-being. I had to ask. It's my responsibility."

"Is that so? Your responsibility?" Her eyebrows rose high over her glasses. "Well, in that case, what were you doing at the inn last night?"

For someone who'd been pretty determined to avoid questions about his current state of affairs, he'd opened the door and walked right on into that one.

He pulled back and folded his arms across his chest, his frown of the day dropping back into place. "Do you and Shep have anything better to do than talk about me? I already got this little lecture from him last night."

His words might've come out a tad harsher than he'd intended, but it wasn't like he and Hannah tiptoed around each other anymore. Not even close. They were family, and thus treated each other as such.

Hannah's eyebrows rose higher in surprise and her mouth got tight. "For your information, Finn"—she poked him in the chest—"your brother and I do not discuss you at length. I didn't even know that he knew you were there." She moved away from him and walked over to her purse on the counter, her hand disappearing inside for just a moment before she pulled it out. "But I did find the keys to Brie Davis's room along with these in the key drop box this afternoon."

His glasses sat in her hand.

"Oh."

"Oh?" she repeated, looking thoroughly displeased. "That's all you've got?"

"Sorry."

Hannah crossed over to him, handing him the glasses. "I'm allowed to be concerned about you, Finn. I'm also allowed to ask questions, any questions. And I really don't want to hear any lip about said questions considering the hell you put me through when I first came down here."

Finn and Hannah had a rather caustic relationship in the

beginning. Though, that was mainly his fault...or *entirely* his fault. It had been a few months after he'd moved back to town himself, and nothing had been the same from when he'd left to go to school.

Owen was gone, Ella was starting to fade, and Rebecca had moved on to Brett. It wasn't exactly the warmest welcome home. Then Hannah had shown up, and Shep was prepared to pack up his life to move to New York to be with her.

He'd blamed Hannah for everything. Totally fair...if you were an asshole. Which Finn had been. He'd gotten over his shit with her, though, and he loved his sister-in-law dearly. How could he not? The woman made his brother happier than he'd ever been.

"You're right." He nodded. Back then he'd questioned almost everything she did, so he was just going to have to deal with her questioning him now. Didn't mean he was going to like it.

"Damn straight I am." She reached up, placing her hand on his chest as the frown twisting down her mouth lessened in its severity. "You know I just want you to be happy. Right?" She patted his chest, and the corner of her mouth quirked to the side.

He reached up, grabbing her hand and gently squeezing before letting go. "I know you do."

She patted his chest again before she dropped her hand. "So does Shep."

"So does Shep what?" The man in question walked into the kitchen. He was carrying a teal box with "Café Lula" printed out on the sides in purple writing. It was their father's birthday cake.

"You want your brother to be happy," Hannah answered.

Shep set the box on the counter before he turned to Finn, the look on his face clearly saying he still might be a little sour about the conversation from the night before. Made sense as Finn had told his brother to go fuck himself.

"Yeah, I do want him to be happy." Shep shrugged before he folded his hands across his chest. "It's just that *he* doesn't want to be happy."

"Can we not get into this right now?"

"Sure. Except you're not going to get into it *ever*. You just do and don't think"—a harsh laugh escaped Shep's mouth—"and damn the repercussions."

"Well, I'm not saying *damn the repercussions* today. OK?"

"Oh yeah? And why's that?"

Maybe it was just the need to tell someone, even if it was his pissed-off brother and well-meaning sister-in-law. Though, Finn had to face facts. Pissed off or not, if there was anyone he was going to talk to, it was Shep.

"Brie is Bethelda Grimshaw's daughter."

Just that fast the look on Shep's face transformed from anger to shock, and his arms dropped from his chest, falling to his sides. "Bethelda had a daughter?"

"Yup. Last thing you were expecting?" Finn asked. "Me too."

"How…how is that even possible?"

"Bethelda gave her up for adoption twenty-eight years ago, and apparently left her everything in the will. She came into the office to pick up Bethelda's cat this afternoon. That's when she told me who she was…and that she wasn't leaving any time soon."

"Well…shit." Shep leaned back against the counter.

"What does it matter?" Hannah's question had both men turning to face her.

"What do you mean *what does it matter*?" Finn asked her, feeling himself starting to get frustrated. "You do remember who Bethelda Grimshaw was, right? Blogger-hag and all-around pain in our asses?"

"Um. Have you looked in the mirror lately, Finn? You're a pain in the ass, and we still love you." Hannah smiled sweetly.

"Truer words." Shep nodded.

"The point is, *Bethelda* did all of those things. Brie is not her mother. And you have absolutely no idea what the woman is going through. Nor, I'm guessing, do you know the finer points of this whole story. She didn't exactly seem overjoyed about her visit the little that I talked to her. Did she seem that way to you?"

No, she hadn't. She'd made it clear that it was unwanted, unpleasant business that brought her to Mirabelle.

Brie, if you say yes, I swear to you, I can make the rest of your night really *pleasant.* A weird sensation kicked low in his gut as he thought about how he'd whispered those words into her ear.

"She wasn't overjoyed, no, but—" Finn started, but Hannah didn't let him finish.

"Exactly. So before you judge her on the actions of others, maybe you should give her a chance. Or maybe you should take a step back and see what the bigger picture is. It might give you a better idea than focusing on one little spot in the corner." She tilted her head to the side, giving him a look that clearly said she thought he was being an idiot. "Obviously there was something you liked about her in the first place, considering the fact that you spent the night with her."

"Yes, there was." His frustration was intensifying. "But you don't get it, that isn't the point."

"Hmmm," she hummed, still giving him that *you're an idiot* look. "I think you're the one who doesn't *get the point*, Finn."

It was then that voices started to carry in from the hallway behind them. Nate senior and Faye came into the kitchen a moment later, a freshly bathed and changed baby Nate the third in Faye's arms. The kid was a spitting image of his father. Same sapphire-blue eyes. Same thick black hair that curled around his ears and the back of his neck. He was giggling in his grandmother's arms, clapping his hands together rather enthusiastically.

"He loves water more than any child I've ever seen." Faye smiled as she looked down at Nate who'd started making a series of nonsensical noises like he was responding to her. "Much more than the two of you. You guys hated baths," she said as she looked between her sons. Her smile faltered as she zeroed in on Finn. "What's wrong?"

"Nothing." Hannah moved in front of Faye, plucking Nate out of her arms and handing him over to his grandfather. "The boys are going to have a birthday drink with their dad while I help you in here."

Finn's frustration with Hannah lessened fractionally in that moment. She'd just given the perfect kind of distraction for his mother. A look of shock—and maybe a little horror—came over Faye's face at the prospect of Hannah helping her cook.

"Hey! I got the water going just fine." Hannah pointed to the pot steaming on the stove. "Just tell me what to do next."

As they left the kitchen, Finn was in an even worse mood than when he'd entered it. He hadn't even known that was possible. Apparently it was.

* * *

Keeping up with the theme of the day, Brie stayed pretty busy since she'd picked up Delores. The cat had wailed the whole ride back to the bungalow. Luckily it had only been about five minutes, because the terrible sound the cat made was close to nails on a chalkboard grating. The second Brie had gotten the carrier in the house, she'd opened the door and the cat had been out of it like a bat out of hell.

That had been about three hours ago and she hadn't seen hide nor hair of Delores since. What she had done was check a number of things off on her to-do list.

Brie had only packed for a couple of days, not a couple of months. There were a number of things that she needed now that she was staying, the most important being her research books. She'd called her friend Lyndsey, one of the few people who had a key to her town house. Lyndsey had said she'd swing by the next day and pack up a few boxes to mail down.

After that, Brie set up her room in the den/library. Maybe it was the whole being surrounded by books thing, but she felt the most comfortable in there. She unpacked the few things she had with her before setting up her makeshift bed on the sofa. Once that was finished, she moved on to cleaning.

The bathroom had been next on the list. It wasn't the first thing she'd gone through that day, but it had been a lot weirder tossing Bethelda's half-used toiletries than it had been throwing away the spoiled food in the refrigerator. It was more personal…more intimate. Brie learned a whole hell of a lot from it, though. And try as she might, she couldn't stop comparing their differences.

Bethelda liked tropical fruit–scented soaps. Brie was more of an herbal girl herself.

Bethelda used spray antiperspirant. Brie used the bar.

Bethelda was all about hairspray…she had thirteen cans of it. Brie's hair product of choice was mousse.

But they did use the exact same brand of toothpaste…and they both squeezed from the middle. That little discovery was a bit of a jolt. Actually, it had been more like getting the wind knocked out of her.

She hadn't let herself dwell on that small similarity, though. Instead she moved on to bigger things, like the woman's makeup collection. Bethelda had enough products to rival a department store beauty counter. Over a hundred palettes of eye shadow; eyeliner in every variety and color; powder, cream, and liquid foundations; mascara for days; probably two hundred plus bottles of nail polish; and her lipstick stash was fifty shades of red.

It was ridiculous.

The bathroom had taken up a good amount of her afternoon, and when she finished it was close to dinnertime. She'd moved on to the kitchen, looking through the options in the pantry and fridge.

It took almost no time at all for her to realize it was a breakfast for dinner kind of night. She was going to cover her feelings in butter and syrup before she ate them. And as she'd worked up a pretty good appetite, she was going to eat a lot of those feelings.

God, she couldn't stop seeing that disgusted look in Finn's eyes. It was completely opposite to how he'd looked at her the night before…when he'd been touching her…when he'd been inside of her.

She pushed the memories away, both good and bad.

Live and learn, Brie. Live and learn and move on.

She flipped the pancakes in the skillet, the sizzle of the un-cooked side hitting the hot metal. A soft pop came from the pan on the back burner, the bacon crisping up as it cooked. Her stomach rumbled as the delicious scents filled her nose.

Movement out of the corner of her eye had her turning her head just as Delores came stalking into the room. Her big fluffy tail was up in the air, slowly swaying back and forth with each step.

"Good Lord you are massive." Brie shook her head as she watched the cat move.

Delores stopped when she was a few feet away, sitting back on her hind legs and looking up at Brie, assessing. Apparently they were both taking a moment to study the other.

"Well, it's nice to see you out and about. Were you bored, hungry, or both?"

The cat's response was a low, rumbly *mrowww* before she licked her lips.

"I'll go with both, so let's get you fed before you decide to eat me."

Brie turned back to the stove, checking that the bacon was done before she flipped off the burner. She picked up the tongs sitting on the counter and pulled each piece out, setting them on the plate covered with a paper towel. Grabbing another clean plate from the cabinet above her head, she flipped the pancakes onto it, slicing off a decent dollop of butter to slide between each one.

While the butter melted, Brie went over to the pantry to grab Delores's food. The cat ate a two-to-one ratio of dry to wet food, something that Brie knew as the proportions along with the feeding times had been tacked onto the wall in the pantry. Delores continued to watch from her position on the floor, her jade-green eyes not leaving Brie.

After everything was measured out, Brie mixed the food in the bright turquoise bowl that was covered in yellow fish skeletons. Delores licked her lips again.

Brie was of half a mind to put the dish on the floor. She wondered if Finn had been messing with her when he'd rattled off that list of the cat's ridiculous preferences. But the second she grabbed the bowl and pulled away from the counter, Delores stood up and headed for the dining room. Brie followed and turned the corner just as the cat jumped up on the cushioned bench that ran the length of the table.

"Hmmm," she hummed, still skeptical, as she set the bowl down on the bench in front of the cat. "You going to eat?" she asked as she placed her hands on her hips.

Delores just sat there as she looked at Brie instead of the bowl of food. The stare-off lasted for a good twenty seconds before Brie gave up and headed back for the kitchen to finish getting her dinner ready.

It was another three minutes or so before she was carrying her plate and cup of steaming tea back into the dining room. The cat hadn't moved an inch.

Brie sat down and settled into her seat. The second she took her first bite of syrup-covered pancake, Delores moved to her bowl and bowed her head to eat.

"Well, I'll be damned."

So Finn apparently hadn't been lying to her…didn't change the fact that he was still an asshole.

Chapter Eight

You Know What They Say About Assumptions…

It was just after four on Friday when Finn pulled up in front of Mirabelle's biggest hunting and camping goods store. Though, *biggest* wasn't exactly saying a lot. Wide Open Spaces was in the building that used to house the Fifty-Nine-Minute Photo and the town's one and only Blockbuster back in the day. Once both of those had shut down, Angelo Rivera bought the building and tore down the dividing wall.

The stores tagline of "If It Flies It Dies, If It Hops It Drops" was stuck on the glass front doors in bold, black lettering. Finn grabbed the door handle and pulled, walking inside and immediately spotting Angelo behind the register. The guy had a phone to his ear and he looked up and waved as Finn passed.

Finn waved, too, heading to the back of the store and toward the fishing supplies. He'd just been out at Sam Johnson's farm checking on a pregnant mare. The store was on his way back to work so he'd taken advantage and stopped by as he needed to restock his hooks, weights, and fishing line for his rod.

Saturday morning was going to start well before the sun came up as he was going fishing with a couple of guys. The cold snap that had settled in that week was starting to let up, and it promised to be a pretty decent day out on the water. Though he wasn't sure if fishing was the right choice to take his mind off of things. *Things* being Brie Davis.

He hadn't been able to get her out of his head. Hadn't been able to stop thinking about the night they'd spent together. The feel of her soft skin under his hands. The faint scent of lemon on her skin, mint in her hair. Her throaty voice in his ear, getting huskier and huskier the closer she got to coming.

But following those excellent thoughts came the not so great ones…like finding out the truth. Then there was the whole conversation in the kitchen between Shep, Hannah, and him. He'd felt pretty justified in his reaction to the news, but his sister-in-law most definitely had not.

There hadn't been an opportunity for a proper conversation with Shep about it. Bethelda had put his brother through the ringer when it came to her stupid blog. The woman had caused them more than a little heartache and grief.

Shep would have to agree with Finn…wouldn't he?

Somewhere in his musings, Finn had wandered over to the nets. He was rubbing the nylon mesh of one between his thumb and fingers. Dropping his hand he moved over to the supplies he'd actually come for.

As he headed up to the front of the store, his phone vibrated in his back pocket. His stride faltered and then stopped as he pulled the phone out and looked down at the screen. It was a text from Shep asking about covering a shift at the Sheep the next week.

Before he had a chance to respond, something—or more accurately someone—collided with him from behind. Holding firm on his phone, the fishing line, box of hooks, and weights all clattered to the ground. A second later they were joined with a good-size box that had hit his side before bumping its way down his leg.

"Oh my gosh, I'm so s—"

But the apology died on the crasher's lips as Finn turned and came face-to-face with Brie.

Her eyes widened—way more brown than golden in that moment—and a flush of red started to take over her neck and cheeks. Though, he couldn't tell if the color was because of embarrassment or anger.

But he didn't need to wonder for long. Tension snapped her back straight, her shoulders going rigid, and her mouth coming together in a pinched purse as she glared at him.

Angry, she was most definitely angry.

Her focus moved from him to the floor before coming back up again. Her eyebrows rose high as she tilted her head to the side. "Out looking for your next catch?"

"Very funny." He frowned. "I'd say don't quit your day job, but clearly you don't have one."

He didn't really know anything about her personal life, but he figured it was a safe assumption. Based off their conversation yesterday, she was staying in Mirabelle indefinitely. There were very few jobs that would allow for that kind of last-minute absence. And if he was wrong? What did he care? There was really nothing to lose.

Besides, she'd poked first.

"Clearly." She said the word slowly, her eyes moving over his face. She studied him for a few more seconds before she shook her head in disgust. "I don't live my life with regrets, Finn. But I guess there's a first time for everything."

Well, that shut him up.

And with that, she bent down and grabbed the box she'd dropped containing an air mattress. She said nothing else as she headed to the register. Finn just watched her walk away, something uncomfortable twisting in his gut.

If he didn't know any better, he'd think he was regretting a few things himself...except it wasn't sleeping with her.

It was something else entirely.

* * *

Well, that had sucked.

Brie should've walked away. She should've picked up the air mattress and walked away without saying a single word to him. It was just that when she'd seen what he was buying, the snide comment had fallen out of her mouth. Like she'd had absolutely no control.

But when it came to Finn Shepherd it was becoming clear that she couldn't control the good or the bad outcomes. Well, what *had* been good outcomes. She hadn't been lying when she'd said he was making her regret her choices.

I'd say don't quit your day job, but clearly you don't have one.

What a dick. He made assumption after assumption with her. *Ass* being the operative word. He could go fuck himself, because he wouldn't be fucking her again.

Her hands shook just slightly as she walked through the parking lot. She tightened her grip—one hand on the bag with the air mattress while the other held her keys—trying to get a hold of herself. Unlocking her MINI, she put the box in the back before sliding into the front seat. As she twisted to reach for the seat belt, her lower back twinged, the pain causing her to suck in a sharp breath. Sleeping on the sofa last night had not been kind to her body. She'd woken with a stiff neck and a sore back. Plus, there'd been the cat that had burrowed under the covers and curled up at Brie's feet, taking up a good amount of the sofa herself.

Thus her investing in an air mattress.

During her initial walk-through of Bethelda's house, she'd found a stash of memory foam mattress toppers among the boxes in the spare room. Four to be exact. All still undisturbed in their original packaging.

She figured layering a couple of those on top of an air mattress (and making it cat-claw proof) would be a much better temporary bed than the sofa. Now she just had to deal with muscle spasms. And to think, a little over twenty-four hours ago she'd woken up feeling sated and relaxed.

That was clearly no longer the case.

No, today's feelings were ones of frustration and tension. Her temples throbbed with a headache that could not and would not be quelled with Advil. The cause of it all lay in a bright purple folder in the passenger seat next to her.

The folder held copies of all of Bethelda's monthly bills, bank account information, investments, deed to the house, keys, and so on. They were all the things that Brie had spent the morning and afternoon dealing with. The bank had been the first stop that morning, Brie giving them a copy of the death certificate to gain access to Bethelda's account.

After that she'd headed over to the cable company. She again showed the proper paperwork for access, paid that month's bill, and got them to reset the Wi-Fi password so she could actually use the Internet. She'd also taken care of the utilities, stopped by the PO box at the post office, and closed out a number of Bethelda's accounts around town.

With each stop that she made her day got worse and worse, and her headache got more and more intense. Every time she mentioned Bethelda's name people went from being helpful to hostile, and then they'd started to give her the third degree on who she was. They wanted to know *exactly* how she was associated to Bethelda.

Brie had long exceeded the max of what she could handle, but she needed to make one more stop to be finished with this particular task.

The GPS on her phone said that Rejuvenate, a high-end spa, was in the downtown area…just a few blocks away from the old Victorian that housed St. Francis Veterinary. She looked resolutely forward as she drove by. She wasn't exactly sure why as she knew for a fact Finn wasn't even in the building.

She pulled into the lot of the spa, her tires crunching against the gravel as she rolled into an empty space. Grabbing the papers she needed and sticking them in her purse, she got out of the car and locked it behind her.

Like a lot of the other businesses in the downtown area, Rejuvenate looked like it had once been a home. Nestled between two massive, mossy oaks, the building was slightly elevated. Five brick steps led to a wraparound porch that held a number of whitewashed rocking chairs. The windows were all outlined with white panels, which made them pop against the deep hunter-green siding. Planters hung from the ceiling of the porch, green leafy tendrils stretching down. Brie bet that when those flowers bloomed in the spring it would be even more of a sight.

She mounted the steps to the front door, pushing it open before walking inside. A bell chimed above her, making another chime as the door closed. Moving farther into the room, her eyes landed on the currently unmanned front counter. There was a glass display off to the left that was filled with a variety of colored stone bracelets, each one promising to bring the wearer a different gift. Wisdom, tranquility, peace, love.

She'd take any of them...except the love. She didn't need that.

To the right was an archway that led to an open room. One side had a wall of massage chairs—about half of them occupied—attached to foot spas while the other had half a dozen stations set up for manicures. Only two of those stations were filled, customers sitting across from women in jade uniforms. The one closest to Brie looked up from buffing her client's nails.

"Someone will be right with you," she said, and smiled before returning her focus to the task at hand.

Brie continued to look around. Multicolored tapestries covered the walls. Some sported animals (elephants, monkeys, tigers), others had flowers, and some had symbols. Jeweled chandeliers hung from the ceilings and rich woven rugs lay across the mahogany hardwood floors.

It was pretty quiet, too. Just the soft voices of the few people getting their nails done. It was a moment later when a curvy woman with black hair and stunning violet eyes came up from a room behind the front counter. She was wearing a jade uniform and a warm smile.

"Hello. Welcome to Rejuvenate. How can I help you?"

Brie pulled a small smile onto her face. It was the most she could muster at the moment. Really she was just preparing herself for the inevitable attitude switch to be flipped, as was the norm for her day. "I'm hoping you can help me. I need to close out an account. And I'm not sure what the refund policy is, but all of February was charged to the credit card on file and none of the sessions will be used."

And for four massages at eighty bucks a pop, that wasn't a small charge, either.

"Do you have the account number or phone number on the account?" the woman asked.

Brie moved to pull her purse from her shoulder, flinching as another twinge tightened her lower back. The run-in with Finn must've agitated it more, or maybe *he'd* just agitated *her* more. Setting the purse on the counter, she pulled out the papers and handed them over. One had the account number along with the automatic monthly charge, the other was the death certificate.

The woman glanced down at the papers for just a second before returning a now shocked look to Brie. "This is Bethelda Grimshaw's account?" she asked, lifting one eyebrow as she set the papers on the counter.

Brie had always wished she could do that, raise just one eyebrow. Whenever she tried she just ended up looking like she was trying not to squint one eye, which was a lot less cool.

"Yes"—Brie nodded—"Bethelda Grimshaw."

The woman continued to study Brie for just a few more seconds, confusion highlighting her features. There was no doubt a myriad of questions running through her mind, but she didn't voice a single one before she cleared her throat and moved to the computer.

Brie had been bracing herself, so the reprieve surprised her.

After a moment of typing, the woman looked back up at Brie. "We actually did an account review yesterday and put in a refund for the February charges. You should see that show back up on the card it was charged to in three to five business days."

"Oh." Brie was slightly taken aback by how simple that had been. Her shoulders slumped in relief, relief that was short-lived as her back spasmed again. She sucked in a sharp breath, her hand automatically moving to her lower back.

"You OK? That's the second time you've done that."

There was actual concern in the woman's voice, and to Brie's horror she felt her eyes start to water.

"Sorry." She blinked rapidly. "I slept on a couch last night, and it wasn't kind to me. I'm exhausted"—physically and emotionally—"and you're the first person today who has seen that paper"—she pointed to the death certificate—"and talked to me like I'm an actual person afterward."

And that was just from the death certificate; those people had no idea that she was Bethelda's biological daughter. But Finn had shown her quite clearly how people were going to re-act to that.

"Yeah, Bethelda wasn't what anyone would really call pop-ular around here. That doesn't justify anyone treating you like that." She tilted her head to the side, the sympathy on her face clear. "I'm sorry."

"Thank you." Brie reached up and swiped her fingers under her eyes. "I didn't even know her and I'm guilty by association."

The woman opened her mouth, inhaling before she spoke. For just a moment, she hesitated at the top of the shallow breath. Brie knew that the words that came out of her mouth weren't what she was initially going to say. She had questions, no doubt about it, but she didn't ask them.

"There are two credits on Bethelda's account. Nonrefundable credits…and I just had a massage cancellation."

"Seriously?" Good Lord a massage sounded absolutely glorious.

"It would be a shame to let those go to waste."

"You're on."

"Good." The woman held out her hand. "I'm Harper."

"Brie." A genuine smile turned up her mouth as she reached up, extending her own hand across the counter.

"Nice to meet you, Brie." Harper grinned back as they shook hands.

Chapter Nine

Pariah vs. Piranha

The sun was just coming up over the water when Finn threw his first cast out over the side of the boat and into the Gulf of Mexico. It really couldn't be a more perfect morning. The view was stunning, yellows, oranges, and pinks painting the sky. The temperature was in the low sixties and it promised to get up into the high seventies.

It was the perfect kind of day for fishing. He'd never get tired of mornings like this out on the water. Never get tired of the beauty that his town had to offer. Not ever.

For the eight years that Finn had been in school, and away from Mirabelle, he'd felt like something was missing. During those years, the longest he'd ever gone without coming home was two months, and that long of an absence had been pretty rare.

He loved Mirabelle. It had always been his home and would always *be* his home. Not everyone felt the way he did about it. All of his close friends growing up had moved away for college and settled down elsewhere. The only person who'd come back was Rebecca.

Finn and his ex met on the first day of second grade. She'd

forgotten her crayons at home, so he'd done the gentlemanly thing and shared his. From that point on they'd been best friends, and it was right before they'd started eighth grade that their friendship became something more.

It had happened two weeks before summer break ended, a rainy Tuesday that had kept them inside all day. They'd spent it having a movie marathon at her house. Her parents had been at work and her older sister had left to go to a friend's house. One minute they'd been watching *The Sixth Sense* and the next he'd been kissing her.

She was his first kiss…she was his first *everything* actually. First girlfriend. First lover. First love.

When college had rolled around they'd both gotten their top picks. His was Auburn, hers was Virginia Tech. They'd made the long-distance thing work. Daily phone calls. Driving halfway to meet up at a hotel in Greenville, South Carolina. They didn't even leave the room on those weekends. Dealing with the distance hadn't been the easiest thing in the world, but what other choice was there?

She was the love of his life…or at least he'd thought she was.

It had always been the plan that after they graduated from undergrad, they'd move back home and get married. They'd shared a mutual love for the small town that they'd grown up in, and that was where they wanted to spend the rest of their lives. Settle down. Have a family.

That had been the plan…but plans change.

During Christmas break of their senior year, Finn told her that he'd decided he wanted to go to school to become a veterinarian. He'd waited to tell her about applying and getting in to his top choice until they could celebrate together.

Rebecca hadn't wanted to celebrate. Instead she'd given him an ultimatum: her or school.

There was no conversation about how they could make their relationship work. She wouldn't even discuss it. Not all that surprisingly, Finn hadn't reacted well to her ultimatum and he'd chosen school.

Fourteen years, all of that history, and she'd just walked away. Admittedly, there was the fact that he'd let her go. But he'd thought she'd come back to him...thought she'd figure out that they were supposed to be together.

Oh, how wrong he'd been. So very, very wrong.

Instead she'd moved on and married someone else: Brett *fucking* Milton. There wasn't an ounce of love lost between Finn and Brett. Not from the time they'd been in the same little league together. Somewhere in that first season they'd started competing *against* each other, odd, as they'd been on the same team.

And the competing had never ended. Sports, academics, their personal lives...and then Brett had gone and gotten the girl. The *only* girl who had ever mattered to Finn.

The thing that had *really* gotten under his skin? Brett was a dentist. After undergrad he'd had to go to school for four more years, too. Meaning he'd come back to Mirabelle at almost the exact same time Finn had.

It had been a bitter pill to swallow, but he'd gotten it down in the end and moved on. And in the years since, he'd gotten over Rebecca...for the most part.

He wasn't in love with her anymore—that was for damn sure—but what happened with her had definitely changed him. How could it not? The only serious relationship he'd ever been in had ended with him getting his heart broken.

Thus him doing a total one eighty on that front. No commitments meant no pain.

That was why he shied away from commitment at all costs these days. He thought that with his three rules—no locals, no staying the night, and no repeats—he could prevent himself from going down that path…and prevent himself from regretting his choices.

Regret. That word kept repeating in his brain on a loop. Sometimes it was accompanied by more words…words from Brie. *I don't live my life with regrets, Finn. But I guess there's a first time for everything.*

Not only that, but when he closed his eyes he'd see her in front of him. See the pain etched on her face…radiating from every part of her.

What the *hell* was his problem? What the *hell* was he doing?

Boots thudded on the deck of the boat, stopping at Finn's left. He pulled his focus from the water—and his thoughts—and turned. Tripp Black stood next to him, an uncast rod in one hand and a disposable cup of coffee in the other. As Tripp had been getting Grant—his stepson…of sorts—set up, he hadn't gotten his line in the water yet.

Tripp wasn't one of Mirabelle's natives. He'd moved to town four years ago when he'd gotten the job of fire chief. He and Finn had gotten to be pretty good friends over the last couple of years. Probably because they'd been the last two remaining bachelors.

There was also the fact that their dogs were siblings. It was going on a year and a half that Tripp had found two puppies abandoned at the fire station. Tripp had adopted the male, Duke, and Finn had kept the female, Frankie.

So they'd had their dogs while everyone else in their close circle of friends had gotten married and started to pop out kids. But then Tripp had gone and fallen in love with his neighbor Beth. They'd started seeing each other last March and been married by December. And not only had Tripp gotten himself a wife, but he'd gotten an insta-family as well.

When Beth's sister and brother-in-law had died in a car accident two years back, she'd gotten custody of their three children. Nora (eighteen and no longer in the terribly rebellious stage she'd been in the year before), Grant (who was nine and hero-worshipped Tripp), and Penny (the sweetest four-year-old on the face of the planet). Tripp had fallen in love with those kids, too, and he was beyond protective of them.

Finn had seen it all happen, from beginning to end. He'd even walked in on them making out like a couple of hormonally charged teenagers. But that wasn't the only thing he got to witness. He got a front-row seat of Tripp being brought to his knees by Beth…and then the rest of the family.

And that was how Finn was left as the only single guy in their group of friends.

"Man"—Tripp shook his head—"that look on your face is *way* too pensive for seven thirty in the morning."

A soft chuckle to Finn's right had him turning in that direction. As his brother's focus was still out on the water, he only got Shep's profile. But Finn knew the signs, the guy was grinning from ear to ear.

"What?" Finn couldn't stop himself from asking.

"Did I say anything?" Shep let out his line.

"No, but you're definitely thinking something." Tripp set his coffee in the cup holder of the chair behind him. "What's going on with our boy here?"

"Could it have anything to do with the pretty brunette who was in your office two days ago?" This question came from Bennett who was on the other side of Shep.

Finn had just known that Bennett witnessing that moment was going to come back and bite him in the ass. And really, this was going to be a big bite. There were seven guys out on the boat that day: Finn, Shep, Tripp, Grant (who was the only one who wouldn't be busting Finn's balls...mainly because he was nine), Bennett, Brendan, and Liam James.

Liam wasn't a Mirabelle native, either, but when he met Harper Laurence—now Harper James—there'd been no turning back for him...something that had been true before he realized he'd gotten Harper pregnant.

He'd been living in Nashville at the time, which was how he'd been able to balance his career of being a country musician. It was a little more complicated for him professionally now that he'd made Mirabelle his home base, not to mention his career had blown up after his hit song "Forever" had gone platinum. But he and Harper were managing.

"Pretty brunette?" Liam asked, his interest clearly piqued. The guy might have just recently become a part of their group, but he could razz with the best of them.

"I think her name was Brie." A smirk started to appear on Bennett's face. "She was there picking up Bethelda's cat."

"Brie from the bar?" Brendan's focus moved from Finn to Shep and then back to Finn. "The one who was staying at the inn? Bethelda left her a cat?" he finished, clearly baffled.

Neither Finn nor Shep—not that he was going to do anything more than stand there and grin—was given the chance to say anything.

"I'm pretty sure Bethelda left her everything," Liam said as he lifted his coffee cup to his lips.

Finn's eyes landed on the man who'd just spoken. "How do you know that?" It was the first thing he'd said since the inquisition had gotten started.

"Harper met her yesterday afternoon. She was going around town tying up Bethelda's accounts, getting access to her finances, and everything else. One of those accounts was at the spa. I guess everyone she'd dealt with before Harper was a jerk."

"That's really unfortunate." Brendan shook his head.

"Yeah, well, apparently Harper was the only one who treated Brie like an actual person. Once everyone else found out what she was trying to deal with in regards to Bethelda, they turned on her. Like a bunch of bloodthirsty piranhas."

That uncomfortable twist—that he was beginning to connect to Brie—tightened Finn's gut. Why did he get the feeling that he'd been the worst piranha of them all?

"So she's guilty by association?" Shep was now frowning, his grin from earlier good and gone.

"That's exactly what Brie said." Liam nodded. "Right after she started crying."

Just that quickly the twist went from uncomfortable to painful. "She was crying?" Finn asked.

"Yeah, I guess she's just had a rough time of it."

"No kidding." Shep's less than pleased focus was now on Finn.

"So wait." Brendan's brow furrowed quizzically. "What about that night at the bar, the night before Bethelda's funeral, she was talking to us like she didn't know the woman."

"She *didn't* know her." The words were out of Finn's mouth before he could stop them.

"And how are you tied into all of this?" Tripp focused on Finn, too.

Actually, everyone now had their eyes on him...well, except Grant who was concentrating hard on the fishing rod in his hands.

"I don't tie into *any* of this." Finn shook his head, his tone final as he looked back to the water.

And for the next few hours on the boat, he said very little and thought way too much. But now his thoughts were on the present instead of the past, and the woman who hadn't been far from his thoughts since the moment she'd walked into the Sleepy Sheep.

* * *

Saturday morning started a little bit later and a lot bit better for Brie. Yesterday's afternoon massage (which had been downright glorious) combined with the new sleeping arrangement (and all of that memory foam stacked on top of the air mattress had been freaking amazing compared to the sofa) had done wonders on her body and her mood.

She'd still had her furry bed buddy that night, too.

Delores hadn't been there when Brie had gone to sleep. But somewhere in the middle of the night the cat had slunk in, burrowed under the covers, and curled up next to Brie's hip. Neither of them moved until well past nine.

Clearly Brie had been exhausted...on many, many levels. Not all that surprisingly as she'd stayed up until close to one in the morning.

After pouring herself a glass of wine the night before, she'd headed into the spare bedroom/office, synced her phone to the Bluetooth speaker (where she proceeded to put all three Adele albums on shuffle), and then started in on some of the boxes in the closet.

She put the ones labeled "Mom's" and "Dad's" to the side, figuring those wouldn't be safe territory for her in her current mental state. Instead she went through the three labeled "Delores," where she no joke found cat costumes for every holiday.

There was one that promised to make the cat look like a giant velvet heart, another of a leprechaun, an Easter bunny, Uncle Sam, a pumpkin, a witch, a turkey, a pilgrim, and Mrs. Claus. There were also non-holiday ones like a bumblebee, a spring flower, a ladybug, a dragon, and a narwhal.

Brie couldn't imagine getting the cat into a single one of those outfits. Though, if there was one she'd pick above any other, it would totally be the narwhal. The unicorn of the sea for the win.

After the costumes, Brie moved on to the cat toys. There were probably over a hundred stuffed, silicone, fuzzy, furry, stringy, or squeaky toys in the box. When Brie had stepped out of the room to refill her wine, she'd come back to find that Delores had gotten into the box. When she'd jumped out there was a little mouse in her mouth.

Once she had gone through the cat boxes, Brie moved on to the things Bethelda had bought in bulk. The lightbulb box promised to keep every appliance and socket in that house illuminated for a decade. There was a three-year supply of air filters, enough toilet paper and paper towels to get a family of five through the next three months, a stock of Bethelda's preferred shampoo and conditioner that would probably last a good two years, and a box of fancy—unused and unopened—lotions and oils that Brie had seen for sale at the spa the day before. Those she set to the side, the first thing she'd actually contemplated keeping for herself.

That was how she'd spent her night, going through a good dozen boxes. The thing was, she'd barely made a dent. Something that was confirmed as she looked to the ceiling to discover that there was indeed an attic.

She grabbed a flashlight—that she'd found in a box with twelve others—and the step stool to take a peek. The attic was filled with boxes, too.

Upon first glance most of the boxes up there were from Bethelda's past: baby clothes, first grade, middle school, high school, and so on. It was at that point that Brie called it quits. She took a shower to wash the day from her skin and passed out on the air mattress.

Now, eight hours later, she stared up at the slowly spinning fan above her trying to gather the momentum to get up and start another day. But she was warm and comfortable under those covers, snuggled up with a cat.

She found one of her hands making its way to Delores's back, her fingers delving into the soft fur. A steady, deep purring began to rumble out of the animal, who was also clearly content with the current moment.

Brie pulled the covers up with her free hand, looking down at Delores. The cat lifted its head at the sudden draft of air, her jade eyes slowly opening. She really was a beautiful animal. There was no doubt about that.

"Am I beginning to meet with your approval?" Brie asked.

Delores closed her eyes and rubbed her head against Brie's arm. Well, at least something liked her. Though, there was the fact that Brie was the one feeding the cat and providing warmth and a soft place to sleep at night.

It was another couple of minutes before Brie dragged herself out of the bed, Delores giving a protesting *meow* when she was no longer being petted. Stopping by the kitchen, she turned the Keurig machine on before heading for the bathroom.

Once her face was washed and teeth brushed she changed into jeans and a clean T-shirt—one of the last she had, which reminded her she needed to do laundry at some point. She should be getting her boxes from North Carolina that day, Lyndsey had FedExed them overnight so she could get them that Saturday. Brie was already starting to feel twitchy that she hadn't worked on her thesis in a week.

The need for a space to work was why she'd decided to tackle the office first. Cleaning it out was going to take some time, though.

Brie headed back for the kitchen, making herself a cup of coffee and getting breakfast ready. She mixed Delores's food together before she poured herself a bowl of cereal. The cat was circling her feet as she made her way to the dining room table, setting both bowls down in their respective places.

Grabbing the list of things she needed to do, Brie crossed out a number of lines while adding just as many. First thing was first; she needed to get rid of the few things she'd already gone through. She wasn't sure if there was a Goodwill in town, but there was most likely a church charity of some sort or another.

She was probably going to need to make a few phone calls

to find a place to bring it all. Once Delores had finished with her breakfast—because heaven forbid she disturb the cat's eating habits—Brie got up and went to grab her laptop.

There were four churches in Mirabelle: Baptist, Methodist, Episcopal, and Catholic.

All four of them had links on their homepages to the CCC—Center for Charity & Compassion. It was the local shelter/food bank/donation station and all of the churches were involved in the running of it.

They were also open on Saturday and taking donations.

She looked over and eyed the stuff she'd dragged to the living room the night before. There were at least three carloads already...well, three of *her* carloads. Only so much could fit into the back of the MINI.

Brie pushed the chair back from the table and stood. "Might as well get started." She grabbed her coffee and headed for the spare bedroom/office. It was go big or go home, and she was going to have that closet cleaned out as much as possible.

* * *

The CCC was yet another place that was located in downtown Mirabelle. However, it was one of the few establishments Brie had been to in the area that was not in an old house. The three-story warehouse was made of brick and was probably over a hundred years old.

Brie pulled her overstuffed car to the side of the building where a large red and white sign read "Drop Offs." Once the car was in Park and shut off, she got out and looked around. There was a little placard by the metal double doors that read

"Ring for Assistance." She walked over to it and pressed the little black button, a droning buzz echoing inside the building.

It wasn't even a minute later when the doors were pushed open and none other than Hannah Shepherd appeared. Brie's mouth rounded in a surprised "O." And she wasn't the only one in shock, either. Hannah's eyes had widened behind her glasses.

Shit. Just what she needed, another Shepherd. Not only that, but the woman had to *know* that Brie had slept with Finn. She'd just had to leave those damn glasses in the drop box. She should've tossed them in the trash.

Not that she was bitter about the whole thing or anything…except she really, *really* was.

But what else did Hannah know? Would Finn have said something to his sister-in-law about it? Or maybe he'd kept his mouth shut because he hadn't wanted anyone to know that he'd spent the night with Bethelda Grimshaw's daughter.

Hannah was the first to get over her shock, pulling what seemed to be a genuine smile onto her face. "Hi, Brie."

"I…hi. What are you doing here?" Brie asked before she could stop herself.

Hannah's smile grew. "I volunteer every once in a while. Today, I'm on receiving duty."

"Oh." Brie nodded, that smile on Hannah's face throwing her off even more.

"What are you doing here?" Hannah asked.

"Well, I…um…I have some stuff to donate," she said, and pointed lamely over her shoulder and to her car.

Hannah's gaze followed Brie's gesture and her eyes got huge again. "Holy crap." She looked back to Brie. "How was there enough room for you in there?"

"I made it work."

"I see that. I'm guessing this is stuff from Bethelda's house?"

Well, Hannah apparently knew something. That was for sure. But was it the truth that Finn knew? Or the partial truth that a number of people around town knew?

That was the question.

"I know what it's like." Hannah put a hand to her chest. "I know what it's like to come down here after the death of someone in your life and be left a house...and a ton of questions."

Compassion vibrated out of every word she spoke, and understanding was there on every facet of her face. How was that possible? It went against almost everything she'd experienced in the last couple of days.

Instead there was no ill will in the woman's eyes. No indication of spite or malice. Instead, she looked sympathetic.

Brie felt like she knew the answer to how much Hannah knew, based off everything the woman had just said, but she had to hear it. So she asked the questions. "Finn told you, didn't he? Told you who I was in relation to Bethelda?"

"He did." Hannah nodded. "He told Shep and me. I know he isn't your favorite person—"

Understatement. *Huge* understatement.

"And sometimes he isn't mine, either." Hannah gave Brie a commiserating smile before she continued. "But I can promise you he hasn't told anyone else about it."

Which brought Brie back to her theory of him wanting to keep his mouth shut about being so intimately connected to Bethelda's daughter.

"I don't know that it matters. I get the feeling it's a secret that won't stay *secret* long."

"It's true in Mirabelle secrets rarely do. Small towns. People like to talk."

Brie took a deep breath and let it out in a huff of laughter. "And they already have something to talk about. I had to go around yesterday to get access to some of Bethelda's accounts while closing out others. So it won't be long before I become the town pariah."

"I mean, it probably will be a little longer than it was before considering…" Hannah trailed off now looking slightly uncomfortable.

Brie finished the thought for her. "Considering the person who liked to tell all of those secrets is now dead?"

"Well…yeah." Hannah paused for a second, not breaking eye contact in the beat of silence. "It isn't an easy thing, dealing with the aftermath of a death, no matter who it was."

"No, *easy* hasn't been a word I would use to describe any part of any of this." Brie shook her head.

It wasn't just dealing with Bethelda's death, though. It was everything. The will, being in that house, the negative reactions, not having someone to lean on, not having anyone to talk to. Her parents were still in the dark as to what was happening; Brie couldn't bring herself to have that conversation with them. She didn't want to add their worry on to everything else.

"You said you lost someone who left you a house?" Brie asked, veering the conversation from herself.

"The inn actually." Hannah nodded. "It was my grandmother. She and I spent a summer here before I went to college…the inn was a bed-and-breakfast then. I met Shep, we fell in love, the summer ended, and I left. She died about three years ago, but before she did she bought the inn, unbeknown to me. And then she left it to me in her will. She said I had *un-finished* business and she wanted me to come down here to deal with it."

"Shep?"

"Among other things." A bittersweet smile turned up Hannah's mouth. "Brie, I also know what it's like to be in this town alone. I know how isolating it is. If you ever want somebody to talk to, about anything, you know how to reach me."

That she did. Hannah's cell phone was the number people called to make a reservation at the inn.

"Thank you." It was all Brie could say. Hannah had shown her more kindness than she'd been prepared for...and she knew the truth of the whole situation, too.

"Anytime." There was so much sincerity in that one word. "Well, let's get you unloaded." Hannah nodded to the car.

"Let's," Brie agreed as they both moved to the back of the MINI.

They made quick and quiet work of unloading the car, pushing through the doors, and setting the boxes and bags in piles along the wall of the hallway. Brie appreciated the time to process as her mind was racing from the conversation she'd just had.

That was now *two* people that hadn't looked at her like she was Satan's spawn. Hannah seemed to understand Brie, more than anyone else had. Not only that, but she'd offered a friendly ear to talk to.

"Do you want a tax write-off form for all of this?"

Hannah's question pulled Brie from her thoughts as they finished with the last load.

"Well, I actually have more at the house. I just couldn't fit it all in my car."

Hannah raised her eyebrows. "How many more loads?"

"Today? Probably two or three." Actually, it was more like four or five. Turned out some of the boxes were awkward fits that took up more of the small space than she'd previously thought.

"OK, well, it doesn't make any sense for you to go back and forth that many times. Let me see if there is a spare truck around." Hannah turned and headed down the hallway.

"You really don't need to do that," Brie objected as she automatically started to follow. "I can get it."

Hannah looked over her shoulder, giving Brie an *oh please* look. "Would you rather spend the next two hours hauling this stuff over? Or just get it done in one trip?"

Well, the one trip was preferable; it was just that she wasn't too sure about people coming to the house. And she was equally unsure of accepting help from people.

Before Brie had a chance to respond, Hannah was asking another question. "You want something to drink? There's some freshly squeezed lemonade and sweet tea." She pushed through a swinging door and into a rather large kitchen.

Industrial, stainless-steel appliances were lined up next to each other. Two massive refrigerators stood side by side on one wall, while two double ovens took up some of another. A blond woman was standing at the center island, chopping fruits and vegetables of all varieties. A woman with black hair was manning a ten-burner stove that had multiple pots of soup bubbling.

The delicious aroma made Brie's stomach rumble. It was after one and she hadn't had lunch yet, not to mention she'd worked up an appetite with everything she'd been doing all morning and afternoon.

The woman at the center island looked up from her chopping, her gaze moving from Hannah to Brie to Hannah again. Brie hadn't met the woman before, but there was something familiar about her, something Brie couldn't quite put her finger on.

"Mom, this is Brie. Brie, this is my mother-in-law, Faye."

Mother-in-law…meaning Hannah's husband's mom…meaning Hannah's husband's brother's mom. Oh good God, Brie was currently standing ten feet away from Finn's mother. No wonder she looked vaguely familiar.

Shiiiiiit.

"Nice to meet you." Faye wiped her hands on a towel before crossing the space. She held a now dried hand out to Brie, smiling.

Something caught in Brie's chest…she had the same smile as her son. A smile that went all the way to her eyes. The blue was different…Faye's more of a sky to Finn's sapphire.

"You as well," she somehow managed to get out as she grabbed the woman's hand and shook it.

"And this is Delilah." Faye let go of Brie's hand and indicated the woman who'd stepped away from the stove.

"Hello." Delilah smiled warmly, also extending her hand.

This woman looked familiar to Brie, too, but it was another face that she couldn't quite place. It was something about the shape of her eyes.

Brie got her answer to the familiarity of the second woman almost immediately. The kitchen door swung open and Harper walked through, her black hair pulled up in a messy bun on top of her head and a box of cans in her hands. There was no doubt in Brie's mind, Delilah was Harper's mother.

Same hair, same full lips, same cheekbones, and those same almond-shaped eyes.

Speaking of eyes, Harper's violet ones widened in surprise when they landed on Brie. "I didn't expect to see you here, Brie." But she didn't sound disappointed at finding Brie in the kitchen. On the contrary, she was pleased by the new development.

"You guys have met?" Hannah asked, looking between the women.

"Yesterday," Harper answered as she slid the box of cans onto an empty space on the counter. "At the spa."

"So what brings you to Mirabelle?" Faye asked.

"I…" Brie hesitated for just a second. What did it matter anymore? People were already learning the reason, so there was no need for her to hedge around it. Besides, she was going to be in Mirabelle for a while, might as well face the music.

"Bethelda Grimshaw left me her house. Actually, she left me everything, so I'm down here dealing with it."

The looks on Faye's and Delilah's faces went from open curiosity to shock.

"I didn't know Bethelda had any living family, in or out of Mirabelle," Faye said, tilting her head to the side as her eyes moved over Brie, like she was trying to figure out the connection.

Well, Brie might as well go for broke at this point. And really, it would be better for people to just hear the truth from the horse's mouth as opposed to coming up with other theories. For whatever reason, this felt like the best place to enlighten them. Maybe because Hannah already knew, and Harper hadn't turned on her yesterday.

"Bethelda was my biological mother. She gave me up for adoption."

"Holy. Shit." The two words came out of Harper's mouth on a whisper.

"Harper!" Delilah scolded her daughter.

"Sorry," Harper apologized. "I just, I hadn't expected that."

"I don't think anyone has expected that." Brie shook her head.

"Well, I'm sorry for your loss." Faye took a step closer to Brie, her body language open…receptive. It was totally different from anything she'd expected in that moment.

"I was under the impression there was no love lost between Bethelda and most of the people in this town."

"There wasn't." The honesty in those two words from Harper wasn't as harsh as it probably should've been. Actually, it wasn't harsh at all. It just *was*.

"I didn't know her." Brie gave a slight shrug of the shoulders.

"Doesn't mean you didn't lose something," Hannah said softly.

Brie's mouth fell open on an inhale, but no words came out. Instead her throat started to constrict, and there was that prickling sensation at the corner of her eyes.

"Thank you." Her voice broke on the last syllable and she forced herself to push the emotion back, clearing her throat before she could speak again. "Anyway, I've started to clean out the house. Bethelda had a lot of things. Way too many things. Things that no normal person would need in that amount."

"Which actually brings us to why we came in here," Hannah said. "Is Nate's truck still around back? Brie has a MINI Cooper and it makes absolutely no sense for her to make a bunch of trips."

"No, he went to go get a sofa that's being donated. But the boys should be here any minute now. I'm sure Finn could go over with his truck."

Finn? *Finn*? No, he was absolutely the *last* person she wanted helping her do anything. She'd make a thousand trips hauling stuff in her car before she asked that man for help.

"That won't be nec—"

But before Brie could even finish turning down the offer, the door swung open again and the man in question walked into the kitchen.

The second Finn's eyes landed on Brie he halted in his tracks. The door swung out and in again, hitting him from behind.

Chapter Ten

Making Up Is Hard to Do
(Making Out, on the Other Hand,
Is Not Hard to Do)

W hy, *why* was Brie everywhere that Finn went? First it had
been his office, then yesterday it had been the store, and today
it was the CCC.

This was why he didn't sleep with locals.

But Brie *wasn't* a local, she wasn't staying in Mirabelle. Well,
at least not for forever. She was just here for the foreseeable future. Though as she hadn't given him an end date, he had no
earthly idea how much longer he was going to have to deal with
running into her *everywhere*. Had no idea how much longer he
was going to have to deal with that jarring jolt that hit him like
a sledgehammer to the gut.

Or like a heavy door slamming him in the ass. And that was
another thing, why was it that running into her meant getting
run into? He was forced to take a step forward from the momentum of the door, moving farther into the kitchen and closer
to Brie. And closer to Brie was the exact opposite direction he
wanted to go.

It wasn't like he could just turn around and hightail it out

of there. Retreat wasn't an option, not with the rest of the audience in the kitchen. And what an audience it was, four women
who knew him better than most.

Delilah Laurence was the wife of his boss/mentor, Paul Laurence. Once Finn had started volunteering at the shelter at the
age of sixteen, and then working summers there in between
college, he'd become a pretty regular fixture at the Laurence
household. He'd probably sat at Delilah's dinner table just as
much as his mother's in those years.

Then there was Harper, who though only a year younger
than him, had always been like his little sister. Speaking of sisters, Hannah was there. Since she knew the finer points of his
time with Brie, she was pretty much the last person he wanted
to witness that moment. Well, second to last. His ever-obser-
vant mother was actually the last person.

Just don't react, he told himself. *Act like everything is fine.*

Except it wasn't fine, for either him or Brie. It was apparent
from the frown now pulling her mouth down that she was less
than thrilled to be in the same room as him, too.

"Just the person we needed," his mother said. "Finn, this is
Brie. Brie, this is my son Finn." She waved a hand between the
two in an introduction. "Brie needs help getting some donations down here. She has a small vehicle so we need a truck to
get it all. Would you mind helping her?"

This was one of those situations where he saw absolutely no
way to get out of it. Saying *no* really wasn't an option, especially
not to his mother. That would've gone over like a ton of bricks.

Before Finn had a chance to respond, Brie was the one
speaking, a forced smile turning up her lips as she looked at
him. "We've met before, actually."

It was such a different smile to when it was genuine. This one was cold, even with the flush taking over her cheeks. But that warmth under her skin didn't reach her eyes, didn't thaw the look she was giving him. He was close enough to see that there was barely a glint of gold in those eyes, and he wondered what it would take to get them golden again.

"Oh?" His mother's eyebrows rose high as her focus went solely on Finn. She wasn't the only one, either. Harper's eyes had narrowed on him, too. He could feel her stare drilling into the side of his head.

"At the Sheep. Brie came in for a drink," Finn answered.

"I sure did." Brie's tone was icy.

Faye looked between the two of them, clearly trying to figure out why the room was now filled with a rather uncomfortable tension.

Brie pulled her gaze from Finn, and the second her focus left him some of the coldness left her face. "I really do appreciate the offer for help, but I'll figure out how to get everything here. There's a lot of stuff that I need to get rid of, and not just today, either. The more I clean, the more I'm going to need to bring down. I'd hate to put anyone out, or force them to do something they really don't want to do."

There was an edge to her words with that last sentence, and Finn couldn't keep the sharpness out of his voice when he spoke, either.

"I didn't say I wouldn't help you, Brie."

Her shoulders went rigid before she looked back to him. "Yes, Finn, but what I'm saying is, I don't want your help."

Her words were a slap and it took everything in him not to flinch from the sting.

She turned away from him again, like that brief moment of looking at him was too much. "Faye, Delilah," she said to the women in turn, "it was nice meeting you. Harper and Hannah, it was good seeing you guys again." She gave a small nod. "Thank you for everything. Now, if you'll excuse me."

And with that she walked around him and left the kitchen, pushing through the swinging door and disappearing from view.

"What did you do?" His mother rounded on him within an instant.

"What makes you think I did something?" His back went up immediately at her tone.

Her eyebrows rose high and she glared at him. "What makes me *know* you did something is because that girl"—she gestured to the door—"was perfectly lovely before you walked in here and brought the Arctic Circle with you."

So he hadn't been the only one to feel the chill.

"Look, you don't know the full story—" Finn started but he didn't get to finish.

"The full story being that she's the daughter Bethelda gave up twenty something years ago?" his mother asked.

"How do you know that?"

"She told us, idiot." This answer was from Harper, and when Finn turned to look at her, it was to find her glaring at him. "You're one of the assholes who was terrible to her, aren't you? One of the people who turned on her when they learned the truth?"

Delilah's eyes went wide at the harshness in her daughter's voice, but then her gaze settled into disappointment that was directed at Finn. He didn't know where to look, so his eyes landed on the only other woman in the kitchen.

Hannah folded her arms across her chest. "You already know how I feel about it all, Finn. I think you're taking an entirely wrong stance on Brie. I also think you should pull your head out of your ass."

"Pull my head out of my ass? Did I not say I'd help her out?"

"Actually you didn't." Delilah shook her head. "What you said was that you didn't say you wouldn't help her. Which is not the same thing."

Good God, his head was spinning. All he'd done was come in the kitchen for a sandwich and a bowl of soup before he started moving furniture around upstairs. But apparently he wasn't going to get either, not that he had much of an appetite anymore.

"Also, you should stop treating every other woman like they are Rebecca two-point-oh," Hannah added.

And that was when Finn's temper flashed to beyond the boiling point. "Low blow."

"Son, if you don't like the truth, then maybe you should change it."

"Mom—" he started, but again, his mother didn't let him finish.

"You should know better, Finn. Kids aren't always a by-product of their parents."

Her eyes narrowed on him at that point, and if looks could kill, he'd be six feet under.

"How many of your friends had a parent walk out on them? Brendan"—she held a finger up in the air—"Grace"—she held up another finger—"Bennett"—she held up a third finger. "Then we get to Jax who would've been better off not knowing his mother or his father."

"Not to mention me"—Hannah put her hand to her

chest—"who had parents who were more concerned about raising the numbers in their bank account than actually raising their children."

Oh, how easy it was to forget all of those facts, especially when Finn had been looking down at Brie from his own high horse. But he wasn't going to get a chance to step down from it. Nope. His mother was going to push him off the damn thing.

"And finally we get to your grandmother who had a mother who walked away from her two kids and never looked back. Did you forget about that fact as well, Finn?" Her mouth went tight as she waited for him to answer.

Shame burned low in his gut, moving to his chest and then through his limbs. His answer was to not respond. What was he supposed to say?

"I didn't raise you this way. Not even close. Fix it, Finn." That last part wasn't a request from his mother, but a demand.

* * *

Brie opened the front door of Bethelda's bungalow and walked inside. The second the door closed behind her she leaned back against the wall and breathed a sigh of relief. Who would've thought that being *in* this house would be better for her sanity than being out of it?

No one, absolutely no one.

She was so freaking tired of running into Finn. So tired of him looking at her like she was the biggest mistake he'd ever made in his life. She'd had enough, didn't need that shit from him or anyone, not on top of everything else she was dealing with. It was too much. *Way* too much.

But there was a little good to come out of the afternoon. There were some people who now knew the truth who didn't despise her…people who didn't hold her accountable for her biological mother. Interesting that two of those people just so happened to be related to Finn. Though that had all happened before he'd walked into the kitchen. There was no telling what their opinion was now that she'd walked out.

She'd had to get out of that room, though, had to get away from *him*. That man had way too much power to hurt her. And sure, some of it had to do with them having sex, but it wasn't just that.

It couldn't be. She'd been intimate with enough men to know that that kind of hold didn't always translate over. With Finn it was something else…something else that she didn't understand in the slightest.

He made her skin prickle, like it was being stretched too tight. Then there was the fact that her head would start to slowly spin, but maybe that was because around him she couldn't take full breaths. The thing was, he'd done all of those things to her before he'd turned into an insufferable ass. It was just that before she'd been smiling. Now when she was around him there were no smiles to be found.

A car door slammed outside the house, echoing through the afternoon air. The closest neighbors to the bungalow were about a hundred yards on either side, and based on the closeness of the sound, she knew someone was outside that house.

A sinking sensation started to move down her body, settling low in her belly. She knew this wasn't going to be good. Just *knew* it.

Pulling away from the wall she slowly walked the few feet

to the peephole only to find Finn was making his way up the paved path. Yup, nothing good. He didn't look any more pleased to be there than she was at seeing him there. His mouth was turned down in a severe frown and those sapphire-blue eyes behind his glasses were filled with a slow burning anger.

Like he had any right to be angry with her about *anything*.

When he got to the door he hesitated for just a second, apparently gathering his nerve before he lifted his hand and pressed his finger to the doorbell.

It was the first time the doorbell had rung since Brie had been there, and she wasn't exactly prepared when the house was filled with the chorus of "Wake Me Up Before You Go-Go." But really, what George Michael super-fan wouldn't have that as their doorbell ringer? Not a true super-fan, that was for damn sure.

Brie could ignore the bell, ignore him. Just stand there and not make a sound until George stopped singing and Finn turned around and left. But really, what would that accomplish? Clearly he'd shown up here to say something, and with the way they kept running into each other, maybe it would be better to hear it in private.

She closed her eyes for just a second, gently resting her forehead against the door as she took a deep, steadying breath. When her eyes opened, her hand moved to the handle. Twisting the knob, she pulled and took a step back, coming face-to-face with the man she apparently just couldn't get away from.

He opened his mouth on an inhale, but no words came out. Instead he stood on the front porch still looking angry and more than slightly confused. Well, he wasn't the only one who was confused.

"Really? Wham!?" Apparently his confusion was the doorbell and not what he was doing there.

Brie chose not to answer his question and asked one of her own. "What are you doing here, Finn?"

"I came here to take whatever it was you wanted to get rid of." He shifted on his feet, moving closer.

He was already too close. Close enough to tower over her and make her feel small. And yes, she was obviously already smaller than him. It was hard not to be with all of his six-foot-two tallness, plus he was wearing boots. But it wasn't just the vertical space he took up…there was the horizontal space, too. The man had broad shoulders, with muscles that her hands knew the feel of.

The memory flashed through her brain, her holding on to him as he moved over her…moved inside her. Her hands on those shoulders, her nails digging into his skin.

What was wrong with her? Sex with Finn was absolutely the last thing she needed to be thinking about. It was something she never needed to be thinking about again.

Her hands went to her hips. She wasn't sure if it was in an attempt to try to make herself seem bigger, or because she needed a place to put them to stop herself from doing something incredibly stupid.

"Did I not make it clear that I don't want your help?" she asked him. "And not only that, but I *never* asked for it."

"I know that. But my mother asked me to help you. And saying *no* to my mother has never really been an option for me."

He never said *no* to his mother. Why in God's name did that fact do something weird to her equilibrium? Because everything about him did something weird to her equilibrium, that was why. It clearly didn't matter that she didn't want to be affected by him. Didn't matter that she knew he was the biggest asshole on the face of the planet.

Never in her life had she felt more confused by a single person. God, she needed him to leave her alone...needed him to just *leave*.

The next words out of his mouth were as if he knew exactly what she was thinking. "Brie, the quicker I get this stuff, the sooner I can go. And you don't even have to say *thank you* at the end of it, either."

Heat crept up her neck and to her face. Yet another memory from them sleeping together, that stupid freaking *thank you*. She'd said it because she'd been so grateful that he'd made her forget...now she wished she could just forget about him.

Her eyes narrowed. "God, you're a jerk."

"So I've been told."

They stared at each other for a few seconds—that felt like an eternity—neither of them blinking or budging. She was capable of being pretty stubborn herself, but fighting his offer to haul off the stuff she wanted to get rid of felt like a waste of her energy and time.

"Fine." She grabbed the door and pulled it open wide, turning around and not waiting for him as she headed down the hallway.

As she walked into the living room, there was a soft snap of the front door closing. Finn followed, his boots making a muffled thud on the carpets that covered the hardwood floors. Reaching the threshold of the living room, he came to a stop, his eyes darting around and taking in all of the pictures and paintings on the walls, the three china cabinets (bears and all),

the covered floors, and the collection of furniture, before landing on the pile of things in the corner.

He hesitated for just a second before moving his gaze to
Brie. "Seriously? You were going to try to haul all of that over
yourself?"

"Do or do not. There is no try." The Yoda quote fell from
her lips automatically. Both of her parents were huge *Star Wars*
fans, and lines from the movies were part of their daily dia-
logue.

Finn's eye widened, and if she didn't know any better she'd
say the corner of his mouth twitched. She couldn't be sure,
though, as he was turning away from her and moving to the pile
of stuff.

"Well, she clearly wasn't a minimalist."

"You have no idea," she muttered, shaking her head. The
living room was barely even a glimpse of the reality of the situation. Not that he was going to get to see the entirety of it.

Nope. Not a chance.

Brie stood back, giving Finn space while he loaded his arms
up with a massive box. It was filled with knitting supplies and
wasn't heavy so much as bulky. Once he'd moved away and
headed out of the living room, she grabbed one of the black
trash bags she'd stuffed with yarn—there were three—and followed behind him.

Neither of them said anything else as they loaded the rest of
the donations, keeping a safe distance from each other as they
passed back and forth from the house to the truck. That was
until the very end when Delores decided to make an appearance.

There'd been two boxes left, one with sweaters that had

never been worn (tags still on and everything), and another of a brand-new set of pots and pans. Brie went for the sweaters and the second she tried to heft the box up, she knew it was heavier than it should be.

Nineteen and a half pounds too heavy to be exact.

Delores sprung out and right into Brie's face. There was no telling what was louder, the cat's yowling or the woman's scream.

The box fell from Brie's hands, flipping over and dumping all of the sweaters onto the floor. And the box wasn't the only thing falling, either. Brie had jumped back when Delores had flown out at her, her feet getting caught in one of the rugs and making her lose her balance. She was going down and right into a glass-fronted grandfather clock.

The crash never happened. Instead two rather steady, masculine hands caught her and changed the direction of the fall. But there was too much momentum to stay up straight and they both hit the floor. Actually, Finn hit the floor while Brie hit the solid wall that was his chest. She was sprawled across him, rather inelegantly, too. Her hands were captured between their bodies, their legs tangled together, and her face pressed into his neck.

One small, unsteady breath and her lungs filled with that incredible soap and aftershave scent that was him. Though, today it was mixed with sun and sea.

She wasn't the only one breathing deep, either. Finn's nose was in her hair and his chest was expanding under her, making her body slowly rise. One of his hands was cradling the back of her head, while the other was planted firmly in the middle of her spine.

Neither of them pulled away, neither of them made a move to get up, and neither of them let go. In fact, she wanted to curl into him, open her mouth over his throat.

"You OK?" His whispered words were strained. Not like he was hurt, but more like he was trying to get a hold of himself.

"Yes, I-I'm fine." Her lips brushed over his skin and he groaned, the vibration rumbling through her.

Well, that was a blatant lie, she wasn't even close to *fine*. If fine was *anywhere* on planet Earth, she was on Pluto. Except it wasn't cold on Pluto, it was hot like the sun, setting every part of her on fire. And she wanted *more*.

How was it possible for everything to change just that quickly? The air around them crackled, the angry tension from moments before gone. Well, the anger was gone, the tension had just transformed into something else. Something sexual and raw.

They both moved at the same time, Brie looking up while Finn's gaze came down. The second their eyes met, their mouths followed, his coming down hard on hers. And just that quickly, she found herself on her back.

She gasped at the sudden change in position, and he took advantage of her open mouth, his tongue thrusting past her lips. The invasion was welcomed and so beyond reciprocated, Brie kissing him back with equal enthusiasm.

Because she was no longer lying across him; her hands had been freed. She took the opportunity to move them to the back of his head, her fingers delving into his hair. Another one of his deep, masculine groans vibrated from his throat as she not so gently pulled, wanting him closer. He complied, giving her his weight and pushing her down into the floor.

She moaned as her breasts pressed against his chest, her nipples hardening under the pressure. And her nipples weren't the only thing that were hard, either. Finn was between her legs now, and his rather prominent erection had decided to make an appearance. She felt every single inch of him on her thigh.

He reached down, grabbing a knee and pulling her leg up and around his waist. The new angle aligned his cock with the apex of her thighs. It was then that they started to *really* move against each other, picking up the rhythm that they'd discovered the other night.

Nothing about how their bodies or mouths moved was gentle. It was grasping desperation for both of them.

But the moment was broken a second later, ending almost as fast as it had begun. The cause? George Michael's voice filled the house for the second time that day. Apparently nothing could completely and totally destroy a moment quite like that damn doorbell.

Finn's body tensed before his mouth left hers. He pulled away and she slowly opened her eyes as realty began to sink back in.

Oh God, what had just happened?

His face hovered above hers, blue eyes wide in shock. She was surprised to find that it wasn't a horrified shock and instead a bemused shock. It was different not seeing that simmering anger behind his eyes and getting a glimpse of the man from a couple of days ago, the man who'd wanted her.

An ache that she wasn't at all prepared for hit her smack in the middle of the chest. Why did she care how this man looked at her? Or what he thought of her?

Her fingers were still tightly twined in his hair, and she

forced herself to loosen her grip and drop her hands. The movement caused some of the confused haze from Finn's face to clear, but it still lingered in his eyes.

"Brie, I…" But that was all he said, apparently unable to figure out the rest of that sentence.

Not that she had any place to pass judgment on the inability to put together a coherent thought, because she was right there with him.

The doorbell rang again, the song starting up and filling the house.

"I—" Her voice caught on that one syllable and she cleared her throat before trying again. "I need to get that."

"Right." Finn nodded, shifting back and off of her.

She had to force herself not to think about the fact that her body immediately missed the weight of him. Once he got to his feet, he stuck his hand out to help her up, too. Before she could think better of it, she grabbed his proffered hand.

The second she was upright and stable he let go and took a step back. It was as if the added contact and close proximity was just too much. Or, at least it had been for her.

"Excuse me." She moved around him, keeping as much distance as possible as she walked out of the room and to the front door.

She wished more than anything she could go into a room and shut the door behind her, take a moment to think without dealing with anyone or anything. But she wasn't going to be allowed that luxury as someone was at the front door and Finn was still in the living room.

Good Lord, Finn. *What. Had. Just. Happened?* The question was running through her mind on a continuous loop of ticker tape.

Brie took a deep, steadying breath, trying to push the last few minutes from her brain. She was unsuccessful. It was going to take a lot more than that to forget. Her lips were swollen. Her cheeks sensitive from his scruff rasping against her skin. Her breasts full and tender. And then there was the fact that she could still feel his hand on her hip, could still feel him moving between her legs, thrusting against her.

Grabbing the door handle, she twisted and pulled it open to find a FedEx deliveryman on the front porch. There was a hand truck dolly that sat at the bottom of the steps, five boxes stacked on top of each other, her friend Lyndsey's loopy handwriting on the side of each.

Her clothes and books were here. At any other time she probably would've jumped with joy at seeing them. Not only could she start working on her thesis again, but her wardrobe had just expanded tenfold. But instead of jumping she was still reeling from what had just happened in the living room.

"Brie Davis?" the delivery guy asked, giving her a lopsided grin.

"Yes."

"I've got a delivery for you." He grinned. "Nice doorbell. Sorry, I had to ring it twice just to hear it again."

The guy was cute in a puppy dog sort of way with his floppy blond hair and light blue eyes. His eyes weren't as pretty as Finn's, though.

No one's were as pretty as Finn's, not even his brother's and grandmother's who had the exact same shade of sapphire blue. It was *his* eyes that did it for her. *His* eyes that had captured every part of her when he looked down at her just moments before.

Nope. Focus, Brie. FOCUS!

"Yeah, the song choice is interesting. It came with the house."

He tilted his head to the side, his grin widening. It was the kind of look that she was sure had gotten him laid many a time. "Yeah, well, I was really more of a 'Careless Whisper' guy myself."

She had to stop herself from rolling her eyes. If this guy was even a day over twenty she'd be shocked. There was no way he'd even been born when that song came out. Actually he hadn't even been alive when George Michael had been in the heyday of his career. Not that Brie could really talk...she only had about eight years on the guy.

"You just move here? I've never seen you before, or delivered to this house for that matter and it's been on my route for a year." His eyes moved from left to right, scanning the space on either side of the front door.

"You never delivered to Bethelda Grimshaw?" The question was out of Brie's mouth before she could think better of it. She just found it incredibly hard to believe that with all of the crap in Bethelda's house, FedEx hadn't made a stop...or five hundred.

As was the typical reaction when it came to most people hearing the name *Bethelda Grimshaw*, the guy's entire demeanor changed. The grin on his mouth disappeared like she'd just spit on him, and a second later he was sneering.

"*This* was that bitch's house?" He looked around the door again as if to double-check that he didn't recognize the place, and then his eyes were back on her. "Who the hell are you?"

What with her defenses being in the state they were in, she

wasn't prepared for the sudden change. Not only that, but his words were filled with so much malice that Brie found herself taking an involuntary step back…and right into the solid wall that was Finn's chest.

"Robbie, I suggest you tone it back, *way back*, and apologize." Finn's words came out low and menacing, his deep masculine voice filling her ears and going to her bones. She had to repress a shiver.

And she wasn't the only one who had a reaction to Finn, either. Robbie was taking a step back, the sneer on his mouth lessening as he looked in confusion from Brie to Finn and back to Brie.

"I…" Robbie trailed off before he shook his head, all of his aggression disappearing with the movement. "I'm sorry, it's just that I didn't like that woman. At all. She always got her packages delivered to her office at the Mirabelle Information Center, anywhere from one to fifteen a week. And every single time I had to deliver to her, she was *terrible*. Complained about everything. Tried to get me fired. I'm sorry," he said again, remorse taking over in his eyes. He really was like a puppy. One who'd bitten in fright and was now cowering in the corner. "It was a knee-jerk reaction, not that that is any legit reason."

"No, it's not a reason. Not only is there no need to talk to Brie that way, but it doesn't matter who she is besides a customer." Finn's voice rumbled through her again, except this time it wasn't a shiver Brie had to push down. No, this time his words had her back going up.

The association with Bethelda didn't matter? It was no reason for what had just happened? It didn't matter who Brie was? Well, this was all news to her. And on top of it all, hadn't Finn *told* Robbie to apologize to her, too? Pretty much demanded it? That little fact hadn't exactly clicked earlier, but it sure had now.

What a sanctimonious son of a bitch.

She pulled away from him, wishing she could put a lot more distance than a foot or two between them. Instead she forced a half smile into place as she focused on Robbie. "I'm learning that kind of reaction is par for the course when it comes to Bethelda. Thank you for the apology."

Robbie's eyes darted behind Brie and she just *knew* he was getting approval from Finn, making sure that the apology was enough to appease the enforcer at her back, too. Apparently it did because Robbie's shoulders relaxed just fractionally in relief.

"If I could just get you to sign," he said before he pulled a black signature pad from a holder on his belt. Looking down, he hit a few buttons on it and then handed it over with the stylus.

Brie grabbed both, scribbling out a signature that was barely legible before handing it back. Robbie gave her another apologetic look before focusing on Finn again.

"I'll see you around." He nodded before he turned around and walked off the porch and to the boxes. Once he had his hand truck out from underneath the stack, he was heading back down the path and to his FedEx van on the curb. The guy couldn't get away fast enough.

Good gravy Brie felt like she had whiplash. It was from everything, *everything* that had transpired in the last ten minutes. The cause of that whiplash? The man behind her. The man who'd been at her back while he apparently *had* her back. And if that wasn't the most confusing part of it all, she didn't know what was.

Something in her snapped and she spun around and headed into the house, thinking that if maybe she put some more space between her and Finn she wouldn't explode like Chernobyl. She was not successful. The second she heard him behind her, she went off and became downright radioactive.

Brie spun around, already yelling before she was even facing him. "What was that?"

Finn came to an abrupt stop, his eyes narrowing. "What was *what*? Me defending you?"

"I don't need you to defend me, Finn. I don't need you to do anything for me. I thought I made that perfectly clear."

"Are you kidding me right now?" His voice was just as loud as hers had been. "You don't need me for *anything*? You think you would've just gotten a concussion from falling into that earlier?" He pointed to the grandfather clock at their side. "Or maybe just thirty-five stitches from all of the shattered glass?"

"I'm not talking about that, I'm talking about you being a raving hypocrite. Robbie's reaction wasn't anything different from what I've already dealt with. In fact, it's not even the *worst* that I've dealt with. How *you've* treated me gets that glowing honor. I can't believe you actually stood there and demanded an apology from him after everything you've said to me."

"I actually know that, Brie." His voice had softened and he didn't break eye contact with her as he took a moment to gather his thoughts. Shaking his head, he reached up and rubbed the back of his neck with his hand. "I was wrong. Really wrong with how I've treated you. I know that...have *known* it. I'm sorry."

The words were sincere, and something about that fact had her coming down fractionally. Or at least just enough for her to stop screaming. But she was still holding on to a fair amount of anger, and she wasn't letting him off that easy. "How many times have you actually admitted to that? Being wrong?"

"Not a lot." He shook his head, taking a second to study her. All of her. His eyes moved from hers and down her body, not in a sexual way so much as just getting the full picture. "I wasn't prepared for you. In any way. I don't do relationships, Brie."

Her eyebrows rose high. "I wasn't aware that I'd asked for one."

"You didn't, but the women that I…" He trailed off, apparently looking for the right words to continue.

But she finished for him. "The women that you sleep with?" She wasn't shocked by the fact that he didn't do relationships and only had sex, not in the slightest. It wasn't like she imagined the man to be celibate. After the night they'd spent together there was no doubt in her mind that he was experienced. Plus, he worked at a bar.

She wasn't naive.

"Yes." He nodded. "The women that I sleep with aren't from around here. Which means that the instances that I randomly run into them again are few and far between."

"And you keep running into me."

"Over and over and over again."

"And that's why you've been an asshole when we've run into each other? Because you don't like seeing your one-night stands out in the light of day?"

"A case could be made that I'm usually an asshole." He gave her a self-deprecating smile.

"Don't I know it."

"I'm sorry, Brie." He repeated those words and she knew he meant them, could see it there in his eyes. God, his eyes. "There's no excuse…no excuse for any of it. It doesn't matter about Bethelda. I mean it matters, but not in the way that I was making it an issue."

Her shoulders slumped, all of the fight leaving her in a rush of air. "God, Finn, you're exhausting."

"There are a number of people in my life who would agree with you." This time when he smiled it reached his eyes. "You're going to be here for a while, and with the way the last few days have gone, I have a feeling we're going to see each other often. I feel like it would be good for both of us to be in the same room and not get into a fight. And yes, I know I'm the one who has to take the first steps in that direction. So I am."

"That's it? Just get along? What about what just happened on the floor over there?" She nodded to the spot where they'd been dry-humping each other.

"Call it a moment of weakness."

A huff of laughter escaped her lips and she tilted her head to the side. In that small moment it felt like it had been at the beginning with him. "A moment of weakness? Really?"

"You have a better explanation?"

"No." She shook her head. She had absolutely no explanation for anything that happened with the two of them.

"In that case, truce?" he asked, holding out his hand.

"I guess so." She nodded, reaching her hand out and grabbing his. "Truce."

That oh-so-familiar warmth spread up her arm, and for just a second she forgot to breathe. Apparently that was how it was going to be when he had his hands on her, even if it was just a simple handshake.

Except nothing with them had been simple. Not from the start.

They both let go and he took a step back. "I'm going to go get those boxes from outside. You want me to just put them in here?"

"Y-yes. That's fine."

"And I'll grab those on my way out," he said, pointing to the two remaining boxes. Well, the one remaining intact box and the pile of sweaters next to the empty box. "Can you just repack it for me?"

She nodded and he turned and headed out of the room. "Finn?" she called out when he got to the threshold of the hallway.

He stopped walking, putting his hand on the frame as he looked back to her. "Yeah?"

"Thank you."

His hand dropped as he turned to fully face her. "I thought I told you I didn't need any thank-you for helping move stuff?"

"I meant thank you for catching me."

His mouth fell open on a breath, his eyes widening. He clearly hadn't expected that. But then that smile of his was back in place, turning up the corners of his mouth. "I wasn't going to let you fall, Brie. Not without catching you." And with that he turned around and walked out of the room.

Chapter Eleven

More People Eating Their Feelings with Pancakes

When Sunday morning dawned Finn was exhausted and more confused than he'd been in his entire life. He'd slept like shit, tossing and turning. It didn't even take closing his eyes for him to see Brie…she was a constant thought, a constant picture, a constant want.

His mind kept replaying everything from that afternoon. The only intention he'd had when he'd driven over to Bethelda's house—scratch that, now Brie's house—was to get the stuff she'd wanted to donate. That was it. Nothing more, nothing less.

He knew it wasn't exactly enough to get his mother, Hannah, Harper, and Delilah to stop glaring at him whenever he walked into a room, but he thought it might be enough to appease his conscience a little. Except he'd gotten there and all of his intentions had gone out of the fucking window.

First off, it had been weird being inside of that house. Seeing where Bethelda had lived and all of the stuff she owned. It was no wonder Brie had no idea how long she was going to be in

Mirabelle with all of the things she had to go through. One glance at one room and he knew she hadn't even made a dent with the load she'd gotten rid of.

The second thing that had happened to throw him off—and the biggest—was when Brie had almost crashed into that grandfather clock. There'd been no thinking when he'd gone to grab her, only action. And then they'd been on the ground and she'd been sprawled on top of him.

Being in close proximity to her had already done funny things to him. But then he'd felt every part of her pressed up against every part of him. His nose had been in her hair, that sweet mint scent filling his lungs. All he'd been able to do was breathe deeper. And then they'd looked at each other and every ounce of his self-control had disappeared.

Kissing her again, tasting her again, it was all he could think about. It was those memories that took control when he'd finally fallen asleep. She'd been in every part of his dreams, except there he'd actually gotten inside of her again.

He'd woken up hard and even after getting himself off in the shower he felt almost no relief. It had barely made a dent in his need. And how could it? He knew exactly what being with her was like. Knew exactly how it felt to have her pulsing around his cock as they both came.

To add insult to injury, his first cup of coffee hadn't done anything to his zombie-like state. He was going to need a lot more and fast.

Luckily for him, that was on the morning's agenda. That Sunday was the first Sunday in February.

Since Finn was five years old, he and Shep had been coming to the Stardust Diner on the first Sunday of every month. It was something they'd always done with their grandfather. There'd been times over the years that either Finn or Shep hadn't been able to make it, but they'd been few and far between. And there'd never been a single instance where Owen had dined alone. Not one.

God Finn missed Owen, more than words could possibly say. He'd idolized the man as far back as he could remember. Finn's very first memory was of him and Shep sitting in their grandfather's lap. Owen reading them *Charlotte's Web* while he moved them all back and forth in his rocking chair.

It used to be that whenever Finn and Shep needed advice with a problem—usually about something that they'd done that was most definitely going to get them in trouble—they turned to their grandfather first. More often than not, Owen always told them to face the problem head on.

There'd been the time they'd burned a hole through their mother's oriental rug. Another time they'd gotten a little too carried away while wrestling in the hallway…and put a shoulder-shaped hole in the wall. They'd broken ceiling fans and bunk beds. Hit a baseball through the window in the kitchen. Gotten caught drinking Jack Daniel's…half of the brand-new bottle gone. Sunk a fishing boat in the Gulf of Mexico. Gotten their father's truck stuck out in the middle of a field while mudding.

And that was just the stuff they'd gotten into together.

As kids they'd snuck stray dogs into their rooms…as teenagers it had been girls. Though, with Finn it had always been Rebecca while Shep had a revolving line.

It was a miracle that they hadn't killed their parents…or that their parents hadn't killed them. They credited their survival to Owen. He'd always stood by them through all of their screw-ups, and had never given up on them even when they were at their worst. But even though he hadn't—and wouldn't have ever—given up on his grandsons, it didn't mean he'd ever minced words when he was telling them what he thought about a situation.

If there was anything that Owen Shepherd was, it was honest. He wondered what his grandfather would say to him now.

The answer to that question came almost immediately, and it was in the form of Shep's words from the other night. *You want to know one of the last things Grandpa said to me? He asked me when I was going to stop messing around with my life and settle down.* It wasn't the first time those words had replayed in his mind...it wasn't even the fifty-first.

But Finn didn't want to settle down. He was perfectly content with his life.

Bullshit. That one word echoed around his head like a rifle shot, Owen's voice loud and clear.

OK, it was true, at one point in his life he had imagined himself with a wife, 2.5 kids, a dog, and a house on the water.

The thing was, the woman in that picture had always been Rebecca. Once that dream had drowned he'd done nothing to bring it back to life. He'd just gone down a new path. One that didn't involve a wife or kids.

He had two out of the four from what he'd imagined of his future...those were odds he'd definitely take to Vegas.

Now you're gambling with your life? Again it was Owen's voice in his head, sounding less and less pleased. Almost six years since his grandfather's death and Finn could still hear him loud and clear.

There was something to that. Even if he wasn't there, the people who remembered him wouldn't let him die. Keeping up with traditions was part of that. Which was why he and Shep continued to go to the Stardust Diner on that first Sunday of the month. They'd done a pretty good job of keeping up with that particular tradition, too, one of them was usually always there, even if they were eating alone.

But neither of them would be eating alone that morning. Shep was already sitting at the booth when Finn walked through the door, two steaming cups of coffee on the table.

"Hey." Finn took the empty seat, immediately grabbing two sugar packets and ripping them open.

"You look like hell."

"Thanks." He dumped the sugar into the mug before grabbing the small metal container of half-and-half and tipping it over the rim. Once the correct ratio had been reached, and the coffee stirred, Finn lifted the mug to his mouth and took a long drink…so long that when he was finished half of the coffee was gone. Setting the mug down he looked up to find his brother frowning at him.

"Look, I'm OK with this unspoken truce we've had going on. I've already said my piece on what I think about things, so it's totally up to you on whether you want me to ignore whatever this is." Shep waved a hand in the air, the motion encompassing Finn's face. "Or do you want to tell me about whatever it is that's gotten under your skin?"

"You mean *who* has gotten under my skin?"

"Oh, I know it's Brie, I'm not an idiot. What happened now?"

"Hannah tell you that Mom ripped me a new asshole yesterday?"

"No." He shook his head. "But Dad did when we were working at the Sheep last night. He said Mom was *in a state* when she got home. I guess Brie told them all the truth about Bethelda."

"Yeah, and none of them cared one little bit about it."

"And now you've finally realized you don't care, either?"

"Why do you think that?" Finn hadn't had nearly enough coffee to be psychoanalyzed by his brother, but he asked anyway. And as Shep's mouth turned up into a knowing smile, he knew he was in for it.

"You mean how do I *know* it?"

Finn didn't answer and Shep just grinned.

"What was your first thought? When you saw Brie standing in your office? After the night you'd spent with her but before you found out about Bethelda?"

"I…" Finn trailed off, thinking back to that moment. "I was glad she hadn't left," he admitted. But not only had he been glad, he'd felt hope. Hope that turned into that balloon, that damn balloon that he'd had to pop.

"Knowing you the way I do, once you thought that, you became set on finding something that was wrong with her," Shep continued. "And once the Bethelda factor was out in the open, you latched on and went with it."

Dammit, Shep had gotten that right.

Finn took a deep breath before he let it out through his nose on a sigh. "Yeah. That's exactly what happened."

"I know just as much as you do how much it sucks when Mom lays into you. Hurts more than anyone else…well, besides when it was Owen."

"God, when Owen was disappointed that was worse than anything."

"I agree with her, though," Shep said honestly. "You know biology isn't always a factor in how someone turns out."

"I do." Finn nodded.

"So why did you act like it mattered with Brie?"

"Because I still wanted her." He paused for just a second before he amended that statement. "I still *want* her."

"That's new and different for you and your *one and done* mentality."

"I know that. First time in a long time."

"You mean first time in eight years?" The part that Shep left out of that question was that it was the first time since Rebecca. But unspoken or not, Finn heard it loud and clear.

"Yeah." He slowly nodded, reaching for the handle of his mug and draining the remainder of the coffee. He was going to need an entire pot brought to the table.

As if thinking it had summoned her, their regular waitress came out from the kitchen, pot in hand.

"Wanda, you are a godsend," Finn said as he offered her a genuine, if not tired, smile.

"Sugar, I've been serving you breakfast for almost a quarter of a century, I know what you want even before you want it." She filled up both coffee cups before setting the pot down on the table.

"Well, in that case, what should I have for breakfast?" He had no clue what he wanted to eat, but what he did know was that he was starving.

"Chocolate chip pancakes, with extra whipped cream and a double side of bacon."

"Done." He nodded.

"And you, honey?" Wanda looked to Shep.

"Same as him."

"Perfect." She grabbed the two untouched menus from the corner of the table and headed back to the kitchen.

"So what happened after the flogging?" Shep asked while they both doctored up their coffees again.

Finn waited to answer until he could take another hit of caffeine before he launched into the story. Shep just sat back and listened, slowly sipping from his own mug.

"Really, Robbie went off?" Shep asked, surprised. "That's pretty out of character for him."

Robbie was actually from the next town over—which was why he hadn't known where Bethelda's house was—where the FedEx distribution center was located. He'd had the job since he was eighteen, but had been delivering to Mirabelle for just over a year. As there were only a few FedEx trucks that came to Mirabelle, most people knew who he was. He'd also turned twenty-one a couple of months back and stopped by the Sleepy Sheep every once in a while.

"It is. At first I came to the door because he was flirting with her, which I didn't like. And then he turned on her when she mentioned Bethelda, and I wanted to shove his head through a wall."

"Interesting." Shep raised his eyebrows but he didn't say anything else as Wanda was making her way back to the table, a tray balanced on her hand.

She unloaded the food with quick efficiency, two pancake plates, two bacon plates, and two bowls of freshly whipped cream. Any expert pancake eater knew that the whipped cream could not be put directly on the pancakes, because it would melt before the food even got to the table.

"You boys need anything else?" she asked as she flipped the tray under her arm.

"No, ma'am. Looks perfect."

"Would I serve you anything less?" She put her free hand on her hip and gave them a sassy look.

"Never."

"Exactly." And with that she turned around and headed for the kitchen again.

Finn grabbed his knife and fork, digging into his pancakes. They were loaded with just enough melted chocolate, and the thick whipped cream had just the right amount of sweetness.

He swallowed, taking another sip of coffee before he asked, "So what was *interesting*, as you put it, about the encounter with Robbie?"

"That you can be mean to Brie, but no one else can." Shep broke off a piece of bacon and popped it into his mouth.

Finn frowned. "Look, I thought we'd already established that I've been a total dick when it comes to Brie. And clearly there's been no logic in my actions whatsoever, so let's move on from that." He waved his hand in a small rolling motion. "Besides, she already pointed out that I was a hypocrite."

"Good for her. You apologize?"

"Yes."

"And she forgave you?" Shep asked as he forked up a bite of whipped cream–covered pancakes.

Finn thought back to the moment. "Not in so many words, but she accepted my truce."

"So what now? The white flag is raised and you stop jumping down her throat every time you see her?"

Was that all that he wanted? Just a cease-fire? "What other option is there? It's not like there's a future or anything."

"Why not?"

"A, she's not staying. And B, I'm not interested in a relationship."

"You know, you could just be her friend. She's going to be here indefinitely, doesn't know anyone, and is having a bit of a tough time. Maybe you could try that as opposed to just getting in her bed again."

"Really?" Finn said that one word slowly, and laced it with a whole hell of a lot of skepticism. "Was that your plan when Hannah came back to town? Just be friends? No sex?" He cut into his pancakes before spearing another bite.

"No, my plan with Hannah was to get her back. Finn, from the moment that woman walked back into my life she was mine. There was no chance in hell I was going to give up until she realized it, too."

Something uncomfortable settled in Finn's gut at Shep's little speech. The food he was chewing going down with an uneasy swallow. It wasn't just a relationship that Shep had wanted when it came to Hannah coming back to town, his brother had wanted marriage, wanted *forever*.

The thought of a long commitment *period* made Finn's lungs constrict and his head spin. The thought of marriage? Well, that was like he was suffocating.

Nope. Not for him. He didn't want it. He was better off alone.

Bullshit. And there was Owen's voice, echoing loud and clear in his head again. He ignored it…or at least tried to.

"What do you want, Finn?"

"I have no fucking clue."

"Well, I suggest you figure it out." Shep made that task sound so simple as he speared another bite of pancakes with his fork.

Finn knew it was going to be *far* from simple.

*   *   *

St. Sebastian's was the one and only Catholic church in Mirabelle. They had three Mass times on Sunday morning: eight, ten, and twelve. As Brie had spent another late night going through stuff in the spare bedroom/office, she opted to go to the ten.

When she'd opened her eyes that morning she couldn't help but notice that some of the massive weight had lifted from her shoulders. Sure, there was still the stress of being in Bethelda's house and dealing with everything, but the truth was out there and not everyone hated her.

There was also the fact that she wasn't feuding with Finn anymore. He'd apologized and she didn't for one second doubt that it had been genuine. She also didn't doubt that there was still something between them. She'd be a filthy liar if she said she hadn't thought about their kiss on the floor of the living room.

Not that it meant anything was going to happen again. She wasn't delusional. The very last thing she needed to do was get tangled up in anything or anyone in Mirabelle. That being said, she also knew she shouldn't isolate herself. She'd never done well being confined to the same four walls, thus her going to church. That and she wanted to experience something that was part of her history. Bethelda had gone to this church and so had her grandparents.

She got there about ten minutes early and a handful of people were outside milling around on the front steps. When she walked inside it was to find that only about half of the seats were filled. There were ten pews on both sides of the center aisle, and each looked like it could seat from eight to ten people. She found herself a spot on the right and toward the center, wanting to be more in the middle of things than on the outskirts.

Brie wasn't what could be described as a practicing Catholic; the last time she'd gone to church was over the holidays. She'd been with her parents in Spain and they'd gone to Christmas Eve Mass at the Basilica in Barcelona.

To say that St. Sebastian's was much, *much* smaller would be an understatement. The Basilica had a capacity of nine thousand, St. Sebastian's was closer to a hundred and ninety. The little, whitewashed, red-doored, steepled building didn't have any of the opulent, gothic architecture, but it was still beautiful in its simplicity.

The crucifix above the altar was different from anything she'd seen, the cross made of driftwood. And then there were the windows. Stunning stained glass, each one depicting a different scene from the Bible. Crisp, clear sunshine shone through, and the colors danced on the mahogany hardwood floors and white walls. Brie got lost in the one closest to her showing Jesus washing the feet of the disciples.

Before she knew it, the choir started singing a hymn and the congregation was standing up. She looked around to see that the church was almost filled, just about every single space taken up by a person.

The priest got to the altar, turning to face his congregation and waiting for the hymn to end. He was probably in his sixties, with white hair and a white beard. Brie wondered how long he'd been there, wondered if he'd known her grandparents.

Petunia and Harold Grimshaw had probably been married in this church…Bethelda had most likely been baptized here. Brie imagined a baby Bethelda, dressed in a white christening gown, crying out as the water touched her forehead. It resembled the picture that Brie had seen many times from her own baptism. She just switched out the background to match this church.

For her, buildings held memories, and the people still existed here. They'd breathed here, lived here. The Grimshaws—all of them—had sat in these pews, warmed these seats.

When everyone went to sit again, her hands moved to the edge of the pew, her fingers curving around the wood and pressing in. It was like she could touch the memory of them here, a memory that wasn't her own.

It was then, right there in that moment, that she knew beyond a shadow of a doubt she'd made the correct choice by coming to Mirabelle. There was so much she had to figure out, so much she wanted to learn.

She also knew it wasn't going to be easy, but it would be worth it.

* * *

There were a number of things that Finn had taken up since moving back to Mirabelle, and going to Sunday Mass with his Grandma El and his parents was one of them. It wasn't just him that now went regularly, either. Shep, Hannah, and baby Nate were all loaded into the pews as well.

Now, just because Finn went to Mass didn't exactly mean he was in good standing with the church. He hadn't gone to confession since he was fifteen and then there were his extracurricular activities. Nevertheless he was still there every Sunday.

After breakfast, he and Shep headed over to St. Sebastian's, meeting up with everyone else in the parking lot. His mother had given him a rather severe frown when she'd seen him, the question clear in her eyes.

"I fixed it, Mom."

"Good." She nodded, linking her arm with his and letting him lead her inside.

So there he stood, Ella on one side and his mother on the other, as everyone listened to Father Duncan read the Gospel. It was then that it happened, a baby on the other side of the church started to cry. When the dad sidestepped out of the pew, it opened up the view to the next row. That was when Finn's eyes landed on a head with unmistakable mahogany hair.

Sunshine streamed in from the stained-glass window behind Brie, highlighting the red tones among all of the deep rich brown in her hair. It was down and around her shoulders, and all he could think about was sinking his fingers between silky strands again.

Someone cleared their throat behind Finn, and he pulled his focus from Brie. It was then that he realized everyone was sitting again…except for him. He glanced over his shoulder as he sat down to find Shep smirking at him. As he pulled his attention forward he saw that his mother was giving him an appraising look. Her eyes moved past him and in the direction he'd just been staring. He knew the second she spotted Brie because her eyebrows rose high.

Not wanting to see whatever look his mother was about to give him, Finn immediately turned to Father Duncan. For the next fifteen minutes he tried his hardest to focus on whatever the man was saying while keeping his eyes resolutely forward.

He failed. Miserably.

Everything going on around him became white noise, and more than once he got a sharp poke from Shep because he wasn't standing, sitting, or kneeling like he was supposed to be. If at the end of the hour he didn't have a bruise on his back—his brother kept poking the exact same spot—and a crick in his neck from straining to look forward, he'd be shocked. Not only that, but he heard nothing except the thoughts in his head. Well, his thoughts that were prompted by stuff that Shep had said at breakfast.

So what now? The white flag is raised and you stop jumping down her throat every time you see her?

Well, he did want to be down her throat, he just didn't want to jump there. No, he wanted to kiss the hell out of her. Feel her lips under his. Taste her mouth. Hear her moan…

Yeah, that wasn't a good track to go on while sitting in a place of God. So instead he moved on to another thing that Shep had said.

You know, you could just be her friend.

Friend. Friend? He'd never in his life been friends with someone that he'd slept with…except Rebecca. She might've been his girlfriend when they'd had sex for the first time, but she'd been his best friend, too.

And now he was on a track that he really didn't want to be

on. Thinking about Rebecca was always a bad choice. *Always.*
So, moving on to something else.

What do you want, Finn?

He hadn't meant to turn and look to where Brie sat, but before he even realized what he was doing, he had his eyes on her again. Her elbows rested on the back of the pew in front of her as she knelt, and her hands were clasped together as she looked forward. She'd pushed her hair back and over her shoulder, giving him an unobstructed side profile of her face.

God she was beautiful.

What did he want? Her. He wanted her, and he was so over fighting it. Over the stupid excuses he'd tried to come up with. As fate kept proving, he wasn't going to be able to stay away from her while she was in Mirabelle. The thing was, he didn't want to stay away. He wanted to see her in whatever way he could.

* * *

The sunshine outside of the church was almost blinding when Brie walked outside. She reached for her purse on her shoulder, digging around for her sunglasses as she walked down the stairs. As her eyes were focused down—both paying attention to every step that she took and trying to shelter her eyes from the sun—she didn't see the solid wall of man that moved into her path.

"Oomph." The startled sound escaped her lips as firm hands landed on her shoulders, steadying her.

Brie would know those hands anywhere. She looked up to find Finn grinning down at her. The sun had nothing on brightness when it came to his smile lighting up his eyes.

"Why is it that running into you around town means literally running into you?"

"I have no idea." She shook her head, unable to stop herself from grinning back at him.

His hands disappeared from her shoulders and she immediately missed them on her body. She'd say that was an interesting development, but the man's touch had affected her from their very first handshake.

Until him she'd never *fully* appreciated just how sexy a man's hands could be. Maybe that was because she'd never seen—or felt—hands as sexy as his. Or maybe it was his hands combined with the rest of the whole sexy package.

Her mind veered to the night they'd spent together…her straddling his legs as she counted his eight-pack, feeling each ridge under her fingertips…

"How was Mass?" Finn's question brought her back to reality.

For heaven's sake, she'd just gone to church and was now thinking about sex with Finn. It would probably be prudent to take a few more steps away from the building behind her before lightning struck her down.

"It was good. I…um…" She hesitated for a second, unsure of how much to say to him. Truce or not, he wasn't a confidant. "I just wanted to get out of the house. If I'm in there for too long I start to feel claustrophobic."

"Understandable. I don't know what I expected when I walked in there yesterday, but it sure wasn't that." He shook his head.

"I think *unexpected* has been the major theme since I got here."

"Brie?" a soft voice said from behind Finn. They both looked over to see Ella making her way over from a group of elderly ladies. She might move a little slowly, but she could walk unassisted.

"Hello, Ella." She smiled.

Finn's head whipped back to look at Brie and he looked dumbfounded. "You know my grandmother?"

"We met at Bethelda's funeral," Ella answered, reaching a withered hand out and grasping Brie's. Withered or not, she had a firm grip, her skin soft and warm. "How are you, deary?" she asked as she let go of Brie.

"I'm good. Just enjoying this beautiful Sunday."

"Excellent." She beamed. "So how do you know my grandson here?"

Brie glanced at Finn to find that stunned expression still on his face as he looked between her and his grandmother.

"We met at the Sleepy Sheep last week."

"Oh." Ella nodded, the brightness in her smile diminishing for just a second as pain flashed through her blue eyes. "My Owen built that bar with his own two hands." As she said it one of her hands came up and she began to rub the gray pearl on her necklace between her thumb and forefinger. "I see you didn't head back to Chapel Hill yet."

"No." Brie shook her head, seeing Finn's reaction become even more astounded. "I've been a little bit delayed."

"I see that. So how long are you going to be delayed for?"

"At least the next month or two I think." She hesitated for only a second before continuing on with the truth. "Bethelda left me everything in her will. She was my biological mother and she gave me up for adoption."

What was the point in not saying it? Pretty much all of Finn's family knew anyway. Besides, Ella had known Brie's grandparents...she'd been close with Petunia. Brie had the sense that Ella would be a wealth of information, and the only way she was going to get it was from laying it all out on the line.

The truth will out.

Ella's blue eyes went wide, her hand letting go of the pearl and coming up to cover her mouth that had dropped open. After a moment she shook her head, moving her hand away. "Bethelda had a daughter? I...I had no idea."

"I don't think anybody did."

"Well, that explains the whole you not knowing her thing but being at her funeral. Who was your—" Ella abruptly stopped, shaking her head as she looked around, realizing it wasn't the time or place.

Brie knew the question that Ella had wanted to ask: who was Brie's father?

Now wasn't that the million-dollar question? One Brie had been asking herself for over twenty years.

"You should come over and talk with me sometime." Ella reached out again, patting Brie's arm. "If I have any answers to any questions that you have...they're yours. And I promise not to pry."

Brie shrugged. "Even if you did pry, I don't know very much."

"How about next Sunday? For dinner?" Ella asked. "You can come over a little early, we can talk, and I can teach you how to make Petunia's cobbler. Peaches aren't in season, so we will have to make strawberry rhubarb. It's delicious, too. And I'm sure one of the bartenders at the house can make us some

Mirabelle Sweet Teas, which coincidentally has very little sweet tea."

"Yes." Brie agreed without hesitation.

"Finn, honey," Ella said, and turned to her grandson, "you'll let Brie know how to get to the house?"

"Yes, I will," he said with a nod.

"OK, well, I'll see you next week, or sooner." Ella patted Brie's hand again. "And I'll see you later," she said as she leaned in close to Finn.

Finn kissed his grandmother's cheek and she smiled at them both before she turned around and walked away. She slowly made her way over to Faye who was talking to some other women. Faye looked over and spotted Brie with Finn, and she lifted her hand and waved as the corners of her mouth turned up.

Brie waved back before moving her attention back to Finn, who was still looking beyond surprised. "You only met my grandmother once? Only had one conversation with her?"

"Yes."

"She has dementia. Some days she's fine, and others…" He trailed off, shaking his head. "Well, other days she thinks it's twenty or thirty years ago. Or really any point in time that Owen was still alive."

"Owen was her husband? Your grandfather?" She could sense a profound sadness from him. It was there in how he held his body, his shoulders down. It was also there in his words and in his eyes. She didn't like seeing that sadness there, wanted to make it go away.

"Yeah. She doesn't usually remember people who she's only met once, and she very clearly remembered you."

"Maybe I'm just memorable." *Oh shit*. What had she just said? It sounded like she was flirting.

Because you are flirting.

But the comment worked, Finn's lips quirking to the side. "I can attest to the fact that you're very memorable, indeed."

Annnnnd he was flirting back.

Flirting or furious, were those the only two modes in which they could interact with each other?

But it was more than just that, there was something about the look in his eyes that made her pretty sure he was remembering something about their night together. His eyes lingered on the small diamond hanging above her breasts. She remembered the way he'd traced his warm lips over the chain, how he'd kissed the pendant. When his eyes met hers again she knew they were thinking about the exact same thing.

"Anyway, I actually had a reason for coming over to talk to you."

"Which was?" she asked, grateful for the change in topic. She was pretty sure her cheeks were taking on a rosy hue that had nothing to do with the sun.

"That you should call me when you need help getting rid of Bethelda's belongings."

"Finn, I really don't think you understand what you'd be getting into with that offer. You haven't seen the full scope."

"I've seen enough. And besides, what are you going to do? Strap the furniture to the roof of your MINI?"

"No," she said as she rolled her eyes. "I could always rent a truck or something."

"That seems like a waste of time *and* money, especially as I'm offering to do it for free. Besides, how is a guy supposed to atone for his sins if you won't let him?"

"Atone for your sins? I already forgave you, Finn."

Something that looked remarkably like relief flashed in his expression. "Good. Now the next goal is making you forget about them."

"Finn, that isn't necessary."

"Actually it is. Let me make it right, Brie. Or at least try to."

Oh good gravy. There he went being all sincere again. How in the world was she supposed to say no to that? She didn't have any idea, so she didn't.

"OK," she agreed, getting the feeling she was saying yes to a whole lot more than his help.

Chapter Twelve

No Strings Attached

When Finn left the church on Sunday, after setting Operation Atonement in action, he wondered just how long he was going to have to wait before seeing Brie again.

It turned out not very long at all. Just a few hours actually. Though this time he was expecting to run into her when he walked into Farmer's Drugs. He spotted her car parked outside as he pulled his truck into an empty space a few down.

On Monday morning he ran into her at the Gas-N-Go. Tuesday found them both standing in line at the bank. Wednesday afternoon was the post office. He helped her carry out a couple of packages, putting a very small dent in his redemption plan. He also knew he made out better from that little encounter as he'd gotten to hear her laugh. Their time together hadn't ended there, though, because she had another truckload of stuff for him to take to the CCC so he'd swung by after work.

The thing was, none of it was enough. He wanted a lot more time with her. Wanted way more than a handful of minutes here and there. He was just going to need to figure out the best way to accomplish that.

There was no running into Brie on Thursday morning, and there wouldn't be as he started his day well before the sun came up. He was out of bed by five, and he and Frankie were out the front door by five fifty. It was cold that morning, too, in the low forties. A cold snap had settled over Mirabelle and it was only going to keep dropping over the next couple of days. His breath misted on the air as he headed down the front steps of his house and to his truck.

Finn's aunt and uncle, Jacob and Marigold Meadows, owned Whiskey Creek Farm. It was about ten miles from the main part of Mirabelle, a stretch of forty acres that was put to good use.

There were currently twenty-eight horses in residence on the farm, some of them owned by the family, and others that were boarded. All of them were getting their first-of-the-year checkups. Since Finn would be spending all day at the farm, he figured he'd do it right and show up early enough to go for a ride.

Both Finn and Shep had horses. His a bay named Nigel, his brother's a white and brown Appaloosa named Springsteen. Both horses had been born on the farm, and both had only known one owner. Nigel was another reason that Finn hadn't really stayed away for longer than a month when he was in college. He loved that horse like a member of the family. The only thing that had eased his mind while he'd been gone was knowing that Shep took good care of Nigel during Finn's absence.

Speaking of Shep, his brother's mustang was parked in the driveway when Finn pulled in. Apparently he wasn't the only one who'd wanted to go for a ride. It was interesting…they rarely ever planned to go riding together because more often than not they'd both show up on the exact same mornings.

There were two barns on the property. The smaller one closer to the house was where they stabled the family horses. The bigger one was farther away and where the boarded horses were kept. Finn found Shep and Meredith, their cousin, in the family barn. They were already starting to get the feed ready.

"Look how that turned out." Shep grinned when he spotted Finn.

"Well, if both of you got these guys, I'm going to go help my parents and Emma. Hi, Finn." She stopped, gave him a kiss on the cheek before she patted Frankie on the head, and headed out the door.

Meredith, and her seventeen-year-old daughter, Emma, moved back to Mirabelle and the farm last summer. Meredith had just gone through a messy divorce from her husband. *Really messy.*

It turned out he'd been having an affair with Emma's high school principal…Emma's male high school principal. For most teenagers it probably would've been hard to pack up and move right before junior year, not so much with Emma. She'd wanted just as much of a fresh start as her mother.

Plus, both Marigold and Jacob were glad to have their girls closer, and not just because of the extra help. They weren't the only ones, either. Marigold was Owen and Ella's daughter, so she was a Shepherd by birth, and Meredith had stakes in the bar, too. Since she'd moved back she pulled shifts behind the counter every once in a while. And that wasn't the only place she was involved with the business, either.

Meredith was not only a graphic designer but a Web designer, too. She'd been the one to create the branding logo for the Sleepy Sheep and the brewery along with completely redesigning the website. She'd done the same thing for the farm, too. The fact that she could work from anywhere was another thing that made relocating easier.

But that was where *easy* pretty much stopped. She'd been very much in love with her husband, and that amount of deceit and betrayal had rocked her to the core. She was doing a lot better than she was a year ago, but he wondered if she'd ever let a man into her life like that again.

Finn understood the whole being gun-shy thing better than anyone else in the family.

Not all that surprisingly, as his mind had the habit of doing these days, he thought of Brie. Gun-shy was not his current mind-set when it came to her.

He'd decided how he wanted to accomplish getting more time with her, and that was asking her out on a date. Part of the problem was he was out of practice on the whole dating front. He hadn't gone on one since he'd moved back to Mirabelle. Besides all of that, there was the whole her saying yes part of the equation.

So he was going to need to figure all of that out. And that was what he was working on as he helped Shep with the horses. They worked seamlessly, as per usual, getting everyone in the barn fed. Once they finished with that, they each led their horses out of the stalls and got them ready for the ride.

By the time they finished their ride and got Nigel and Springsteen cooled and brushed down, it was close to nine. Finn headed inside for a quick bite before starting his rounds on the farm, while Shep headed home to eat breakfast with his wife and son.

The rest of the day proved to be a long one, and thoughts of how to win Brie over for a date were pushed to the back of his mind. On top of the usual yearly checkups for everyone, he had to contend with an aggressive new stallion, a pony that panicked when it was away from its pasture mates, a fidgety pregnant mare, and two horses both recovering from recent bouts with a cold and colic. He barely even paused the rest of the day, just a quick lunch in his aunt's kitchen where he scarfed down some gumbo and then he was out the door again.

Before he knew it, it was close to six. He stuck around for the nighttime feeding, spending a little bit more time with Nigel before he and Frankie were loading up into his truck and heading home.

The second they walked in the door, Frankie headed for the kitchen knowing full well it was dinnertime. Finn scooped up an overflowing cup of dry food and poured it into her container before checking on his own food situation.

The refrigerator proved to be slim pickings: a container of raspberry yogurt, half a carton of eggs, and a lemon. He was an OK chef, but that just didn't seem like something he could make a meal with. He opened the freezer to find marginally better offerings: a frozen pizza and a bag of broccoli.

"We need to go to the store, Frankie."

Her head came up from her bowl, and she looked at him for only a moment before she returned to her dinner. He was pretty sure that was her version of a doggy eye roll.

The very last thing he wanted to do was cook anyway. It was one of those evenings where nothing sounded better than a burger and a beer. He grabbed the neck of his shirt and pulled it up, taking a deep breath.

Yeah, a shower would need to happen before food. As he'd been in a barn all day, he smelled like he'd been rolling around *with* the horses.

Leaving Frankie with her dinner, he headed for the stairs and up to his bedroom and the shower.

* * *

Bubba's Burgers was pretty busy when Finn pulled into the parking lot. He found an empty spot up front, which was lucky as cars lined the lot all the way to the back. Apparently he wasn't the only one who wanted a burger.

He walked quickly to the front door, shoving his hands in the pockets of his jacket in an attempt to shield them from the cold air and bitter wind whipping off the Gulf behind the restaurant. Once he got inside, he found a spot at the bar, ordering a beer from Twila Thomas who was working behind the counter. She was a few years older than Finn, caramel skin and her long black hair twisted in small, intricate braids.

"I'll give you a minute for your dinner order," she said as she slid a full beer down in front of him.

Finn took a sip of his beer before he grabbed the menu in front of him. It took him less than a minute to decide on the applewood-smoked bacon burger with cheddar cheese and a side of fries.

As he set his menu back in the holder, he took a quick glance around the restaurant and his eyes landed on none other than Brie. She was sitting in a booth by the windows, looking down at a menu on the table. Her brow was furrowed like it was the most complicated selection she'd ever made in her life.

Though in truth, Bubba's had a wide variety of options and they were all delicious, so Finn got it.

"You ready to order?"

Finn turned back to Twila who was standing in front of him again. Her eyebrows rose as she looked between him and Brie, a smirk turning up her mouth. "She isn't on the menu, honey."

"I'm aware of that."

"You know she's in town dealing with Bethelda's estate? Brie…" She trailed off.

Damn, but word traveled fast in this town.

"Brie Davis," he finished for her. "And I'm aware of that, too. She order anything to drink yet?"

"Nope."

"Can you get her one of these?" He held up his beer. "And put it on my tab."

"Sure thing." She grabbed another glass and moved it under the tap, the golden brown liquid moving up and filling it. "You delivering this or am I?"

"I am. And I'll order my dinner over there."

Twila's eyebrows rose high as she slid the other glass in front of him. "Well, aren't you sure of yourself?"

"Wishful thinking, actually." He flashed her a smile before he slid off the bar stool and made his way to Brie, both beers in hand.

Interestingly enough, he found that he was slightly nervous as he walked across the room. He hadn't been nervous when it came to a woman in God only knew how long. Probably his first time with Rebecca…which had also been his first time period.

That was almost fifteen years ago. He should be over that by now…and yet his heart was beating a little bit faster and his mouth had gone dry. For good measure he took a sip of beer before he got to the table, attempting to loosen his tongue.

She must've sensed someone approaching, because her head came up. The second her eyes landed on him, a smile tipped up the corner of her lips. And just that quickly his heart picked up an even faster tempo.

"Imagine seeing you here." She shook her head, leaning back in the seat as she looked up at him.

"I know, apparently we can't go a day without running into each other."

"Apparently not. You double-fisting it tonight?" She nodded to the two glasses in his hand.

"No. I saw you over here looking like you were trying to figure out quantum physics instead of your dinner order." He set the full glass down in front of her. "And I thought that since I did so well with your drink selections before, I'd try it out again tonight."

"Oh really now. Well, let's see." She grabbed the glass, lifting it to her lips and taking a sip. Her eyes narrowed on him as she lowered the glass. "How do you do that? It's perfect."

"A magician never reveals his secrets, nor does a part-time bartender. Can I join you?" he asked as he indicated the empty seat across from her.

"You paid the toll," she said, and nodded as she lifted the glass to her lips again and took another drink.

At her yes, a sense of relief rolled through him. It wasn't a small sense of relief, either, not by any means. He moved into the seat across from her, feeling like he'd just won. His evening was only going to get better and better with her sitting on the other side of that table.

"Do you want to choose what burger I should get for dinner, too?" She pointed to the menu.

"Well, do you want sweet or salty, or both?"

Her nose wrinkled. "Sweet on a burger?"

"The peanut butter and jelly one is actually pretty good."

"I'll pass," she said, shaking her head.

"Also in the slightly sweet category is the goat cheese, with onions caramelized in a balsamic vinaigrette, and arugula."

"Now that is more up my alley. Side?"

"Sweet potato fries are the clear pairing here."

"Perfect." She grabbed her menu from the table and moved it to the stand behind the salt and pepper shakers.

"So what happened today that made food selection beyond you? More Bethelda boxes?"

"No actually." She shook her head. "I didn't go through any of her things today. Yesterday, I got the office cleaned up enough to where I could finally work at the desk."

"What are you working on?"

Her mouth opened on an inhale and she hesitated for just a second. "I…I'm working on my thesis."

"Your thesis? You're getting your doctorate?"

"That's the plan. I took this semester off of teaching to work solely on it. Clearly that's not going to happen."

"No," he said as he shook his head slowly, a certain insult that he'd thrown at her replaying in his head.

I'd say don't quit your day job, but clearly you don't have one.

"What?" She tilted her head to the side. "What are you thinking about that has you frowning so intensely now?"

"Just thinking about how big of an asshole I've been to you."

Her eyebrows rose in question.

"The job comment."

"Finn, it's water under the bridge. And if I'm remembering correctly, I started that particular battle of words."

Actually, she'd started it *and* finished it, effectively putting him in his place before she'd walked away from him in Wide Open Spaces.

"Plus"—she lifted her glass in the air—"you bought me a beer."

Finn lifted his glass, too, and they gently clinked them together before taking a sip. As they set the glasses down on the table, Rosalie Simpson came to the table, strawberry-blond ponytail bouncing as she smiled at the two of them.

"Do you guys know what you want?" she asked. They both gave her their food orders before she nodded and walked away.

"So what are you getting your doctorate in?" Finn asked before he took another sip of his beer.

"History. The subject always fascinated me. I think it was because I never knew mine."

Fascinated...that was a good word. He found that the more she talked the more he became fascinated, and the more he wanted to know. "Where are you going to school?"

"UNC Chapel Hill."

"Go Tar Heels."

"Damn straight."

"What about undergrad?"

"Well, when I was born my parents lived in Miami, and they actually taught at the University of Miami. But then when I was five, we moved to Atlanta when they both got jobs at

Emory. I grew up loving that school, so I always wanted to go there. What about you?" Her head tilted to the side, her hair falling over her shoulder. "Where did you learn to become a doctor?"

"Auburn. All eight years."

"War Eagle."

"Damn straight," he repeated her sentiment from a moment before, making her grin. "Where are your parents now?"

"They are actually in Italy. They're both at the American University of Rome."

"Really? What do they teach?"

"Well, my mother teaches art history and my dad economics."

"Only child?" The question was out of his mouth before he could think better of it. "Sorry, I—"

"No, it's fine," she said as she waved him off. "With my parents, yes. With Bethelda? Who knows. She kept me a secret, but I don't know if that happened more than once. It's possible. And then there is the mystery of who my biological father is."

"You don't know who he is?"

"His name wasn't on the original birth certificate. And the one and only time I met her, we didn't get far enough into the conversation for me to ask. I figure there have to be some answers in that house. Somewhere. I just have to find them."

"You found anything yet?" he asked before he took another sip of his beer.

"Finn, I haven't even really started looking. The stuff that I've gone through, and gotten rid of, she bought in bulk. The things that don't have ties to anything. Well, unless you count all of that yarn I got rid of."

"I see what you did there."

Her mouth turned up in a half smile. "I don't do well with clutter, and there is so much of it there. That's why I couldn't work until I got the office cleared out a little. Sometimes it's been hard for me to breathe in that house, let alone focus."

"That makes total sense. So that's your plan while you're here? Working on your thesis in between going through Bethelda's stuff?"

"Yeah." She nodded.

"And what about when you're not doing either of those things?"

"What do you mean?"

Well, he'd started on this track, he might as well barrel on through it. Full steam ahead. "Have dinner with me."

Her eyebrows rose in surprise. "I thought that was what we were doing now."

"I mean a date. I pick you up. I take you out."

"Finn, I..." She stopped for a second, giving a slight shake of her head. "I don't know if that's a good idea."

"Why not?"

"Because you and I tend to run hot...especially in unsupervised situations where there can be, how did you word it? Moments of weakness?"

"What's wrong with moments of weakness?" The memory of them kissing on the floor after he caught her came to mind...quickly followed by one from the night they'd spent together where she'd been riding him.

"I don't get you." Her eyes narrowed as she studied him. "First you like me, then you don't like me, and now you like me again?"

"See, that's the thing. There was never a point where I didn't

like you. I was just *trying* not to like you. You should take that
as a compliment."

"Oh really now?" She laughed.

"Yeah. Try as I might, I failed miserably."

She leaned back in the seat, her eyes not leaving his. "Was
the you *trying* not to like me part of your whole *you don't do relationships* thing?"

"Part of it."

"What's the other part?"

"I don't do repeats." His answer might've been a little too
honest, but he figured that was the best way to proceed with
Brie at this point. Especially given his end goal.

"So you never want seconds?"

"No." He shook his head. "Except with you."

"Is that supposed to be a compliment, too?"

"Take it how you will, but it's the truth."

"Hmmm," she hummed, her mouth slightly pursing together and distracting him for just a second. "So what's the
deal? As long as I'm in town, we what?"

"Have as many moments of weakness as possible."

"And when I leave we just both go on our merry way? No
strings attached?"

"In effect."

"It's just that simple?"

"Why can't it be?" he asked, resting his elbows on the table
as he leaned forward and dropped his voice. They weren't exactly talking in an unbreakable code here, and the place was
busy. "We know we're compatible. I also get the feeling that
with what you're dealing with being in town, you might need
more nights of forgetting."

"Is that so?"

"It's just a hunch. Besides, you might need a friend every once in a while. No man is an island." He gave her one of the grins he'd given to many a woman, the ones that always got him exactly what he wanted.

Her eyes narrowed and she laughed, shaking her head. She wasn't in any way oblivious to what that look implied. "Yes, but you aren't exactly offering *just* friendship."

"I'm not. But if that's all that you want, then that offer is on the table, too." Though he had a pretty good idea they'd end up sweaty and naked anyway.

The heat that flashed in her eyes said she was thinking the exact same thing. But quickly following that heat was hesitation.

"How about we start off smaller. Not a one-on-one date, but more of a group thing. Come to the Sleepy Sheep, maybe one night when a Stampede game is on; those are always guaranteed to attract a crowd. You can get out of the house, meet a few more people in town."

"Make friends?" she asked.

"Yes, just not the type of friends that I'm offering to be."

She laughed, turning her head for just a second. When her gaze met his again she was smiling. "OK," she agreed.

Finn had never been happier at one single word in his life, because he knew it wasn't just her agreeing to come out to the Sheep.

* * *

Thursday night was bitterly cold. Well, bitterly cold for Florida that was. It was in the low thirties and the next night promised to drop to the twenties. Brie's plans of sleeping by the gas-lit fire in the den had been dashed as she couldn't get the stupid thing started. She couldn't get the one in the living room to light, either.

Instead she turned the heater to sixty-five and hunkered under the covers with Delores, or Lo as she was now referring to the cat.

As Brie tried to go to sleep her brain—not all that surprisingly as it had done it every other night that week—found its way to Finn. She replayed their dinner through her head. The easygoing look on his face as she'd looked up at him, that sexy smile he'd kept shooting at her, the look of determination when he'd tried to convince her of his proposal.

Or maybe *plan* was a better word. *Idea?* She wasn't sure, but *proposal* seemed too…too something else. *Something* being a territory that neither of them were going to wander into, no matter what happened.

What was going to happen? What did she *want* to happen?

The more she'd seen Finn the more she realized she liked seeing him. It was like it had been when she'd first gotten to Mirabelle. Those two evenings that she'd walked into the bar and he'd made her forget.

And what he'd promised that night was to make her forget again…and again…and again.

But then it was hard for her to forget those few days in between them sleeping together and him apologizing. All of those days he'd been an asshole.

"How is a guy supposed to atone for his sins if you won't let him?"

"Atone for your sins? I already forgave you, Finn."

"Good. Now the next goal is making you forget about them."

And he *wanted* her to forget about him being an asshole. She didn't think he'd turn on her again, but as the saying went: *once bitten, twice shy.* If anything, this week had made her realize that Finn would be a pretty good ally in this town.

Except, he hadn't used the word *ally*. He'd used the word *friend*. What he'd meant was friends with benefits. Brie had never dabbled with that particular arrangement before. She had more than one doubt that it would actually remain in the realm of *no strings attached.*

Way more than one doubt.

But did she really want to spend the rest of her time in Mirabelle alone? *No man is an island.* Yeah, that was something else she was beginning to realize more and more. Especially as she spent most of her time with a cat.

Isolating. That was the word Hannah had used about being in a similar situation.

Brie was suddenly uncomfortable…fidgety. She rolled over to her back, the air mattress groaning under her as she moved. She stared up at the ceiling not knowing what she wanted except that she didn't want to spend the next month alone.

She knew that for damn sure.

Chapter Thirteen

Chicken Potpie, Fuzzy Fox Slippers, and Fate

Brie woke up bright and early on Friday morning. She made herself a cup of coffee, had breakfast with Lo, and then sat down at the desk in the office. Before she knew it, it was almost one and she was starving. She was used to getting tunnel vision when she was working, especially when she was on a roll.

Even with the sun shining brightly, the temperature outside had barely cracked forty. A chill lingered in the house and Brie was in the mood for good soup and a hot sandwich. As she really had no desire to stand in front of a stove to prepare said soup, she decided to venture out.

Besides, she had a few errands she needed to run. She hadn't gone to the grocery store in a week and she needed to pick up a few things she was getting short on. There was also the fact that a number of packages had apparently built up at the Mirabelle Information Center where Bethelda used to work. Someone who worked there had found out about Brie taking over Bethelda's estate and left a message on the house phone. She'd sounded more than slightly hostile, saying if the packages weren't picked up she was going to throw them in the Dumpster.

After washing her face and running a brush through her hair, she touched up with a little concealer and put on mascara. Once she put on a clean pair of jeans and a thick sweater and scarf, she was out the front door.

As she'd yet to go to Café Lula she decided to head down to the beach to try out what they had for lunch…and maybe get herself something sweet while she was at it. There were a good number of cars in the lot when she pulled in and parked in front of the brightly painted cottage.

The building was salmon, the shutters yellow, and the eaves lilac. A large green sign hung over the turquoise door, big black letters reading "Café Lula." Brie made her way up the green stairs—the same green as the sign—and pushed the door open. A bell rang as she walked in, finding the inside of the café to be much like the outside.

The walls were turquoise and displaying a variety of beautiful paintings and pictures and works of art. The doors and windows were yellow. The tables and chairs scattered across the blond hardwood floors were all painted in a variety of colors from the same palette of pinks, periwinkles, greens, and oranges. But what really got Brie was that the whole place smelled like coconut and chocolate.

Her stomach rumbled as she made her way to the line. It didn't take too long for her to get to the counter, just long enough for her to figure out what she wanted to eat: crab bisque, a fried green tomato grilled cheese, and sweet tea.

Didn't matter how cold it was outside, it was *always* the time for sweet tea.

"For here or to go?" the woman at the register asked.

"For here," Brie said as she handed over her credit card.

But before the girl at the counter could grab the card, Brie heard a familiar voice. "Hello, Brie."

She turned to see Harper and Grace standing off to the left on the other side of the counter, both of them smiling wide. Brie hadn't seen the pretty blond since the morning of the funeral…when she'd fled like a bat out of hell.

"H-hi." Something about that memory had her feeling slightly off balance.

"That one is on the house, Lillian." Grace nodded to the register.

Brie shook her head. "Oh, that's not necess—"

"I know it's not necessary. I want to do it anyway. But I will take you joining us for lunch as payment." She pointed to a door behind the counter, a door that they had clearly just materialized out of.

Brie's gaze moved from the door back to the women, hesitating for just a moment. There was that initial voice in her head that questioned if lunch was a good idea. But then she reminded herself that Harper knew the truth so there most likely wouldn't be any unpleasant surprises. She also reminded herself that the only conversation she'd had that day had been with her cat.

Her cat…that was a new development. One she wasn't going to focus on at the moment. Not that she could focus on it because it was then that another—louder—voice was speaking…a voice that sounded a lot like Finn. *No man is an island.*

Besides, it was only Grace and Harper. She could handle two people no problem.

"OK," she agreed.

"Perfect." Grace beckoned Brie with her hand, waving her through the open space between the counters. "They'll bring your food with ours."

Grace led the way, her blond ponytail swinging back and forth as she pushed through the door and into the back. Brie followed behind her, while Harper took up the rear.

Brie barely got a glimpse of the kitchen—stainless steel appliances and countertops, yellow and blue tiles on the floors and climbing up the walls, an island in the center—before her eyes moved to the table and chairs in the corner where two other women sat. She recognized Paige immediately, but she had yet to meet the curly haired blond with a baby on her shoulder.

So much for it being just two people…the unknown had just doubled in size. Well, more than doubled including the baby, but as the child was sleeping, Brie wasn't too worried. Besides, she was wearing a pink onesie with little giraffes in tutus on it.

There was nothing intimidating about giraffes in tutus.

"Ladies, we have a guest joining us," Grace announced.

"Brie, this is Mel and her daughter, Juliet. Mel, meet Brie." Harper moved to Brie's side, waving her hand to the woman with the baby.

"Nice to meet you," Mel beamed at her.

"You too."

"And you remember Paige." Grace indicated the brunette from across the table as she sat down next to Mel.

"I do." Brie nodded, moving to the empty chair next to Paige and hanging her purse on the back. She wasn't exactly sure what to expect as she took her seat, but there was that part of her that was bracing for the worst. She couldn't help it. "Thank you for letting me join you guys."

"No thank-you necessary." Mel shook her head. "We like new people around here."

Paige scoffed.

"Well, we do." Harper moved her hand in a circle, encompassing everyone at the table. "There are some people in this town who can be a bit more resistant." Her mouth pinched as she said it, taking a seat next to Grace.

"Which we've heard you've experienced a little of." Mel nodded.

"Or a lot of," Paige said as she turned in her seat to face more toward Brie. "Believe me, I get it. Unlike the rest of these ladies, I'm not from Mirabelle, either. Philadelphia, born and raised."

"On a playground was where she spent most of her days."

"Thank you, Will Smith." Paige rolled her eyes at Grace. "Anyway, I moved down here about five and half years ago, and I had no intention of staying."

Brie had followed the conversation like a tennis match, and she couldn't help but smile at the rapid fire and easy comfort with which they conversed. It made her miss her own friends. But at the mention of permanence in Mirabelle, she finally spoke up.

"Oh, I'm not staying." Brie shook her head. "At least not beyond the spring."

"Well, while you're here, you'll at least know a few friendly faces," Mel said.

"That's for damn sure," Harper agreed. "And none of us will be judgey or ask questions you don't want to answer."

"But we will be more than happy to lend an ear when one is needed," Grace added.

"So you're offering everything and demanding nothing, even though you don't know me?"

"My grandmother used to always say you could spot a kindred spirit immediately." Harper rested her elbows on the table, leaning forward just slightly.

"Besides," Grace said as she shrugged, "we've got nothing to lose being nice to you. And all of us know what it's like to be targeted…singled out. Some of us more than most."

"I get that." Brie nodded slowly. "But I get the feeling that a lot of those instances in which you were targeted and singled out have to do with the person that brought me to this town in the first place."

"You're not her." Paige said it like it was the simplest thing in the world.

"Yes, but she was my biological mother." That Band-Aid was getting easier and easier to rip off. She wasn't sure if she was just getting used to it, or if she was just developing nerve damage.

A moment of stunned silence went around the table, everyone looking surprised except Harper. Brie's eyebrows rose as she looked at the raven-haired beauty.

"Not my business to tell." Harper shrugged. "Or Hannah's."

Apparently there were some people in Mirabelle who didn't talk.

"It doesn't change anything," Grace said simply. "You talk when you want to talk. *If* you want to talk."

Brie sat there in stunned silence, amazed with what these women had just offered her. She'd never experienced anything like it in her life, and there was some part of her that thought she never would again.

Just as quickly as that thought came she pushed it away, focusing on the moment.

As the next thirty minutes went by—and Brie enjoyed every delectable bite of her lunch—all of her apprehension disappeared. Every woman at that table was friendly beyond measure, an easy smile on their faces as they told her about themselves and asked questions that were surprisingly not all that prying.

Before Brie knew it, thirty minutes turned into an hour, which turned into two. Harper was the only one who had to leave after lunch, needing to get back to the spa for her next massage client.

Mel had only had her daughter a month ago, so she was still on maternity leave. She was taking advantage of her days off from teaching high school students math. Having regular lunch dates with her friends was both a nice treat and it got her out of the house, a need that Brie completely understood. Mel's husband, Bennett, was a carpenter. He did custom woodwork, refurbished antique wood pieces, and made some of his own furniture. He'd also recently remodeled their house.

"It was only a two-bedroom, one-bath and he built us a brand-new master suite. He'd started before I even found out I was pregnant." Her hand moved to Juliet's back who was currently fast asleep. "But once he found out? He wouldn't sit still until he had everything finished. People always say that women nest when they're pregnant, but I swear to you, my husband was worse than any woman."

Brie found out that Paige only worked at the funeral home three days a week. Her days off were spent working on her art, the same art that was displayed on the walls of the café. Brie made a mental note to take a closer look later.

Paige and her husband Brendan had three kids. Trevor would be four that summer, and the twins—Sarah and Molly—were almost a year and a half. Apparently when Paige had come down to Mirabelle all of those years ago, it had only been for her to find her feet again. She'd lost her job, her apartment, and her boyfriend. She'd had no choice but to head south to stay with her parents who'd retired in Mirabelle. Then she'd met Brendan and the rest was history.

Speaking of Brendan, he was Grace's older brother. Grace had married Brendan's best friend Jax. Or, more accurately, one of his best friends, as that title was taken by both Jax and Shep. Grace and Jax had a little girl, and apparently Rosie Mae was two and a half going on thirty.

Though Grace did need to go back to work, her working involved moving to the center island and whipping up a batch of lemon cookies. Brie ate four…and a double chocolate, coconut cupcake. Said cupcake had been the source of the mouthwatering smell in the café when Brie had walked in. It tasted even better than it had smelled…something she hadn't thought was possible.

Grace and her grandmother, Lula Mae, were the ones who owned and ran the café. Though, Lula Mae wasn't at the café that afternoon as she was taking a mini vacation and had gone on a cruise with her husband, Oliver King. Brie also found out that Oliver and Brendan owned their shop King's Auto.

There were so many locally owned family businesses in the area. She found it refreshing and more than kind of amazing. It was no problem for her to sit there and appear interested because she was beyond fascinated with it. People learning a craft that had been passed down, some of them for generations.

It was after three when Brie finally left the café with a box of the double chocolate coconut cupcakes and a whole chicken potpie. She'd bought it before she left, knowing she'd want something hot and comforting for dinner. Not that she was even remotely hungry at the moment, but it was good to be prepared. And good food wasn't the only thing she left with, either. She had new phone numbers programmed in her phone and the promise to go to a girls' night the following Saturday that would include dinner and then drinks at the Sleepy Sheep.

Well, she'd be fulfilling her promise to Finn to come out to the bar and hang out with a group of people…and see him. The thing was that was more than a week away. She'd yet to go a single day without seeing him so far. She wondered how long those coincidences of fate were going to continue.

Or when one of them was going to have to take matters into their own hands.

As Brie headed to the Mirabelle Information Center, she felt light…recharged…happy. So happy that the snarling woman who'd worked with Bethelda didn't affect her one little bit. Instead, Brie grabbed the pile of boxes (there were eleven) and loaded them into her car. As she was passing the post office on the way to the Piggly Wiggly, she figured she'd see if anything had been delivered there, too.

Four boxes had come in since she'd last visited the post office on Wednesday afternoon. That brought her grand total to fifteen for the day. If Brie hadn't already thought it before, it was confirmed now. Bethelda had had an addiction for shopping, an addiction that hadn't been maintained on the salary she'd made at her job. Nope, she funded this little habit with the money she'd made selling Harold and Petunia's property after they died.

Harold had bought the three acres of oceanfront land for next to nothing back in the early fifties. When Bethelda had inherited it thirteen years ago, she'd sold it for a little over half a million dollars. It was a lot of money, and Bethelda had spent seventy-five percent of it. To be fair, Bethelda had in fact paid off her own house, but that only accounted for about a third of the money spent. The rest of it was now in all of the things she bought, filling up her house. The last thing that house needed was more stuff. Brie was going to need to put a stop to these packages coming.

So many things to do, so little time.

Brie pushed it to the back of her mind; she could worry about that later. Now she needed to focus on getting in and out of the store and crossing the staples she needed off the list. When she walked out of the Piggly Wiggly half an hour later, it felt like the temperature had dropped another ten degrees. That might've been because the sun was now completely blocked by the overcast skies, followed by the wind that was whipping around her.

Breath fogging up the air with every exhale, she quickly headed to her car and loaded up the few bags. The ride back was barely enough time for the heater to kick in, her exposed fingers only getting a moment to defrost before she was back at the bungalow.

And that warmth didn't last very long at all, because when she walked in the front door she was greeted to a house that was only slightly warmer than it was outside.

OK, so maybe *slight* wasn't the right word. It was thirty-two degrees outside while the house had slipped down to fifty-one. Brie looked at the thermostat—watching as it dropped yet another degree—checking that it was still set to sixty-five, and it was. Except there was absolutely no hot air blowing out of the vents and the unit wasn't humming at all outside.

Her eyes darted to the clock above the stove: it was after five o'clock on a Friday. She wasn't in any way hopeful of getting someone on the phone to come out there and look at the unit.

She was going to need to figure out those damn fireplaces. It was that or freeze her ass off. But after an hour of trying to figure it out—why yes, she did have a stubborn streak every once in a while—she gave up and pulled Finn's number up on her phone.

* * *

Friday proved to be another long day for Finn as he'd had more first-of-the-year checkups. Though these horses hadn't been on Whiskey Creek Farm and instead had been all over Mirabelle and the surrounding county. It was almost six when he and Frankie finally walked in the front door.

After feeding Frankie, Finn unloaded his pockets, setting his phone and wallet on the counter next to his keys. Then he headed directly for the shower. He needed to wash the barn smell and chill from his skin. He lingered under the hot spray for longer than usual, letting the water work over his back and hoping that some of the tightness in his muscles would wash away, too.

He headed downstairs twenty minutes later feeling a whole lot better. Well, except for the rumbling in his stomach as he was starving. He opened his refrigerator to find the exact same offerings as the day before. Why he thought it would be magically full, he'd never know. He'd meant to stop by the store on his way home…clearly that hadn't happened.

"I guess it's frozen pizza tonight," he told Frankie as he pulled the box out of the freezer.

As he walked over to the stove his cell phone started ringing, vibrating against the counter where he'd left it earlier. He grabbed it, glancing down and seeing Brie's name flashing across the screen.

And just that quickly he was grinning like an idiot. That day had been the first that he hadn't seen Brie since she'd been in town. As the day had gone on, he'd definitely been aware of the absence.

He'd been exhausted just moments before, but as he slid his finger across the screen and put the phone to his ear, he suddenly got a second wind. "Hey. What's going on?"

"Hi." That one word came out slightly breathless, like she was nervous. "Are you busy?"

"Nope. About to make dinner."

"Oh, well, I don't want to bother you. I can let you go."

"First of all, you are in no way bothering me." He was starving and he'd rather talk to her than eat. "Second, it's a frozen pizza, so it really doesn't require that much brain capacity. What's going on?" He repeated the question.

"So it would appear that the HVAC unit stopped working. The house has dropped to tundra temperatures and I can't get the gas fireplaces to light. I was wondering what the odds were that you—or someone you know—know something about the latter? I don't have high expectations about the former for the evening."

"The odds are very high for the latter."

"In that case, I don't know how high your hopes were set on that pizza."

"Not very high."

"Then I have a proposition for you. You help me with the fireplace and you can have some Café Lula chicken potpie."

"Deal." He grabbed the pizza box and walked back to the fridge to put it away.

"Well, that took a lot of arm twisting."

"Brie, I would've come over to help without the prospect of food. Dinner is just icing on the cake. You mind if I bring Frankie?"

"Not at all. See you guys soon."

"See you soon," he agreed before he hung up.

He and his dog were out the door three minutes later. It was another five after that when he was ringing the doorbell to the bungalow, George Michael's voice echoing on the other side of the door.

Brie was opening up for him before George even finished the first verse. She stood in the threshold wearing a knit beanie in UNC blue, an old gray sweatshirt that read "Talk Nerdy to Me" across the chest, black yoga pants that molded to her ass and hips, and fuzzy fox slippers on her feet.

He'd never met a woman who managed to pull off sexy and adorable to this level. It was impressive. He liked it a lot...he liked *her* a lot. That much was beyond clear, and fighting it had proven to be impossible.

"Hey." The smile that turned up his mouth could not be helped, nor could the heat that settled low in his abdomen before moving up to his chest and out to his limbs. He was wearing jeans, a pullover fleece over his T-shirt, and a jacket. He was suddenly feeling the need to take off his jacket and pull at the collar of the fleece.

If that reaction was just at the sight of her, he was in for an interesting night.

"Hi." She stepped back, making space for him and Frankie to come into the house. He gave her just enough room to close the door, stopping in front of her. The new position had her tilting her head back so she could look up into his face.

"Thank you for coming over."

"No thank-you necessary." He grinned, and before he could think twice about it, he leaned down and pressed a kiss to her cheek. Her skin was warm under his lips.

The unexpected move had clearly caught her off guard, and she took a startled breath. He wanted more than anything to push her back against the wall and capture her mouth. Taste her lips.

Instead he pulled back, taking a step away and giving them both space. It was the very last thing he wanted to do, but he knew if he kissed her, he wouldn't want it to stop there. Not only did he come over there to figure out her heating situation, but he didn't want to push her. She knew his offer, so he'd wait for her to accept…even if it killed him.

"I'm glad you called," he said as he took another step back. "If you hadn't we would've broken the streak."

"What streak?" She shook her head slightly, like she was trying to focus.

"Of seeing each other every day. Also, I wouldn't have gotten to see those rather fantastic slippers on your feet."

"You like my foxes?"

"I do indeed." He glanced down as she wiggled her feet in the slippers, making the foxes move.

"They were an impulse buy. Apparently I had a premonition I'd need them."

"Apparently. Well, let's get some heat in this place."

Brie turned around and headed down the hallway. Finn couldn't stop his eyes from moving down, getting a good look at her from behind. God bless yoga pants.

Frankie followed by his side, nose in the air, no doubt smelling Delores. But she didn't leave him, and she wouldn't until he gave her permission.

"So there is one in here," she said as they walked into the living room. "And another that backs against it in there." She pointed to a door a few feet away from the fireplace.

"There are two. Nice." He pulled off his jacket, laying it down on the sofa. "That should keep you warm enough until you get the heater running again. You might need to sleep in one of these rooms, though, so you don't get cold."

"I already sleep in the den." She moved through the space and to the door she'd just pointed to.

"You do?" He followed behind her just as she flipped on the light switch, illuminating the room.

"Well, I'm sure as hell not sleeping in Bethelda's bed. Too weird."

His eyes widened as he took in the space. Almost all of the walls were taken up with bookcases, and all of those bookcases filled with books and magazines. A sofa was pushed off to the side while an air mattress took up much of the floor space. It was covered in blankets, a big lump right in the middle.

"That's Lo." Brie pointed to the lump. "She hasn't come out since I got home. Too cold for her out here."

Frankie, who was still at Finn's side, whined as she looked

between the lump and Finn. "Do you mind if she goes near the bed?"

"Not at all."

Finn barely nodded his head in that direction before she was off, leaning over the side and nudging the lump with her nose. Slowly, *very* slowly, the lump began to inch over through the covers until her nose poked out. It was then that Frankie's big tongue darted out, licking the cat in greeting.

Or bathing her.

Frankie collapsed down on the rug next to the bed, and Delores was out and curling into the dog's side a second later.

"Lo?" Finn turned to Brie, his eyebrows high at the new name she'd called the cat.

"Yes. I think it fits her better than Delores."

"She respond to it?" He glanced back at the cat who was now barely visible as she was pretty much burrowing under Frankie's warm body.

An amused expression took over Brie's face as she glanced at the cat and dog, but she looked back to Finn before she answered. "About as much as she responded to Delores. But I've learned that she pretty much does what she wants, when she wants."

"That sounds about right. But she's getting used to you?"

"I think so," she said, giving a slight shrug of the shoulders. "She sleeps next to me every night, but I feel like that's more about staying warm than affection for me."

"With cats you never know."

Brie leaned her hip against the side of the sofa, her body faced to him. "I heard this story one time about this lady who had a pet python, and every night when she went to bed the python would stretch out next to her. She told her vet, thinking that the story about her snake wanting to be close to her was cute. The vet told her it was because the python was trying to figure out if it could eat her or not. Lo stretches out next to me every night."

Finn grinned. "You think she wants to eat you?"

"It's crossed my mind."

"I think you're safe, Brie."

"Didn't you just say that with cats you never know?"

A laugh burst from Finn's mouth. "I did, but I still think you're safe. Now I just need to get you warm."

"Well, why you figure it out, I'm going to go put dinner in the oven. I don't know what tools you need, but I found those in the laundry room." She moved away from the sofa as she pointed to a red metal toolbox on the floor. "Also, feel free to take your boots off as you're staying awhile."

"Will do."

"Shout if you need anything."

Finn's eyes stayed on her as she walked out of the room, his eyes automatically moving to her ass again, watching until she disappeared from view. It was only after she was out of his line of sight that he made himself focus, and he moved to the fireplace to figure out what he was working with.

But in his focusing, there was a thought that crossed his mind. He wondered if it wasn't fate that had broken the heating system that night, guaranteeing he got to see her.

Chapter Fourteen

Cupcake Surcharges

Brie was screwed. So totally, beyond a doubt, screwed. From the second she'd opened that door it had taken everything in her to concentrate and not lose her mind. His hair was slightly tousled, like he'd run a towel through it after a shower and then hadn't bothered after that. She wanted to reach up and run her fingers through it.

Shiiiiiit.

She hadn't even lasted three seconds after seeing him before she was already thinking about getting her hands on him. This boded well for her. *Really* well.

Not.

Then he'd gone and kissed her cheek. She'd felt that simple brush of his lips everywhere. If that hadn't been enough to distract her, she'd gone and taken a deep breath, filling her lungs with his scent. A scent she couldn't get out of her head. Clean. Fresh soap mixed with that potent scent of *him*. He'd totally just showered. All she'd wanted to do was move closer to him, wanted to press her face into his chest and breathe deep.

So yeah, it went without saying that she couldn't exactly think straight.

Oh, who the hell cared? A properly working brain was entirely overrated. Luckily for her she'd already preheated the oven before Finn had gotten there. This had been partly in the hopes that warmth from the oven would get rid of the chill in the house. Too bad for her she had to set the timer now.

It took her three tries, but she managed in the end.

After that she went in search of a drink. She'd been pounding hot tea since she got home, but now she needed some alcohol.

There were a few clangs from the living room, and Brie leaned to the right to see Finn crouching down in front of the fireplace.

"You want a drink?" she called out.

"Sure. What do you have?"

"Well, there are a few hard liquor options, wine, and some of the Sleepy Sheep's grapefruit IPA is in the fridge."

Finn turned and looked over his shoulder. "When did you buy beer from the Sleepy Sheep?"

"I didn't. Bethelda did."

"Seriously?"

"It was here when I got here."

"All right. That's interesting, and a conversation for later, but I'm kinda in the mood for something not chilled. You have any red wine?"

"It just so happens that I do."

She grabbed the opened bottle—she'd had some the night before—on the counter. The aerator sat on the sideboard by the sink and she fitted that into the top before pouring two glasses.

Taking a deep, somewhat calming, breath, she grabbed both glasses and headed for the living room.

Her eyes landed on the fireplace, where a healthy flame was already going around the logs.

She stopped in her tracks, staring. "How the hell?"

The smile on Finn's face was more than slightly cocky, but she was so grateful she chose to ignore it.

He walked over to her, now bootless, his sock-clad feet moving across the floor. "There was a key hole off to the side, one that I knew about only because the one at my house is exactly the same. It just needed an Allen wrench that you had in the toolbox. I got both of them going now."

"You know"—she shook her head handing him one of the glasses of wine—"I don't even care that I couldn't figure it out after an hour and you did it in three minutes. Cheers." She held her glass in the air, and Finn raised his, clinking them together.

"Cheers," he said before they both took a sip. "This is pretty good." Lifting the glass to his nose he took a deep breath. "What is it?"

"An Argentinian blackberry Malbec. It was in the wine cabinet. She had a stock of it, but she has a stock of a lot of things, so that isn't saying much."

"No kidding." He took another sip as he looked around, his focus landing on the dining room table. "Are those more packages?" he asked, turning back to her.

"Yup. I picked the majority of them up at the Mirabelle Information Center today. When I showed up, Winnie Lanore looked like she'd been sucking on a pickle all day her expression was so sour. Just another person that Bethelda left an impression on."

Finn's eyebrows narrowed. "Was she rude to you?"

"She barely spoke to me. Just pointed to the pile of boxes and made sure I didn't take anything I wasn't supposed to."

"That sounds about right. I wouldn't take that one personally...she's like that with everyone."

"Well, that's a small comfort. Why is it that the least friendliest people in Mirabelle work at the welcome center?"

"A mystery we will never know the answer to. So what is it that she's getting delivered? You'd think the packages would be slowing down considering the fact that she's been..." he trailed off, looking uncertain.

"Dead for two weeks?" Brie finished for him. "You don't need to tiptoe around it...or her...or anything. I don't know what I am, but I'm not overly sensitive. And the packages *are* slowing down, kind of. I think the ones that keep coming in are the whatever-of-the-month subscriptions. I need to figure all of them out and cancel. It's on the list of things to do this weekend."

"What did she subscribe to?"

"The Fairfield Farms fruit and vegetable of the month—luckily both were in jars when I opened that box. Pickled beets and roasted pumpkin puree. There is also Chester's Cat Costume Emporium. If you felt the desire, we could dress Lo up as a manatee tonight."

"I'll pass on that one."

"You sure? It could be fun. There's a whole box of cat costumes in the closet."

"I'm good." He laughed, shaking his head. "You didn't donate those?"

"To the Triple C? I really don't think people who need charitable items are looking for cat costumes. I was going to try to sell them all on eBay. Anyway, you want to help me open those?" She nodded to the packages on the table. "We can see what other ridiculous things Bethelda gets delivered. Besides, we have about thirty minutes to kill before the pie is done."

"Absolutely." Finn nodded, taking another sip of wine as they both headed to the dining room. He was a few steps in front of her and her eyes moved down, admiring how his jeans cupped his ass.

She couldn't help herself.

"Which one first?" he asked, setting the glass on the table before pulling a pocketknife from his pocket.

"That one is a cooler from Cheeses and Crackers." She pointed to a medium-size one. "Winnie was at least nice enough to tell me that it had been delivered this afternoon."

"Talk about timing," Finn said as he slid the blade under the tape and popped the seal. When he pulled the cardboard flaps back it was to reveal a white Styrofoam box. It squeaked noisily as he pulled it free from the cardboard.

"Let's see." He lifted the lid. "Still cold so that's a good sign. Now you've got goat, Irish cheddar, butterkäse, gouda, and"— he looked up at her grinning as he pulled a small round package out—"Brie for Brie."

"Well, look how that turned out. Open whichever box you want," she told him as she grabbed all of the cheese and headed for the kitchen to put them in the fridge.

She could just hear the sound of him slicing through more tape before his deep voice filled her ear. "Oh, I like what's in this box."

"What's that?" she called out.

"More wine. Well, this most certainly wasn't a dry house. That's for damn sure."

When Brie walked back into the dining room, Finn was pulling each bottle out one by one, looking at the labels. "It's an assortment of reds and whites. I think you're set for a good long while."

"Clearly." She nodded, moving around him to the Bluetooth speaker—Bethelda had one in every room of the house—pulling up a playlist of random music for them to listen to while they worked.

They spent the next half hour opening each and every box. Bethelda had some pepper jelly from JPJ (Jams, Preserves, and Jellies), a box of assorted chocolates, three scarves (because the woman had needed more of those), a collection of Valentine's-themed bear outfits (appropriate as Valentine's Day was the following Tuesday), artichoke and sun-dried tomato pasta, a box that contained five envelopes of different spices, a bag of honey-roasted macadamia nuts, a spiced orange–scented candle, a can of loose-leaf green tea infused with pomegranate, and two different kinds of hard salami.

"Geez," Brie said as she looked over everything laid out on the table. "It's no wonder the woman's pantry is full with the amount of food she subscribes to. This is ridiculous."

"Yeah, but that pepper jelly would probably pair really well with the goat cheese."

Brie turned to look at Finn, slightly incredulous.

"What, I'm hungry." He shrugged.

As soon as the words were out of his mouth, a loud beep sounded from the kitchen. "You and your timing." She shook her head as she grabbed both empty wineglasses. "You want me to open another bottle of this? Or do you want to try one of those?" She nodded to the selection on the table.

"How do you feel about merlot?" he asked, grabbing the bottle and holding it in the air.

"I feel good about it. Want to play part-time bartender?"

"Lead the way."

Brie did just that, turning toward the kitchen, Finn following behind her.

She was feeling that glass of wine just a little bit, making her comfortable…at ease…good. She liked Finn being there. Liked talking to him. Liked flirting with him. Liked that it wasn't weird or awkward with him anymore. She liked him.

Good Lord did she like him. She'd liked him even when she hadn't liked him. That didn't exactly make a lot of sense, but nothing had made sense since she'd been in that town. But she was done trying to make sense of things for the evening.

She was just going to enjoy it, come what may.

* * *

Lo left Frankie just long enough to eat her dinner. She took her spot on the bench, digging in when Finn and Brie sat down. As soon as the cat was done eating, she was back at the dog's side. They were now both sleeping in front of the fire in the living room.

As for Finn and Brie's dinner, it was a relaxed affair, both of them talking as they ate their meal. He wanted to know more about her PhD in history, which led to her telling him the focus of her thesis.

"Post-World War II. How it changed the country. How it changed the people…those who fought in it and those who stayed behind."

"You have a lot more stuff you can talk to Ella about. She and Owen met after the war."

"He fought?"

"Yup."

Recognition flashed in her eyes. "Are those his dog tags? The ones tattooed on your chest?" She made a motion to her own chest, putting her hand close to her heart.

"They are. Shep has a tattoo that's identical."

"Tell me about him," she said before she speared a piece of crust and chicken on her fork.

"Shep?" He asked jokingly. "He's obnoxiously right most of the time, which makes him think that he's annoyingly superior, and—"

"No." Brie laughed. "Owen. Tell me about your grandfather. Unless you don't want to," she amended.

"I don't mind talking about Owen, not at all." He shook his head. "If anything, talking about him makes his memory live on in a way. If that makes any sense."

"To me it makes perfect sense. It's one of the reasons I love history so much. When did he join?"

"About two years before America got involved. His family had been hit hard by the Great Depression. For him, the military was his only way out…"

Finn told Brie about how Owen had met Nathanial Franklin, Ella's older brother. The two had become the best of friends, and soon they were more like brothers. Their bond was so strong that Nathanial died saving Owen's life. Once the war was over, Owen had gone to find Ella, the girl he'd heard Nathanial talk about more than anyone.

Ella and Nathanial hadn't had the easiest of lives growing up. Their parents had married young—they'd had to. They were seventeen and sixteen years old when they got pregnant with Nathanial. Ella had come along two years later, and their parents still had no idea what they were doing. Ella and Nathanial's father died in a factory explosion shortly after she was born. Four months after that, their mother ran off with a man ten years older than her.

Apparently the new guy had given her the perfect get-out-of-jail-free card, because she totally looked at the two kids she'd never wanted as jail. Ella and Nathanial had been left in the care of their grandmother, and though she didn't abuse them, her three sons had.

"When the war ended, Owen knew exactly where his first stop was going to be. And that was Ella. When he showed up, he took one look at her and knew he was going to marry her."

"And what did she think?"

"She made him work for it. It wasn't the easiest for her to let anyone in again. Nathanial had been her family, and when he died it almost destroyed her. But he won her over in the end."

"Clearly. Otherwise you wouldn't be sitting here." She gestured to him with a wave of her hand.

"No I wouldn't." He shook his head.

"So Owen built the bar, and it became a family business."

"It did."

"And yet you became a veterinarian."

"I always had a love for animals. But I think it was getting my horse that really tipped the scale."

"You have a horse?"

"Yup, a bay named Nigel…"

He told her all about growing up with him; his pride and joy in the animal clear. It was apparent when he talked about animals—his and any others—where his passion was. Brie found herself drawn to each and every word that he spoke, fascinated with him.

Before she knew it, she realized they'd been sitting there talking for a good long while. They had to have finished eating almost an hour ago, but neither of them had moved from the table. They just sat there—Brie with her chin in her hand as she leaned close. Finn turned toward her, his posture open—continuing to talk as they worked through the bottle of merlot.

The house had warmed up significantly by that point…or maybe Brie had just warmed up significantly. She was pretty sure it had less to do with the alcohol and fire and more to do with the man in front of her.

"So, what did you do today?" he asked as he leaned back in his seat, at ease.

She raised her glass to her lips, taking another sip of the lush, full-bodied wine before answering. "Worked on my thesis for a while, and then lunch at Café Lula turned into an afternoon with the girls."

"Oh really now?" His eyebrows rose high.

"I ran into Harper, Grace, Mel, and Paige. They were lovely."

His eyes were on her face, looking for something she wasn't sure of. "You had a good time with them."

"I did. I told them the truth about Bethelda and they just accepted it. Didn't question me at all. Said if I wanted to talk the door was open. It was nice. I've also been invited to Girls' Night Out next Saturday."

"Oh, that's bound to be entertaining."

"Why's that?"

"Because it's always entertaining when that group of girls gets together to drink."

"Well, entertaining will be nice." She nodded. "And anyway, you were right, it's good to have a friend—or friends—every once in a while."

"If for nothing more than to get the fireplace going."

"Exactly."

"Well, you might get even more friends. I called Brendan on the way over here and asked if he could come by tomorrow to look at your system. It isn't just cars that he knows how to fix."

"Thank you. You didn't have to do that, but I really appreciate it."

He shrugged like it was no big deal. "It's going to be pretty cold the next couple of days. For you to get someone out here to fix the heater on the weekend would be ridiculously expensive."

"Well, I could just pay in canned goods or dish sets. You think that would be acceptable?"

"Probably not." He shook his head.

"What about chicken potpie and wine?"

"No. That's my payment. That along with one of those cupcakes in the kitchen."

"Oh really now? I don't remember offering those in the negotiations." She tried to fight the smile playing at her lips. She failed. Miserably.

"Dessert is a hidden fee. If you read the fine print you'll see the surcharge."

"Are there any other hidden fees?"

"Nope, just that one."

"Good to know." She shook her head, a small laugh on her lips as she lifted her wineglass and took a sip.

Finn's focus lingered on her eyes, something she noticed him do often.

She lowered the glass. "What? Why do you keep looking at me like I'm a math problem you're figuring out?"

"Not a math problem," he said as he shook his head. "More like a science experiment."

"And why is that?"

"I've noticed something about your eyes."

"What?"

"They change colors based off of your mood. When you're upset they're more brown than gold. When you're happy, they're more gold than brown. Well, happy or—" He stopped himself, shaking his head as a sly grin took over his mouth.

"Happy or what?" she pressed.

He cleared his throat, but when he spoke his words were more than slightly amused. "Your eyes turn really gold when you're turned on."

A slight blush crept into her cheeks, though it was less about embarrassment and more about the pleasure in that observation. Not very many people had figured that fact out about her eyes, that they changed color based on her mood. And yet he had.

"You would know that from experience." She nodded before she lifted her glass to her lips and finished off the last of her wine. Probably not the best idea as she was just adding fuel to the fire…her fire.

"You want more?"

For just a second she thought he was referring to more sex, but then he nodded to the empty glass in her hand.

"As your part-time bartender for the evening, I'm going to need to open another bottle."

"Yeah, let me…uh…clean up while you do that." She was still a little flustered from where her mind had gone initially at his question. Mainly because she'd wanted to say yes to that, too.

"But you cooked."

"I stuck a pie in the oven. It was hardly a complicated task." Besides, she needed a second to think without his focus on her. She pushed her chair back to stand, leaning over the table and grabbing his empty plate.

"Find one that pairs well with chocolate." She nodded to the wine cabinet/liquor bar that took up almost the entire wall behind him. It might take him a bit to look through the supply as there were close to three hundred bottles. And that wasn't counting what they'd just opened.

"Yes, ma'am."

She turned around and knew his eyes were on her back, watching as she left the room. As she entered the kitchen she took a deep breath and let it out. It did very little in the realm of steadying her. Turning the water on and letting it heat up, she grabbed on to the edge of the sink and bowed her head.

Your eyes turn really gold when you're turned on.

She had no doubt her eyes were way more golden than brown at that moment.

The music that had been playing softly in the dining room got loud enough for her to hear in the kitchen, Finn apparently turning the volume up. She pulled herself back to the present, trying to focus on cleaning up. It was a lost cause. As there was very little to clean up—and it was a fairly mindless activity— her mind stayed on the man in the other room…and his offer from the night before. She'd thought about it a lot in the last twenty-four hours…especially that evening. It was hard not to when he was that close.

And why was it that just talking to this man was foreplay? Not just the last part of their conversation, but the whole thing. Just listening to him speak, the sound of his voice, the way his mouth moved, how he'd reach up and rub his palm against his jaw, his smile when he talked about something or someone he loved.

She wanted that mouth on her again. Wanted his lips moving over hers. Wanted to feel his scruff on her skin…between her thighs.

Before she knew it, she had the dishwasher loaded and running, the counters wiped off, and the last of the chicken potpie covered with aluminum foil and in the fridge. Grabbing the hose, she rinsed out the sink, and flipped the garbage disposal on for a couple of seconds before shutting it off again. She was just washing her hands in the warm water when she felt Finn's presence behind her.

Looking over her shoulder, she found him leaning back against the counter watching her, his eyes on her swaying hips. She hadn't even realized she was moving to the beat of the music until that moment. She shut the water off before she grabbed the dishtowel next to her and turned, leaning back and mimicking his posture.

"You know, I have to keep reminding myself that I'm supposed to wait."

"Wait for what?"

"For you to accept my offer."

"Your friends-with-moments-of-weakness offer?" Apparently she hadn't been the only one thinking about it.

"Yes." He nodded, heat flickering in his eyes. "I think I have a handle on how much I want you, and then a second later you prove me so unbelievably wrong. Like just now, I walked into the kitchen to find you dancing along to the music, and all I wanted to do was put my hands on your hips to feel you move."

Brie set the towel down before she pushed off the counter and crossed over to him. She stopped when she was only inches away from him, reaching out and grabbing his hands.

"Like this?" she asked as she put his hands on her hips, starting to move them to the beat of the music again.

Finn's nostrils flared as he took a deep breath. "Say yes, Brie."

Her mind flashed to another night that he told her to say yes, her second day in Mirabelle. They'd been at the bar and he'd promised to make her night a very pleasant one. There was no doubt in her mind that evening would be another repeat of that promise.

Her hands landed on his chest, moving up and around his neck. "Yes," she whispered.

The word was barely out of her mouth before she found herself spinning around, Finn pushing her back against the counter as his mouth covered hers. Her hands moved to the back of his head, her fingers fisting in his hair, pulling him closer. He must've taken that as a sign that she wanted more, and his tongue pushed past her lips, devouring her.

Just that quickly Brie was lost. Lost in him. Lost in his hands on her body, how they were pushing up under the hem of her sweatshirt, his warm palms on her bare skin, his fingers wrapping around her sides, holding her to him.

One of his hands disappeared from her body as he pulled away from her mouth. She slowly opened her eyes, it taking a good few seconds for her to regain her focus. He was breathing hard as he reached up, taking his glasses off and setting them on the counter. And then he was reaching up again, pulling the knit beanie from her head and tossing it to the side.

"You're so fucking beautiful." His hand gently moved to the back of her head, his fingers delving into her hair as he lowered his mouth to hers, his lips hovering. "So sexy I can't see straight."

"That's because you took your glasses off."

His mouth curled into a grin. "Brie, I could be blind and know you were sexy. It's in how you talk." He lightly pressed his lips to hers before he moved them across her cheek, and to her ear. "It's in how you listen. In how just the scent of you drives me crazy." He bent his head, his nose skimming her throat. "In how you feel under my hands. Your soft skin, your hair." His grip tightened where he held her. "You make me want in ways I've forgotten…make me want in ways I didn't know I could want." His mouth opened on her neck, his teeth lightly raking before his tongue moved over the spot to soothe.

"Finn." Brie's moan filled the kitchen, and her fingers flexed in his hair. "Please."

His hand dropped from her hair as he moved, mouth covering hers as he gripped her waist and lifted her up. Her legs wound around his hips and he moved his grip to her ass, holding her to him as he pulled away from the counter and started moving through the house and to the den.

Chapter Fifteen

Gold, Diamonds, and Wine Straight Out of the Bottle

It took a whole hell of a lot of concentration for Finn to navigate through the house while carrying Brie. There were certain obstacles he had to contend with, like the furniture and the cat and dog sprawled on the floor. Then there was the way Brie's mouth was moving against his, her tongue tangling with his. Another thing that was taking up a good portion of his focus was how she moved against him.

Somehow, miracle of miracles, he got them to their destination.

His grip on her ass loosened, and she dropped her legs from around his hips. She oh-so-slowly slid down him, pressing against his erection and making him groan. God, he was going to lose his mind.

He needed to get her naked. Needed to get her under him, or above him, or anything at this point. He just needed her.

She was of the same mind-set, both of them attacking the other's clothes, their mouths separating only long enough to pull sweatshirts and shirts over their heads. Her hands moved over his bare chest as he worked at the back of her bra. Once her breasts were free, he dropped his head, sucking an erect nipple into his mouth.

He didn't stop undressing her as he tasted her, hooking his fingers into the sides of her yoga pants and pulling them down, leaving her standing there in a pair of simple black cotton panties.

Simple or not, the whole picture was perfect. Her body was illuminated by the fire behind them. Her hair down and around her shoulders, her cheeks flushed, her eyes golden.

Her hands went to the front of his jeans, tugging at his belt buckle before unsnapping the button and pulling the zipper down. Her hand moved under the waistband of his boxers, wrapping around his cock.

"Brie." He sucked in a sharp gasp of air as she slowly moved her hand over him, giving just the right amount of pressure.

She leaned into him, her breasts against his chest as she kissed the side of his jaw. "Take your pants off, Finn," she whispered, her lips moving against his skin.

Finn didn't need to be told twice, nor did he hesitate in the slightest. The second she let go of his cock he moved, pushing his pants and boxers down his legs and taking his socks off while he was at it.

Brie moved back to him, taking him in hand again, as she started to stroke. "Do you like this?" she asked as she swiped her thumb over the tip.

"God, yes."

"Well, then you're going to love this."

He grinned as she used his words from their first night together, but a second later all thought left his brain. Brie dropped to her knees and proceeded to take him into her mouth...and blew his fucking mind.

That was when he experienced the second miracle of the night and was somehow able to keep his legs beneath him. How he didn't fall to his ass he'd never know, but he didn't care. He let himself go over to the feel of her warm, wet mouth moving over him. She'd take him deep before moving back up, swirling her tongue over the tip before moving back down.

His hand went to the back of her head, his fingers in her hair, feeling her move over him. The pleasure was unreal, but he kept his release at bay, not wanting their first round that night to be over that quickly. He tried to think of different things besides Brie's lips wrapped around his cock. He did as best as he could, holding on to the last ounce of his control right up until she reached up and squeezed his balls.

That was his breaking point, and he pulled from her mouth, almost panting. "Come here."

He reached for her arms, lifting her to her feet. His mouth covered hers as he hooked his fingers in her panties and pushed them down her legs. Once she was free of them, he had them both down on the air mattress, him between her legs. He reached down, finding her wet.

"Is this from having me in your mouth?" he asked as his fingers slipped inside of her.

"Yes." Her body arched as she moaned.

"I need to taste you." He rolled their bodies, pulling her on top of him. His hands went to her hips, moving her up his chest before settling her on her knees on either side of his head.

"Finn, wh—" But whatever she was going to say was cut off

by her cry of pleasure filling the room. His mouth was on her, his tongue moving over her drenched folds.

"So good." He found her clit with his lips, sucking before lapping at it.

She cried out again, her body falling forward to hold on to the sofa behind the mattress. He held on to her hips, guiding her movements above him, but it didn't take long for her to start to move on her own, seeking more pressure as she rode his face. He didn't let go of her hips, didn't stop giving her exactly what she wanted, and she didn't stop giving him what he wanted.

Her pleasure. Her moans. Her body.

"Oh God, Finn!" She screamed his name as she came, her legs shaking, her body pulsing.

He didn't stop moving his mouth or tongue over her until she was good and truly done, milking her first orgasm for all that it was worth. He kissed the inside of her thigh as he felt her hands in his hair. She tugged lightly, bringing his gaze to hers.

"That was—" She swallowed, shaking her head. "That was phenomenal."

"I think you'll like what's next on the agenda, too."

The sexy grin she gave him was one that had the ability to make his heart stop. He stood by his statement from earlier…she was so beautiful it was insane.

Helping her move off of him, he sat up, reaching for his jeans and the wallet in his back pocket. He found a condom and pulled it out, throwing his wallet to the side.

"How many do you have tonight?"

He turned to her, finding her lying back on the bed, her head on the pillows. She bent her knees, planting her feet flat and spreading her thighs.

If his heart had stopped earlier, this sight was enough to get it going again. "Four." He moved across the bed, kneeling between her legs.

"That sure I was going to say yes?"

He shook his head, opening the package. "Hopeful. I was *hopeful* that you would say yes. Now I don't think I brought enough."

"Finn, if we run out I'm sure we can figure something out." Her eyes dropped, watching as he rolled the latex down his length.

"I'm sure we can. Lift your hips," he said as he grabbed a pillow.

She did as he told her, and he put it underneath her, elevating her pelvis. He shifted closer, the tip of his erection at her entrance. "But let's see how creative we can be with the four." And with that he thrust into her.

"OK." Her golden eyes closed as she pulled air into her lungs on a sharp inhale. When she opened them a second later they were dazed with passion.

He gripped her hips as he moved in and out of her, setting a rhythm. Her breasts bounced with each push and pull, her chest rising and falling with uneven breaths. Both of her hands were fisted in the blankets on either side of her body, twisting the fabric in a death grip.

He watched her writhe around beneath him, enjoying each and every slick slide of his cock inside of her. Her eyelids dropped to half-mast, as her body arching up to meet him became more insistent.

Finn moved one of his hands from her hip, bringing it between their bodies as he found her clit and began to circle. He knew she was close; he could feel her orgasm building.

"Finn," she gasped his name. "Harder. I need more. *Please.*"

He pulled his hand away from between their bodies. Grabbing one of her hands, he moved over her. Giving her his weight and his mouth, he stretched their hands above their heads. He used the angle for leverage, giving her what she wanted as he thrust into her harder.

"Yes!" Her free hand wrapped around his back, her nails biting into his shoulder as she came. Her core pulsed around his cock and Finn let his own orgasm rip through him.

Well, *let* was probably the wrong word. He'd had no choice, because Brie had grabbed him before she'd fallen over the edge, dragging him with her.

Their bodies rocked together, slowing as they came down. He didn't stop kissing her, didn't stop tasting her mouth, didn't stop touching her.

Because he couldn't. It was impossible. Just like fighting his attraction to her had been. Just like trying to not like her had been. Just like forgetting her would be. Just like getting over her would be.

Impossible.

* * *

Brie was nice and warm snuggled up to Finn's side, her head on his shoulder, her hand resting on his chest. He'd set up a stack of pillows behind him, using the sofa as a makeshift headboard so he could sit up.

They'd spent the last three hours talking while passing a bottle of red wine back and forth. Neither of them had wanted to bother with the glasses. Nor had they bothered with plates or napkins of any kind when they'd eaten cupcakes. Finn had just licked the frosting from her fingers afterward…and then licked some of that frosting from certain parts of her body after that.

They'd already worked through a second condom, Brie coming spectacularly with her feet resting on Finn's shoulders.

"I think I'm going to need to open another bottle soon," he said as he took another sip. "We're down to a fourth of this one."

She looked up at him, her cheek moving across his warm skin. "I think I'm going to need to hydrate some more." She'd grabbed an armful of water bottles earlier, tossing them onto the sofa behind them. She'd already drank two, Finn three. "Between the wine and your stamina, I'm getting dehydrated."

He grinned, reaching up and pushing a strand of her hair back and behind her ear. "Really? I'm just trying to keep up with you."

"Well, you're doing spectacularly." She patted her hand against his chest.

"As are you." His hand was up and under the shirt—his shirt—that she was wearing, his fingers trailing up and down her spine.

She moved her head back down, resting it on his shoulder. "Can I ask you a question?"

"Yes."

"Last week you told me you don't do relationships. Why don't you?"

Finn was quiet for a moment as he took a deep breath and let it out. "It's not exactly my favorite topic of conversation, but as you've shared things that I have no doubt aren't your favorite, here goes. Rebecca was my childhood sweetheart…"

They continued to pass the bottle back and forth as he told her all about the woman who broke his heart. All the while that he talked, he didn't stop moving his hand up and down her back. She got the feeling that being able to touch her was comforting to him.

Brie wasn't sure how she felt about what Finn told her. On one hand, she hated that he'd been hurt. On the other, if he'd still been with Rebecca, he wouldn't be there with her in that moment. She preferred him there with her.

"Thank you for answering me."

"You're welcome." He kissed her on top of the head. "Now I have a question of my own, one I've been thinking about for a while now."

"What's that?"

"Why would someone buy that many cat costumes?"

Brie burst out laughing at the drastic change in conversation. "You've been thinking about Lo's cat costumes for a while?"

"Well, when you had that gorgeous mouth wrapped around my cock, I had to think about something while you worked me over."

"And it was cat costumes?" She laughed again.

"I had to focus on something."

"Clearly. So where else did your thoughts go with these cat costumes?"

"Well, I feel like there have to be pictures of Lo in them. Why else would Bethelda get these cat costumes unless she was documenting them for posterity? And I feel like that album has to be in here among the hundreds of other books."

Brie put both of her palms flat on his chest, pushing up so

that she could look around the room. There was enough light from the fire and the lamp in the corner to illuminate some—but not all—of the shelves.

"Hold on." She pulled her legs up and under her, leaning over Finn to reach the lamp on the side table. His hand moved from her spine down to her bare ass, squeezing lightly. She turned and looked at him over her shoulder. "Really?"

"Couldn't help myself." He smiled wide.

She shook her head, turning back to the lamp and stretching just a bit farther to turn it on. The lamp more than doubled the light in the room, clearly showing the bookshelves. Brie moved back, her hands resting on Finn's shoulders as she looked at the shelves behind him. As Finn was now seductively running his hands up and down her bare hips, she doubted he was doing anything besides looking for the outline of her nipples through the shirt.

It took her a minute—Finn's wandering hands really didn't help—before she focused on a cluster of photo albums in the back right corner.

"Hold please." She kissed his lips before she pulled away and got out from under the covers.

Frankie, who was sprawled out in front of the fire with Lo, barely lifted her head at the movement before resettling and closing her eyes.

The house wasn't nearly as cold as it had been before Finn got there and turned on the fires. Just a slight chill in the air. It wasn't terrible, but it was enough to make goose bumps break out on her bare legs and arms. She grabbed the stack of albums before she quickly made her way back to Finn.

Dropping them on the floor next to the air mattress, she

climbed back under the covers that Finn held up for her. Though this time she settled herself on his lap, straddling him. She sat back on his legs, making herself comfortable—and warm—before she grabbed the first album on the stack.

Finn pulled the T-shirt to the side, kissing her shoulder before he, too, grabbed an album. The first one Brie opened had a picture of a newborn that she was going to guess was from forty-seven years ago.

She barely glimpsed the pink, pudgy child in all white before she closed it. There was no need to open that can of worms right now. She tossed it onto the sofa behind them.

"Baby Bethelda," she said as she grabbed another album.

"She's probably about five years old when this one starts." Finn tossed his on top of the sofa, too.

"Let's grab from the bottom then," she said as her fingers closed on the one in question and she tugged. Opening the cover she found a photo of a Christmas tree decorated in white and red, candy canes, sparkly snowflakes, and balls covered in red glitter. She flipped to the next page to see another tree covered in plums of peacock feathers and decorations corresponding with the blue and green color scheme. She turned to a page toward the back to find an all-white tree with silver and gold ornaments.

"Christmas," Brie muttered as she threw the album on top of the others.

But before she could grab another, Finn said, "Jackpot." He moved the album so that Brie could see the first photo. A kitten Lo was sitting in front of a neutral backdrop, looking pissed as she wore a hippopotamus costume. He flipped to the next photo to show the cat just slightly bigger and wearing a lion outfit, complete with a big furry mane.

"Oh. My. Gosh." Brie reached over and turned to the next page to see Lo dressed as an elephant.

"Clearly the first couple of outfits had a safari theme," he said as they looked at a picture of Lo as a gorilla.

"Clearly."

From there they moved on to a year of birds: flamingos, ostriches, owls, blue jays, cardinals. After that were flowers: rose, hydrangea, daisy, sunflower...it went on and on. And in every single one of them she looked angry.

Brie looked over her shoulder to where Lo lay. She was on her back between Frankie's paws, fast asleep.

"Don't worry. I won't put you in anything like that again."

"Oh come on, this is gold," Finn said, and Brie turned back to see him pointing to the photo of Lo in the narwhale costume.

"OK, that one I am most definitely keeping."

"I really don't think you have any other choice. You're going to need to put this one on the wall."

"In a frame covered in sequins." She pulled the book from his hands, tossing it on the sofa with the other albums.

"What other way would there be to display it?"

"Clearly no other." Placing her hands on his shoulders she slowly moved farther up his lap.

He took a sharp breath as she pressed the apex of her thighs against the erection growing behind the fabric of his boxers. "So you're keeping her. Keeping Lo?" His hands settled on her hips. "I got the sense when you picked her up that you weren't too sure about her. There is also the fact that you apparently think she's gearing up to eat you."

"Well, you know." She shrugged her shoulders. "I like to live dangerously." She was quiet for a moment before she said, "You know what great mystery I can't figure out?"

"What's that?"

"Bethelda never got anything delivered here. Everything went to her PO box or the Mirabelle Information Center. She didn't have any friends, at least not any who have made any effort to contact me. There wasn't really anyone at the funeral, either. So I don't see anyone coming for a visit. Yet, she had this specialized doorbell. So I wonder how often she actually heard it ring."

"I'd wager not all that often at all." His hands moved from her hips, his palms at her ribs, fingers wrapping around her sides.

"Me either." She shifted even closer. "Finn, thank you for ringing that doorbell." Her arms wrapped around his neck, leaning close as she pressed her mouth to his.

"What is it with you and your *thank-yous*?" He slowly shook his head, his hands continuing their journey up as he pushed the shirt up her body. She lifted her arms so he could pull it over her head.

"I'm just glad you're here…mainly because of the body heat."

"I figured as much." He reached up, tracing the chain of her necklace with his fingertip. Goose bumps broke out on her skin again, but this time they had nothing to do with being cold. "What's the story behind this?"

"How do you know there's a story?"

"Because you always wear it."

"The day my parents brought me home, my dad had two necklaces, one for my mother and one for me. They gave it to me on my tenth birthday."

"I like it…I like seeing you in only it." Leaning forward, he pressed a kiss to the diamond before moving down and covering one of her breasts with his mouth.

He sucked her nipple deep, making her moan, before laving it with his tongue. He spent ample time admiring every inch of her chest, her holding on to his shoulders while she rocked her hips against his now hard cock.

They were both good and truly worked up by the time he pulled his mouth away, leaning back just slightly as he watched her move. She reached between their bodies, pulling him from his boxers before she started to stroke him.

"God, you're good at that."

"I want you inside of me, Finn." Her words came out just a little bit desperate…or a lot desperate. She reached behind him, grabbing one of the remaining condoms from the stash on the end table. Ripping it open with her teeth, she pulled the latex out before slowly rolling it down his length.

"For someone who wants me inside of them, you sure are taking your time."

"Just making sure I do it right." She stroked him one more time for good measure…and to torture him a little bit.

He groaned, lifting her hips as she positioned him at her entrance. And then she moved down, letting out a satisfied cry as he filled her. His hand came to the back of her head, hands in her hair as he pulled her mouth to his.

The kiss was long and deep, their bodies starting a slow rhythm. Finn held on to her hips as she started to really move. "Ride me, baby," he demanded against her mouth before he nipped at her bottom lip.

And ride him she did, enjoying every last moment of it.

Chapter Sixteen

Wine as Currency

When Brie woke up on Saturday morning her first conscious thought was one of being wonderfully satisfied, the next was how incredibly warm and comfortable she was. Hard not to be when she had a solid wall of man at her back, his arm wrapped around her. His hand was under the T-shirt—his shirt—that she wore, possessively holding her breast.

Slowly opening her eyes, it was to find the room bathed in a dim glow. She hadn't drawn the curtains, and the sun pushed through the thin blinds on the windows as much as it could. Based off of the amount of light in the room, she'd wager it was well after eight...probably close to nine.

It had been almost one in the morning when they'd finally gone to sleep. Understandably they'd both been exhausted with their activities of the night. Though, Brie wasn't feeling all that exhausted at the moment. She was feeling well rested and deliciously sore.

The only downside to the moment was that her mouth felt like a sandbox. Damn that red wine. They'd gone through two and a half bottles, and the only reason she wasn't sporting a hangover was because she'd downed another bottle of water before they'd gone to bed.

Which meant she really needed to use the bathroom now.

Gently pulling Finn's hand from her breast, she slid away from him. She was careful not to jostle him as she got off the bed. He barely stirred before he rolled over onto his back, sound asleep. She smiled as she watched him for a moment, a little impressed with herself that she'd wiped him out so thoroughly.

A chill ran down her spine, making her entire body shiver. Though they'd left the fire burning all night—its warmth filling the air and doing a decent job of combating the cold—it wasn't enough compared with the warmth of the bed and the man she'd just pulled away from. Her thick robe lay on a chair in the corner and she slipped it on, grabbing her yoga pants from the floor, before sliding her feet into her fox slippers by the door.

She made quick work in the bathroom, pulling the yoga pants on, brushing her teeth, and washing her face. When she opened the door, it was to find Frankie sitting in the hallway.

Brie reached down to rub the dog's head as she whispered, "Do you need to go outside, pretty girl?"

Frankie got up at the word *outside* and headed for the back door off the kitchen. Brie followed, smiling as she watched the dog's fluffy tail wag back and forth. Twisting the lock and opening the door, Brie stepped outside and onto the back porch while Frankie tore off into the backyard.

Brie liked it out there, had spent a couple of evenings—that weren't freezing—on the wooden porch swing, enjoying the view at sunset. It really was a beautiful view. Three massive oaks provided shade, moss hanging down from the long branches. Either Bethelda had a green thumb, or she paid someone to maintain it. There were well-cared-for flower bushes all along the paved path that led down to Whiskey River. She could just imagine those bushes bursting with flowers in the spring.

She wondered if she'd even get to see that happen.

Another chill ran down her spine, making her body shiver. As the sun was shining bright, and the wind wasn't really blowing, Brie could only just handle the cold air. Her fuzzy robe and slippers were helping matters considerably. But what really helped was when Finn came out of the house about two minutes later.

Brie turned around at the sound of the door opening to find him wearing his jeans, the fleece pullover, and socks. His hair looked thoroughly tousled and there was still the vestiges of sleepiness behind his eyes. But maybe that look was from him still not wearing his glasses.

He moved in behind her, arms wrapping around her belly and pulling her back against his chest. His head came down and over her shoulder, and he covered her lips with his, his mouth tasting like mint.

He must've gotten ahold of the mouthwash in the bathroom.

"Morning." That one word came out warm and raspy, and she felt it move over her skin like she was sliding into a hot bath.

"Morning." She repeated his greeting, her hand coming up to cup the side of his jaw, running her thumb against his beard. "How'd you sleep?"

"Better than I have in a really long time. You?"

"Well, as someone put me to bed thoroughly well-used, I slept fantastic."

"Good." The grin that turned up his mouth was enough to make her just a little bit weak in the knees.

Good thing his arms were around her.

"So what are you doing today?" he asked as he nuzzled his nose across her cheek.

"Attempting to tackle something in that house."

"You want help? I'm good at taking orders."

She leaned back so that she could look into his eyes. "You have nothing better to do today?"

"Than spending time with you? No."

Brie turned in his arms, her arms moving up and wrapping around his neck. Her hands went to the back of his head, pulling down until she had his mouth again.

"I didn't like waking up without you next to me," he whispered against her lips.

His words sent a thrill of pleasurable warmth down her spine. He'd wanted her there. Wanted her next to him when he'd woken up. That little fact wasn't so little at all. It was *everything* in that moment. She pulled back just enough to see his eyes, her fingers moving up and down through the hair at the back of his neck.

"I've done a number of stupid things in my life, but leaving you that first night is close to the top."

"Finn—"

"I'm sorry, Brie."

She stretched up, pressing her lips to his in a soft, slow kiss. "I forgive you. *Forgave* you."

"I still want you to forget."

It was at that point that Frankie came back up on the deck, clearly done with her morning business and ready to go back inside.

Brie pulled Finn's bottom lip between her teeth, gently nipping at it before letting go. "Well, you know how to make me forget more than anyone else. Make me forget again, Finn."

His hands moved down to her thighs, pulling her up to that she could wrap her legs around his waist. Turning around he carried her into the house and back to the den. He used that last condom making her forget everything except him. Making her forget everything except the way he touched her, kissed her, the way he held her while he moved inside of her.

He made her forget everything except for how he made love to her.

* * *

After Finn and Brie's morning sex session, they took a shower. The setup wasn't nearly as large or luxurious as what he had at his house, but as he got to see Brie all wet and soapy, he wasn't complaining one little bit.

They'd taken their time under the hot spray, and now out of condoms, they had gotten rather creative. After that, they'd gotten dressed and had breakfast.

What with Finn's career, he never knew when he was going to need a change of clothes. When it came to working with animals, there was no telling when he'd get something on him that would require him to change. There was also the fact that he'd been known to crash at the farm on some nights, waking up early to go for a ride with Nigel. Not to mention there were times when he was at Shep and Hannah's when he'd drink more than was safe to get behind the wheel.

Because of all of these factors, he not only always had a duffel with clothes in his truck, but he also always had food for Frankie. He never left the dog by herself overnight, so if he was sleeping elsewhere, so was she.

Both Finn and Brie had worked up an appetite that morning, and while she fried bacon and scrambled eggs, he buttered toast and made coffee. By the time everyone in the house was fed and he and Brie were good and caffeinated, it was half past ten.

As Brie's first goal was still cleaning out the office for her to work in, that was where they started.

"Let's pack up George and all of his belongings first," Brie said as she walked into the room with two smaller boxes in her hands.

"You donating this stuff?"

"Nope, sold it all. I took pictures of everything and posted it on eBay Wednesday morning with a forty-eight-hour time window. It was all sold by Friday to the same person with the screen name *Freedom!!!!1978*."

"How much did you get for it all?" he asked, taking both of the boxes from her hands.

"Close to six thousand."

"Holy shit."

"Bethelda had a lot of signed things in there, and all of them with proof of authenticity. And pretty much everything was an original. Then you have to add in the fact that Mr. Michael is no longer with us, and this stuff is worth even more."

"I know, but geez, that just seems like a lot to pay."

"It does indeed. But *Freedom!!!!1978* will get way more enjoyment out of this stuff than me. I've learned all that I need to learn from it, Bethelda was a George Michael super-fan."

"She was indeed." Finn nodded. "OK, so how do you want to tackle this?"

"With a lot of bubble wrap." She grabbed a role that sat on the desk, holding it in the air.

But Finn's eyes weren't on the bubble wrap; they were on the cedar desk. It was the first time he'd actually looked at it, and just one glance made it clear to him where it had come from.

"This is one of my friend Bennett's," he said as he reached out, running his hand along the wood of the top. "He does wood work and custom furniture."

"Mel told me yesterday at lunch. But I didn't know that was one of his. It's beautiful, one of my favorite things in the house."

"Everything he does is amazing. I just can't believe she bought a piece."

"He another one of her victims?"

"Brie." Finn lifted his hand from the desk as he turned to look at her. "Over half of this town was on the receiving end of one of her blog posts at one point or another."

"So it would be hard for her to avoid everyone she ever wrote about. Hell, she took Lo to St. Francis."

"She did…it's just…I don't know, I can't wrap my head around her."

A half smile pulled up the corner of Brie's mouth. "Join the club."

It took them a couple of hours to get everything efficiently and safely packed in the boxes. But they worked together, figuring out the best system. There were fifteen packages in total, and by the time they got all of those packages loaded up in Finn's truck and to the post office, it was just in time before they closed at one o'clock.

He took her to a light lunch, prefacing that even though he drove and paid, it did not count as the date he'd requested previously. Not at all. He wanted their date to leave an impression, an evening she'd always remember. Even long after she was gone.

That thought had an unpleasant—and unexpected—sinking sensation settling low in his gut, but he forced himself to push it away.

After a quick stop at the drug store—to stock up on much needed latex supplies—they were driving back to the bungalow. Finn called Brendan, letting his friend know they'd be at the house for the rest of the day so he could come over to see what he could do about the HVAC unit.

Brendan looked slightly uneasy when he first walked through the door. Probably the sense most people had when first entering Bethelda's house, but he relaxed after a little bit. He found the problem with the unit—a blown fuse—within ten minutes, and he had it fixed ten minutes after that.

"You're good to go, Brie," he told her as he walked back into the house—warm air now blowing through the vents—but he stopped in his tracks when he looked through the open door to Bethelda's bedroom. "No shit," he whispered, shaking his head.

"What?" Finn asked, setting a box of musical snow globes down on the dining room table.

Brendan looked over at them, his astonishment clear on his face. "That's one of Paige's paintings." He pointed into the room. "Mirabelle Beach at sunset. I remember watching her paint that; she was seven months pregnant with the twins."

"She has one of Bennett's originals in there, too. A cedar desk." Finn pointed to the office.

"Seriously?"

"That isn't all, either." Brie leaned her hip against the door frame of the kitchen, folding her arms across her chest as she looked between the two men. "Bethelda had beer from the Sleepy Sheep in the fridge, frozen cookie dough from Café Lula in the freezer, Harper's lotions and oils in the bathroom, along with that painting and the desk. She's a conundrum wrapped in an enigma."

"Well." Brendan looked to Brie. "If you ever figure the woman out, I'd be more than interested to know."

"I'll keep you posted." She unfolded her arms as she gestured around the house. "Might take me awhile, though."

Finn hoped it took her as long as possible. "No kidding."

"Anyway, what do I owe you for coming here?"

"Nothing," he said, and shook his head.

"Oh come on, you came down on your day off." She pushed off the door frame and took a step closer to Brendan.

"Brie, I called him, I can take care of it," Finn said.

"Actually, neither of you need to do anything. It took me less than half an hour. It really isn't necessary."

"What if I pay you in wine? Two bottles. You'd actually be doing me a favor as there is no way I'd be able to get through Bethelda's supply anyway. It's less things for me to get rid of in the end."

Not for the first time that day, Finn thought about Brie leaving town. He really, *really* didn't like the idea of it. But he never had liked the idea of her leaving. Even that very first night when he'd met her, he'd felt a sense of disappointment when she'd said she would only be in Mirabelle for two nights.

Now two nights had turned to indefinitely and he could hear the ticking clock that was hanging over his head.

"Deal." Brendan's voice brought Finn back from his thoughts.

Brie grinned as she walked past him to the floor-to-ceiling wine cabinet. He had the urge to put his hands on her as she passed, to pull her close, to not let her go.

"You have a preference?" She opened the doors and gestured to the mostly filled cubbyholes. The squares were large enough for a regular-size bottle of wine, twenty across and fifteen high.

"Damn, that's a lot of wine."

"Exactly. So see, you're helping me out."

"Clearly. Well, Paige likes pinot grigio and she's been on a red wine kick lately."

"I'd give him one of these." Finn crossed over to her on the pretense of helping. Really he just took the opportunity to be near her. Coming up behind her, he kissed her neck as he reached around her, grabbing a bottle of pinot that Bethelda had five of. He handed it to Brie before reaching up and to the left, his free hand at her side, holding on to her hip. "And that Malbec we had last night."

She turned to look over her shoulder at him, her eyes golden. "Good choices."

"Part-time bartender, remember?"

"Oh, I remember. Why else do you think I keep you around?"

"That and because of my fire-lighting skills." He grinned.

Brendan cleared his throat, causing them both to turn. He didn't look uncomfortable so much as amused as he looked at them. "You know, if you just give me the wine, I can go so you two can continue whatever it is that you want to continue." His eyes glowed with humor.

"I'll help you out." Finn shook his head as he grabbed both bottles. "You don't have enough hands with your tool kit, and it would be a shame to break one."

"It really would be," Brie agreed. "And thank you again, Brendan. I really do appreciate you coming over."

"It's not a problem. Also, Paige told me to say hi, and that she really enjoyed lunch with you yesterday. She also said she was looking forward to you coming out next week with her and the girls. To be honest, so am I."

"Why's that?"

"Because, whenever the girls get together, it's always interesting."

"Should I be nervous? Finn said the exact same thing."

"No, not nervous." Brendan shook his head, grinning. "It just always makes for a good night."

Yeah, Finn would just bet his friends enjoyed their wives going to Girls' Night Out. A number of their children had been conceived after those evenings.

"Anyway, I'll see you later, Brie. And don't hesitate if you need help with anything else. I'll gladly take more wine as payment."

"Noted." She laughed, waving good-bye as Finn led Brendan to the door and outside.

"I like her," Brendan said as he headed to his truck. It was parked at the end of the driveway, right behind Finn's.

"I do, too."

"You should know Paige told me about Bethelda being Brie's biological mother. Not because she wants to go far and wide with the information, but because she wanted me to understand the full scope of the situation." He opened the backseat door behind the driver's seat, setting his toolbox on the floor before he turned to Finn. "And you have to know, man, none of us are going to hold that against her."

"I know." Finn nodded, wishing more than anything that *he* hadn't made it into such a big thing when he'd found out. But he was going to continue on his mission of making Brie forget about all of that.

And as he'd been a pretty big ass, there was a lot to forget.

"Good." Brendan grabbed both wine bottles from Finn and stuck them in the pouch behind the driver's seat. "Enjoy the rest of your day."

"I'm spending it with Brie, so that's guaranteed."

"Good man." Brendan clapped Finn on the shoulder before he got in his truck and pulled out of the driveway. And as Finn headed back to the house, the smile on his face was one that couldn't be messed with.

* * *

Church on Sunday morning was an interesting affair. Brie had only gone the previous week to get out of the house. It had also given her the opportunity to connect with her past in a way, being in that building. She hadn't exactly had any intention of going again that weekend.

That was until she'd spent all of Saturday with Finn. By the time Sunday rolled around and he'd asked her if she wanted to go, she figured she might as well go for broke and just spend the whole weekend with him. Well, going to church with him led to her sitting with his family…his *entire* family.

It wasn't just his parents and grandmother who were there,

either. Shep, Hannah, and baby Nate sat in the pew in front while Finn's aunt Marigold, uncle Jacob, cousin Meredith, and Meredith's daughter Emma were in the pew behind them.

Brie got a rush introduction of everyone she hadn't met before Mass. After Mass they all went into the parish hall for doughnuts—she had one with chocolate frosting—and coffee. It was there that everyone was able to chat a little bit more at leisure, and Hannah took the opportunity to introduce Brie to Meredith.

Finn's cousin had inherited from the fairer side of the Shepherd family, or more accurately the Franklin family, with her blond hair and light complexion. She also had Ella's sapphire-blue eyes, and so did her daughter Emma. And yet that blue had completely skipped both of Ella's children who had the stormy gray, which—Finn told her later—was from his grandfather Owen.

There was something about eye color that always fascinated Brie…maybe because she'd always wondered where she'd gotten hers from. Who had given her golden brown eyes that changed with her mood? Maybe she'd learn the answer to that question while she was in Mirabelle.

Maybe…maybe…maybe. So many maybes.

"Well, we won't keep you, darling," Faye said as she patted Brie's arm. "Finn said that he's been helping you clear out a room this weekend, and that you still have a ways to go."

"Yes, ma'am. He's been a big help. I'm sure there will be at least one more truckload of donations before the day is over."

"Excellent. That's what we like to hear for the Triple C."

"I hope you enjoy the cobbler," Meredith said, tossing her empty coffee cup into the trash. "For whatever reason, Grandma Ella's is better than anyone else's."

"That's how it works, right? My mother's chicken enchiladas are other-worldly, and I follow the recipe to a tee, but somehow, they lack a little something. Still good, just probably a nine and a half to my mom's ten."

Once everyone said their good-byes, Finn slid his hand to the small of Brie's back—a gesture that wasn't missed by anyone in his family—and led her to the door.

"Tell me more about these chicken enchiladas," he said as they stepped outside.

"So good you'll forget your name," she told him as she tightened her coat around her waist.

"Well, I think I just figured out what I want my next meal payment to be."

"Deal." She leaned into him, both wanting more body heat—the temp hadn't cracked forty—and using his body as a shield against the wind.

Finn's hand moved from the small of her back and to her waist, pulling her in close. She couldn't help but smile as they walked, because as she was learning, she really liked to be close to this man.

* * *

Finn thoroughly enjoyed the rest of the day, which was saying a lot as he spent most of it in Bethelda's house...cleaning Bethelda's house. But no matter how not great the task at hand was, it was made exponentially great because he was doing it with Brie.

He never once hesitated to touch her, brushing up against her, coming up behind her, wrapping his arms around her waist as he kissed her neck.

It was one of the best afternoons he'd had in a long time. Well, since before the previous afternoon with Brie, because that afternoon had been phenomenal, too. But besides the times he'd had his head up his ass when it came to her, *all* of the time spent with her was pretty fucking phenomenal.

Before they went over to his parents' for dinner, they sat at the dining room table, making sure that both Lo and Frankie ate their dinner before they left. Once the animals were good and full of food, Brie bundled herself up in her black leather jacket, and they were out the door with Frankie by their side.

It was going to be a full house that night with his parents, Ella, Shep, Hannah, baby Nate, Finn, and Brie. None of the Shepherd men would be at the bar because they'd given the reins to Reggie Chambers for the evening.

Reggie was born and raised in Mirabelle. Joined the army right out of high school and had been serving for the last fifteen years. He'd gotten out four months ago and moved back to Mirabelle in need of a job.

As the bar had been going through some changes over the years, mainly Shep taking a step back from bartending as much and focusing on beer brewing and his family, they'd had to hire someone else full-time. So Reggie, along with two of the other part-time bartenders, would all be able to hold it down just fine.

When they got to the house, it was immediately clear to Finn that his grandmother was having an incredibly good day. Ella was chatty and smiling, moving around the kitchen a little bit more spryly than even on her best days. Finn had been given the job of cutting strawberries—along with Hannah who wasn't allowed near a measuring cup—while Ella walked Brie through the cobbler mixing. Shep just supervised the whole thing while holding baby Nate in his arms.

After that, Ella instructed Brie through cooking the strawberries and rhubarb down in the sugar syrup. Once everything had been put together in the baking dish, and the dish in the oven, it was time for a refill on their Mirabelle Sweet Teas. By the time his dad had another batch ready, the pot roast that his mother made had rested long enough and it was time for dinner.

Ella ate like a bird these days, so she took control of the conversation during the meal, telling Brie about her grandparents. Brie hung on her every word, listening about how Petunia loved to cross-stitch, how her favorite flowers were yellow daffodils, how she loved Elvis, how she secretly read Harlequin romance novels…and then gave them to Ella to read when she was finished.

Harold was very much a good ol' southern boy. He wore his blue jeans everywhere, except Mass on Sundays. He smoked one cigar a week, which was always on Saturdays. He loved Johnny Cash, Johnny Carson, and Johnnie Walker Red. He also loved his girls more than anything in the world.

Something, or more accurately someone, that Ella didn't really talk about was Bethelda. She was mentioned here and there, mostly when she was a baby or in adolescence. But she was never really the focus, and adult Bethelda was avoided all together.

Maybe that would be a conversation for a later date, at a time when everything wasn't as light. Because as they sat around eating warm cobbler—that Brie declared was the best she'd ever had—with ice cream melting over the top, it definitely wasn't the time for a Bethelda convo.

It was close to nine when Finn finally got Brie out the front door, with a load of leftovers from his mother. Finn was also greeted to a parting smirk from Shep, who'd been more of an observer that evening. An observer of how Finn and Brie interacted. Sure his mother had paid plenty of attention to them, too, but she'd been slightly preoccupied with trying to impress Brie. Not all that surprising as Finn hadn't brought a girl to that house since Rebecca.

He was pretty sure his mother was ignoring the fact that Brie wasn't staying in Mirabelle…like mother like son.

Once he got Frankie in the back—and set the bag of leftovers on the floor—he moved to the front and got inside. But the second he shut that door behind him, he felt the mood in the cab of his truck change.

It was like Brie had been holding her breath for the last few hours and finally let it out, and with the release of that breath she deflated. Maybe it was because he'd spent a solid forty-eight hours with her that he was so attuned to her, he wasn't sure, but all he knew was she was going through something painful in that moment.

He wasn't an idiot; he knew that even with the good history she'd been given she was probably going to have a hard time processing it all. Anyone would. This was the family she never knew…never had a chance to know.

"You OK?" he asked, his voice low.

Brie looked over to him, a sad smile on her mouth. "No." She shook her head. "I mean, don't get me wrong, I want to learn everything I can. And what Ella told me, what she knows about all of them, experienced with them…it means everything to hear it. But it's a lot. You know? I just wish I'd known them." Her voice cracked just slightly on the end, and he knew she was trying to keep her emotions in check. "Just for a moment."

Finn reached over, grabbing her hand and pulling it up to his lips. "I have absolutely no idea what it's like to be in the situation you're in. But what I do know is that for as long as you want me around, I'll be here for you."

"Can you take me somewhere? Not back to the house. I just want to be anywhere else. With you."

"Absolutely." He gently pulled her closer as he leaned over, pressing a kiss to her mouth. It took an effort of will to pull away from her, but he managed. He started his truck and backed out of the driveway, knowing exactly where he wanted to take her.

Chapter Seventeen

Unsteady

The five-minute car ride was a quiet one, Brie's hand in Finn's, his thumb moving back and forth in a gentle, comforting stroke. She liked his hands on her body, was becoming more and more accustomed to it. Not in a way where she was becoming immune to his touch, just that it felt right.

She looked out the window, not seeing much out into the night. But she wasn't really paying attention to what she saw as her mind was going through all of the things she'd just learned.

Petunia and Harold had tried for kids for years before they finally got pregnant with Bethelda. Petunia had been thirty-nine, Harold forty-three. According to Ella, they'd doted on their one and only daughter. Ella had also said that Brie's grandfather had loved his girls more than anything in the world.

Yet from everything Brie knew about Bethelda, she seemed incapable of love. *That* was what she couldn't wrap her mind around.

It was the truck coming to a stop that pulled her from her thoughts, and Brie moved her gaze from the side window to the windshield. The headlights from Finn's truck illuminated the two-story A-frame in front of them. Because of the dark, she didn't pick up much on details besides the fact that it stood on ten-foot pylons and had a waist-high white picket fence running around the perimeter.

She turned to him as he shut off the engine, more than slightly surprised. "You brought me to your house?"

"Yeah, I figured we could stay here tonight if you want. Lo will be fine, she's eaten dinner and—"

"Yes." She cut him off. "God yes."

They were out of the truck a moment later, Frankie leading the way and Finn slightly behind her as they made their way up the stairs. The sensor light turned on, illuminating the bright red front door and the windows on either side, also sporting the bright red paint. She was pretty sure the house itself was gray, but besides that she couldn't tell anything else.

Finn opened the front door, Frankie heading in as Finn reached in to flip a light on. He held back outside, waiting for Brie to proceed him into the house. As she walked down the hallway—mahogany hardwood floors creaking slightly under her feet—she passed a small den on the left, spotting a desk and half-filled bookcases. To the left were two doors, one that she guessed to be a closet, and the other door opened to where she could just make out that it was a bathroom.

The end of the hall opened up to the living room, Finn flipping another switch that filled the room with light. A dark gray sectional sat in the middle of the room, facing the brick fireplace in the corner and the massive flat screen TV above it. Off to the right was a wall of windows, blackened from the night. As the back of the house faced the water, she had no doubt in her mind those windows provided an excellent view of the water in the daylight. Frankie had already taken up her spot on the massive dog bed in front of those windows.

"Let me put these away." Finn came up behind her, kissing her on the back of the head before he headed to the left of the living room and to the kitchen.

He passed the thermostat on the wall, and he hesitated for just a moment as he turned the heat up higher. When he got to the kitchen he flipped on the light to reveal a beyond beautiful kitchen. Black appliances, black countertops, black cabinets. Everything else was white. A white subway tile backsplash, white walls, white tile floors. A rectangular ebony dining room table with four chairs sat in front of the wall of windows.

"Holy crap," she whispered as she looked at the area. "That kitchen is gorgeous."

Finn set the bag on the counter and started pulling out the Tupperware containers. "Shep remodeled it a few years ago, when he lived here."

"Shep lived here?"

"Yeah, this was Owen and Ella's house. Owen built it, just like he built the bar. When he died, it was Shep's. Then Hannah came down, Shep moved in with her, and he gave it to me." Finn explained as he put all of the food in the refrigerator.

"Owen built this house?" Brie asked as she looked around again, taking in the open floor plan and how most of the downstairs had been designed for whatever view was beyond those windows.

"He did indeed. You want something to drink?"

"Yeah." She nodded as she looked over her shoulder to him. "Something hard?"

"I have whiskey," he said as he tossed his jacket onto the dining room table, pushing up the sleeves of his sweater.

"Perfect."

"You want it on ice?"

"No. Just give it to me straight." Brie moved farther into the living room, pulling off her jacket and tossing it on the sofa. "So what else has been remodeled?"

"Mainly just the bathrooms," Finn told her as he grabbed two tumblers from a cabinet and moved to a waist-high liquor cupboard off to the side of the kitchen. "The layout is the exact same that he built, floors are originals. We did have to replace the windows, but that was when Owen and Ella still lived here. He upgraded to ones that were better for storms."

Brie listened as she sat on the arm of the sofa, unzipping her boots and pulling them off along with her socks. Finn had his back to her, so he didn't see when she unsnapped the top of her jeans and shimmied out of them. Nor did he see when she grabbed the bottom of her sweater and pulled it over her head. She was standing directly under a vent, the heat blowing out, moving across her skin.

"The plumbing has been updated, along with the electricity, but again those were changes that Owen made when he—" Finn stopped talking the second he turned around and saw her.

She stood in front of him wearing a red lace thong and black bra.

"Damn." His eyes moved over her hungrily, like it had been years since he'd had her as opposed to just that morning. "How do you do that every time?"

"Do what?"

"Make it impossible for me to think." He grabbed both

glasses of whiskey, each holding a little more than two shots' worth, and moved toward her.

He handed her a glass, and she didn't hesitate to tip her head back and drink it all. It burned its way down her throat and to her belly, but she didn't stop until she'd swallowed every last drop.

"OK." Finn nodded his head before he mimicked her, tipping his own glass back and downing his whiskey. Then he reached forward, taking her glass out of her hand and setting both empty tumblers on the end table next to them. He moved closer to her, his hand sliding to the small of her back. His fingers were spread wide at the base of her spine as he pulled her against him. He dipped his head low, his mouth going to her ear. "What do you need, Brie?"

"I need you to make *me* not think for a moment, Finn. Or a lot of moments."

"And how do you want this forgetting to go? Soft and slow? Hard and fast?" He pulled her earlobe into his mouth, lightly dragging his teeth across the delicate spot.

She gasped at the sensation, her hands grabbing on to his waist and holding on. "All of the above."

"That can without a doubt be taken care of." He moved his mouth to hers, his tongue thrusting past her lips as he very thoroughly kissed every thought out of her mind.

He tasted like whiskey and oblivion.

Brie loosened her death grip on his shirt, her hands moving up so she could wrap her arms around his neck. "Take me to bed, Finn."

He didn't hesitate, his body swooping low for a second, one of his arms coming behind her knees as he lifted her up. Her hold around his neck tightened as he moved through the room and to the stairs. The man had absolutely no trouble navigating up to the second floor with her in his arms. In fact, he moved like he'd done it a number of times.

She pushed the thought to the back of her mind that he probably had. This was not the time for her to think about him with other women in this house.

The only light in the hallway came from a small night-light on the wall, and Finn carried her down and to a door at the very end. He only took a few steps across the room before he gently lay her down on the middle of a bed. His hands left her body and he moved away. A few seconds later there was a low clicking noise before the room was filled with a soft light from the lamp on a nightstand.

Brie did a quick sweep around the room, taking in the dark brown furniture and another wall of windows that she was sure faced the water. That was all she processed before her eyes were on him.

Finn tossed his glasses onto the nightstand before he reached behind his back, grabbing a fist full of his sweater and pulling it over his head. He was kicking off his boots in the process, his hands at the front of his jeans as he made quick work of getting himself undressed. Besides the sweater coming over his head, his eyes didn't leave her. His gaze was hot and hungry as it stayed on her body.

Once he was completely naked, he knelt down on the bed, moving over to her. He reached for her thighs, his fingers hooking in the straps of her panties before he slowly pulled the thin material down her legs. He lingered over spots as he moved, his fingers trailing across her skin, circling her knees, massaging the back of her calves.

"So pretty," he whispered, shifting forward as his hands moved back to her knees and pushing her legs wide. "So perfect."

He leaned over her, his hands sliding under her back and to the clasp of her bra. Once it was unhooked he pulled it from her body and lowered his head, sucking one of her nipples into his mouth. Her back arched off the bed, her hands delving into his hair as she held him to her.

Apparently this was the slow part of the forgetting, because he took his time admiring her breasts. She enjoyed every moment of it, too. But not as much as she enjoyed one of his hands moving between her legs, his fingers tracing over her slick folds before he slid two inside of her. *Deep* inside of her.

"Finn." Her fingers tightened in his hair, her back arching again, her hips pumping.

He kept working her over but when she'd get close to coming, he'd pull back and slow down, leaving her feeling even more desperate, something she hadn't even thought possible. All the while his mouth never left her breasts, his tongue laving, teeth nipping, lips sucking.

"I need you inside of me." She whispered the words, mainly because she didn't have enough air in her lungs to speak any louder.

Finn leaned to the side, reaching for the nightstand next to him. He grabbed a condom, sitting back on his knees as he ripped it open and rolled it down his cock. "Do you still want slow?" he asked as he ran his hands up the inside of her thighs.

"No. Hard and fast."

"Roll over and get on your hands and knees."

Her pulse quickened at his words, her breath catching in her throat. She moved her legs, shifting so she could do as Finn had just told her. The second she had her ass in the air, Finn moved in behind her, his palms moving up and over her.

"I like you in this position." His voice was low and raspy, like he was barely holding it together. "Then again, I like you in every position." Both of his hands gripped a cheek before he massaged them, making her moan. "You have the sweetest ass, baby."

At his words one of his hands let go before it came back down with a sharp smack. Not enough to hurt, but enough to make her moan again. It was then that she felt the blunt tip of his cock at her entrance. His hand came down on the other cheek as he thrust forward and filled her.

All of the air left her lungs with the movement, and at the same time Finn groaned. Both of his hands were now on her hips, his fingers pressing in as he held her. "God, you feel good."

"So do you." He was so thick inside of her, every inch of him buried deep, but he wasn't moving. She needed him to move. "Finn, please fuck me."

"Yes, ma'am." He moved his hips, slowly pulling out before he moved back in. But he didn't stick with slow for very long at all. Once they'd both adjusted to the new angle, he started to pick up the pace, thrusting in harder and faster.

She had absolutely no idea what incoherent words or sounds came out of her mouth. That might've been because she'd fallen forward, her face pressed into the bed as her arms stretched out, hands fisting in the comforter on the bed. Her legs started shaking and she was beyond lucky that Finn still had her hips firmly in hand, holding her up.

If anything, her mission of not thinking had been accomplished. The only thought on her mind, her sole focus, was that of the orgasm building at her very core. All of the playing and retreating that Finn had done earlier made her beyond primed. She screamed into the mattress as she found her release, Finn pounding into her from behind as he let go and came inside of her.

It was a moment or two later, when her body had stopped pulsing around his, that he pulled from her body. He gently guided her hips down to the mattress, her entire body flat.

"I'll be right back," he whispered as he kissed her shoulder and slid out of the bed.

Somehow, she wasn't sure as to the how, she opened her eyes and watched as Finn's fine ass disappeared through a door that she guessed was the bathroom. She grinned...she couldn't help it. The pleasure had been mind-numbing, more intense than anything she'd felt with him.

More intense than anything she'd felt with anyone.

When Finn came out of the bathroom a couple of minutes later, he grinned seeing her in the bed and in the exact same position he'd left her in, before he headed for the chest of drawers off to the side. Brie again enjoyed the view of the back of him, right up until he pulled on a pair of loose boxers.

"You want a T-shirt?"

"Yes please." She pulled herself up into a sitting position as he crossed over to the bed and handed her a folded black shirt.

"I need to run downstairs and let Frankie out before we go to bed. Do you want anything?"

"Water."

He placed both of his hands on either side of her hips, leaning close and pressing his mouth to hers in a long, lingering kiss.

He'd just brushed his teeth as he tasted like mint. Brie dropped the shirt in her lap as she reached up and held on to the side of his head.

When he finally pulled back enough for her to speak, she whispered against his lips. "Thank you."

"For what this time?"

"Everything."

He grinned as he gave her another kiss, this one quick, before he pulled back from her. "Help yourself to whatever you need in there. Towels are in the cabinet."

"OK." She nodded, again watching as he turned around and walked out of the room. Even covered, she wasn't going to miss an opportunity to look at him from behind. Or more accurately to look *at* his behind.

He was at the stairs when she finally made a move to get out of the bed and crossed over to the open door, shirt in hand. She turned the light on and looked around to find more black and white.

The entirety of the walls was covered with white subway tile, the floors a white and black checker pattern. A cast iron tub was in the corner, white on the inside, black on the outside. A standing glass-fronted shower was off to the very back. Double white pedestal sinks were on the wall right when she walked in, matching mirrored medicine cabinets above each of them. A black cabinet sat in the space between the sinks, and her eyes landed on a spare toothbrush that Finn left out for her, still in the packaging.

For the second time that night she thought about the other women he'd brought here…that he had spare toothbrushes at the ready for whenever someone spent the night with him.

God, what was wrong with her? He wasn't hers. He didn't belong to her. This was just a temporary thing…for as long as she was in town. Besides all of that, she'd never been the jealous type before. And yet thinking about him with other women made her chest ache.

She reached up and pressed her hand to her heart, her eyes landing on her reflection in the mirror. Her hair was good and truly a mess from all the writhing around she'd done. Her lips swollen from his kisses. Her neck and chest were still tinged red from both the flush that hadn't abated and from the rasp of his scruff moving across her skin. And then there were her breasts and the light marks he'd left on both with his mouth.

Brie dropped her hand, shaking her head. She needed to stay in the moment with him. The past didn't matter and there was no future. It was just the present, and she was going to have to accept that.

* * *

When Finn came back upstairs with Frankie, Brie was still in the bathroom, light shining from underneath the door and the water running. He set both glasses of water on the nightstand before he grabbed the top of the comforter and pulled it down to climb in the bed.

Pushing the pillows against the headboard, he lay back, slightly propped up. Brie walked out a moment later, flipping the light off as she stepped into the bedroom.

"The Stingrays?" she asked, grabbing the shirt on both sides, pulling it forward and looking down at the logo on the front.

"Local baseball team that I'm on with all of the guys."

"Oh." She nodded, dropping the fabric so that it fell down to her thighs again.

Good Lord he liked the sight before him, Brie in his shirt and nothing else. Brie in his bedroom. Brie in his house. Now he just wanted her in his bed again. He lifted the blankets next to him, invitation clear to climb in. She crossed the room, her bare feet moving across the hardwood floors. Stopping by the nightstand, she grabbed a water glass and took a long drink. Once she was finished, she set it back down and slid between the covers, right up beside him.

"I like your house," she said as she rested her head against his chest, her arm wrapping around his waist as she tangled their legs together. "And that bathroom is perfection."

"Now that one I remodeled." He pulled his hand up, trailing his fingers through her hair and down her back. "It was shortly after I moved in. Where the shower is was a rather large linen closet, so we pulled that out. The floor-to-ceiling subway tiles are new, but the floors and the rest of the fixtures are all originals."

"I want to take a bath in that bathtub."

He turned his head to the side, kissing her temple. "You play your cards right and you just might get to." It was a pretty picture to imagine, her surrounded by hot soapy water, her nipples peeking through the floating foam. Her head resting back against the rim, eyes closed, neck stretched out as she relaxed.

Yeah, he'd very much like for her to be in that bathtub. But as he'd very clearly discovered, he liked her anywhere that was near him.

Like it had earlier in the cab of the truck, he felt her mood shift. She was going back into her head and he was pretty sure she was thinking about that evening at his parents'. Thinking about what she'd learned. He knew if she wanted to talk, she'd say something. Until then, he'd just hold her, continuing to move his hand up and down her back, tracing her spine as they lay there.

She was quiet for so long, her breath steady against his chest. If she hadn't been running her fingers slowly up and down his abs, he would've thought she was asleep.

"I just don't get it," she finally said.

"Don't get what?"

"How did someone so *mean* come from people who were so *good*? I mean, don't get me wrong, I know that with certain people what you see is *not* what you get. People put on acts, façades, a show for the public, and then they are terrible behind closed doors. But what Ella said feels right, what she said about Harold and Petunia, that they were good people, that they weren't terrible." She paused for a second and when she started speaking again, her voice had dropped low, her words thick with emotion. "Or maybe it's just that I so desperately want to believe I come from something good."

"Brie." He said her name softly, feeling the pain in her words.

Her hand stopped moving on his abs as she tipped her head back to look up at him. The wetness in her eyes was clear, almost brimming over.

"Bethelda was *not* good, Finn." Her voice was even smaller. "You know that. Everyone in this town knows that. *I* know that. My one and only experience with her was awful... just *awful*." She shook her head as her gaze dropped from his.

He wasn't sure if she wanted to keep discussing it, but he

wasn't going to push her. And he didn't need to; it was only a few moments later when she started to talk again.

"I was eighteen, it was the second semester of my freshman year at Emory. One of my professors had been talking about genealogy, and it pushed me to pursue the wild hair of finding out who my birth parents were. Part of it terrified me, and part of it thrilled me. I just wanted to know. The only name I got was Bethelda's. My father's name wasn't on any of the documents."

She paused for a second, resuming the movement of her fingers on his stomach.

"I looked her up online. Found out she lived down here and was working for the town newspaper. So I came down here. When I walked into that building and asked for Bethelda, the receptionist looked beyond surprised. Maybe because I was calm while I asked, and didn't follow up the request with something snarky or aggressive. I'm assuming that was why most people would go down to see her at the newspaper."

"Probably."

"The woman pointed me in the right direction and I made my way to her desk." Brie paused for a second, taking a deep breath before she slowly let it out. "She looked up at me and the second her eyes landed on mine, she knew who I was. I saw the recognition clear as day. There was something about me that made it instantaneously obvious who I was. Whatever that was I will never know."

It was then that something warm and wet hit his chest, and this time when Brie took a deep breath it was unsteady. His arms tightened around her, and God he felt his own heart hurting as the words fell from her mouth.

"Even though she knew who I was, I still introduced myself.

I was nervous, hands shaking and sweaty. The moment I said my name her expression changed from that initial look of recognition to one that was totally unreadable. She spent twenty-eight seconds looking at me. I know because I was counting in my head the entire time. It was all I could do."

More tears hit his skin and she sniffled.

"And then she spoke. I will never, in my life, forget those words. She said: 'I know exactly who you are and I don't care. Nor do I care why you're here. I don't know what heartwarming scene you were expecting when you showed up here, but I can promise you, you aren't going to get it. You aren't going to get *anything* from me now or ever. I didn't want you in my life eighteen years ago and that fact has not changed today. Nor will it change tomorrow. Or the next day. Or the day after that. So what you need to do is turn around and take your little ass out the way it came in. Don't bother ever coming back either.'"

"I'm so sorry, baby," Finn whispered, closing his eyes as he turned his head, pressing another kiss to her temple.

God he hated that spiteful, mean, vengeful, vindictive, hateful woman. Never in his life had he wanted to spit on someone's grave… but he wanted to spit on hers. Too bad she hadn't been buried.

"It was probably a total of two minutes," Brie said after a moment. "That's it, that's all the time I will ever know of the woman who gave birth to me."

She looked up at him again and the pain in her streaming eyes almost broke him in two, right then and there. He also hated himself for how he'd treated her at first. God he was an idiot. The thought that he'd spend the rest of his life making it up to her crossed his mind. Much like many thoughts when it came to Brie, he didn't know where it came from. So he did what he always did and pushed it to the back of his mind.

He did, however, tell Brie the truth when he spoke. "She didn't deserve you, Brie. She didn't deserve *any* part of you."

"I know that." She blinked and more tears fell from her eyes. "But *I* deserved more. I deserved a lot more than that. And I will *never* get it from her. I don't know that I'll ever learn the things that I want to know. Things that I have spent most of my life wondering. God, Finn, I don't know who my biological father is and I might never find that out."

She pressed her face to his chest again as sob after sob broke from her mouth. Finn wished he could do something, *anything*, to take away her pain. But he had no clue how to do that.

So he held her, one hand in her hair, the other on her back, trying to soothe her.

It took a bit, but her sobs subsided and she was finally able to speak. "I just want to come from something good, Finn. I *need* to come from something good…someone good."

He moved his hand to her chin, pushing up until he had her eyes. Apparently crying made them gold, too.

"Your genes don't always define you." His hand went from her chin to her jaw, cupping the side of her face. "You *are* something good. God, Brie, you're amazing. In so many ways. You're strong and smart, funny, thoughtful, and so beautiful. You come from something good." After a few seconds, he added, "Your parents, the people who raised you, are they good?"

"They're the best people I know."

"You come from something good." He repeated the statement, wanting her to believe it.

Needing her to believe it.

"I haven't told them I'm here…in Mirabelle. That Bethelda died, that she left me everything to deal with."

"Why not?"

"They'd worry, hop on a plane and fly here the first chance they got."

"They love you, worrying comes with the territory."

"I know, I just wanted to do this on my own. I can't explain it. And I hate not telling them what's happening. They know how it all destroyed me before. You know, I haven't cried like that…cried over *her* like that, since that day."

"In ten years?"

"No." She shook her head. "I wouldn't let myself."

"You can't bottle that stuff up. You were due to let it out."

"Maybe I was. I think it's also because since I've been here, since I've been in that house, I haven't really been dealing with things that have had history. At least not a history that I want. Everything that I've gotten rid of so far, it's been *extra*. All of the things she bought in bulk. Or obsessions that didn't really mean anything to me."

"Like Michael."

"Like Michael," she said, and nodded. "Like I said, I learned everything I needed to know from that stuff. So it didn't hurt to sell it. I feel like I am just clearing off the dust on everything right now, and I haven't really opened anything up."

"Except today with Ella, learning about Harold and Petunia, that was opening something up that you weren't exactly ready for."

"Not ready for it at all. And I didn't realize I wasn't ready for it until after it was over." She sat up a little bit, not enough to pull away from him, but enough to reach up and palm his jaw with her hand. "Thank you for dealing with my breakdown."

"Brie," he said, and leaned into her touch, "you really need to stop thanking me for things like that. I'm here for you. No questions asked. For as long as you want me."

"In that case, will you hold me while we sleep?"

"As long as you're in my bed, or I'm in yours, I'll have my arms around you."

"Perfect." She stretched up, her mouth landing on his in a soft, slow kiss. He could taste the salt from her tears on her lips.

Chapter Eighteen

Getting Down with My Gnomies

Over the next week, Brie spent her mornings working on her thesis. The office was becoming more and more of a comfortable place for her both as she adjusted to it and cleared it out. She'd call it quits around lunchtime, which was when Finn would come over to the bungalow and eat with her. When he'd head back to work, Brie would start in on tackling more of the stuff in or around the house.

First on her agenda had been going through the charges on Bethelda's credit cards and canceling all of her mail order services. There'd been enough to deal with there that it had taken up the rest of her Monday. By the time she'd finished she had to start making dinner for her and Finn.

He helped her a little bit after they ate that evening, packing up more of the trinkets and knickknacks on the bookshelves in the office. Around nine o'clock he'd grabbed her hand and pulled her into the den and down onto the air mattress.

Tuesday was Valentine's Day, and Brie spent it on Operation DeGnomeing. The little figurines weren't exactly her thing, let alone an entire village of them. So she took multiple pictures of the collection and posted it on eBay. There'd been a bidding war between Gnomeaste62 and GnomePlaceLikeHome that bumped the total price to six hundred and ninety-two dollars. Gnomeaste62 won at the very last minute. Apparently, a lot of the stuff was limited edition pieces for aficionados of *Gnome Life Village* collection.

And Brie clearly was *not* an aficionado.

She also started to go through the dresser and armoires in Bethelda's room. After Finn got off work, he and she loaded up Finn's truck and took it all over to the Triple C. There were nine trash bags filled with Bethelda's clothes and the entire collection of scarves.

"I don't know who would even want clothes that were Bethelda's," Brie said as she dropped a bag into the back of Finn's truck. "Though, a lot of them are brand new."

"Most of the people who benefit from the CCC don't really even know about Bethelda. Or not enough to care. There are a lot of migrant workers who work on the farms or on the boats. They don't exactly have access to computers, let alone the Internet. The stuff will be put to good use, better use than if they were just sitting in her closets."

"That's true," Brie agreed. When people needed things, they usually weren't choosy on where those things came from.

Once they dropped everything off, Finn took her to dinner at the Floppy Flounder. He wouldn't let her pay, but he also said that it didn't count as their date. "You can't add a donation drop into the mix. Our date will be errand free."

After that, he took her back to his house where they spent the rest of the evening watching a movie and making out. Then she'd grabbed his hand and pulled him upstairs to his bedroom. It was one of the better Valentine's Days she'd ever had…maybe even the best.

On Wednesday Brie decided to tackle the hat collection. They were fancy hats and fascinators, like the ones worn to the Kentucky Derby or an English wedding. All were stored in hatboxes and in pristine condition. Brie put all of those on eBay, too. Her new favorite website. By Thursday she'd sold twenty-one out of fifty-four to various buyers. And on Friday she was down to just five.

After her thesis morning marathon, Brie loaded up all of the boxes she needed to ship and headed to the post office. She'd been so many times that week that she and Celine, one of the workers, now knew each other by name.

Once Brie's car was unloaded, she drove down to the beach and to Café Lula. Grace had texted her the day before inviting her to lunch again. When she walked into the building she was immediately greeted by an older woman with white hair and Grace's blue eyes.

"I've heard so much about you!" Lula Mae exclaimed as she pulled Brie into an ample embrace. When she let go and stepped back to look into Brie's face, she grinned and added, "All good things of course."

"Same. I love your place. And your food is amazing."

"Darling, praise will get you everywhere with me. The girls are already in the back, so if you tell me what you want I will bring it out with theirs."

"Any recommendations?"

"How do you feel about chicken salad?"

"That sounds like perfection."

"Coming right up."

When Brie walked through the door and into the back kitchen it was to find Grace, Paige, Mel, and Beth, who Brie had not met before.

Beth was a pretty blond with light blue eyes and a sweet smile. She was an obstetrics nurse at the hospital, which explained why she was wearing hot pink nurse scrubs. Introductions were made, and as was Brie's routine now with this group of girls, she told Beth exactly why she was in town.

Beth didn't flinch at the news. It was clear to Brie that she hadn't known, but it didn't affect her opinion whatsoever.

"I was the only one who hadn't met you yet." Beth grinned. "So when Grace texted me you were coming today I took a longer lunch so I could meet you. I'll be at dinner tomorrow night, too, but everyone will be there, and I wanted to meet you in less of a crowd. Besides I can't promise I will be staying very long at the Sleepy Sheep. Bars aren't as fun when you can't drink."

"Beth's husband knocked her up on their honeymoon." Paige smirked.

"He did indeed. He was very much about adding to our family with more children. It's not like we've ever known a quiet house since we've been together."

"Why's that?"

"Because we already have three. Almost two years ago my sister and brother-in-law died in a car accident."

"Oh my gosh, I am so sorry." Brie put her hand to her chest in a show of sympathy.

Brie hadn't experienced the death of a loved one in her life. All of her grandparents were still alive. Her parents were still there. Aunts and uncles and cousins. She'd experienced loss in a different way, but not like that. God, she couldn't even imagine.

"Thank you. It's still hard some days, and even harder on others, especially for the kids. Nora is eighteen now, Grant's nine, and Penny is four. When I moved back to Mirabelle to take care of them, I did not think that love was going to be in my future. And then Tripp moved in next door."

"And then they had many run-ins over Tripp's dog," Mel added.

"Finn's dog, Frankie," Beth said to Brie. "Well, she has a brother, Duke. As in *the Duke*. Tripp is a huge John Wayne fan. Anyway, someone abandoned them as puppies at the firehouse about a year and a half ago. Tripp is the fire chief and he was working that day, so he took them to St. Francis. Tripp adopted the boy, Finn the girl."

"Finn mentioned something about Frankie's brother being bigger than her."

Beth took a sip of her water before she continued with the telling of her story. "Oh, Duke is bigger all right. And he kept getting into my backyard, destroying my flowerbeds, and rolling around in the mud. I blamed Tripp. Turned out it was Grant who was taking the dog out of Tripp's yard. So I apologized the only way I knew how."

"And how was that?"

"Baked goods. That man has a sweet tooth. I think that's the only reason he fell in love with me."

"Sure it was," Paige said slowly, and didn't even attempt to keep the sarcasm out of her voice.

"Oh, hush. Your husband fell in love with you because of your shoe habit."

"This is true," Paige confirmed to Brie. "He got one look at me in a pair of high-heeled wedges and he was a goner."

The rest of the lunch passed with the same easy conversation, and when Brie left she was in a particularly good mood. So good that she stopped by the Piggly Wiggly on her way home, getting all of the ingredients she needed to make chicken enchiladas for Finn.

* * *

The last week had proven to be a very different experience for Finn. Waking up next to Brie every morning, whether it was her bed or his. Starting the day off by making love to her. Eating lunch with her, though he hadn't been able to that afternoon as he'd been at a farm all day.

He found that his day had been missing something without her being there in the middle of it. Which was probably why he was so eager to get home to her.

Well, get *back* to her…not *home* to her. Bethelda's house was neither of their homes.

He was surprised at how comfortable he was in the space. Maybe because there was no chance of Bethelda walking through that front door…or maybe he was just able to get over a lot of things when it came to Brie.

It was interesting, though, as Brie always referred to the house as the bungalow. Very rarely did she ever call it Bethelda's house. And absolutely never did she say it was her mother's house. Made sense as she never referred to Bethelda as her mother. There was always a *biological* preceding it and an explanation after.

The real reason Finn found this interesting was because Brie *never* slipped when it came to Bethelda. But sometimes when they were talking she would refer to Petunia and Harold as her grandparents and had—more than once—referred to whoever her biological father was as just her father.

It was almost six when Finn and Frankie walked through the front door of the bungalow. Frankie broke off from him, no doubt looking for Lo. Music was playing from the kitchen, so Finn followed the sound, along with the scent of something enticingly spicy on the air.

Brie was standing in front of the stove, hips swaying, as she stirred a sauce simmering in a pot. He watched her for a second, eyes trained on her ass. She was wearing yoga pants again. Those things were going to be the death of him.

But what a way to go.

As much as he liked watching her move, he needed her under his hands. Crossing the space, he came up behind her, his hands settling on her hips before wrapping around her. She didn't jump, wasn't startled at his sudden appearance in the slightest.

Instead she hummed a *hello* as she pressed back into him, her head stretching to the side and giving him ample access to her neck. He took the invitation, kissing his way up her throat and to her ear.

"Hello. God, you smell amazing. Food smells pretty good, too."

She turned and looked over her shoulder. "Flatterer," she whispered right before he caught her mouth in a kiss.

His tongue pushed past her lips and his hold on her waist tightened. It was a good moment or two before he finally ended the kiss and pulled back, Brie just a little bit breathless.

She shook her head at him, cheeks a bright pink, before she turned back to the stove. "If you don't stop that I'm going to burn dinner."

"What are you making?"

"My mother's chicken enchiladas…I made the tortillas from scratch and everything. I figured what with all of your hard work this week, you earned them."

"Is that so? What else have I earned?" One of his hands moved up and he cupped her breast through her shirt, squeezing lightly.

She sucked in a small gasp of air. "That hasn't been decided yet. The night's still young, possibilities are endless."

"That they are." He dropped his hand from her breast, kissing her neck one last time before he let go of her and took a step back. "You want a drink? Might as well get to my bartender duties."

"That you should. Corona and limes are in the fridge."

"Excellent choice."

Finn grabbed two beers and a lime from the fridge, purposely brushing up against Brie as he moved to the cutting board on the counter. A moment later, she brushed up against him as she grabbed the bowl of grated cheese before moving away. She just so happened to be standing right next to the drawer in front of the bottle opener. He had one on his key chain, but where was the fun in that?

They continued on back and forth until Finn was handing her a beer. They tapped the necks together before they both tipped their heads back and drank.

"Thank you," she said as she set the bottle on the counter and went back to setting up what looked like an assembly line of ingredients.

"Can I help you do anything?"

"You can set the table."

Finn grinned as set his own bottle down, sidling up behind her. As the plates were all stacked above her head, they were apparently continuing on with their little game. A game that Finn absolutely loved to play.

* * *

"Holy hell, those were phenomenal." Finn tossed his napkin onto his empty plate. He'd had two helpings, and could totally go for three if he didn't plan on moving for the rest of the night.

But he did plan on moving. A lot of moving.

"I'm glad you enjoyed them." Brie ran her fingers down the neck of her bottle of beer before wrapping those fingers around the base and lifting it to her lips.

"*Enjoyed* isn't exactly the word I'd use. You've ruined me for chicken enchiladas, Brie. Actually, I think you've ruined me for Mexican food all together."

"That's high praise."

"It's the truth." He leaned back in his chair, his focus on her face. He was becoming accustomed to eating his meals with her. It would be an understatement to say that he very much enjoyed her sitting across the table from him. It was a phenomenal experience. Something else she'd ruined him for.

She'd ruined him for a lot of things.

"Well, thank you." She pushed her chair back, making a grab for his plate, but he pulled it away.

"You are not cleaning up tonight." He shook his head as he stood up.

"Finn, come on."

"No, you come on. You just cooked me the best Mexican food I've ever had in my life. I can clean up." He walked around the table, taking the plate from her hand before he headed for the kitchen.

"Well, then what am I supposed to do?"

"You can play bartender if you want. Limes are already cut."

"Deal."

Brie got both of them fresh beers and Finn cleared the table. While he loaded the dishwasher and put all of the food away, she leaned back against the counter, sipping her Corona as she told him about her second lunch date with the girls.

"I met Beth today. She was delightful."

"She is indeed. Her kids are great, too. If you meet Penny, be prepared to be wrapped around her tiny finger."

"Noted."

Finn shut the dishwasher and started it, grabbing his own beer from the counter and leaning back. "So by my count, you've had two dates with the girls and none with me."

"Um, I'm sorry, you're the one who disqualifies everything we do as a date."

"Because they aren't dates. I need to one, pick you up"—he held up his thumb—"two, bring you chocolates or flowers"—he held up his pointer finger—"what is your favorite flower by the way?"

"Daisies," she said on a laugh.

"OK, so I bring you daisies." He nodded as his middle finger came up to join his pointer and thumb. "Three, I need to take you to dinner somewhere without any of my friends or family around"—his ring finger popped up—"four, I need to stare at you across a candlelit table, where we drink wine that has been marked *way* up"—his pinky came up, all five of his fingers in the air—"and five, we need to stand on the front porch while I kiss you, and I hope for an invitation to stay the night."

"Well, why haven't you asked me yet?"

"What are you doing next Saturday?"

"Hmm, let me check my busy, busy schedule. Oh wait, I'm free."

"Are you sassing me?" Finn moved across the kitchen until he was in front of her. He pulled the beer bottle from her hands, before he set his and hers down on the counter. And then he was closing all of the distance between them, hands on either side of her, caging her in against the counter.

"I am."

"You're the one making friends left and right all over town."

"Weren't you the one telling me to make friends?" She placed her palms on his chest, the warmth of her hands coming through his shirt.

"I do remember saying that at one point. But that was before I had you all to myself for extended amounts of time. Turns out, I don't like sharing."

"Well, as you're working at the Sheep tomorrow night, technically girls' night isn't taking away from our regularly scheduled programming."

"That is true." His hands moved from the counter and to her hips, pushing up under the fabric of her shirt. "Well, I have another night I'd like to book you for."

"What's that?"

"Three Saturdays from tomorrow, the second weekend in March, there's a charity dinner. There's this kid, well, he's nineteen now, so maybe *kid* isn't the right descriptor. Anyway, his name is Dale Rigels. He had brain cancer two years ago. Totally in remission now, clean bill of health."

"Oh good." The worry that had shown in her eyes a second ago faded.

"Well, they're doing a charity dinner and live concert in his honor. Proceeds go to the hospital to help out other kids in the county affected by life-threatening diseases. And I was wondering if you would go with me."

"You sure you're still going to want me around in three weeks? You could get sick of me." And now her eyes lit up with humor. Finn was sidetracked for a moment at the sudden influx of gold.

"I'd bet good money that I won't." His head moved down, his lips hovering just above hers.

"Then yes," she whispered.

He closed the remaining space, his mouth covering hers. God he loved the taste of her. Loved the way her hands moved up and around his neck, fingers delving into his hair. Loved the way her breasts pressed against his chest.

Yeah, he wasn't getting sick of her anytime soon.

* * *

Saturday night was the first time Brie had been with *all* of the girls: Paige, Grace, Mel, Hannah, Harper, Beth, and Meredith (Finn's cousin). If she hadn't been around all of them in much smaller groups, she might've been slightly intimidated.

They were all seated around a round table in the corner of Caliente's. It was a good thing that Brie liked Mexican food. Plus she got steak tacos and they were all drinking margaritas (except for Beth), so it was different enough from her meal the previous night.

The next two hours were filled with good conversation, a lot of laughs, and a number of refills on margaritas. Brie was on her third when the tequila started to kick in and she started talking…about everything. The more she talked the more she felt a weight lifting off of her shoulders.

Sure, she had Finn to talk to, and she was opening up to him more and more. But there was something about sitting with that group of women, talking freely, and with no judgment that was freeing. By the end of the dinner everyone had promised to lend a hand in helping clear out the museum of stuff in Bethelda Grimshaw's house.

"And I can pay you guys in wine," Brie promised. "Well, except you." She looked to Beth.

"Hey, I will gladly take an unopened bottle and crack it open in seven months."

"Deal."

It was then that Brie broached the pink elephant that had been sitting at the table. The topic of Finn had been hedged around. Brie had mentioned him when it came to helping her at the house, catching a few raised eyebrows, but nobody pressed.

The thing was, she needed to talk about it. Talk about what was going on with someone. Her biggest confidant in Mirabelle *was* Finn. So she couldn't exactly talk to Finn *about* Finn. And she still hadn't told her parents about this little trip down south, not that Finn would be brought up there, either.

Hey, Mom, let me tell you about this guy I met who I'm currently having mind-blowing sex with.

That conversation would *not* be happening. No, every time

she talked to her parents she artfully avoided what was going on. She told them about where she was with her thesis, that she'd adopted a cat (she even sent them pictures of Lo from when the cat was being particularly snuggly), and told them about the show she and Finn had started watching on Netflix...she just left out the part about Finn.

As for her friends back home, that communication had pretty much just been texts.

Lyndsey was currently dealing with a newborn baby in between teaching that semester. Brie's other friend Ashlynn was planning her wedding for the summer. And Lauren was packing up her life to move across the country to start a new job in San Francisco. Everyone was dealing with their own lives.

There was also the fact that anytime that would've been open for a phone call—the evenings and weekends—was now being taken up spending time with Finn. Brie had no complaints about that, either. She wasn't much of a phone talker anyway. She liked the face-to-face interaction, seeing reactions, feeling the mood.

Besides all of that, none of her friends back home knew Finn. None of them had met him. Sure they could give insight on men in general, but not *that* man. So now she was sitting at a table, in a little Mexican restaurant, with a table full of women who could provide insight.

She was diving in. "So about this charity dinner in three weeks...I have a date, but no dress."

"And who is the date with?" Grace pressed, clearly already knowing the answer.

Brie hesitated, filling the moment by taking a sip of her margarita. "Finn."

"*Finally.*" Harper drug out the word like it had been killing her not to ask about the man in question. "Are we now allowed to talk about what's going on there?"

"For as long as I'm in town, we're seeing each other."

"I made that deal once," Hannah said.

"And how did that turn out for you?" Brie asked before she took another sip from her glass.

Hannah's mouth formed a bit of a smirk. "I married him."

Brie choked, setting her glass on the table as she grabbed a napkin and coughed into it.

Grace reached over, patting Brie on the back. "To be fair, the second Hannah came back into town there was no chance in hell Shep was letting her leave unless he was with her."

"This is very true," Meredith agreed. "My cousin pined for Hannah for thirteen long years."

"Also, true," Mel said before she took a sip and set her glass on the table.

"So, OK, what does *seeing Finn* entail?" Paige rested her elbows on the table as she leaned in closer.

"Well, it only really started last Friday, he came over to help me with my heating issue."

"Is that a euphemism for sex?" Harper asked.

A burst of laughter escaped Brie's chest. "No, the HVAC unit went out and I couldn't get the fireplaces started."

"Oh." Harper's mouth moved to the side in a pout of disappointment.

"He did stay the night though."

"Oh?" The pout disappeared and her eyes went wide.

"We spent the weekend together. And then after dinner at his parents' house on Sunday, he took me over to his house—"

Brie stopped talking as every woman at the table reacted to those words, looking stunned. "What?"

"He took you to his house?" Grace asked.

"Yeah."

"And did you guys stay the night there?" This question from Beth. "Both of you?"

"Yes."

"Wow." Meredith leaned back in her chair, looking at Brie in amazement.

"What?"

"Brie, Finn has been back in Mirabelle for three years. Ever since he graduated." Hannah lifted her hand in the air, holding three fingers up for emphasis. "He's owned that house for almost that long. He's never once brought a girl home with him."

And now it was Brie's turn to be stunned. That would mean Finn hadn't carried any other woman up those stairs and to his bedroom…that would mean Finn hadn't had another woman in his bed…or had spare toothbrushes laying around for his one-night stands.

"You're serious? Never?"

"Never." Hannah shook her head. "He'd break one of his rules if he did that."

"He has rules? Why?"

"Well, let's just leave it at he had his heart broken once, and this is how he deals with it."

"You mean Rebecca?"

"Yes. You know about Rebecca?" Harper asked, surprised.

"Yes. He'd told me he didn't do relationships and I wanted to know why."

"All right, that's beyond interesting that he told you about that. But moving on, yes he has rules, and you've broken all of them," Grace said as she gave Brie an admiring and approving look.

"What are they?"

The women all gave each other quick glances, before Harper shrugged her shoulders. "It isn't like they're exactly secrets. Especially as Finn has prescribed by them pretty much since he moved back."

"True." Hannah nodded. "First is no locals."

"Oh, that one I knew. He mentioned it to me when he said he didn't do relationships. The thing is, I'm not a local."

"But you're in town indefinitely," Paige said.

"Yes, but I'm not *staying* in Mirabelle." It wasn't the first time Brie had said that, hell it wasn't even the twenty-first time. Why did she feel the need to keep saying it like a mantra?

"Ladies? Consensus?" Grace looked around the table.

"Sorry, honey, I'd say you qualify." Harper gave a commiserating head tilt.

"Me too." Paige agreed.

"Me three." Mel nodded.

"And that's because the whole point of his *no locals* rule is so that he doesn't run into them after he…" Hannah trailed off, suddenly looking uncomfortable.

"He sleeps with them? Don't worry. No need to hedge. I know what I'm dealing with there."

"Yes, after he sleeps with them. And since he can run into you, it counts."

"OK, I'll give it to you." Brie put her hands in the air in a conceding gesture. "What's his next rule?"

"No spending the night. Which is why he never brought

girls to his house…until you, apparently. If he did, then *he* couldn't exactly leave and he isn't that big of an ass to kick someone out after."

"Just big enough to walk out on them while they're sleeping." The words were out of Brie's mouth before she could stop herself. *Damn*. She really needed to remember that loose lips sink ships.

"Is that why things were weird with the two of you in the beginning?" Harper asked. "You two…and then he…?"

Well, she was apparently *in* this conversation. No backing out now. "Yes."

"Well, as he's used *all* of his rules on you, I don't feel badly in the slightest that we are telling you about them." Harper made a sassy pout with her mouth this time. "His last rule is no repeats."

"He actually told me that rule, too." And they'd broken it. Over and over and over again. In fact, the last time had been before he'd dropped her off at dinner. He'd backed her against the wall, pulled her legs around his waist, and…

"So for almost three years he's lived by those rules," Hannah said, bringing Brie back to the moment. "And you broke them in a little over a week."

"Bravo." Grace held her margarita glass in the air in a salute to Brie before she took a drink.

Brie wasn't exactly sure how she felt about those three rules, but she held her own glass in the air and took a sip. It wasn't that she was upset by them, because she wasn't. Well, not exactly. She couldn't blame him for anything he did in the past. Just like she couldn't get upset for anything that happened in the future.

Because she wasn't the future. She was the present, which was what she would be until she became the past, and that was all she'd asked for when she walked into that bar.

"To be fair to him, that first night we spent together was the day of Bethelda's funeral, and I maybe wanted a bit of a distraction. He had absolutely no idea why I was upset, but he provided that distraction." *With gusto.*

"Of course he did." Paige shook her head as she smiled.

"That wasn't exactly something I was accustomed to doing, picking up a guy at a bar. But then I met him, and he made me forget what I was dealing with…" She trailed off, suddenly feeling a little unsure of herself and where this conversation was going. It was like the plug had been pulled and now everything was spilling out.

"Sweetie." Grace reached over and touched Brie's hand. "It's OK, you don't need to explain yourself."

"Seriously, there is no judgment at this table," Harper agreed. "My husband is the result of a one-night stand, one in which I, too, was trying to forget something."

"What was that?"

"My fiancé called off our wedding three months before the day we were supposed to be married. I of course didn't want to be here on that weekend. So I went up to Nashville to stay with my aunt. Met him at a bar…and now we're married."

Wow…that was two parallels from Brie and Finn's current situation, and both of those parallels had included marriage for the couples in question.

Not that Brie was marrying Finn. That was ridiculous. Where in the world had that thought even come from? Good Lord how much had she drank?

She reached across the table, grabbing the almost full glass of water and taking a long drink of it.

"So dresses for the charity dinner." Brie changed the subject, going *way* back to the beginning of that particular conversation.

None of the girls commented on said subject change and went with it, telling Brie they hadn't gotten dresses, either.

"Since I have so many, I was thinking about wearing one of the bridesmaids' dresses I have," Mel said.

"See, you *can* wear them again." Grace laughed.

"You guys want to scrounge through our closets and see what we have? We could do a girls' night again next week. Have a fashion show at someone's house." Paige looked around the table for agreement.

"I can't on Saturday. Finn is taking me out somewhere."

"Oh really?" Harper raised one of her eyebrows high. "How fascinating. What about a Friday fashion show then?"

"That works for me."

"Me too."

"Perfect." Grace nodded. "And if we can't find anything in our closets, maybe a trip up to Tallahassee will need to be booked."

"Agreed." Everyone nodded.

"Yeah, agreed," Brie said as she downed more of her water.

She'd only been half listening to the conversation, her mind still reeling from that ridiculous marriage thought…and the image she'd gotten in her head of walking down the aisle of St. Sebastian's, Finn at the altar wearing a tux.

Yeah, she'd definitely had *way* too much to drink.

Chapter Nineteen

Surprise Yourself

The Sleepy Sheep was pretty busy that Saturday night. There were three bartenders behind the bar: Finn, Shep, and Reggie. All of them were keeping up a constant pace of refilling drinks and clearing away the empty ones.

But even with how busy they were, Finn was aware of every single person who walked through that front door. Why? Because he was waiting for Brie.

He thought about another night when he'd watched that door like a hawk, the second night she'd been in Mirabelle, the night she'd come back to get a drink and see him. Unlike that night he *knew* she'd be walking through that door…knew he'd be going home with her.

Home, to his house. They hadn't spent much time there that week, but they'd been there enough for him to realize just how much he liked her there. An image from the other day popped into his head, one of Brie asleep in his bed, hair spread across the pillow. Then he saw her the following morning, standing by the windows as the sun rose over the water, a steaming cup of coffee in her hands, wearing nothing besides one of his T-shirts. And then them in the shower, steam billowing around them as he moved inside of her.

Yeah, he really liked her in his house and he was looking forward to sleeping in with her the following morning. Looking forward to lingering over coffee before making breakfast together.

Very much looking forward to it. Not all that surprising as he enjoyed every minute he spent with her.

"How's it going?" Shep asked as he moved into the space text to Finn, helping him stack clean glasses.

"Fine. Just trying to keep up with everyone."

"Not what I was talking about. I meant with Brie."

Finn paused in his cup stacking for a moment. "It's good. Really good. Actually, I wanted to talk to you about something."

"What's that?"

"I'm going to cut back on taking shifts here for a bit."

"How long is a bit?"

Finn took a deep breath before he turned to his brother. "For the next month or two."

"Or for as long as Brie is in town?"

"Yeah." Finn returned his attention back to the glasses.

"OK." There was a moment of silence before Shep spoke again. "You know, it's been a while since I've seen you like this."

"Like what?"

"Happy."

Finn looked over at his brother in surprise. "I've been happy."

"Hmm." Shep shook his head. "Not like *that* you haven't.

And it's more than the look of happiness a man gets when he's having regular sex. It's the look a man gets when he's having regular sex with a woman he cares about. Cares *a lot* about."

"I like her."

"I've seen that. Up close and personal. Our friends over there haven't." Shep tilted his head to the side of the bar where Brendan, Jax, Bennett, Liam, and Tripp sat. "You know everyone is going to be watching the two of you tonight like you're a tiger exhibit at the zoo. Girls included."

"Oh, of that I have no doubt." That was the norm when it came to anyone in their group seeing someone. The new person always had to be vetted and approved of if they were going to be sticking around.

But Brie *wasn't* sticking around. A fact that Finn was ignoring more and more as the days went by.

"It's going to be an entertaining night," Shep said as the front door opened and the group of girls in question all trailed in.

Brie was right there in the middle, looking beyond beautiful in a pair of jeans and her black leather jacket. Her cheeks were slightly pink, perhaps a result of alcohol or the cold air outside, or both. She was too far away for him to see her eyes, but he knew beyond a shadow of a doubt that they were gold.

"A *really* entertaining night." Shep clapped his hand down on Finn's shoulder before he moved off.

* * *

Brie stopped walking as all of the girls headed off for a group of empty tables in the corner. The reason she stopped walking?

Because Finn's eyes had met hers and she forgot *how* to walk.

OK, maybe she didn't *forget* how to walk. She just chose to stop because he was walking across the room to her and she wanted a moment with him. A moment with him surrounded by a room of people. All of her doubts and worries and concerning thoughts from the evening were suddenly gone. He made everything else disappear.

How long was it until they got to leave again?

"Hi." He didn't hesitate for a second, lifting his hand to the back of her head and pulling her in for a kiss.

"Hi," she whispered against his lips.

"The girls all treating you well?"

Brie turned to look at the group to which Finn was referring. They were all standing around the table, watching them. But the second she looked over they started moving again, pulling their gaze and sitting down.

"Safe to say all of them know what's going on?" he asked as he reached up and pushed a strand of her hair back and behind her ear.

"You *might've* come up in conversation."

He laughed, the sound of it rich and real, warming her up from the inside out. Then again, he always made her feel warm.

"On a scale of one to ten, how drunk are you right now?"

"One being I've only been drinking water, and ten being I'm about to black out?"

"That's a good rating," he said with a nod.

"I'm about a five. Five and a half. Those ladies sure know how to drink their margaritas."

"They do indeed. But it looks like you're keeping up."

"By the skin of my teeth."

He laughed again and it took everything in her not to push herself up against him. She wanted *all* of the warmth he could provide.

"Come on." He grabbed her hand, pulling it to his lips and placing a kiss on her knuckles before he turned and started leading her to the table where everyone was sitting and watching them with the biggest freaking smirks Brie had ever seen in her life.

"Ladies, what would everyone like to drink?" Finn asked as he pulled the chair out for Brie and then pushed it back in when she sat,

"How about something with more tequila?" Paige requested.

"I can do that. And a cranberry and ginger ale for you?" he asked Beth.

"You know it."

"I'll be right back." He squeezed Brie's shoulders gently before he turned and headed back for the bar.

"Well that was fascinating." Mel's smile got even bigger.

"Beyond fascinating," Grace agreed.

Brie looked over her shoulder, too, watching as Finn walked away. As he went behind the counter her eyes went to the row of men who were all looking over at their table. She'd met—or seen—most of them at one point except for the two at the end with dark brown hair. Both were beyond attractive with a decent amount of scruff growing on their strong jaws, but Brie's focus stayed on the one at the far end.

"Holy shit," she whispered.

"What?" Meredith asked, and out of the corner of Brie's eye she saw the woman turn and look, too.

"That…that's Liam James."

Brie loved music of all genres and decades, country music being one of them. Liam James had been around for years, Brie liking him when he was doing small concerts for less than two thousand audience goers. He was now selling out arenas as the headliner for twenty thousand. He'd made it big a couple of years back with his hit song "Forever," which just so happened to be one of Brie's favorite songs ever.

A collective laugh moved around the table and Brie turned back to the women.

"What?"

"My one-night stand that ended in marriage?" Harper said, grinning. "Liam's my husband."

"Holy. Shit." Brie couldn't help but repeat the words. *Violet eyes and the lips of a goddess*—she heard the lyrics in her head— *I knew I'd want more than just one kiss.* "The song 'Forever' is about you."

"It is." She nodded.

"My mind has just been sufficiently blown."

"Finn didn't tell you about Liam?" Hannah asked. "Or that Liam's brother, who we're also friends with, *and* who Paige's best friend is married to, is Logan James? Who plays for the Jacksonville Stampede?" She gestured to the TV behind them.

"No." She shook her head. Which was interesting as the second night she'd come to the bar they'd watched a Jacksonville Stampede game and he'd explained the rules of hockey. They'd also had on many games in the background while he helped her pack up stuff at Bethelda's house.

He didn't use other people's fame—fame of his friends—to impress people. That wasn't exactly the usual. Most guys she'd dated would've totally used that as a pickup. But he'd just used all of his own natural charm.

And damn did he have a lot of charm. Charm she really needed to distract herself from at the moment. Luckily for her there was a readily available topic, one that she was more than interested in.

"OK." Brie leaned over the table as she looked at Harper. "I'm going to need to hear this whole story from the beginning. I love that song and want to know as much as you'll tell me about the conception of it."

"So there I was, sad, depressed, and alone," Harper started. "When this weirdo with a neck tattoo that read *Bubba* walked up and started hitting on me…"

Brie settled in, beyond excited as she listened to Harper and Liam's story. Beyond happy that she was surrounded by a group of wonderful women who wanted her at that table. Beyond thrilled that Finn was just a few yards away from her.

* * *

The crowd at the Sleepy Sheep had started to lessen once the Stampede game finished. Shep said he could handle closing with Reggie if Finn would just drop Hannah off at the inn. It was close to eleven when Brie and Finn walked in the front door of his house. Well, he walked, Brie stumbled a little bit. He grabbed on to her waist, steadying her, and she turned to him, laughing as she wrapped her arms around his neck.

She wasn't terribly drunk; the drinks she'd had at the Sheep had only bumped her up by a point. She'd been pretty diligent about keeping up with drinking water.

"You keep catching me," she whispered against his mouth.

"I can't very well let you fall." He kissed her before he pulled back enough to look into her face. Something flickered in her gold eyes, something he couldn't quite put his finger on. "What?"

"I just like you, that's all."

"That's all?" He grinned.

"Mmm hmm. Now go let Frankie out"—she said of the dog who was now circling their legs—"so I can show you just how much I like you."

"Yes, ma'am." He pulled away from her and headed back to the front door while she moved farther into the house.

It was less than two minutes later when he and Frankie walked back inside to hear music playing from the living room. They headed down the hallway to find Brie dancing around the room. She'd taken off her shoes and socks and was now barefoot, her jacket on the sofa and her long hair swaying around her as she moved.

"Come dance with me," she said as she lifted her arms above her head, showing a strip of her stomach as her shirt rose up.

Finn tossed his jacket next to Brie's before he kicked off his boots and pulled off his socks. Then he crossed over to her, pulling her into his arms. They moved with each other easily, like they'd done this a thousand times. Maybe it was because they were just so used to each other's bodies. Either way, it might've been the best foreplay of his life.

The simple caress of her palm moving over his chest. How her hair wrapped around his forearm, tickling his skin. Then there was her mouth at his ear, slightly breathless. She laughed when he spun her in a circle before pulling her back against his chest. Her ass pressed into his erection as she continued to move her hips.

He had no idea if they danced to one song or five. He stopped paying attention to the music, following her lead as they moved. Not caring about anything but her. When he reached his max he pulled her up into his arms and carried her upstairs to his bed.

Brie let him take charge right up until the moment he was about to push inside of her. She shook her head. "I want to be on top."

A request he wasn't going to deny, not for a second. He rolled them, holding on to her hips. Once she was straddling him she lifted up, wrapping her hand around his cock and lining him up with her entrance. Then she was slowly lowering herself down, hands on his chest as her entire body arched back.

He watched her move over him, watched her breasts bounce, watched the flush that crept up her chest and her neck, darkening as she got closer and closer to her orgasm. He listened to her moans and cries of pleasure. Felt her body flex under his hands, felt her core pulse around his cock as she came.

She was magnificent. She was everything…but she wasn't his.

* * *

Sunday started off pretty low key with Brie and Finn sleeping in. She had a slight headache from all the drinking the night before, but nothing that a couple of Advil and a strong cup of coffee wouldn't fix.

After Mass with his family, they picked up Frankie and

headed to the bungalow to have brunch with Lo. Once everyone had full bellies, it was time to tackle another project around the house. Brie decided that Sunday would be Bethelda's closet.

She tried to go through everything section by section. The unworn shoes—which comprised about half of the hundred or so boxes, all with price tags still on—were all taken to the office to be put on eBay. The used ones, which were also in pretty excellent condition, Brie donated to the Triple C. It was the same with the clothes, new or used; they were put in bags and loaded in Finn's truck.

That was until she got to the very back corner of the closet to find black garment bags hanging up. She only opened a few, finding dresses with sequins, taffeta, organza, silk, satin, and some truly eye-popping colors.

"Leave these here," she told Finn as he left with an armful of bags.

She pulled her phone out of her back pocket and snapped a picture. She sent a group text to the girls saying: *Jackpot. That is if you don't mind wearing a dress of Bethelda's.*

It was Paige who responded with, *I think showing up in some of Bethelda's dresses would be poetic justice in a way. Maybe that's just me, though.*

Nope. I agree, Grace responded.

Friday Fashion show @ Bethelda's @ 6:30, Hannah typed out.

Well, that's going to be an interesting night, Mel said, sending a wineglass emoji.

No doubt about that, Harper texted, adding about ten wineglass emojis.

Don't worry, I'll be the sober one taking pictures of this drunk fashion show, Beth told the group.

Perfect, Meredith said. *I'll bring pizza. Let me know topping requests.*

Brie felt eyes on her and looked up to find Finn in the doorway of the closet, leaning against the door frame and grinning.

"What? What's with that smile?"

He pushed off the frame and crossed the few steps to her. "You smile and I can't help but smile, too."

"The girls were just being funny."

"Oh were they?" He reached up to her chin, pushing up as he leaned down and kissed her. "And what were they being funny about?"

"They're coming over on Friday, for drinking and dress-trying-on for the dinner thing."

"Another night of you drinking with the girls. I'd say I'm more than a little jealous that they get your Friday night, but as I will no doubt benefit greatly once they leave, I'm not going to complain."

She put her hands on his chest, moving her palms up and out. "Are you saying you enjoyed last night?"

"Very, very much."

"I did, too." She stretched up for another kiss and he didn't hesitate to give it to her.

"You don't stop that and we're going to have to take a break so I can have you."

"Well as the closet is empty besides those dress bags, I'd say you deserve a break."

The sentence was barely out of her mouth before he was bending down and throwing her over his shoulder in a fireman's hold.

"Oh my gosh, Finn! I can walk."

"This is faster," he said as he turned around and carried her to the air mattress in the den. And really, what was the point in arguing? There was something so beyond sexy about the ease with which the man could pick her up and carry her off to whatever flat surface he wanted to take her on.

No point in arguing at all.

* * *

The week that followed was fairly similar to the previous week. Brie would wake up next to Finn (either in her bed or his), they'd have breakfast with Lo and Frankie (always at the bungalow), Brie would work on her thesis until lunch with Finn, and then when he left she'd work on clearing something out.

One thing that did change was *what* she was clearing out. There were few things left in that house that were what she'd deemed "extra" or "trivial." And she didn't use the word *trivial* lightly; it was just that she really didn't believe she was going to discover anything from her past in Bethelda's bear collection. Which had also all been packed up and sold on eBay.

And yes, just about every buyer had a bear-themed name: BreakingTheSoundBearer, BearNecessities, BadNewsBears13, ConanTheBarBearian, BearFootMama69, GrandeBearista, ThreadBear72, and—Brie's personal favorite—BearItAll, who believed that bears were not made to be clothed and should be naked as God intended.

No freaking joke.

Anyway, once all of those things had been cleared out, Brie had to move on to some of the more questionable items. As there were so many dish sets she decided to start there. There was also the question of where all the furniture had come from. And who better to look over those things than Ella?

Brie and Finn cooked dinner on Thursday night for Ella and Faye; Nate senior didn't come as he was working at the Sheep that night. While the manicotti finished baking, Brie showed Ella around the house.

"The only rug that was Petunia's is the oriental one in the den; the rest of these are ones that Bethelda acquired. That"— Ella pointed to the grandfather clock that Finn had saved her from crashing into—"was a thirtieth-anniversary gift from Harold. But those clocks"—Ella nodded to the display on the wall—"were probably also all Bethelda's. That was Harold's." Ella waved to the old record player in the corner. "That was your great-great-grandmother's," she said of one of the china cabinets in the dining room.

And so went the evening, Ella telling Brie everything that had been her grandparents', or Bethelda's when she'd been growing up. The dish sets and tea sets were all tackled after dinner, Ella pointing out just three of the thirty-five tea sets that had been Petunia's, and only one of the seven displayed dish sets that had been Harold and Petunia's wedding dishes.

Brie ended up spending all of Friday taking pictures, looking the sets up online and seeing how much they ran for, and posting each one on eBay. Once she was done with that, she packed everything up that she wasn't keeping and labeled all of the boxes so that when they sold, she knew exactly what was what.

Out of all of those particular possessions, the only thing Brie kept that hadn't been Petunia's was a royal blue tea set with delicately painted emerald-green leaves. She didn't know why, but she just couldn't bring herself to get rid of it. So she followed her instinct and set it aside.

When Finn got off of work, he stopped by the house to spend time with Brie before he went out and got a burger with Tripp and Liam. It was Finn who answered the door when Beth, Hannah, and Harper rang the doorbell, "Wake Me Up Before You Go-Go" filling the house.

"Hello, ladies," Brie heard him say as she walked through the dining room and toward the front of the house.

"Is that doorbell seriously George Michael singing?" Harper's voice floated down the hallway.

"It is indeed."

"I feel like I've stepped into a parallel universe," Hannah said as she walked into the living room.

"Oh, you just wait, dear sister. You. Just. Wait."

"Holy shit," Beth whispered under her breath as she looked around at all of the stuff. "How much have you gotten rid of already?"

Brie looked to Finn, tilting her head to the side. "You think it's a quarter?"

"If that. But hey, you guys are going to work on the rest of those dresses and the wine tonight. So that's gonna help," he said as he pointed to the dining room where the wine cabinet doors were opened.

He'd taken the time while he was there to pull a few bottles of red forward that he thought might be good selections, and he'd also stuck a good assortment of white in the refrigerator.

"Holy. Shit." Beth repeated the words as she looked at the wine cabinet. "There might've been no love lost between Bethelda and me, but I *have* to admire that wine selection."

"It is rather impressive, isn't it?" Brie asked.

"It is indeed."

"I should get going." Finn moved over to Brie, leaning down and kissing her lips before he pulled away. "Have fun tonight." He grinned and she knew without a doubt just how much fun he hoped she had.

"You too. I'll see you later."

"Later." He nodded to all of the other ladies just as George started singing again. "I'll let them in."

Brie turned back to the other three women in the room, three women who all had their eyes on her. They were the kind of assessing looks that made her feel like she was under a magnifying glass.

"Wine?" She didn't wait for any one's answer before she turned around and headed for the kitchen.

The more time she spent with Finn, the less she wanted anyone looking closely at it...probably because she was avoiding looking too closely at it. That was because it was starting to get too hard to look too closely at it.

* * *

When all of the girls got there they wanted a tour of the house, wanted to see the sheer magnitude of belongings Bethelda had. None of them could believe it. When Paige got there, she stared at her painting hanging above Bethelda's bed, sipping on her glass of wine with the most confused expression on her face.

"I just don't understand," she said, and shook her head. "That woman did not like me, and yet, she bought one of my paintings? How does that make any sense at all?"

"Paige, as I'm learning when it comes to Bethelda, nothing makes sense. *Nothing.*"

Once they'd eaten all of the pizza—one thin crust mushroom, one vegetables and sausage, and one three cheese with tomatoes—they could, they opened another bottle of wine and moved into the living room with the butterscotch cookies Grace had brought.

They used this space for the runway, the lighting good and there was more room. Plus it was cold and Finn had started the fire, and Frankie and Lo were spread out in front of it sleeping.

Once Brie had sent the picture of the dress bags, everyone wanted to see what those options were before crawling through closets or climbing into attics. And they had a lot to choose from, too. Seventeen dresses in sizes ranging from two to fourteen.

Paige's was royal blue with a strapless top made of sequins and a knee-length blue taffeta skirt. Grace picked a red polka dot number that looked like it would be appropriate for a flamenco dancer. Mel's was a yellow lace dress that went down to the floor with a rather impressive slit up the side. Hannah's was an emerald-green, silk, mermaid dress.

Harper chose a dress that was also floor length and covered with purple sequins. With the right altering (which everyone was going to need to do to their dresses anyway) it was going to look perfect on all of her curves. Beth picked a flowy hot pink dress with a silver, sparkly halter. While Meredith went with a one-shoulder baby-pink dress made of shiny satin.

"OK, you're up," Harper said as she looked between the remaining options. "I want to see you in this one. Mainly because if it had been my size I would've picked it for myself. Plus it's pretty."

The dress was two pieces, a black lace top and a long black skirt. It actually was the dress Brie had her eyes on from the start.

"You know? I'm surprised that these dresses are so pretty, and fun, and have never actually been worn before," Mel said as she grabbed her wineglass.

"I'm not." Brie shook her head as she moved her hand in a circle, indicating the house. "Bethelda liked to buy nice things and then not use most of them. That's the theme of her life."

"Clearly. Now go try the dress on." Harper thrust it toward her.

Brie grabbed it and headed for the bathroom. She pulled off her jeans and sweater before she shimmied into the skirt of the dress and struggled for a few moments to get the invisible zipper up. Brie studied the top for a second and realized a bra was useless, so she pulled that off, too. It had a solid, corseted piece underneath the lace with a solid strap at the back. She slid her arms into the long sleeves, the black lace on her skin with no barrier, before she reached around and snapped the strap together.

Taking just a second to look at herself in the mirror, Brie adjusted everything into place. The skirt was high-waisted, the top cropped, and there was a good two inches of skin showing. It was just the right amount of sexy.

She took a moment to fiddle with her hair before she stepped back out and into the living room.

"I was right," Harper said. "That's the perfect dress."

"It fits you like a glove." Mel got up from her seat and moved closer.

"You don't need to get a thing altered." Grace shook her head.

"Holy crap, you look awesome." Paige tilted her head to the side, studying Brie. "You're going to rock that dress."

"We are all going to rock these dresses," Meredith said just a tad bit tipsily. "I just need to find a date, because I refuse, *refuse* to go stag."

"What about Reggie?" Hannah asked, referring to the caramel-skinned, sky-blue-eyed bartender Brie had met the other night. "I'm sure he doesn't have a date. You should ask him."

"He works at the bar and is about six years younger than me." Meredith frowned.

"And?" Beth waved her hand in the air. "He also kept looking at you from across the bar last Saturday night. And as I was the only one not drinking, I was *way* more observant than anyone else."

"Fact," Grace agreed.

"I-I will need to think on this," Meredith said. "Brie, go take that dress off so we can drink more wine."

"Yes, ma'am." Brie grinned.

Chapter Twenty

The Death of a Bachelor

It was at four thirty on Saturday evening when Finn left the bungalow and headed home with Frankie. He gave Brie a kiss before he told her he'd be back at six to pick her up.

As Finn had asked her on this date over a week ago, she'd had plenty of time to order a new dress for the night. Sure, she could've probably made something she had down there work, but it was a special night, so she wanted a special dress.

Hair curled around her shoulders and makeup done, she reached for the dress hanging on the back of the door to the bathroom. It was a silvery purple, satin, wrap dress. The sleeves went down to the middle of her forearms, the hem hit her about mid-thigh, and the V of the neck where the material met went low enough to give more than a hint of her cleavage. She paired it with a pair of black heels and her leather jacket.

It didn't matter how much time Brie had spent with Finn over the last couple of weeks, when that doorbell rang, a wave of butterflies took flight in her belly. She grabbed her clutch, gave Lo a good scratch behind the ears, and headed for the front door.

Opening the door, she found Finn on the other side wearing dark gray slacks, a white button-up shirt, and a black blazer. She was about to tell him how nice he looked, but then her gaze met his sapphire eyes behind his glasses. The amazed look on his face made her forget how to talk for a second.

He spoke first. "You look beautiful."

"I…thank you. So do you."

His lips turned up. "I look beautiful?"

"Yes, you do. Men can look beautiful, too."

"Well, thank you." He took a step forward, reaching up to touch her elbows. "Now do you have more of that lipstick you're wearing in that tiny purse?"

"Yes. Why?"

"Because I'm about to kiss off what you're wearing. Come here." He pulled her in close as he lowered his mouth to hers and did precisely that.

Finn took Brie to dinner at LaBella, a high-end resort on Mirabelle Beach that boasted an upscale restaurant, too. He told her it was also the only place in town that met all of his requirements for the evening: candlelit dinner, white tablecloths, someone playing the piano in the corner, and overpriced wine.

As the hostess led them through the restaurant, his hand moved to the small of her back, sliding under her leather jacket so it rested directly on the silk. The heat from his palm seeped through the thin material, making her warm all over.

"Oh wow," Brie whispered when they got to the table.

It was in the corner by a bank of windows that looked out to the water. It was just before sunset, the sun hovering right above the horizon. Bright oranges and pinks painted the sky.

He said something to the waitress—she didn't hear exactly

what as she was so focused on the view outside of those windows—before he moved behind her, helping her pull off her jacket. He leaned in close, kissing her neck before he moved his mouth to her ear. "I figured we could enjoy our first glass of wine while we watch the sun disappear into the Gulf of Mexico."

She turned and looked at him over her shoulder. "That sounds perfect."

He kissed her lips this time before he pulled her chair out from the table and helped her sit. And then he was taking the spot across from her.

It hadn't even been ten minutes since he'd picked her up, and it was already the most romantic date she'd ever been on.

And it didn't stop there. Somehow the man managed to just make the night more and more perfect. His focus never strayed from her. He didn't get distracted by the other people coming and going. Didn't miss a word she said. Didn't for one moment make her feel like anything less than the most important person in the room.

That wasn't something she'd ever experienced before, and that right there would've made the evening perfect. But then there was the food, which just added even more perfection to the evening.

They had a fancy salad course with fried green tomatoes, goat cheese crumbles, and pickled onions. Then there were the main courses—that they shared—of steak with rosemary mashed potatoes, and oysters with biscuits. And tiramisu for dessert, which just so happened to be Brie's favorite.

When dinner was done, Finn paid the bill, helped her pull her jacket back on, and slid his hand into hers, interlocking their fingers as they walked outside. When they got to his truck, he pulled her against him, leaning down for a lingering kiss.

He tasted like the wine they'd had with their dessert.

"Thank you." She smiled against his mouth. "Dinner was perfect. Everything was perfect."

"You're welcome, Brie." And then he was kissing her again, his hands at her waist, fingers pressing into her hips.

"Finn?" His name came out breathless as she pulled back, her hands fisting on the sides of his blazer, holding on to him as she looked up into his face. "You know how you said you wanted part of the evening's agenda to include kissing me on the porch of the bungalow and hoping for me to invite you inside?"

"Yes."

"Since you already kissed me on the porch at the beginning of the date, can we just skip that part and you take me back to your place? I want to be in your bed tonight." She wanted to be surrounded by everything that was him while he made love to her.

"It would take a foolish, foolish man to say no to a request like that."

"And you aren't foolish?"

"No, not in that regard."

"Then take me home, Finn."

He pulled a sharp breath in through his nose, his chest expanding out. Something flashed in his eyes at the same moment, something deep and intense in those dark blues. His grip on her waist tightened fractionally in a flex before he loosened it.

And just that quickly, whatever it was, was gone. It was replaced by that smile of his, the easygoing one that had charmed her from the very start.

"Yes, ma'am. But I want to dance with you again."

"Deal."

He kissed her lips one last time before helping her into his truck.

When they got back to his house, Finn let Frankie out while Brie searched through her iPhone to make the perfect playlist. She wasn't sure how long he'd last before taking her upstairs, but she figured five songs would be good.

"Perfect."

Brie looked up as Finn walked into the room. "What?" she asked, plugging her phone in and starting the first song before setting it down.

"You kept your heels on." He pulled off his blazer and tossed it on the sofa next to her leather jacket, then he was crossing over to her.

The whole thing was déjà vu to the last time they'd danced in that very living room a week ago.

"I did leave them on."

He reached out, those hands of his that she loved so much sliding across the silk of her dress as he pulled her close and started to move their bodies to the slow beat of the music. "Have I told you how unbelievably beautiful you are?"

"Not in the last"—she turned toward the clock on the wall before looking back to him—"twenty minutes."

"Well, you're so beautiful I can't think straight. So beautiful that all I've cared about tonight is looking at you."

"Finn." She reached up, her hand covering his jaw as she

leaned up and pressed her mouth against his. It was a habit now, when his mouth was close enough—hell, when he was in the same building—all she wanted was to feel his lips on hers.

When she pulled away from him she saw that same intense look in his eyes that had been there in the parking lot of LaBella. But then she couldn't see his eyes anymore as he leaned in, his hand sliding to her lower back as his mouth moved to her ear.

"Dance with me, Brie."

And that was exactly what they did, *danced*. Him holding her close as they moved around the room. He made it through four of the five songs before he pulled her upstairs and un-wrapped her like she was a Christmas present.

* * *

Take me home, Finn.

Those words kept replaying in his head, over and over and over again. It had been hours since Brie had fallen asleep, thoroughly exhausted, pressed up against his side. Her head was on his chest, her breath hitting his skin and moving out with every slow, deep exhale. He stared up at the ceiling, the limited light in the room illuminating the slowly spinning ceiling fan.

Take me home, Finn.

It had been there, right there in that moment when she said *home*, that he realized he wanted his house to be more than just his. Wanted that with *her*. And just as that thought had entered his mind the reality set in. It wasn't going to happen.

She's leaving.

More words that kept repeating in his head. Words that made

his chest tighten. Words that made it hard for him to breathe. It was to the point where thinking about her leaving, thinking about not seeing her every day, not talking to her, not kissing her, not waking up next to her, caused him physical pain.

He was in love with her. How the hell had this happened to him?

He tightened his arms around her, pulling her close as he brushed his mouth across her temple. He couldn't let her go...not now, not ever. Now it was just a matter of making her realize she couldn't let *him* go, either.

He was in love with her.

* * *

Sunday morning started off nice and slow, with Brie and Finn sleeping in and then lingering over a few cups of coffee as they snuggled on his sofa. After Mass, though, was busy busy busy. Brie and Finn drove back to the bungalow to eat with Lo before the moving party got there. There were ten guys coming over with five trucks.

They hauled off all of Bethelda's bedroom furniture: bed, mattress, nightstands, armoire, two cabinets, and two dressers. They loaded up the emptied bookcases in the office, six of the china cabinets (she kept her great-great grandmother's), and rolled up the rugs upon rugs on the floor...except for the oriental one that had been Petunia's. At first it was weird for Brie walking around the house and seeing the bare hardwood floors in all of their glory.

"I don't understand why she'd cover these up." One of the guys named Preston shook his head as he looked around.

"I'm telling you right now, you aren't going to understand a lot of things when it comes to that woman." She shook her head.

"I guess not." Preston laughed.

Brie had met him, along with his husband Baxter, that afternoon. She decided they were the most adorable couple she'd ever met in her life. Something that was compounded when they showed her pictures of their two-year-old daughter Nikki, who they'd just adopted.

Brie also met Hamilton O'Bryan, Mel's little brother, and the famous Dale Rigels. Both boys—though she used that word loosely as the nineteen-year-olds were just as big as the adult men in the room—were handsome beyond all reason and almost painfully polite.

"I've heard a lot about you." Brie smiled when she shook Dale's hand.

"Hopefully good."

"All good," she confirmed with a nod.

It turned out that Finn had a really big soft spot for the young man, something she'd figured out after just a few conversations.

Dale's father had been killed in Afghanistan when he was twelve. He'd acted up and out until he was fifteen and had been taken under the wing of Bennett...along with everyone else. Brie also learned that when Dale had his battle with cancer, he'd met hockey player Logan James—Liam's brother—who became a mentor to the boy. Not only that, but Logan had paid for all of Dale's medical bills.

Just that last summer, Dale had worked with Finn at St. Francis and out on the farm. Apparently he wanted to be a veterinarian.

It was an all-in-the-family operation with this community, because if you were friends, you became family. Clearly as Brendan, Jax, Bennett, Shep, Liam, and Tripp were all part of the moving party, giving up a few hours on their Sunday to clear out what they could.

Their payment? Five bottles of wine each. Well, everyone's payment except for the two teenagers. They got to take first pick of the pile of DVDs. After that it was a free-for-all on who got what. Brie would've gladly given anyone whatever they wanted, but it was clear that when it came to owning the more personal possessions of Bethelda, they were all good.

By five o'clock all of the trucks had everything dropped off at the Triple C, and all of the guys were heading home to their families. She and Finn picked up a pizza for dinner and headed back to his house. After they ate, they both took a long, glorious soak in the bathtub.

Brie didn't know what she found more relaxing: the hot soapy water working into her sore tired muscles or Finn wrapped around her.

Definitely Finn. She could lie in that man's arms every day for the rest of her life and not get tired of it.

But that wasn't going to happen.

She knew that wasn't a reality, didn't mean she couldn't want it. At the thought of leaving him, that oh-so-familiar ache welled up in her chest. Not all that surprisingly, when she blinked her eyes, tears slid down her cheeks, disappearing into the water. She was thankful Finn was behind her and couldn't see her crying.

She needed to stay in the present…and stop thinking about after.

* * *

It was an odd thing in life that when someone wanted time to slow down, it just sped up, faster and faster.

As the days went by, every time Finn was at the bungalow, he noticed more things gone. More closets emptied. More cabinets cleared out. More things missing from the walls.

It felt odd that the more Bethelda disappeared from the house, the less he liked it. Actually, he hated it. But he tried not to focus on that, and put all of his energy in Operation Brie Falling in Love with Him.

He wasn't exactly sure where he was in that process, but he was fighting the good fight. It had been eight years since Rebecca, eight years since he'd had to work at anything beyond one night. He'd felt like he'd done pretty well with the dinner at LaBella's. But when he'd planned that, it hadn't been about wooing her, it had been about giving her a night she wouldn't forget.

Turned out it was a night he wouldn't forget as that was when he'd figured out he was in love with her. Figured out she was it for him.

Since he hadn't brought her flowers the night of the date, he had a bouquet of purple and white daisies delivered to her while he was at work one day. When he walked through the front door she'd pretty much pounced on him and he'd taken her right there up against the wall.

So that had been successful.

Some of the things he did were small. Others he wasn't sure if they were stupid or not, but he did them anyway.

On another day he kidnapped her at lunch and took her to

the Stardust Diner for fried green tomato BLTs, crispy french fries, and milk shakes. She got cookie dough while he enjoyed cookies and cream.

He left Post-it notes for her to find around the house during the day. He brought her coffee in bed. He cooked her dinner— tacos were his specialty and he added on his homemade guacamole. He also made her Owen's jambalaya, and, as she was a breakfast-for-dinner kind of girl, french toast.

He let her pick whatever she wanted when they decided to watch movies. He fixed her grandfather's record player and they'd dance every night to the stash of records on the shelf. There was Bing Crosby, Ray Charles, Joni Mitchell, Frank Sinatra, Marvin Gaye, and so many more. The collection was extensive, and there'd been a few nights where they'd danced to an entire album. He'd get so lost in her, and the music, that an hour would pass before he even knew it.

And then there were their nights together, when he'd put everything he had into making love to her. Desperate for her to realize it was love for him.

The thing was, all of the things he was doing, none of them would change if he got her. If she were his, he'd do everything and more for the rest of his life.

He knew he was going to have to tell her. Knew he couldn't just continue with the track he was on. It was said that actions speak louder than words—which was part of what he was doing—but he was going to have to say something at some point. He just wasn't ready to do it yet. Wasn't ready to lay it all on the line.

Wasn't ready to get his heart broken again.

The one and only time he'd dealt with heartbreak, he'd been

burned so badly that he ran away from ever putting himself in that situation again. Sex without love. That had been his MO. But now? Now he wanted more. He'd had a taste of what life could be like with a woman who was everything.

Now he wanted it all, and he wanted it with her.

When the next Sunday morning rolled around, Finn left a still sleeping Brie at the bungalow and headed for the Stardust Diner. It was the first Sunday in March

Where had the month gone? It felt like he'd just been there, sitting across from Shep and asking his brother advice about Brie. Looked like that Sunday wasn't going to be any different.

Though the topic was not the same. Before it had been about Finn figuring out what he wanted. Now he knew what he wanted. *Brie.*

Finn had barely sat down when Shep leaned back in the booth saying, "So you've finally figured out that you're in love with her."

"How the hell do you do that? You see me for a total of five seconds, and you fucking figure it out?" Finn asked, slightly annoyed but more impressed than anything else.

"Man, over the last few years I've watched my closest friends fall in love around me. I got the love of my life back. And fell in love with her all over again, deeper and more intense than anything I could've ever thought was possible. You don't think I know what it looks like when I witness the death of a bachelor?"

"Death of a bachelor?" Finn repeated, unable to stop the corner of his mouth from pulling up.

"Yeah, that's what I've termed it when you get to the point of no return."

"No arguing with that."

Their conversation was interrupted as Wanda came to the table, carafe of coffee in hand. "Hello, boys." She grinned as she filled up the cups they'd just flipped over.

"Hello," they said in unison, giving her smiles back.

"What can I get you for breakfast?"

"You recommend anything?" Finn asked her.

"Belgian waffles with strawberry compote."

"With a side of bacon, please," Shep said as he grabbed two sugars.

"Two sides," Finn added.

"Coming right up," Wanda said, and nodded before she left the table.

"Speaking of strawberries, Brie is going over after Mass today to help Mom and Hannah make strawberry jam?"

"Hannah make strawberry jam?" Finn raised his eyebrows as he started to doctor up his own coffee.

"Hey, she washes and cuts the strawberries, which is still part of the process. Just because she isn't allowed near the stove doesn't mean she isn't involved. Anyway, what's your plan with Brie?"

"So far? Getting her to fall in love with me."

"That's a good plan." Shep nodded in agreement. "And what happens after that?"

A question Finn had asked himself more than once. His life was here, Brie's was in North Carolina. "I don't know yet." Finn shook his head. "I'm trying to focus on the first part, because until that's accomplished, nothing else matters."

"Fair enough."

"I do know that I want to spend the rest of my life with her."

Shep grinned knowingly. "Figuring that out is half the battle."

Figuring out...those words triggered something that Shep had said earlier. "When I first got here, you said, *you've finally figured out that you're in love with her.*"

"Yeah, I did."

"Like *you've* known that I'm in love with her."

"Yeah." Shep said that one word like it had been a beyond obvious observation.

"When? How?"

"That night at the Sleepy Sheep, when the girls all had dinner and then came after. I told you that it had been a while since I'd seen you look happy, and it had been. But when Brie walked through the door? You lit up like a fucking Christmas tree. And I've never, *ever*, seen that look on your face before. Not even with Rebecca. And then Hannah told me that Brie had been staying at your house, and that just sealed the deal."

"Well you figured it out a week before I did."

"I was looking for it, Finn. You weren't," Shep said simply.

But it wasn't simple at all. Not even close.

"I was in the middle of it before I even realized what had happened. And when I did realize it, it wasn't a matter of *falling* in love with her. I was well past that point. By then it was a matter of bracing for impact."

"At least you're preparing for the crash. Now tell me more about this plan of yours to get her to fall in love with you."

And that was how they spent the rest of their breakfast, Finn telling his big brother about the woman he was in love with, and how he planned to win her over.

Chapter Twenty-One

Fools Rush In

It was weird to Brie that as more and more of Bethelda's possessions left the house, the smaller it felt. She would've thought it'd be the opposite, that it would feel bigger. Nope. Not even a little bit.

As Bethelda's bedroom and closet had now been emptied, Brie turned it into a staging area of sorts. Everything she had to go through was pulled into the room. Stuff that she was selling would be boxed, labeled, and put in the closet, and everything that could be donated was taken to the Triple C.

Brie had to give Bethelda credit for one thing…there was very little that had to be thrown away. The most that had been trashed in one go were all of the opened/used cosmetics and toiletries Brie had gone through when she'd first gotten the house.

Her next project to tackle was Christmas, and there was a lot of it. As Brie was more of a real Christmas tree kind of girl, the three fake trees were easy enough to decide to donate. The more modern/newer decorations were also put into the donate pile. Brie had no use for multicolored feather boas or fifty light-up snowflakes. The only stuff she cared about were things with a past. Ella and Faye came over for lunch one afternoon, Ella doing a thorough look-over again and pointing out what had been Petunia's.

Once that had been dealt with, it was on to the attic. Every night, Finn would climb up and hand down boxes for her to go through the following day. This was the part where things were a little tougher for Brie…or a lot tougher. Most of the boxes in the attic were filled with possessions that were part of Bethelda's history.

A box filled with memories from each year she was in school, her old baby clothes and toys, an antique cradle, and so on. She was only able to go through so much of that before she'd have to move on to something else.

By the end of the week she was maybe just a little bit emotionally exhausted and very much looking forward to going to the charity dinner with Finn. Every time she thought about it she couldn't help but smile. But that was just par for the course as she couldn't think about Finn and not smile.

The night of the dinner, Brie got ready at the bungalow. One, because that was where all of her stuff was, but mainly because she wanted that moment of Finn picking her up again.

So she shaved her legs, curled her hair just right, and did her makeup to perfection. She was just sliding her new gold, strappy heels on when the dulcet voice of George Michael filled the house.

She opened the door to find Finn in a tuxedo, and for a moment, she forgot how to breathe. Her brain flashed to that thought she'd had of him, standing at the end of the aisle of St.

Sebastian's. Except her imagination hadn't done justice to the reality of him in a tux. He looked *goooooood*.

"OK." His voice brought her back, and when she moved her focus to his face she saw that the look he was sporting was stunned. "I'm torn between saying I just write a check and we stay in tonight, and wanting everyone in this whole damn town to see you on my arm."

Brie grinned. "Why? You like me in this dress?" she asked as she did a slow turn.

"*Like* isn't even close to the right word. God, Brie, you're stunning."

"Thank you." She reached out, grabbing the sides of his jacket and gently pulling him close to her. He followed with barely a tug. "You look handsome."

"Just trying to impress you."

"It worked." She kissed him lightly.

"You ready?"

"Yes." She grabbed her clutch and shawl from the table by the door and let him lead her to his truck, grinning from ear to ear.

* * *

There weren't very many places in Mirabelle that were big enough for an event like the charity dinner. The high school gymnasium was off limits because they were serving alcohol, so it was held at the Mirabelle Community Center. When Finn walked into the room, he felt like he was at his high school prom again. It was decorated in all white and with so many hanging lanterns and twinkling Christmas lights (which over half had been from Bethelda's stash that Brie had given Mel) that it wasn't necessary for the overhead lights to be turned on at all. There was music playing lightly, just loud enough to be heard over the chatter of everyone in the room.

Finn didn't even bother looking at the seating chart as he'd just spotted Shep, Hannah, and Paige across the room. His hand at Brie's back flexed as he guided her through the crowd of people. Out of the corner of his eyes, he noticed more than a few heads turn as they walked by.

Of course they did, because Brie was the most beautiful woman in the room...not that Finn was biased or anything. Not at all. Especially when it had to do with anything that involved Brie. But even with all of that established, he wanted to make it perfectly clear who Brie was with for the evening. And hopefully all evenings for the rest of his life.

His hand moved out and to her side, pulling her possessively closer to him. Brie turned to him, a knowing smile on her face. "Don't worry, Finn, I'm going home with you."

Home. That word again. That word that made him hope for so much more. That word that made him hope for *everything.*

"Yes, you are," he said with a nod. Just like she'd gone home with him every night that week. There were no words to describe how much he liked having her in his bed every night. Absolutely no words.

He paused for a second, bringing her to a stop, too, as he leaned down and kissed her temple. Then he started walking again, leading her to the table.

When they got to everyone who was already there, it was Hannah who spoke first. "Damn, girl," she said as she shook her head. "That dress is killer on you."

"No kidding," Paige agreed.

"Look who's talking." Brie looked between both ladies.

"It's true, we all look fabulous," Beth said as she and Tripp joined the group. Tripp was holding Beth's hand, and she'd practically dragged him over from wherever they'd come because he was looking over his shoulder. Beth glanced at him and rolled her eyes, shaking her head on a smile before she tugged hard on his hand to get his attention. "Stop it. They're fine."

Tripp looked back to her, a severe frown on his face. "He's a nineteen-year-old boy, Beth. I know what nineteen-year-old boys want. I was one. They are *not* fine."

Finn looked over in the direction Tripp had just been looking to see a young couple in the corner. The boy's arms were wrapped around the girl's waist as he smiled down at her, twirling one of her curls around his finger.

Finn grinned as he looked back and turned to Brie who was also looking in the direction of the couple. "So Hamilton, who you've met, is dating Nora, Beth's eighteen-year-old niece. Tripp, who is in all respects Nora's stepfather, likes to worry incessantly when it comes to her…or any of those kids."

"First off"—Tripp looked to Finn—"wait until you have kids and then you can mock me. Second, are you aware of who Emma came with?"

"Who?" both Shep and Finn said in unison as they started looking around the room.

Growing up, their cousin Meredith had always been more like a sister than anything else. So Meredith's daughter Emma was more like their niece, who they were exceptionally protective of.

It was Finn who spotted them first. Emma's back was against the wall as she looked up into Dale Rigels's face. He had one hand against the wall next to her shoulder, the other at her waist as he leaned down and kissed her.

"No. Shit." Shep muttered the words, next to Finn.

"Nathanial and Finn Shepherd, if either of you go over there, I will hurt you both."

The two men turned to see Meredith on Reggie's arm, both of them with drinks in their hands. As Nate senior and two other part-time bartenders were working that night, Reggie had been given the evening off, but neither Finn nor Shep had known he was bringing Meredith to the charity dinner.

"OK, first I want to know about how and when that happened." Finn gestured to Emma and Dale.

"And second, we're going to get to this." Shep indicated Meredith and Reggie.

"How and when that happened," Meredith repeated, "was when Dale was at the farm all of last summer."

"That was eight months ago."

"Exactly." Meredith nodded. "And you don't get to ask questions on the second part."

Reggie bowed his head just slightly, smiling at the ground. Finn was going to have to question him later, when Meredith wasn't around. If something was going on with the two of them, there was no way he wasn't going to say something. Not with everything Meredith had gone through in the last year.

He didn't care how big of a hypocrite he was, either.

"Hey, there's someone I want you to meet," Reggie said to Meredith as he looked to a group of people to their left.

"We'll be back." Meredith smiled to the girls. "You two behave," she added to Finn and Shep with a stern look before she let Reggie lead her away.

And as two people left the group, two more joined it as Abby and Logan James walked up.

That evening's event had been specifically scheduled for a time that hockey players from the Jacksonville Stampede could attend. Logan wasn't the only player from the team who had come; there were eleven guys there that night who'd wanted to show their support for Dale and the cause.

Logan had his hand at Abby's back as they walked up, leaning down and whispering something in her ear that had a slight blush creeping up her cheeks. Finn might think that Brie was the most beautiful woman in the room, but all of his other female friends were tying for second, and Abby was one of them.

She was wearing a red beaded gown that in no way hid the baby bump at her belly. It was then that Finn had the brief image of Brie pregnant...pregnant with *his* child.

"Hello," Abby said as she looked around the group, her eyes landing on Brie, the only person she hadn't met before.

"Abby, Logan, this is Brie." Finn introduced her.

"Brie, this is Abby and Logan James."

"Oh, it's so lovely to meet both of you," Brie said as she shook both of their hands. "And I know you had a big hand in tonight's event, Abby." She gestured around the room. "It's beautiful."

When Abby and Logan had met, she'd been doing PR for the hockey team. Now she was working for St. Ignatius, a major hospital in Jacksonville. As this particular event had involved Dale, she'd partnered with Atticus County Hospital to do as much PR for the event as she could. She'd been successful, too. There were over a thousand people there that night and more than three hundred and fifty thousand dollars had been raised before the evening had even started. There was a silent auction going on in the corner that would no doubt pull in some money.

Then there was the evening's main event that had created a massive draw from all over. Not only was Liam playing a live concert, but he was doing it with Isaac Hunter. The country duo was a Grammy–winning powerhouse with a massive fan base. People had shelled out a lot of money to see them that night.

"Thank you. It's been a good amount of work, but it's a good cause."

"It's an excellent cause," Brie agreed. "I've also just recently become a hockey fan," she said to Logan. "Finn has spent a lot of time explaining the game to me."

"Good. And your favorite team?"

"The Stampede of course."

"Damn straight." Logan grinned.

"Have you guys seen Harper and Liam?" Abby asked, looking around the room.

"Liam was getting drinks with Bennett and Jax." Hannah nodded to the bar. "And Harper is checking out the silent auction with Adele, Mel, and Grace."

"We're actually done checking out the silent auction," Harper said as she and Adele James joined the group. "Mel and Grace went to track down some appetizers."

Finn had only met Adele a handful of times, and every time she was dressed to fit into a different era. Tonight she was in a dress that looked like it belonged in the sixties with dark blue lace over white satin. Her brown hair was pinned up in a style fitting the time, the bright red streaks showcased accordingly.

But as Adele was head costume designer for a hit period drama, it was no wonder she was a master at fashion in any time period.

"Brie, this is Adele, Liam and Logan's little sister." Finn made the introductions. "Adele, this is Brie."

"Oh, lovely to meet you." They both shook hands.

"Speaking of drinks"—Logan looked down at his wife—"Red, what do you want?" he asked, using the nickname he'd given her due to her red hair.

"Ginger ale and cranberry."

"Hey, that's my drink," Beth said to Abby.

"Well, then make that two," Abby told her husband.

"I'll go help." Tripp kissed Beth on the head before he pulled away.

"You want white wine?" Finn looked down at Brie.

"Please." She nodded.

"Oh, me too." Hannah said to Shep.

"We'll be back." Finn flexed his hand on Brie's hip before he let go and went with the guys to the bar.

* * *

Brie watched Finn walk through the crowd, looking at the back of him in that tux. It was almost as nice as the front of him. She turned back to the group of girls, now consisting of Hannah, Harper, Adele, Abby, Paige, and Beth. As was the usual whenever Brie and Finn were around his family or friends, they were all silently observing.

"What?"

"Nothing," Hannah said as everyone else shook their heads.

"You two are just fascinating to watch, that's all."

Paige looked between Abby and Adele. "Brie here has tamed Finn."

"I have not tamed Finn." Brie shook her head.

"Oh, yes she has," Harper immediately disagreed.

"Really now?" One of Adele's dark eyebrows shot high. "Do tell. I could use some pointers."

"Who are you trying to tame?" Paige asked.

"No one in particular. It's just good to know these things. So what tricks can you impart to the only single girl in this circle."

"Oh, Finn and I aren't together. I mean, that is to say, we are together *here*. Just not together permanently."

"I don't exactly know what that means." Abby looked confused.

Heat infused Brie's cheeks. Yeah, that wasn't the best explanation; it was just an odd thing to explain. "I'm not from Mirabelle. I'm only in town for a couple of months to deal with an estate that I was left."

"So you and Finn are only together for as long as you're in town?" Adele asked for clarification.

"Yes."

"You know," Adele started to say, her entire focus on Brie, "you can tell me to shut up if this is going too far for the first five minutes of meeting you, but Brie? That man did not look at you like he was only in this for a couple of months."

"Oh, good, even outside observers see it," Beth said.

"I…I mean…I care about him."

Care? Really? Was that it? Or was it well past that point? Was she in love with him? It was the first time she'd asked herself that question. Actually, it was the first time she'd *allowed* herself to ask that question.

"But I'm not staying here." Brie wasn't sure who she was trying to convince with that statement anymore.

She couldn't stay in Mirabelle…could she? Did Finn even want her to stay? Was it possible that he loved her? When they'd started this whole thing there'd been an expiration date attached to it. The promise of no strings…but now things were stringy.

Oh, who was she kidding? They'd been stringy for a while now.

And don't get her wrong. She knew she felt something for this man that she'd never felt for anyone in her life before. She wasn't impulsive, and she never really led with her heart. She'd always led with her mind. Well, before him that was the case.

It was different. Everything was different with him. And what exactly was it that she felt for him? She wasn't quite ready to fling herself off that cliff…yet.

"Ladies," Shep announced as all of the men, along with Mel and Grace, joined the group again. The sudden onslaught of new people effectively shut down the conversation they'd been having.

Not that Brie would've been voicing any of the thoughts that were now rolling around in her head. Finn slid into place next to her again, handing her a glass of white wine before his free hand moved to wrap around her lower back.

"Thank you." She looked up at him, still trying to process.

His eyes narrowed on her face. "You OK?"

"Yeah. Yeah, I'm good." She nodded slowly.

"A toast," Logan said, drawing everyone's attention.

Finn's focus lingered on Brie's face for a moment longer before they both turned to look at Logan, too.

"To getting kids the medical help they need, and to everyone who put this event together."

"Cheers!" Everyone clicked their glasses together before they all took sips of their drinks. But Brie had to stop herself from downing her wine in one go.

Was she in love with Finn? Was she really and truly in love with a man for the first time in her life? The kind of love where she'd give up everything to be with him? The kind of love to build a life on? The kind of love to *last* a lifetime?

* * *

Something was up with Brie, Finn knew it. He didn't think it was bad, just that she was in her head for most of the dinner, doing way more listening than talking. He wanted to know what was in her head. Wanted to know what she was thinking about.

But he *always* wanted to know what she was thinking about.

Once they were done with dinner, her hand moved to his knee, her fingers moving back and forth and driving him out of his ever-loving mind. Which was entirely typical whenever she had her hands on him.

He was pretty sure she was OK, but he wanted a moment alone with her, a moment where they could talk.

He leaned over, his mouth moving to her ear. "You want to dance with me?"

Brie turned to look at him. "No one is even on the floor yet." That was because everyone was waiting for the dessert course; not only that, but none of the evening's musicians were on stage yet. The song currently playing through the speakers was a female musician talking about someone never letting her go. It sounded pretty perfect to Finn.

"I know. Doesn't mean we can't go out there."

"You're right, it doesn't."

Finn stood, and Brie gave him her hand as he pulled her up beside him and led her out to the empty dance floor. Eyes followed them as they moved through the room, but the second he had her in his arms, everyone else disappeared. In a room of over a thousand people, it was just the two of them.

"Have I told you how beautiful you look tonight?" he asked her.

"You have, indeed."

"Just checking." He spun her around in a slow circle before he pulled her back in close. "You having a good time?"

"I am."

"You've been quiet. What are you thinking about?"

She didn't hesitate before she said, "You."

"What about me?"

"I'm glad I met you." She reached up, her hand on his jaw, thumb rasping against the scruff of his beard. "I'm glad I walked into that bar and you were there."

"I'm glad I was there, too."

"I was also thinking that I like the way we dance."

It was then that the song ended, and Brie stretched up, pressing her mouth to his. Before their kiss had ended, the sound of a piano playing filled the air, chords that Finn recognized immediately.

When he and Brie pulled apart it was to see Liam onstage, and he started to sing Elvis Presley's "Can't Help Falling in Love."

Neither of them said another word as they started to dance again. People began to get up from their seats and file onto the floor. But like before, everyone else disappeared, and it was just Finn and Brie moving together, alone in a room filled with a thousand people.

* * *

It was close to midnight when they got back to the house. They stood on the porch while Frankie walked around the yard, sniffing everything in sight. Brie's hands were on the railing while Finn had his arms wrapped around her waist, his chin resting on her shoulder.

There was a spell over them. A spell that had been over them since they'd started dancing. A spell that hadn't broken in the last few hours.

Brie had decided she wasn't going to contemplate any life-changing questions. She'd made that decision when Finn had asked her to dance. Instead she let herself just be in the moment with him, be in the moment and not worry about a thing.

Choosing not to overthink something like if she was in love with him wasn't the easiest thing she'd ever done. But as per usual, Finn had the ability to make her forget about everything except him, even when she didn't ask him to do it.

Frankie was heading back up the stairs not five minutes later, her big paws hitting the boards and echoing through the cool spring air.

"Come on." Finn grabbed Brie's hand and led her back into the house, locking up before he pulled her upstairs.

She hadn't known it was possible to be completely and totally comfortable *anywhere* in Mirabelle, but she was in Finn's house. She could breathe easy there, could just *be*.

When they got to his bedroom they took their time undressing each other. Finn was down to his black pants, Brie running her hands across his chest and over his arms, before he reached behind her and pulled down the zipper of the skirt of her dress. It fell down her thighs and legs, puddling on the floor at her feet. He let his eyes move over her body once, lingering on her black lace thong for a moment, before he moved his hands up to the snaps at the back of her top. Once those were all undone and the material pulled away, he grabbed her hips and took a step forward, pressing his bare chest to hers.

"I've never wanted a woman the way I want you. Sometimes it's so much I can barely control it. This constant *need* for you is something I've never known."

"Finn." She whispered his name as she stretched up and pressed her lips to his. "I've never experienced anything like it, either." It was in that moment that she was almost certain she never would again. Not to this extent. "Make love to me."

The rest of their clothes hit the floor in quick succession and Finn lay Brie down on the bed, covering her with his solid body. He kissed his way down her throat, over her chest, and across her belly before he pulled her legs apart and covered her with his mouth.

It took him absolutely no time at all to get her writhing and moaning, gasping for air, and then screaming his name as she came…twice. She could barely breathe when he was done, kissing his way back up her body.

He made a move to reach for the nightstand but she caught his hand.

"No. I don't want anything between us. I...I'm on birth control."

His eyes widened at her words, his nostrils flaring as he took a deep breath through his nose. "Brie, baby." His forehead came down, resting against hers. "Are you sure?"

She'd never been more sure of anything in her life. She'd also never had sex without her partner wearing a condom before, but she wanted to now, with him. Wanted him to be the first man she'd ever been with without barriers.

"I want to feel you inside of me, Finn. I'm clean."

"I'm clean, too." He pulled up to look down into her face, the look he gave her one of complete adoration.

"I trust you," she whispered, reaching down and wrapping her hand around his bare cock and lining him up with her entrance. "I trust you, Finn." She repeated the words before he thrust into her.

Brie almost sobbed at the sensation, whereas Finn let out a long low groan.

"You're perfection." He closed his eyes as he rested his forehead against hers again, breathing deep as he tried to steady himself.

It was a moment before he started to move with deep, slow strokes. The pleasure he built inside of her was mind numbing, otherworldly. Her hands gripped his biceps, nails digging into his muscles. Her legs were wrapped around his waist, feet at the small of his back. Each time he pulled in and out of her, he rocked her body. The speed built, intensity ratcheting up, the pleasure building.

"Baby," Brie moaned, eyes closing as her back arched, right there on the precipice of coming.

"Look at me," he demanded.

Her eyes opened almost instantly at his words to find his sapphire gaze right there, focused with intensity on her face. It was then that she fell over the edge, her core clenching tight and pulsing around his still thrusting cock.

Even in the throes of the most intense orgasm she'd ever had in her life, she watched Finn let go with his own release. The pleasure on his face was one of a man who'd found ecstasy.

He collapsed onto her, bracing some of his weight so as not to crush her, and she reveled in the feel of him pushing her down into the mattress. His face was pressed to her shoulder, his mouth at her neck as he kissed her skin.

Brie held him, one hand running through his hair while the other traced over the top of his back. She had absolutely no idea where it came from, but as she lay there with him in her arms, her in his, she felt the burning sensation at the corner of her eyes. When she blinked, warm tears fell down the sides of her face, hitting the pillow.

Chapter Twenty-Two

The Grim Truth

The very last thing Finn wanted to do was go out of town and leave Brie behind. But as he'd agreed to go to a veterinarian's conference in Houston, and committed to speaking for his alma mater months ago, he felt like he didn't really have a choice. He just kept telling himself it was only six days. His flight left early Monday morning, and he'd be back by Saturday afternoon.

The thing was, six days felt like too long to be away from her, especially with the current time line they were on.

He'd felt like he and Brie had made real progress both emotionally and physically since the night of the charity dinner. That had been over a week ago. And yes, part of that progress was the newest addition to their sex life…or would that be the newest subtraction from their sex life? Either way, the whole no barriers thing had been a pretty massive step for them.

At least he thought so.

He still hadn't told her that he loved her, probably because there was a part of him that was terrified she wouldn't feel the same way. And he had every right to be because he'd had his heart broken before, and it had taken him eight years to bounce back.

Or maybe he'd just been in a holding pattern until Brie came into his life. Whatever it was, he was going to have to figure out what he was going to do. As it just so happened, he had a long flight there and back to think about things. There was also all of that time in between that he'd be gone, too.

Six days, he had six days to figure it out. When he got back to town on Saturday, got back to Brie, he was going to need to have a game plan.

"You'll call me when you get there?" Brie asked as they stood in the driveway of the bungalow. He had his hands at her waist as she leaned into him.

"I will."

"I'll miss you." She smiled as she looked up at him.

Those three words had his heart in his throat. "I'll miss you, too."

"Good." Her hands tightened in his shirt as she stretched herself up for a kiss.

He complied because he wasn't an idiot. He'd always want her mouth like a man dying of thirst would want water. "I'll be back."

"Promise?"

"Yeah. You have my dog." He reluctantly let go of her as he took a step toward his truck.

"This is true," she said as she nodded.

He hadn't asked her if she'd watch Frankie, she'd volunteered to do it. And as Frankie was beyond comfortable with Brie and Lo it was the perfect situation. Plus he liked the fact that if he couldn't be there with Brie, at least his dog was.

Frankie might be friendly, but she was protective of her people, and Brie was her people now.

Just like Brie was one of Finn's people…maybe the most important person.

* * *

The first night Finn was gone, Brie slept horribly. Since that first night he'd stayed at the bungalow when he'd come over to start the fires, she hadn't slept alone. Apparently she was now accustomed to him being next to her. Accustomed to his big, solid, warm body wrapped around hers.

She pulled herself out of bed around six on Tuesday morning, giving up on sleep. She was in absolutely no mood or state of mind to sit behind the computer and work on anything academic, so instead she decided to work on packing some boxes in the den/library.

She thought the task would be good for her, something physical and mostly mindless that would allow her to focus on another topic, like how she felt about Finn. *What* she felt about Finn.

As she'd promised, she did miss him. A lot. He hadn't even been gone for a full twenty-four hours and she was fully aware of his absence. That day would be the first since she'd been in Mirabelle that she would not see him.

She didn't like it. Not one little bit.

It was becoming clear to her, that leaving this town, leaving him, was becoming less and less likely. Well, that was if he even wanted her to stay. She hadn't broached the subject, mainly because there was no need yet. She still had at least a couple more weeks of work at the house…she'd bring it up then.

OK, maybe she was a bit of a coward, but really, she was leaps and bounds further than she'd ever gotten before. Not all that surprisingly as she'd never willingly handed her heart over to someone else like this.

It was terrifying.

Closing the box she'd just filled with crime novels, she lifted it from the side table, knocking over a stack of leather-bound classics.

"Dammit," she muttered to Lo, who barely lifted her head from the pile of blankets she was curled up in.

Brie moved the box to the other side of the room before she dealt with the books scattered on the floor. When she looked down she noticed that a few had fallen open showing pages filled with a curvy handwriting that she immediately recognized as Bethelda's. She grabbed the book and stood, reading what had been written.

I got first place in the statewide writing competition. Mom and Dad couldn't be more proud…

Brie's eyes moved to the date on the top of the page. It was from twenty-eight years ago. Bethelda would've been seventeen and a junior in high school. Brie's focus moved back to the passage, reading about how Petunia and Harold had taken Bethelda out for a celebratory dinner. She'd gotten shrimp scampi and her favorite dessert…tiramisu.

Flipping to another page, Brie read about the prom and how Bethelda had gone with Billy Granger and they'd danced to "Can't Fight This Feeling" by REO Speedwagon.

Brie's hands were shaking when she closed the book and

looked at the front of it. The cover was dark blue leather, embossed with gold and reading *The Great Gatsby* by F. Scott Fitzgerald.

"What in the world?" She set that book on the table before she reached for *Jane Eyre*, this one a deep burgundy leather, embossed with bronze. Her heart was racing out of her chest when she opened to the first page.

The date at the top was from New Year's Day thirty-five years ago. Bethelda would've been twelve.

A few months ago, I was looking through a mail order catalog of Mom's when I found these journals that look like classic books and immediately fell in love with them. I told Mom about them for a potential Christmas present, but with the price tag on them, I wasn't too hopeful.

When I opened my presents on Christmas Day, I opened this, the best present a girl could ask for…

Brie set that book down and grabbed *Alice in Wonderland*, which was emerald green and with silver embossed writing. That one had Bethelda's last semester of middle school and her first semester of her freshman year of high school. *David Copperfield*—which was in black leather with copper detailing—was from her last semester in college and when she'd moved back to Mirabelle.

Brie would've been three years old when that had been written. She closed the book and looked to the shelf where a whole row of the green, blue, burgundy, and black books sat.

"Holy shit."

This was the history she'd been looking for. This was the

past she'd been trying to figure out. And she knew, *knew*, that her father was in one of them. She was going to have to find him.

As it wasn't even after eight o'clock in the morning, it was too early for Brie to take a shot of something, so she made herself another cup of coffee. After that, she pulled every single leather-bound journal—posing as a piece of classic literature—down from those shelves and brought them to the dining room table. Then she went through and put them all in order. There were thirty-five, one for each year from when Bethelda started them at the age of twelve. Each book was probably three hundred and fifty pages long, but not all of them were filled to capacity. Some had a few empty pages at the end while others had folded pages stuck in the back.

Brie stared at the one Bethelda had written when she was eighteen, *A Tale of Two Cities*.

Should she start there? Start with the one where Brie would've been conceived? Or should she start at the beginning? Get the full evolution of Bethelda? She'd waited most of her life to get the answers she knew were in that book. But would she fully understand those answers unless she started at the beginning?

No, she wouldn't. Besides, she'd already waited this long, what was a few more hours? She reached for *Jane Eyre* before she grabbed her cup of coffee and headed for the living room.

* * *

By six o'clock, Brie had made it through six of the journals. She was a bit of a speed reader, and because right now this was about information gathering, she was fine with going through them quickly. She'd have these to reread when she needed to really analyze.

Her conclusions so far? Well, if Bethelda had been honest with her writing, then she'd been raised by two parents who doted on her, never left her wanting for anything, and loved her with all of their hearts.

She seemed fairly well rounded if not a little naive, which was understandable for a teenager. She was boy crazy—which was actually very hard for Brie to picture—but she never wrote that she was in love. It was always infatuations and when they ended, she moved on. Well, except for George Michael. There were many entries about Bethelda's love for the musician.

But the woman was impulsive when it came to relationships...something Brie had never been. Well, except with Finn, but she wasn't going to focus on that at the moment.

Bethelda was also a big reader of all things: classics, mystery, sci-fi, romance, *everything*. She'd started sneaking her mother's Harlequins when she was fifteen. When Petunia found out, she just started giving the already read books to Bethelda with the warning of, *just don't tell your father*. It was no wonder she'd fallen in love with the covers of the journals she wrote in—she loved books.

That love of reading ended up fueling Bethelda's real passion. She wanted to write, so much so that she devoted all of high school into getting a full-ride scholarship to the University of Florida. She got it, too.

There was a difference between Bethelda's academic writing—there was a folded copy of her paper that won her the statewide writing competition as well as the paper that got her into UF—and her journal writing. Her academic writing was very precise and scholarly…her journal writing was care-free and fun.

Bethelda's UF acceptance was the last thing Brie read in *The Great Gatsby* journal. Which meant that a *Tale of Two Cities* was next. It was the last semester of her senior year, that summer, and the first semester of college.

Brie had been sitting in the chair in the den for the last hour, and she got up and headed for the kitchen.

She'd spent almost a solid ten hours reading that day. She'd moved around the rooms, lying on the sofa in the living room for a bit, sitting at the desk in the office, taking some time on the swinging bench outside to enjoy the spring air, staying at the dining room table for a bit after she ate her lunch. She'd also paced around the house while she read. This was now possible without fear of getting hurt as there wasn't furniture or stuff at every turn.

And now it was time for some wine and food before she started journal seven, thus her journey to the kitchen.

As she was still in the information stage of things, she wasn't at the processing part yet. And really, how could she process anything? So far Bethelda seemed *normal*. She wasn't terrible or twisted, wasn't mean and vengeful. She was hope-ful…happy.

Brie's cell phone started vibrating against the counter, and she looked down to see Finn's name. She swiped her finger across the screen to pick up the call and put the phone to her ear. "Hey."

"Finally. I was about to call in reinforcements."

"What?"

"I've been texting you all day. I called earlier, too, but you didn't answer."

"Oh, I…I got caught up in some stuff around the house." Her voice sounded off to even her, maybe because she hadn't really used it all day besides talking to the dog and cat.

"You OK?"

"Yeah. Just tired; I didn't sleep well last night without you." At least part of that was the truth. Yet she felt like it was the biggest freaking lie. Why didn't she tell him what she'd found? Why was she keeping it to herself? What was she afraid of?

"Same here," Finn agreed. "It's been nonstop since I got here. My old director had an itinerary for me when I met with him this morning."

"That sounds delightful."

"Yeah, not so much. I'm going to dinner tonight with one of my buddies who lives up here…" He kept talking, telling her about his day, that he missed her, that he'd rather be there with her.

There was something about listening to his voice that made her feel her feelings. She'd been able to block it off, shut it down all day. But now, with his voice in her ear, she was trying desperately to not start crying.

She should tell him, but when she opened her mouth to, the words wouldn't come out. Maybe it was better to wait until she knew everything. Yeah, that was why she wasn't saying anything.

Instead she leaned against the counter and sipped on her wine while he talked. By the time they got off the phone she was pouring herself a second glass and grabbing a bag of chips. Dinner of champions.

When she walked into the dining room to get the journal, she stared at it for a full five minutes. "It's now or never." She grabbed the book and headed for the living room again.

* * *

May 25

I've met him, the man of my dreams. Daniel Fernandez. He's beautiful. Dark brown hair, golden brown eyes, big smile, tall. Oh man is he tall, six-foot-three.

OK, so maybe MET isn't exactly the right word. I saw him from across the room at the CCC and knew he was it for me. I'm saying it now, it was love at first sight. He was loading furniture while I was sorting boxes...

* * *

June 7

DANNY TALKED TO ME! We were passing in the hallway and he told me he liked my red hair and my glasses...

* * *

June 19

Danny calls me Betts. Isn't that the most perfect nickname on the face of the planet? No need to answer, I already know that it is. Anyway, I learned he's twenty-one and in town this summer working with his uncle at the marina. They go out on the boats in the mornings to catch fish, and when they get back in the afternoon, Danny works at the CCC for some extra money.

He's from Cuba. Well, his parents were from Cuba. They came over here before he was born. His dad died when he was fifteen and his mother passed away four months ago, that's why he's up here with his uncle. He wants to have his own boat someday...

* * *

June 22

DANNY KISSED ME!!!!!!!!!!! We were outside splitting a coke when he leaned over and just kissed me. It was perfection. He is the world's absolute best kisser. This is not hyperbole either...

* * *

June 28

It's official, Danny has asked me on a date. We're going on Saturday night. I didn't tell Mom and Dad about it, mainly because they most likely would not approve. Dad wants me to stay focused before I go off to school in a couple of months. Plus, there is the fact that Danny is three years older than me. So I told Mom I was going out with Lacy...

* * *

July 3

I am on cloud nine. Danny picked me up last night at five in his uncle's truck. We drove over to Alligator Lane to go for a walk and a picnic. He held my hand the whole time.

How can it be that something as simple as hand holding can be the absolute best thing in the world? And he did that thing where his thumb moved back and forth across my hand. It was such a small thing, but I felt it everywhere. Like, goose bumps across my skin, butterflies in my stomach, lungs tightening everywhere.

And then it started raining. Pouring. We were soaked by the time we got back to the truck, and my dress was sticking to every inch of me. He kept apologizing. Why? I don't know. It wasn't like he controlled the weather, and that storm blew in out of nowhere. But then he was kissing me in the rain, pushing me back against the truck. He whispered in my ear that I was the most beautiful woman he'd ever met.

HE CALLED ME A WOMAN. Not a girl, a w-o-m-a-n. How freaking amazing is that?

Danny's plan had been for us to have a picnic outside, but clearly the storm stopped that from happening. So we sat in the cab of the truck, eating ham and cheese sandwiches and potato chips, and drinking the cokes he packed…

* * *

July 4

All I have to say is fireworks. Fireworks everywhere. After the church picnic we went down to the beach (I told Mom I was going with Claudia) to watch the show and Danny brought a blanket for us to spread out on the sand. We lay there for a while before the fireworks in the sky started, me in his arms while he kissed me. That was actually the first set of fireworks.

I'm not going to lie, I liked the first show much more than the second…

* * *

The next two weeks of entries were all about the places that Danny took Bethelda around Mirabelle. How he'd tap on her window before the sun was even up to go down to the beach with her and watch the sunrise. How he'd pick flowers and bring them to her when they were both working at the CCC. How Danny's favorite movie was *Back to the Future* and that he wanted to own a DeLorean one day.

Brie looked over at Lo (Delores) at this point, and wondered if that was where Bethelda had gotten the name.

* * *

July 9

I know I have my moments of jumping in to things without looking. More so with boys than anything else. But there is

*a difference between jumping and falling, and I've now offi-
cially fallen in love with Daniel Emmanuel Fernandez.*

*Last night we got caught in the rain again. We were walk-
ing at Alligator Lane (which I still don't know why it is
named that as there aren't alligators there). Anyway, it was
close to dusk when the clouds blew in off the water. We started
back for the truck but the skies opened up before we got back.*

*I pulled Danny into the backseat and told him I wasn't
ready to go home yet. We were kissing for a while, and then
we were pulling each other's clothes off. I thought about
my first time many times. How it would happen. When it
would happen. When I pictured it, it was always on my
wedding night, my husband helping me out of my pretty
white dress. What else was to be expected of a good virgin
Catholic girl?*

*Instead it was impulsive. Reckless. Both of us soaked to
the bone in the back of an old truck. It was perfect…*

* * *

The month of entries that followed were all about Bethelda and
Danny sneaking around town to be together. Bethelda had gotten home late one night and was caught sneaking in by two very
disapproving parents. She'd been grounded for a week in which
she agonized about not getting to see Danny.

Though there was one day that her dad was at work and
her mom went to the grocery store that she snuck Danny into
her bedroom. Bethelda had gone from boy-crazy virgin, to sex-
crazed teenager at the drop of a hat. But it was more than just
the sex…or so Brie thought from what she was reading.

Bethelda went down to Gainesville to start school at the end of the summer. She and Danny were still constantly talking to each other, writing letters between phone calls. Brie wondered where those letters were. If Bethelda had kept them. If they were still in the house.

Even without seeing it from her father's side of things, it really did seem like the two loved each other. Danny told Bethelda he loved her all the time. Told her he wanted to marry her. That after she was done with school they'd get a house wherever she wanted...as long as it was on the water. That way he could work from the fishing boat that was his, and she could write.

So what happened to her father? And she knew that Daniel Fernandez was her father. Bethelda had said it at the beginning: he had golden brown eyes. So where did he go? Did he bail when the inevitable pregnancy happened?

Because Brie knew that particular spoiler to the story. She'd been preparing herself for it when she got to that passage. Something she knew was just around the corner. But even with preparing herself, it still was jarring when she got there, like she'd missed a couple of steps on the stairs.

* * *

September 12

I'm late, like ten days late. And no, I'm not the most consistent in that department but I have never been TEN DAYS LATE. We've used protection every time we've been together. Well, there was that one time on the beach, but that was just once.

Oh God.

I haven't told Danny yet. I know I need to, but I'm scared. This was not part of the plan. Nowhere near part of the plan...

* * *

September 13

I told Danny last night, I was sobbing on the phone, but he was totally and completely calm. In fact, he seems excited about the baby. Like, by the end of the phone call he seemed overjoyed.

He said we'd figure it out. We have a little over two months until I come home for Thanksgiving break. I might or might not be showing, but it's fall, so I can just wear baggy sweaters to cover up any bump I do have.

That's when we'll tell my parents...

* * *

September 23

I got a package in the mail yesterday. Danny mailed me a tiny yellow onesie with a family of ducks on the front. He put a note in there that said, It works if we have a boy or a girl...

* * *

October 30

Danny came down to visit me this weekend. It's the first time I've seen him since I left at the end of August. He got a ride with his uncle who was going down to Tampa. He went with me to my doctor's appointment on Friday. There's a clinic in town that I've been going to. We got to hear the baby's heartbeat.

Allison is out of town this weekend, so Danny and I had the whole dorm room to ourselves. I snuck him in, not that it was all that difficult as our RA doesn't exactly keep us under a close watch. That first night we lay in bed and he had his hands on my stomach while he talked to the baby.

I'm pretty sure he wants a little girl as he kept saying her and she…

* * *

November 19

I'm nervous. Dad is coming to pick me up today. They haven't seen me in months, so I'm sure the weight that I've gained is going to be obvious. Maybe I can just push it off as the freshman fifteen. Though, it might be closer to the freshman twenty at this point.

I also haven't heard from Danny in a couple of days. He always calls on Thursday night and he didn't this week. When I tried him at his uncle's house the phone just rang and rang.

Dad and I should get back in enough time today for me to go over to his uncle's house…

* * *

That was where the journal entries for that year ended. There were a couple of pages with a big black ink dot at the top. Like Bethelda had set the pen down to start writing, but hadn't been able to move the pen, the ink soaking into the paper. There were other pages where the lines had blurred, watermarks scattered across the paper.

Tears. There were tears everywhere.

Brie didn't hesitate in grabbing the next journal *The Scarlet Letter*. How freaking appropriate. The first couple of entries were full of starts and stops, the words almost illegible.

* * *

January 1

I can't

* * *

January 2

Why

* * *

January 3

He's gone.

* * *

January 19

I don't know where to start. It's been two months since it happened.

Two months since everything ended

Two months since my world ended.

Danny's gone.

There was an accident out on the water. A guy was on his speedboat, drunk and not paying attention. He crashed into Danny's uncle's fishing boat. Seven people were killed that day, including Danny.

I don't know how to breathe anymore. I feel dead too. How can I be here without him? What am I supposed to do now? He left me behind. I can't live without him.

* * *

Brie had known at the first glance of the passage that it was going to be a blow. Bethelda's normally neat handwriting was messy, like her hand had been shaking as she wrote. There were also tearstains all over the page, blurring the lines and the words written in pen.

Reading the facts of the accident was jarring, seeing it all laid out like that. Brie wondered how many times Bethelda had recited those facts, reminding herself of the harsh reality. The heartbreak of it all leaked off the page with every word.

Her father hadn't left Bethelda…hadn't left Brie. He'd been taken from them.

* * *

It was close to eight that night when Brie put the journal down, leaving off with Danny's death. That was as far as she was going to be able to go into Bethelda's writings for the night. But she wasn't done trying to learn more about her past.

She had her father's name now: Daniel Emmanuel Fernandez.

From the journals, Brie had learned that Danny's parents were Inés and Leandro Fernandez. They'd come to America with Inés's brother Rafael in 1958. Leandro and Rafael had been fishermen back in Cuba, so that was what they did while they lived in Tampa. Inés had been a nanny/cook/maid. After Leandro and Inés had died, both Rafael and Danny had wanted to get out of Tampa, so they came up to Mirabelle.

Brie wasn't all that hopeful that a computer search was going to come up with anything on any of them, and she was right. The only thing she found was an archived article from the *Mirabelle Newspaper* on the boating accident. Danny's uncle had died in the accident, too.

There wasn't even a picture of her father...

Brie stood up so fast from her seat that the chair went rolling out behind her, hitting the wall with enough force to startle Frankie who'd followed her into the room.

"Sorry." Brie patted the dog's head before she walked out of the office and headed for the den/library.

Since that night she and Finn had gone through the photo albums looking for the Lo costume pictures, Brie hadn't touched the photo albums. She hadn't wanted to dive into that particular pool. Hadn't been ready.

She sat down on the floor and started searching through them. She set aside the Christmas tree collection, the ones of Bethelda as a child, another of Petunia and Harold pre-baby. When she got to the ones of teenage Bethelda she started to flip through them slower.

Bethelda had thick, long red hair that was rather beautiful. It had been hard for Brie to say that her biological mother had been beautiful, mainly because the one and only time she'd met her, she'd been sneering. But looking at these photos, with a smiling and happy Bethelda, it was easier to see what Danny had fallen in love with. *Who* Danny had fallen in love with.

Brie got to the photo of Bethelda at her high school graduation, wearing her cap and gown and with Petunia and Harold on either side of her, proud as could be.

The next photo was of Bethelda in a red bathing suit on the beach, and she was rocking it pretty hard-core. She had a figure all right, a figure that was pretty similar to Brie's.

The next photo was of the church picnic, Fourth of July banners hanging in the background while Bethelda and two girls showed off blueberry pie.

And there he was, her father. He was in the background looking at Bethelda. His eyes weren't clear in the picture, but she knew it was him. She could just tell that she had his nose. He was handsome, just like Bethelda had described.

Brie would swear her heart actually stopped beating for a moment.

It was her father. Her fingers moved over the photo, a photo that started to blur the longer she looked at it. He was there, right there. Proof that he existed.

The pain she'd been holding back for the last few hours finally escaped, she couldn't fight it anymore, and she wept as she sat on the floor.

* * *

The next twenty-four hours were not the easiest of Brie's life. It had taken her awhile to get a hold of herself after she found the photo of her father, and by that point she was so mentally and emotionally exhausted she went to bed, her head pounding something fierce.

Her dreams that night were ones of Bethelda and Danny, a young couple so incredibly in love. If there was one thing she believed, it was that they'd loved each other.

When Brie woke up the next morning she was still exhausted. She hadn't been able to entirely recoup the energy she'd depleted the previous day, but at least she wasn't running on empty.

After she took care of Lo and Frankie—which was oddly painful as they reminded Brie of Finn—the first part of her morning was spent looking through more of the picture albums. Brie got to see the transformation of Bethelda from happy, to miserable.

There was a picture of Bethelda outside of her dorms at UF, looking excited but nervous. The next one was Thanksgiving, where a slightly heavier Bethelda was looking at the camera with a blank stare. There was no light in her eyes. After that was a picture at Christmas. Bethelda wore a big, baggy black sweater, her gaze vacant. Like she wasn't even there.

The next picture was the following summer, a no longer

pregnant Bethelda standing at a table outside the church selling raffle tickets. She looked miserable.

The photos became less and less as the years went. Just holidays and random events. Bethelda's expressions went from looking slightly annoyed to downright hostile before they just stopped. Brie guessed the last one was probably when she was in her late twenties. Harold and Petunia were in it, so Brie guessed it was shortly before he died.

There weren't any more pictures of Danny. Brie suspected this was because these albums were most likely put together by Petunia. Which meant any other photos of Danny would be somewhere else.

After some more coffee, Brie started reading the journals again. Bethelda was in so much pain after losing Danny that it was almost debilitating. What got her through it was focusing on school and nothing else. And Brie meant *nothing* else.

Bethelda didn't really talk about the baby growing in her belly. The little she did was very disconnected, like the child wasn't a part of her, wasn't a part of anything. People either believed she was just getting fat, or they didn't ask questions. She continued on with her baggy-clothes strategy, which got a lot harder when May rolled around and it was starting to warm up outside.

The only person Bethelda did tell was her roommate. The night Bethelda went into labor, Allison drove her to the next town over where a convent of nurses-turned-nuns helped her have the baby.

After that, she signed the adoption paperwork and left. Just like that.

Bethelda's descent into what she became was not quick.

It was a slow progression of shutting people out, letting her pain turn inward and making her hateful. By the time Brie was finished reading for the day, she'd gotten through nine more journals. The last one she read was when Bethelda was twenty-eight...the same age Brie was now.

That night when Finn called Brie, she didn't answer.

Chapter Twenty-Three

When You Find Me

Something wasn't right. Finn knew it, felt it in his gut. When he'd called Brie the night before she hadn't answered…nor did she answer that morning when he'd called.

He'd just finished up with a panel when his cell phone started buzzing in his pocket. His moment of hope that it was Brie was short-lived when he looked at the screen to see Hannah's name.

"Hey, I'm glad you called. Have you talked to Brie? I can't get a hold of her."

There was silence on the other end of the phone before Hannah cleared her throat uncomfortably. "Finn, I…she was just here." The tone in her voice was one he was familiar with; it was the same one he got when he was about to deliver bad news to the owner of a pet.

"What happened?"

"She dropped off Frankie and Lo, and asked me if Shep and I could watch them until you got back. Finn, Brie left. Left Mirabelle and she wouldn't tell me where she was going."

Right then and there his world came crashing down around him. Everything he'd realized he wanted since Brie had walked into his life was gone. Just that quickly.

He'd been left.

Again.

* * *

Growing up, Brie and her parents would always go on vacation in Helen, Georgia, at least once a year. Whether it was a week in the summer, during spring break, or sometimes at Christmas, they'd stay in a cabin and just get away.

Brie needed to get away now, so that was where she went. The little one-bedroom cabin she rented was right on a river, surrounded by trees.

It was after six when she got to the cabin that night—she'd stopped for groceries in town first. The sun still had about two more hours in the sky, so she preheated the oven for the frozen pizza she'd just bought, poured herself a glass of wine, and went outside on the deck.

As she'd reached the max of what she could handle, she decided to take a journal-free day. Though she hadn't left them behind. Nope, she'd packed up all of them and brought them with her. They were like little Pandora's boxes, all waiting to let loose more pain and heartache.

The journals weren't the only thing she'd taken a break from, either. She'd turned off her phone, but not before she'd sent Finn a text. All it said was, *I had to leave. I'm sorry. I can't do this.*

She was a coward. She knew it. But she'd had to get out. Had to get away. Had to *run away*.

So there she was. Alone.

No man is an island. That wasn't true. Bethelda had been her own island. Isolated herself to the point where she had no one. She'd taken the love for the man she'd lost and turned it into something else. Something dark and twisted. Something vengeful.

When other people had love and happiness, she'd made it her job to make them miserable. She also liked to rub salt in the wound of those that were hurting. Her vengefulness had started well before the blog; she'd been a menace at the *Mirabelle Newspaper*, too. Though, where Brie was in the journals, Bethelda hadn't been fired yet. That wouldn't come for another eight or nine years…right after Brie had met her.

The low beep filled the air, pulling Brie from her thoughts. She turned from the river and headed back inside to put her dinner in the oven.

* * *

Finn landed at the Tallahassee airport just after six o'clock on Thursday night. It hadn't even been eight hours since that phone call from Hannah, but it had been the longest eight hours of his life.

He'd called the airline the second he got off the phone with her, heading up to his hotel room so he could shove all of his clothes into his suitcase. It had taken the taxi an hour to get to the airport (where he'd tried calling Brie again. He'd gone to voice mail before she'd sent him that text that made him want to throw his phone out the window), two hours to get onto the first flight, one hour in the air, another two hours in the Dallas Fort Worth airport, and two more hours in the air.

By the end of the flight he was about ready to come out of his skin. Sure, it was about three hours less than if he'd driven, but at least if he'd been behind the wheel he would've felt more in control of the situation. Instead he'd had to do a whole lot of waiting.

When Finn walked out of arrivals it was to find Shep standing there. He was both equal parts relieved and frustrated at seeing his brother. They'd already had a long conversation during Finn's layover where Shep and been trying to be the voice of reason.

Finn didn't want the voice of reason…he wanted to know what the fuck was going on, and Shep didn't have any of those answers. Finn was done talking about stuff. He wanted to start taking action.

"Tripp dropped me off." Shep took a step forward holding out his hand. "I couldn't let you drive home."

"Why's that?"

"Because if Hannah had left me like that I would've driven my Mustang into a ditch. Give me your keys."

Finn pulled them from his pocket and tossed them in the air. Shep caught them and the two brothers headed out of the building.

* * *

Finn had a key to Bethelda's house. It had been a weird addition to put on his key chain a few weeks ago, but it had been necessary. Just as it had been necessary to give Brie a key to his place. They were constantly in and out of the houses at different times, so it had just made sense.

Now, nothing made sense.

He and Shep looked around, and the two most glaring things Finn noticed were that Brie had taken the books she was using for her thesis, and that there was a pile of photo albums scattered on the floor of the library/den. Besides that, almost everything had looked the same from when he'd left.

Well, that and Brie was gone. Which was the most glaring difference.

"What do you want to do?"

He wanted to shove his fist through a wall. Scream. Anything. Instead he couldn't do anything except look around the empty house. Because if Brie wasn't there, none of the other stuff mattered.

He didn't want to go home, either. Go home to another house that was Brie-less. Go home to his bed that had sheets that probably still smelled like her. He wanted to be anywhere else. Be anyone else at that moment.

"I don't know." Finn shook his head, feeling a tightening in his throat that he refused to let himself give in to.

"Come back to the inn. Eat some dinner."

"I'm not hungry."

"Yeah, well, I'm not going to let you drink the amount of whiskey I know you're going to get into until you eat. Let's go."

With one more look around the room, Finn followed, because he didn't have the first clue of what else to do.

* * *

Brie woke up at five in the morning. She was so tired of being wide awake and exhausted. But what else was to be expected?

She wasn't sleeping well at all, hadn't in days. Last night had by far been the worst, though, as she couldn't stop thinking about Finn. Couldn't stop thinking about how she'd walked away.

Run away.

Who did that to someone? Apparently she did have something in common with Bethelda. She'd been cruel. Cruel to the man she loved. And yes, she did love him. She knew it now. Had figured it out at the worst possible moment.

Which was the reason she'd left. Because she was a coward.

It was probably a good ten minutes before she gave up on falling asleep and dragged herself out of bed. She got into a fight with the coffeemaker, but won in the end. While it brewed she moved to the box of journals and lifted the lid.

She wasn't even halfway through. Apparently this was a marathon, not a sprint.

When she reached in to grab the next book in the series— *Wuthering Heights*—her hand brushed another book in the box—*A Brave New World*—on the way out. As the pages fluttered she caught a flash of something shoved into the middle of the book.

Setting the journal she'd grabbed down, she reached in for the other one. Flipping to the front page she saw that it was the one from this year. Bethelda had only written in a handful of pages before she'd died in late January.

Brie let the book fall open to where she'd seen the papers shoved into the middle. There looking up at her was a close-up picture of Danny, golden brown eyes and everything.

Her legs suddenly felt wobbly and she had to brace herself against the table as she moved to a chair, almost falling into it.

She stared at the picture, taking in every part of him. His

golden brown skin, almost the same shade as hers. His nose that was identical to hers. She also had his mouth…and his ears. He looked so happy as he smiled at the camera. Brie knew beyond a shadow of a doubt that Bethelda had been on the other side of that camera, taking the picture.

Brie flipped to the next picture. Bethelda and Danny were at the beach; he had his arm around her shoulders as he leaned in and gave her a kiss on the cheek. She was laughing. The kind of laugh that started deep in a person's belly. The kind of laugh that was filled with joy.

The next picture was one of Bethelda in a white dress, looking over her shoulder and giving a slightly seductive smile to the camera. Brie wondered why Bethelda had kept that picture. Maybe to remind herself of a time when she was happy?

Who knew?

Brie flipped to the last picture in the stack to find the second shock of her morning. It was a picture of Brie. It was her senior graduation photo, the one that graced the pages of her high school yearbook. She was wearing the black velvet shawl thing that exposed her shoulders, and a string of pearls. Her hair was curled and hanging down.

It was the picture that had been put in the newspaper when Brie had been named valedictorian. Behind it was a piece of folded light blue paper, and when she unfolded it she got her third shock of the morning.

It was addressed to Brie and dated a little less than a year ago, and on her birthday.

May 12

Brie,

I don't know if you will find this letter when I'm gone. I don't know if you will take the time to find these journals. Not that this is a test or anything, I just don't know you. I don't even know if you will come down here when I die, and yes, I do know that I'm going to die.

But, we're all dying in some way or another.

The doctors found the brain aneurysm a week ago. It's inoperable and there's no telling when it will burst. It could be a day, it could be a year. If the people in this town knew about it, I'm sure they'd put a wager on when I'd die. It almost makes me tempted to do it.

Anyway, I know that our one and only encounter was not pleasant, but I'm not a pleasant person. I haven't been since Danny died. That's because I died then, too. You know that saying, "It's better to have loved and lost than never to have loved at all"?

Well, I call bullshit. I would rather have never known what it was like to have that man in my life if he was going to be taken away from me. I'm completely and entirely selfish that way.

I don't expect you to understand me at the end of this. And I really don't expect you to forgive me, I don't deserve it. In fact, I'm not asking for your forgiveness. I'm not asking for anything. I'm just saying my piece, and in doing that I show just how selfish I really am, because I never allowed you to say your piece.

But there's something you should know.

I wouldn't hold you the day you were born. I wouldn't even look at you. It was because I knew you'd look like him.

That day you walked into my office, you proved me correct in every way. You are without a doubt your father's daughter. I don't know if you take comfort in that fact or not, and I wasn't trying to offer it. It's just a fact.

It was beyond painful to look at you that day, but at the same time, whatever part of me still capable of feeling any sort of genuine happiness might've liked the fact that there was something of my Danny in this world.

—Betts

The very first thing that came to mind when Brie finished that letter was Finn. All she could think about was how she didn't want to lose out on what they could have. Didn't want to spend her life thinking about the *what-ifs* or *might've-beens*. Didn't want to spend her life apart from the man she loved more than anything.

What had she done?

* * *

When Finn woke up on Friday morning, scratch that Friday afternoon, he had the hangover from hell. He didn't even want to think about how much worse it would've been had he not eaten the pizza Hannah had waiting for them when they got home.

An ordered in pizza of course.

As Finn hadn't been in any mood or state of mind to talk, he and Shep just drank, until four o'clock in the morning. That was why it was almost noon when he woke up with the mother of all headaches.

But it wasn't what hurt the most. Not even close. He knew that people loved with their mind and that the heart wasn't really what should hurt when someone had their heart broken, and yet his did. There was a physical pain in his chest that made it difficult to breathe.

Brie had left and all she'd said to him was, *I had to leave. I'm sorry. I can't do this.*

He'd been through this once before, had the person he was in love with bail on him. As impossible as it sounded, Finn had fallen deeper in love with Brie in the last two months than he had in the fourteen years he'd had Rebecca in his life.

And Brie had just left him without an explanation, without anything. What the hell was that? Whatever it was, it was brutal.

He should've known better. He should've known that love wasn't for him. He *had* known it actually, and then Brie had come into his life and changed his mind.

It took a pretty big effort to get out of bed and stumble across the room to the shower. Frankie lifted her head from where she slept on the floor and let out a soft whine before she got up and followed him into the bathroom, lying down right by the shower. She hadn't left his side since he'd gotten to the inn.

Finn kept the water cold, hoping to clear some of the fog from his mind. It was minimal.

When he came out of the shower he had to dump out the clothes he'd shoved into his suitcase to find a clean pair of jeans and a T-shirt. After he got dressed, he and Frankie walked to the kitchen and into the smell of coffee brewing.

"Oh, there is a God," Finn groaned as he rubbed his eyes before sliding his glasses onto his nose and trying to focus.

"It should be ready in a minute," Hannah said as she pulled out some mugs from the cabinet and set them on the counter.

Finn went to the back door and tried to let Frankie outside, but she wouldn't go.

"I let her out earlier," Hannah said. "She should be fine."

"She eat?"

"Nope. Didn't even touch her food. Just went back to lie down next to you."

"Loyal girl." Finn patted the dog's head as they headed for the kitchen. "Did Lo eat?"

"Yes, with me this morning. She's currently lying on the dryer while I'm finishing a load of towels. She really is the strangest cat."

"The strangest." Finn agreed.

"You guys must've drank a lot last night. Shep just got up, too."

"I was drinking to forget. It takes a lot of whiskey to get there."

"And how does it feel to remember now?"

"Worse." He pulled up a bar stool and sat down, Frankie resting her head in his lap.

"Oh, honey." Hannah reached over and grabbed his hand. "I'm sorry I didn't stop her from leaving."

"What were you going to do? Let the air out of her tires?"

"That would've been a smart idea. Why didn't I think of that?"

A low chuckle filled the room as Shep came into the kitchen and walked up behind her, wrapping his arms around her waist as he kissed the top of her head. "Babe, you aren't as devious as Finn and I are."

"Clearly not."

Finn had to turn away, the sight of his brother and sister-in-law in a moment of genuine affection was too much for him.

Way too much for him.

"I'll be back…I need to check on your son who's taking a nap."

Finn lifted his head just as Hannah kissed Shep and headed out of the kitchen.

"Go eat." Finn told Frankie. She gave him a reproachful look and he pointed to the bowl. She nudged his hand before she got up and headed over to her food.

"How you feeling?" Shep asked as he leaned back against the counter.

"Like death."

"Sometimes you have to hit rock bottom before you can pull yourself back up. Believe me, I know better than anyone."

Finn did believe his brother, mainly because he was there the night Shep hit rock bottom with Hannah. Watched as his brother drank himself into oblivion before he begged Finn to take him back to her.

"What's your plan?" Shep asked.

"I don't have one."

"You just going to let her walk?"

"What choice do I have?"

"Go after her." Shep said it like it was the simplest answer in the world.

"How the hell am I supposed to do that? I don't know where she is. She won't answer her phone."

"So you just give up?"

"I don't have the first clue where to start."

"Go to her house. In North Carolina. Find out who her friends are. Maybe they know where she is. Maybe they'll talk to her. You've got nothing to lose except for her."

"Yeah, except for her." Finn repeated.

"You know, I realized something three years ago with Hannah. Sometimes there are loves in your life that you can't forget, and others that you can't let go of. My first time around with Hannah? She was the girl I couldn't forget. When she came back? She was the woman there was no chance in hell I was letting go of. Rebecca was a girl you couldn't forget. What's Brie? Are you just going to let her go?"

Brie was the love of his life.

"No." He wasn't going to let her go without a fight.

* * *

It was close to two in the afternoon when Brie's MINI Cooper crossed the county line into Mirabelle. If she thought she was terrified when she left, it was nothing, *nothing*, to how she felt now.

After reading that letter—fourteen times—Brie had quickly packed all of her things and was on the road by seven. She'd made the biggest mistake of her life. Love didn't destroy people. That was a choice. Bethelda made that choice…she'd given up on life. Instead of seeing what a gift she'd been given, even for a brief moment, she saw it as a curse. That wasn't how Brie wanted to live.

She'd prescribed by no regrets, and she'd just made the biggest mistake of her life. If she couldn't fix this with Finn, she'd have regrets all right.

If? No ifs. She *was* going to fix this. There was no other possible outcome.

It was then that it happened, her steering wheel started to vibrate—along with the rest of the car—as the telltale sound of *whap whap whap whap* echoed from outside.

"No. No, no, no, no."

Brie pulled off to the side of the road and got out of her car. She rounded to the back to see that she very clearly had a flat tire. The kind that not even Fix-a-Flat could help, which was all she had as MINI Coopers did not have spare tires.

And in that moment she was now regretting most of her life choices.

"Shit."

She went back to the front seat, leaning over the console and searching for her phone in her purse. She hadn't powered it up since she'd turned it off the day before, she'd been so focused on just getting back to Finn.

When it finally got to the home screen—it took for freaking ever—there was so signal.

"*Dammit!*"

OK, so she could either stand there and wait for someone to drive by…or start walking. Luckily for her, it was towards the end of March and rather pleasant outside for a spring afternoon. She'd just made the decision to start walking when she spotted a car coming around the bend about a mile off.

"Well, that was luck."

But as the car got closer she realized it was a truck…a big black truck, and that Finn was behind the wheel.

* * *

Finn stared through the windshield for a full ten seconds—or was it ten minutes?—trying to convince himself what he was seeing was real. That Brie was in fact standing in front of him wearing a little white dress and hot pink Converse sneakers.

After that morning's conversation with Shep, Finn had gone home, packed another bag, swung by Bethelda's house to find the boxes Brie had shipped there, and got the address of her friend in North Carolina.

He was going to go after Brie. Find her.

Turned out he didn't have to go very far. Just ten miles up the road.

Brie's mouth had fallen open in a startled "O" when she saw that it was him behind the wheel of the truck. Well, she wasn't the only one who was surprised.

He unbuckled his seat belt and got out, slamming the door behind him as he took a few steps forward. She was probably a good five yards away from him.

"Hi."

He had to swallow down the response that burned his throat. He wanted to yell *What the fuck, Brie?* But somewhere in the back of his mind, he knew that wasn't the best idea. "Hi? I get a *hi*? Do you have any idea what the last twenty-four hours have been like for me?"

"I'm sorry, Finn. I messed up. You can't possibly know how much I know that."

"Why? Why did you leave?"

She took a deep breath through her nose before she let it out through her mouth in a rush. "I found these journals. Bethelda's journals from when she was thirteen until now. Each one was a year in her life. And then I got to the one where she met my father." Her voice broke when she got to that part, and she closed her eyes, turning her head away for a moment. When she looked back to him there were tears on her cheeks.

That was it, that was all it took for him to move the remaining distance to her.

He reached up to her face, cradling her jaw with his palm and running his thumb across her wet cheek. She leaned into his touch and let out another breath, like his touch eased her.

"You found out who your father was?"

"Yes." She nodded. "His name was Daniel Emmanuel Fernandez. He called Bethelda Betts, and he loved her."

"What happened?"

"He died. He died and it destroyed her. She was about four months pregnant when it happened. She couldn't keep me because she couldn't look at me. *I* reminded her of him. And if she couldn't have him, she didn't want anything." She blinked again and more tears fell from her eyes. "So, she became the way she was. For her, being alone meant you didn't lose anyone."

"Why didn't you tell me you found the journals? I would've come back."

"I know you would've. You know, when I decided to come down here, for the funeral, I thought it was something I was going to have to deal with all on my own. And then I walked into that bar, and I met you." She gave him a sad smile as she reached up and touched his jaw with her fingertips, trailing them across the scruff of his beard.

"When I found the journals, I went back to that old mentality. I needed to do it on my own, stand on my own without anyone's help. Then it became all too much for me to handle and I ran. I ran because I saw how thoroughly love destroyed Bethelda and it scared me more than anything."

"Why?"

"Because I was in love with you...I *am* in love with you."

At her words, at her declaration, Finn pulled her against his body and covered her mouth with his. He kissed her like his life depended on it. Actually, his life *did* depend on it.

"I love you, Brie," he whispered across her lips. "Love you more than I've loved anyone."

"I'm so sorry that I left. I won't ever do it again. I swear to you. I don't want to do things on my own, Finn. I don't want to be alone."

Finn moved his hands into her hair, tilting her head back as he looked into her golden brown eyes. "What do you want?"

"You."

Epilogue

No Better Love

Sometime later…

Clean, crisp sunshine streamed through the bedroom windows. Finn had forgotten to close the blinds the night before, not all that surprisingly as he'd been thoroughly distracted with making love to Brie.

She was curled into his side that morning, her head on his chest as she slept. Her hair was a riot of tangled curls on the pillow. She was still the most beautiful woman he'd ever seen. No matter how many times he woke up with her in his arms, he still considered it one of the greatest gifts of his life.

He didn't want to wake her, *really* didn't want to disturb the peaceful expression on her face, but it was Sunday and they needed to have breakfast before they went to church.

"Baby," he whispered, brushing his fingers across her cheek.

"Hmm," she hummed, slowly blinking her eyes open.

"We have to start the day."

"I don't want to." She burrowed in closer to him, pressing her lips to his chest. "Let's just stay in bed all day."

Finn laughed...he couldn't help it. "You know that isn't going to happen."

She sighed, her breath moving out and over his skin. "I do know that. We probably only have another sixty seconds."

"My guess is thirty."

It was more like twenty seconds before the sound of feet running down the hallway echoed through the house. A moment later the bedroom door burst open and a thirty-six-pound ball of terror—along with his constant canine companion Frankie—burst into the room.

Owen launched himself onto the bed, landing on Brie and Finn with a squeal of laughter. "Time to get up!"

Finn grabbed his son and rolled so that Owen was on his back, limbs flailing as Finn tickled him.

"No, Daddy. Nooooo!" Owen giggled harder.

Finn leaned down and blew a raspberry on Owen's stomach, another high-pitched squeal of delight filling the room. The tickle torture stopped a moment later and Finn lay back down, Owen climbing up on his father's chest.

"Morning." He gave each of his parents a big, loud, smacking kiss on the cheek before he sat up again. "Can we have pancakes? With chocolate chips? And whipped cream? Puh-leeaseee."

"Only because you asked so nicely. You going to help Daddy make them?" Brie grabbed Owen's foot and tickled the bottom.

"Yes." He grinned, his golden brown eyes lighting up.

"Deal," Finn agreed, getting out of bed and padding over to his dresser in a pair of boxers. He grabbed a T-shirt and pulled it on before he grabbed Owen's outstretched hand.

"Mommy." He looked over his shoulder when they got to the door. "Meet you downstairs?"

"Give me five minutes."

"OK." He nodded before he started walking again.

When Finn got to the baby gate at the top of the stairs, he saw Lo patiently waiting. The cat always slept with Owen and Frankie in Owen's room, but unlike his son and dog, the cat did not take part in the morning barrage into his and Brie's room.

Finn unlatched the gate and Lo and Frankie headed down while Finn helped Owen conquer the stairs one step at a time. He let Frankie outside before they went into the kitchen and he started the coffeepot, which was always priority number one. Owen watched his father measure out the grinds, telling him about the dream he'd had with Captain America and Iron Man.

Once the coffee was brewing, they headed for the pantry, Owen looking up at the shelves that were just out of his reach. None of the pancake-making ingredients were within a three-year-old's arm's length anymore. They'd learned that lesson the hard way, finding a box of mix scattered around the kitchen like snow one morning.

Finn lifted his son in the air and put him on his hip. "What do we need?"

"This." Owen reached out and touched the box of pancake mix. "And this." He jabbed at the bag of chocolate chips.

Finn handed Owen the bag before he set him back on the ground. Finn grabbed the box and moved back into the kitchen just as Brie walked in, her hair thrown up in a messy bun on top of her head. She was wearing her dark purple bathrobe and carrying their eleven-month-old daughter Annabella on her hip.

The name was a combination of Anastasia (Brie's mother's name), Brie, and Ella.

The little girl would never get to meet her great-grandmother. Ella had passed away a few months after Finn and Brie had gotten married. It had been exactly seven years to the day that Owen had died.

What Annabella did get was her grandmother's sapphire-blue eyes…Finn's sapphire-blue eyes.

"Morning, sunshine." He leaned in and gave his daughter a kiss on the cheek. She giggled and gave him a big smile.

A light scratch at the back door signaled that Frankie wanted to come inside. "I got it!" Owen said as he bolted for the door.

When the dog came back inside, Owen started playing with her. Finn was fine with that. It gave him a chance to get some coffee.

"You know," he started as he pulled the creamer out of the fridge and set it on the counter. "I had a dream about you last night."

"What dream was that?" Brie looked up from where she was getting Annabella settled in the high chair.

"That day you came back to Mirabelle. That day you came back to me."

Brie straightened before she slowly crossed over to him. She rested her hands on his chest as she looked up at him. "It's where I was supposed to be. With you. Always with you."

Finn leaned down and pressed a kiss to her lips, knowing there was no better love than what she'd given him. His family. This life. Her.

Missing Mirabelle? Don't fret. See the next page for an excerpt from UNDONE and see how Shannon Richard's A Country Road series began!

Available now

Chapter One

Short Fuses and a Whole Lot of Sparks

Bethelda Grimshaw was a snot-nosed wench. She was an evil, mean-spirited, vindictive, horrible human being.

Paige should've known. She should've known the instant she'd walked into that office and sat down. Bethelda Grimshaw had a malevolent stench radiating off her, kind of like road kill in ninety-degree weather. The interview, if it could even be called that, had been a complete waste of time.

"She didn't even read my résumé," Paige said, slamming her hand against the steering wheel as she pulled out of the parking lot of the Mirabelle Information Center.

No, Bethelda had barely even looked at said résumé before she'd set it down on the desk and leaned back in her chair, appraising Paige over her cat's-eye glasses.

"So you're the *infamous* Paige Morrison," Bethelda had said, raising a perfectly plucked, bright red eyebrow. "You've caused *quite* a stir since you came to town."

Quite a stir?

Okay, so there had been that incident down at the Piggly

Wiggly, but that hadn't been Paige's fault. Betty Whitehurst might seem like a sweet, little old lady but in reality she was as blind as a bat and as vicious as a shrew. Betty drove her shopping cart like she was racing in the Indy 500, which was an accomplishment, as she barely cleared the handle. She'd slammed her cart into Paige, who in turn fell into a display of cans. Paige had been calm for all of about five seconds before Betty had started screeching at her about watching where she was going.

Paige wasn't one to take things lying down covered in cans of creamed corn, so she'd calmly explained to Betty that she *had* been watching where she was going. "Calmly" being that Paige had started yelling and the store manager had to get involved to quiet everyone down.

Yeah, Paige didn't deal very well with certain types of people. Certain types being evil, mean-spirited, vindictive, horrible human beings. And Bethelda Grimshaw was quickly climbing to the top of that list.

"As it turns out," Bethelda had said, pursing her lips in a patronizing pout, "we already filled the position. I'm afraid there was a mistake in having you come down here today."

"When?"

"Excuse me?" Bethelda had asked, her eyes sparkling with glee.

"When did you fill the position?" Paige had repeated, trying to stay calm.

"Last week."

Really? So the phone call Paige had gotten that morning to confirm the time of the interview had been a mistake?

This was the eleventh job interview she'd gone on in the last two months. And it had most definitely been the worst. It hadn't even been an interview. She'd been set up; she just didn't understand why. But she hadn't been about to ask that question out loud. So instead of flying off the handle and losing the last bit of restraint she had, Paige had calmly gotten up from the chair and left without making a scene. The whole thing was a freaking joke, which fit perfectly for the current theme of Paige's life.

Six months ago, Paige had been living in Philadelphia. She'd had a good job in the art department of an advertising agency. She'd shared a tiny two-bedroom apartment above a coffee shop with her best friend, Abby Fields. And she'd had Dylan, a man who she'd been very much in love with.

And then the rug got pulled out from under her and she'd fallen flat on her ass.

First off, Abby got a job at an up-and-coming PR firm. Which was good news, and Paige had been very excited for her, except the job was in Washington, DC, which Paige was not excited about. Then, before Paige could find a new roommate, she'd lost her job. The advertising agency was bought out and she was in the first round of cuts. Without a job, she couldn't renew her lease, and was therefore homeless. So she'd moved in with Dylan. It was always supposed to be a temporary thing, just until Paige could find another job and get on her feet again.

But it never happened.

Paige had tried for two months and found nothing, and then the real bomb hit. She was either blind or just distracted by everything else that was going on, but either way, she never saw it coming.

Paige had been with Dylan for about a year and she'd really thought he'd been the one. Okay, he tended to be a bit of a snob when it came to certain things. For example, wine. Oh was he ever a wine snob, rather obnoxious about it really. He would always swirl it around in his glass, take a sip, sniff, and then take another loud sip, smacking his lips together.

He was also a snob about books. Paige enjoyed reading the classics, but she also liked reading romance, mystery, and fantasy. Whenever she would curl up with one of her books, Dylan tended to give her a rather patronizing look and shake his head.

"Reading fluff again I see," he would always say.

Yeah, she didn't miss *that* at all. Or the way he would roll his eyes when she and Abby would quote movies and TV shows to each other. Or how he'd never liked her music and flat-out refused to dance with her. Which had always been frustrating because Paige loved to dance. But despite all of that, she'd loved him. Loved the way he would run his fingers through his hair when he was distracted, loved his big goofy grin, and loved the way his glasses would slide down his nose.

But the thing was, he hadn't loved her.

One night, he'd come back to his apartment and sat Paige down on the couch. Looking back on it, she'd been an idiot, because there was a small part of her that thought he was actually about to propose.

"Paige," he'd said, sitting down on the coffee table and grabbing her hands. "I know that this was supposed to be a temporary thing, but weeks have turned into months. Living with you has brought a lot of things to light."

It was wrong, everything about that moment was *all wrong*. She could tell by the look in his eyes, by the tone of his voice, by the way he said *Paige* and *light*. In that moment she'd known exactly where he was going, and it wasn't anywhere with her. He wasn't proposing. He was breaking up with her.

She'd pulled her hands out of his and shrank back into the couch.

"This," he'd said, gesturing between the two of them, "was never going to go further than where we are right now."

And that was the part where her ears had started ringing.

"At one point I thought I might love you, but I've realized I'm not *in* love with you," he'd said, shaking his head. "I feel like you've thought this was going to go further, but the truth is I'm never going to marry you. Paige, you're not the one. I'm tired of pretending. I'm tired of putting in the effort for a relationship that isn't going anywhere else. It's not worth it to me."

"You mean I'm not worth it," she'd said, shocked.

"Paige, you deserve to be with someone who wants to make the effort, and I deserve to be with someone who I'm willing to make the effort for. It's better that we end this now, instead of delaying the inevitable."

He'd made it sound like he was doing her a favor, like he had her best interests at heart.

But all she'd heard was *You're not worth it* and *I'm not in love with you*. And those were the words that kept repeating in her head, over and over and over again.

Dylan had told her he was going to go stay with one of his friends for the week. She'd told him she'd be out before the end of the next day. She'd spent the entire night packing up her stuff. Well, packing and crying and drinking two entire bottles of the prick's wine.

Paige didn't have a lot of stuff. Most of the furniture from her and Abby's apartment had been Abby's. Everything that Paige owned had fit into the back of her Jeep and the U-Haul trailer that she'd rented the first thing the following morning.

She'd loaded up and gotten out of there before four o'clock in the afternoon.

She'd stayed the night in a hotel room just outside of Philadelphia, where she'd promptly passed out. She'd been exhausted after her marathon packing, which was good because it was harder for a person to feel beyond pathetic in her sleep. No, that was what the following eighteen-hour drive had been reserved for.

Jobless, homeless, and brokenhearted, Paige had nowhere else to go but home to her parents. The problem was, there was no *home* anymore. The house in Philadelphia that Paige had grown up in was no longer her parents'. They'd sold it and retired to a little town in the South.

Mirabelle, Florida: population five thousand.

There was roughly the same amount of people in the six hundred square miles of Mirabelle as there were in half a square mile of Philadelphia. Well, unless the mosquitoes were counted as residents.

People who thought that Florida was all sunshine and sand were sorely mistaken. It did have its fair share of beautiful beaches. The entire southeast side of Mirabelle was the Gulf of Mexico. But about half of the town was made up of water. And all of that water, combined with the humidity that plagued the area, created the perfect breeding ground for mosquitoes. Otherwise known as tiny, blood-sucking villains that loved to bite the crap out of Paige's legs.

Paige had visited her parents a couple of times over the last couple of years, but she'd never been in love with Mirabelle like her parents were. And she still wasn't. She'd spent a month moping around her parents' house. Again, she was pathetic enough to believe that maybe, just maybe, Dylan would call her and tell her that he'd been wrong. That he missed her. That he loved her.

He never called, and Paige realized he was never going to. That was when Paige resigned herself to the fact that she had to move on with her life. So she'd started looking for a job.

Which had proved to be highly unsuccessful.

Paige had been living in Mirabelle for three months now. Three long miserable months where nothing had gone right. Not one single thing.

And as that delightful thought crossed her mind, she noticed that her engine was smoking. Great white plumes of steam escaped from the hood of her Jeep Cherokee.

"You've got to be kidding me," she said as she pulled off to the side of the road and turned the engine off. "Fan-freaking-tastic."

Paige grabbed her purse and started digging around in the infinite abyss, searching for her cell phone. She sifted through old receipts, a paperback book, her wallet, lip gloss, a nail file, gum…*ah*, cell phone. She pressed speed dial for her father. She held the phone against her ear while she leaned over and searched for her shoes that she'd thrown on the floor of the passenger side. As her hand closed over one of her black wedges, the phone beeped in her ear and disconnected. She sat up and held her phone out, staring at the display screen in disbelief.

No service.

"This has to be some sick, twisted joke," she said, banging her head down on the steering wheel. No service on her cell phone shouldn't have been that surprising; there were plenty of dead zones around Mirabelle. Apparently there was a lack of cell phone towers in this little piece of purgatory.

Paige resigned herself to the fact that she was going to have to walk to find civilization, or at least a bar of service on her cell phone. She went in search of her other wedge, locating it under the passenger seat.

The air conditioner had been off for less than two minutes, and it was already starting to warm up inside the Jeep. It was going to be a long, hot walk. Paige grabbed a hair tie from the gearshift, put her long brown hair up into a messy bun, and opened the door to the sweltering heat.

I hate *this godforsaken place.*

Paige missed Philadelphia. She missed her friends, her apartment with its rafters and squeaky floors. She missed having a job, missed having a paycheck, missed buying shoes. And even though she hated it, she still missed Dylan. Missed his dark shaggy hair, and the way he would nibble on her lower lip when they kissed. She even missed his humming when he cooked.

She shook her head and snapped back to the present. She might as well focus on the task at hand and stop thinking about what was no longer her life.

Paige walked for twenty minutes down the road to nowhere, not a single car passing her. By the time Paige got to Skeeter's Bait, Tackle, Guns, and Gas, she was sweating like nobody's business, her dress was sticking to her everywhere, and her feet were killing her. She had a nice blister on the back of her left heel.

She pushed the door open and was greeted with the smell of fish mixed with bleach, making her stomach turn. At least the air conditioner was cranked to full blast. There was a huge stuffed turkey sitting on the counter. The fleshy red thing on its neck looked like the stuff nightmares were made of, and the wall behind the register was covered in mounted fish. She really didn't get the whole "dead animal as a trophy" motif that the South had going on.

There was a display on the counter that had tiny little bottles that looked like energy drinks.

NEW AND IMPROVED SCENT. GREAT FOR ATTRACTING THE PERFECT GAME.

She picked up one of the tiny bottles and looked at it. It was doe urine.

She took a closer look at the display. They apparently also had the buck urine variety. She looked at the bottle in her hand, trying to grasp why people would cover themselves in this stuff. Was hunting really worth smelling like an animal's pee?

"Can I help you?"

The voice startled Paige and she looked up into the face of a very large balding man, his apron covered in God only knew what. She dropped the tiny bottle she had in her hand. It fell to the ground. The cap smashed on the tile floor and liquid poured out everywhere.

It took a total of three seconds for the smell to punch her in the nose. It had to be the most fowl scent she'd ever inhaled.

Oh crap. Oh crap, oh crap, oh crap.

She was just stellar at first impressions these days.

"I'm so sorry," she said, trying not to gag. She took a step back from the offending puddle and looked up at the man.

His arms were folded across his chest and he frowned at her, saying nothing.

"Do you, uh, have something I can clean this up with?" she asked nervously.

"You're not from around here," he said, looking at her with his deadpan stare. It wasn't a question. It was a statement, one that she got whenever she met someone new. One that she was so sick and tired of she could scream. Yeah, all of the remorse she'd felt over spilling that bottle drained from her.

In Philadelphia, Paige's bohemian style was normal, but in Mirabelle her big earrings, multiple rings, and loud clothing tended to get her noticed. Her parents' neighbor, Mrs. Forns, thought that Paige was trouble, which she complained about on an almost daily basis.

"You know that marijuana is still illegal," Mrs. Forns had said the other night, standing on her parents' porch, and lecturing Paige's mother. "And I won't hesitate to call the authorities if I see your hippie daughter growing anything suspicious or doing any other illegal activities."

Denise Morrison, ever the queen of politeness, had just smiled. "You have nothing to be concerned about."

"But she's doing *something* in that shed of yours in the backyard."

The *something* that Paige did in the shed was paint. She'd converted it into her art studio, complete with ceiling fan.

"Don't worry, Mrs. Forns," Paige had said, sticking her head over her mother's shoulder. "I'll wait to have my orgies on your bingo nights. Is that on Tuesdays or Wednesdays?"

"Paige!" Denise had said as she'd shoved Paige back into the house and closed the door in her face.

Five minutes later, Denise had come into the kitchen shaking her head.

"Really, Paige? You had to tell her that you're having *orgies* in the backyard?"

Paige's father, Trevor Morrison, chuckled as he went through the mail at his desk.

"You need to control your temper and that smart mouth of yours," Denise had said.

"You know what you should start doing?" Trevor said, looking up with a big grin. "You should grow oregano in pots on the window sill and then throw little dime bags into her yard."

"Trevor, don't encourage her harassing that woman. Paige, she's a little bit older, very set in her ways, and a tad bit nosey."

"She needs to learn to keep her nose on her side of the fence," Paige had said.

"Don't let her bother you."

"That's easier said than done."

"Well then, maybe you should practice holding your tongue."

"Yes, mother, I'll get right on that."

So, as Paige stared at the massive man in front of her, whom she assumed to be Skeeter, she pursed her lips and held back the smart-ass retort that was on the tip of her tongue.

Be polite, she heard her mother's voice in her head say. *You just spilled animal pee all over his store. And you need to use his phone.*

"No," Paige said, pushing her big sunglasses up her nose and into her hair. "My car broke down and I don't have any cell phone service. I was wondering if I could use your phone to call a tow truck."

"I'd call King's if I were you. They're the best," he said as he ripped a piece of receipt paper off the cash register and grabbed a pen with a broken plastic spoon taped to the top. He wrote something down and pushed the paper across the counter.

"Thank you. I can clean that up first," she said, pointing to the floor.

"I got it. I'd hate for you to get those hands of yours dirty," he said, moving the phone to her side of the counter.

She just couldn't win.

* * *

Brendan King leaned against the front bumper of Mr. Thame's minivan. He was switching out the old belt and replacing it with a new one when his grandfather stuck his head out of the office.

"Brendan," Oliver King said. "A car broke down on Buckland Road. It's Paige Morrison, Trevor and Denise Morrison's daughter. She said the engine was smoking. She had to walk to Skeeter's to use the phone. I told her you'd pick her up so she didn't have to walk back."

Oliver King didn't look his seventy years. His salt-and-pepper hair was still thick and growing only on the top of his head, and not out of his ears. He had a bit of a belly, but he'd had that for the last twenty years and it wasn't going anywhere. He'd opened King's Auto forty-three years ago, when he was twenty-seven. Now, he mainly worked behind the front counter, due to the arthritis in his hands and back. But it was a good thing because King's Auto was one of only a handful of auto shops in the county. They were always busy, so they needed a constant presence running things out of the shop.

Including Brendan and his grandfather, there were four full-time mechanics and two part-time kids who were still in high school and who worked in the garage. Part of the service that

King's provided was towing, and Brendan was the man on duty on Mondays. And oh was he ever so happy he was on duty today.

Paige Morrison was the new girl in town. Her parents had moved down from Pennsylvania when they'd retired about two years ago, and Paige had moved in with them three months ago. Brendan had yet to meet her but he'd most definitely seen her. You couldn't really miss her as she jogged around town, with her very long legs, in a wide variety of the brightest and shortest shorts he'd ever seen in his life. His favorite pair had by far been the hot-pink pair, but the zebra-print ones came in a very close second.

He'd also heard about her. People had a lot to say about her more-than-*interesting* style. It was rumored that she had a bit of a temper and a pretty mouth that said whatever it wanted. Not that Brendan took a lot of stock in gossip. He'd wait to reserve his own judgment.

"Got it," Brendan said, pulling his gloves off and sticking them in his back pocket. "Tell Randall this still needs new spark plugs," he said, pointing to the minivan and walking into the office.

"I will." Oliver nodded and handed Brendan the keys to the tow truck.

Brendan grabbed two waters from the mini-fridge and his sunglasses from the desk and headed off into the scorching heat. It was a hot one, ninety-eight degrees, but the humidity made it feel like one hundred and three. He flipped his baseball cap so that the bill would actually give him some cover from the August sun and when he got into the tow truck he cranked the air as high as it would go.

It took him about fifteen minutes to get to Skeeter's and

when he pulled up into the gravel parking lot, the door to the little shop opened and Brendan couldn't help but smile.

Paige Morrison's mile-long legs were shooting out of the sexiest shoes he'd ever seen. She was also wearing a flowing yellow dress that didn't really cover her amazing legs but did hug her chest and waist, and besides the two skinny straps at her shoulders, her arms were completely bare. Massive sunglasses covered her eyes and her dark brown hair was piled on top of her head.

There was no doubt about it; she was beautiful all right.

Brendan put the truck in park and hopped out.

"Ms. Morrison?" he asked even though he already knew who she was.

"Paige," she corrected, stopping in front of him. She was probably five foot ten or so, but her shoes added about three inches, making her just as tall as him. If he weren't wearing his work boots she would've been taller than him.

"I'm Brendan King," he said, sticking his hand out to shake hers. Her hand was soft and warm. He liked how it felt in his. He also liked the freckles that were sprinkled across her high cheekbones and straight, pert nose.

"I'm about a mile up the road," she said, letting go of his hand and pointing in the opposite direction that he'd come.

"Not the most sensible walking shoes," he said, eyeing her feet. The toes that peeked out of her shoes were bright red, and a thin band of silver wrapped around the second toe on her right foot. He looked back up to see her arched eyebrows come together for a second before she took a deep breath.

"Thanks for the observation," she said, walking past him and heading for the passenger door.

Well, this was going to be fun.

* * *

Stupid jerk.

Not the most sensible walking shoes, Paige repeated in her head.

Well, no shit, Sherlock.

Paige sat in the cab of Brendan's tow truck, trying to keep her temper in check. Her feet were killing her, and she really wanted to kick off her shoes. But she couldn't do that in front of him because then he would *know* that her feet were killing her.

"I'm guessing the orange Jeep is yours?" Brendan asked as it came into view.

"Another outstanding observation," she mumbled under her breath.

"I'm sorry?"

"Yes, it's mine," she said, trying to hide her sarcasm.

"Well, at least the engine isn't smoking anymore," he said as he pulled in behind it and jumped out of the truck. Paige grabbed her keys from her purse and followed, closing the door behind her.

He stopped behind the back of her Jeep for a moment, studying the half a dozen stickers that covered her bumper and part of her back window.

She had one that said MAKE ART NOT WAR in big blue letters, another said LOVE with a peace sign in the *O*. There was also a sea turtle, an owl with reading glasses, the Cat in the Hat, and her favorite that said I LOVE BIG BOOKS AND I CANNOT LIE.

He shook his head and laughed, walking to the front of the Jeep.

"What's so funny?" she asked, catching up to his long stride and standing next to him.

"Keys?" he asked, holding out his hand.

She put them in his palm but didn't let go.

"What's so funny?" she repeated.

"Just that you're clearly not from around here." He smiled, closing his hand over hers.

Brendan had a southern accent, not nearly as thick as some of the other people's in town, and a wide cocky smile that she really hated, but only because she kind of liked it. She also kind of liked the five o'clock shadow that covered his square jaw. She couldn't see anything above his chiseled nose, as half of his face was covered by his sunglasses and the shadow from his grease-stained baseball cap, but she could tell his smile reached all the way up to his eyes.

He was most definitely physically fit, filling out his shirt and pants with wide biceps and thighs. His navy blue button-up shirt had short sleeves, showing off his tanned arms that were covered in tiny blond hairs.

God, he was attractive. But he was also pissing her off.

"I am so sick of everyone saying that," she said, ripping her hand out of his. "Is it such a bad thing to not be from around here?"

"No," he said, his mouth quirking. "It's just very obvious that you're not."

"Would I fit in more if I had a bumper sticker that said MY OTHER CAR IS A TRACTOR or one that said IF YOU'RE NOT CONSERVATIVE YOU JUST AREN'T WORTH IT, or what about WHO NEEDS LITERACY WHEN YOU CAN SHOOT THINGS? What if I had a gun rack mounted on the back window or if I used buck piss as perfume to attract a husband? Would those things make me fit in?" she finished, folding her arms across her chest.

"No, I'd say you could start with not being so judgmental though," he said with a sarcastic smirk.

"Excuse me?"

"Ma'am, you just called everyone around here gun-toting, illiterate rednecks who like to participate in bestiality. Insulting people really isn't a way to fit in," he said, shaking his head. "I would also refrain from spreading your liberal views to the masses, as politics are a bit of a hot-button topic around here. And if you want to attract a husband, you should stick with wearing doe urine, because that attracts only males. The buck urine attracts both males and females." He stopped and looked her up and down with a slow smile. "But maybe you're into that sort of thing."

"Yeah, well, everyone in this town thinks that I'm an amoral, promiscuous pothead. And you," she said, shoving her finger into his chest, "aren't any better. People make snap judgments about me before I even open my mouth. And just so you know, *I'm not even a liberal*," she screamed as she jabbed her finger into his chest a couple of times. She took a deep breath and stepped back, composing herself. "So maybe I would be *nice* if people would be just a little bit *nice* to me."

"I'm quite capable of being nice to people who deserve it. Can I look at your car now, or would you like to yell at me some more?"

"Be my guest," she said, glaring at him as she moved out of his way.

He unlocked the Jeep and popped the hood. As he moved

to the front he pulled off his baseball cap and wiped the top of his head with his hand. Paige glimpsed his short, dirty-blond hair before he put the hat on backward. As he moved around in her engine his shirt pulled tight across his back and shoulders. He twisted off the cap to something and stuck it in his pocket. Then he walked back to his truck and grabbed a jug from a metal box on the side. He came back and poured the liquid into something in the engine and after a few seconds it gushed out of the bottom.

"Your radiator is cracked," he said, grabbing the cap out of his pocket and screwing it back on. "I'm going to have to tow this back to the shop to replace it."

"How much?"

"For everything? We're looking at four maybe five hundred."

"Just perfect," she mumbled.

"Would you like a ride? Or were you planning on showing those shoes more of the countryside?"

"I'll take the ride."

* * *

Paige was quiet the whole time Brendan loaded her Jeep onto the truck. Her arms were folded under her perfect breasts and she stared at him with her full lips bunched in a scowl. Even pissed off she was stunning, and God, that mouth of hers. He really wanted to see it with an actual smile on it. He was pretty sure it would knock him on his ass.

Speaking of asses, seeing her smile probably wasn't likely at the moment. True, he had purposefully egged her on, but he couldn't resist going off on her when she'd let loose her colorful interpretations of the people from the area. A lot of them were true, but there was a difference between making fun of your own people and having an outsider make fun of them. But still, according to her, the people around here hadn't exactly been nice to her.

Twenty minutes later, with Paige's Jeep on the back of the tow truck, they were on their way to the shop. Brendan glanced over at her as he drove. She was looking out the window with her back to him. Her shoulders were stiff and she looked like she'd probably had enough stress before her car had decided to die on her.

Brendan looked back at the road and cleared his throat.

"I'm sorry about what I said back there."

Out of the corner of his eye he saw her shift in her seat and he could feel her eyes on him.

"Thank you. I should have kept my mouth shut too. I just haven't had the best day."

"Why?" he asked, glancing over at her again.

Her body was angled toward him, but her arms were still folded across her chest like a shield. He couldn't help but glance down and see that her dress was slowly riding up her thighs. She had nice thighs, soft but strong. They would be good for... well, a lot of things.

He quickly looked back at the road, thankful he was wearing sunglasses.

"I've been trying to get a job. Today I had an interview, except it wasn't much of an interview."

"What was it?" he asked.

"A setup."

"A setup for what?"

"That *is* the question," she said bitterly.

"Huh?" he asked, looking at her again.

"I'm assuming you know who Bethelda Grimshaw is?"

Brendan's blood pressure had a tendency to rise at the mere mention of that name. Knowing that Bethelda had a part in Paige's current mood had Brendan's temper flaring instantly.

"What did she do?" he asked darkly.

Paige's eyebrows raised a fraction at his tone. She stared at him for a second before she answered. "There was a job opening at the Mirabelle Information Center to take pictures for the brochures and the local businesses for their Web site. They filled the position last week, something that Mrs. Grimshaw failed to mention when she called this morning to confirm my interview."

"She's looking for her next story."

"What?"

"Bethelda Grimshaw is Mirabelle's resident gossip," Brendan said harshly as he looked back to the road. "She got fired from the newspaper a couple of years ago because of the trash she wrote. Now she has a blog to spread her crap around."

"And she wants to write about me? Why?"

"I can think of a few reasons."

"What's that supposed to mean?" she asked, her voice going up an octave or two.

"Your ability to fly off the handle. Did you give her something to write about?" he asked, raising an eyebrow as he spared a glance at her.

"No," she said, bunching her full lips together. "I saved my freak-out for you."

"I deserved it. I wasn't exactly nice to you," Brendan said, shifting his hands down the steering wheel.

"You were a jerk."

Brendan came to a stop at a stop sign and turned completely in his seat to face Paige. Her eyebrows rose high over her sunglasses and she held her breath.

"I was, and I'm sorry," he said, putting every ounce of sincerity into his words.

"It's...I forgive you," she said softly and nodded her head.

Brendan turned back to the intersection and made a right. Paige was silent for a few moments, but he could feel her gaze on him as if she wanted to say something.

"What?"

"Why does buck urine attract males and females?"

Brendan couldn't help but smile.

"Bucks like to fight each other," he said, looking at her.

"Oh." She nodded and leaned back in her seat staring out the front window.

"You thirsty?" Brendan asked as he grabbed one of the waters in the cup holder and held it out to her.

"Yes, thank you," she said, grabbing it and downing half of the bottle.

"Who were the other interviews with?" Brendan asked, grabbing the other bottle for himself. He twisted the cap off and threw it into the cup holder.

"Landingham Printing and Design. Mrs. Landingham said I wouldn't be a good fit. Which is completely false because the program they use is one that I've used before."

Now he couldn't help but laugh.

"Uh, Paige, I can tell you right now why you didn't get that job. Mrs. Landingham didn't want you around Mr. Landingham."

"What?" she said, sitting up in her seat again. "What did she think I was going to do, steal her husband? I don't make plays on married men. Or men in their forties for that matter."

"Did you wear something like what you're wearing now to the interview?" he asked, looking at her and taking another eyeful of those long legs.

"I wore a black blazer with this. It's just so hot outside that I took it off."

"Maybe you should try wearing pants next time, and flats," he said before he took a sip of water.

"What's wrong with this dress?" she asked, looking down at herself. "It isn't that short."

"Sweetheart, with those legs, anything looks short."

"Don't call me sweetheart. And it isn't my fault I'm tall."

"No, it isn't, but people think the way they think."

"So southern hospitality only goes so far when people think you're a whore."

"Hey, I didn't say that. I was just saying that your legs are long without those shoes that you're currently wearing. With them, you're pretty damn intimidating."

"Let's stop talking about my legs."

"Fine." He shrugged, looking back to the road. "But it is a rather visually stimulating conversation."

"Oh no. You are *not* allowed to flirt with me."

"Why not?"

"You were mean to me. I do *not* flirt with mean men."

"I can be nice," he said, turning to her and giving her a big smile.

"Stop it," she said, raising her eyebrows above her glasses in warning. "I mean it."

"So what about some of the other interviews? Who were they with?"

"Lindy's Frame Shop, that art gallery over on the beach—"

"Avenue Ocean?"

"Yeah, that one. And I also went to Picture Perfect. They all said I wasn't a good fit for one reason or another," she said dejected.

"Look, I'm really not one to get involved in town gossip. I've been on the receiving end my fair share of times and it isn't fun. But this is a small town, and everybody knows one another's business. Since you're new, you have no idea. Cynthia Bowers at Picture Perfect would've never hired you. Her husband has monogamy issues. The owner of Avenue Ocean, Mindy Trist, doesn't like anyone that's competition."

"Competition?"

Mindy Trist was a man-eater. Brendan knew this to be a fact because Mindy had been trying to get into his bed for years. He wasn't even remotely interested.

"You're prettier than she is."

Understatement of the year.

Paige was suddenly silent on her side of the truck.

"And as for Hurst and Marlene Lindy," Brendan continued, "they, uh, tend to be a little more conservative."

"Look," she said, snapping out of her silence.

Brendan couldn't help himself, her sudden burst of vehemence made him look at her again. If he kept this up he was going to drive into a ditch.

"I know I might appear to be some free-spirited hippie, but I'm really not. I'm moderate when it comes to politics," she said, holding up one finger. "I eat meat like it's nobody's business." Two fingers. "And I've never done drugs in my life." Three fingers.

"You don't have to convince me," he said, shaking his head. "So I'm sensing a pattern here with all of these jobs. Are you a photographer?"

"Yes, but I do graphic design and I paint."

"So a woman of many talents."

"I don't know about that," she said, shaking her head.

"Oh, I'm sure you have a lot of talent. It's probably proportional to the length of your legs."

"What did I tell you about flirting?" she asked seriously, but betrayed herself when the corner of her mouth quirked up.

"Look, Paige, don't let it get to you. Not everyone is all bad."

"So I've just been fortunate enough to meet everyone who's mean."

"You've met me."

"Yeah, well, the jury's still out on you."

"Then I guess I'll have to prove myself."

"I guess so," she said, leaning back in her seat. Her arms now rested in her lap, her shield coming down a little.

"I have a question," Brendan said, slowing down at another stop sign. "If you eat meat, why do you have such a problem with hunting?"

"It just seems a little barbaric. Hiding out in the woods to shoot Bambi and then mounting his head on a wall."

"Let me give you two scenarios."

"Okay."

"In scenario one, we have Bessie the cow. Bessie was born in a stall, taken away from her mother shortly after birth where she was moved to a pasture for a couple of years, all the while being injected with hormones and then shoved into a semi truck, where she was shipped off to be slaughtered. And I don't think that you even want me to get started on that process.

"In scenario two, we have Bambi. Bambi was born in the wilderness and wasn't taken away from his mother. He then found a mate, had babies, and one day was killed. He never saw it coming. Not only is Bambi's meat hormone free, but he also lived a happy life in the wild, with no fences.

"Now you tell me, which scenario sounds better: Being raised to be slaughtered, or living free where you might or might not be killed."

She was silent for a few moments before she sighed.

"Fine, you win. The second sounds better."

"Yeah, that's what I thought," Brendan said as he pulled into the parking lot of King's Auto. "How are you getting home?" he asked as he put the truck into park.

"I called my dad after I called you. He's here actually," she said, pointing to a black Chevy Impala.

They both got out of the truck and headed toward the auto shop. Brendan held the door open for Paige, shoving his sunglasses into his shirt pocket. His grandfather and a man who Brendan recognized as Paige's father stood up from their chairs as Brendan and Paige walked in.

Trevor Morrison was a tall man, maybe six foot four or six foot five. He had light reddish-brown wispy hair on his head and large glasses perched on his nose. And like his daughter, his face and arms were covered in freckles.

"Hi, Daddy," Paige said, pushing her glasses up her nose and into her hair.

Brendan immediately noticed the change in her voice. Her cautious demeanor vanished and her shoulders relaxed. He'd caught a glimpse of this in the truck, but not to this extent.

"Mr. Morrison," Brendan said, taking a step forward and sticking his hand out.

Trevor grabbed Brendan's hand firmly. "Brendan," he said, giving him a warm smile and nodding his head. Trevor let go of Brendan's hand and turned to his daughter. "Paige, this is Oliver King," he said, gesturing to Brendan's grandfather, who was standing behind his desk. "Oliver, this is my daughter, Paige."

"I haven't had the pleasure," Oliver said, moving out from behind his desk and sticking out his hand.

Paige moved forward past Brendan, her arm brushing his as she passed.

"It's nice to meet you, sir," she said, grabbing Oliver's hand.

Oliver nodded as he let go of Paige's hand and looked up at Brendan. "So what happened?"

Paige turned to look at Brendan too. It was the first time he'd gotten a full look at her face without her sunglasses on. She had long dark eyelashes that framed her large gray irises. It took him a second to remember how to speak. He cleared his throat and looked past her to the other two men.

"It's the radiator. I'm going to have to order a new one, so it's going to take a few days."

"That's fine," she said, shrugging her shoulders. "It's not like I have anywhere to go."

Trevor's face fell. "The interview didn't go well?"

"Nope," Paige said, shaking her head. The tension in her shoulders came back but she tried to mask it by pasting a smile on her face. He desperately wanted to see a genuine, full-on smile from her.

"Things haven't exactly gone Paige's way since she moved here," Trevor said.

"Oh, I think my bad luck started long before I moved here," she said, folding her arms across her chest. Every time she did that, it pushed her breasts up and it took everything in Brendan not to stare.

"I don't think it was Paige's fault," Brendan said and everyone turned to look at him. "It was with Bethelda Grimshaw," he said to Oliver.

"Oh," Oliver said, shaking his head ruefully. "Don't let anything she says get to you. She's a horrible hag."

Paige laughed and the sound of it did funny things to Brendan's stomach.

"Told you," Brendan said, looking at her. Paige turned to him, a small smile lingering on her lips and in her eyes.

God, she was beautiful.

"Things will turn around," Oliver said. "We'll call you with an estimate before we do anything to your car."

They said their good-byes and as Paige walked out with her father she gave Brendan one last look, her lips quirking up slightly before she shook her head and walked out the door.

"I don't believe any of that nonsense people are saying about her," Oliver said as they both watched Paige and her dad walk out. "She's lovely."

Lovely? Yeah, that wasn't exactly the word Brendan would have used to describe her.

Hot? Yes. *Fiery?* Absolutely.

"Yeah, she's something alright."

"Oh, don't tell me you aren't a fan of hers. Son, you barely took your eyes off her."

"I'm not denying she's beautiful." How could he? "I bet she's a handful though and she's got a temper on her, along with a smart mouth." But he sure did like that smart mouth.

"That's a bit of the pot calling the kettle black," Oliver said, raising one bushy eyebrow. "If all of her experiences in this town have been similar to what Bethelda dishes out, I'm not surprised she's turned on the defense. You know what it's like to be the center of less than unsavory gossip in this town. To have a lot of the people turn their backs on you and turn you into a pariah," Oliver said, giving Brendan a knowing look.

"I know," Brendan conceded. "She deserves a break."

"You should help her find a job."

"With who?"

"You'll think of something," Oliver said, patting Brendan on the shoulder before going back to his desk. "You always do."

Acknowledgments

I've never written *the end* when finishing any of my books. That's because for me there is no end when it comes to these stories. They live on inside of my head even after I've stopped writing them. That might sound a little crazy, but it is what it is.

That being said, I was slightly tempted to write it at the end of *Untold* as it's the last chapter in the Country Roads series. I know how much my readers love to get glimpses of past couples, so I tried to do all of them justice while tying up every loose end...which is why this book is the length that it is. I hope beyond hope it's a satisfying way for all of you to say good-bye.

I started this journey in November 2011 when I began writing *Undone*. Now, almost six years later, there are so many people I have to thank for getting me where I am. First, my parents who've supported me from the very start and are proud of what I've accomplished. And to my brothers, Ronald and Jonathan Richard, and their wives (the sisters I wasn't born with but was blessed with), Sammi and Julie Richard.

To my beta readers, and oh, how there have been a lot of you. Thank you for all of the time you've taken in reading these stories and helping me along the way. I'd like to especially thank Gloria Berry and Katie Crandall, who've lived with me at one point or another, and know how I am when on deadline…and still love me afterward.

To my agent, Sarah E. Younger. What else can I say that hasn't already been said? I wouldn't be here without you. Plain and simple. Thank you for taking a chance on me. And thank you to everyone at the Nancy Yost Literary Agency. All of you are amazing. And a shout out to Nicole Fischer, thank you for seeing something in my writing.

To all of my editors: Megha Parekh for the years you put into this series, Selina McLemore for fighting to sign me, Jessica Pierce for your kindness and patience, and Michele Bidelspach for coming in at the end and waving me back to home base. Also, to everyone at Grand Central who has put time and effort into these books. I had no idea where I was going with this series when it started, or how many books would come out of my head in the end. Thank you for sticking with me, letting me see this vision through, and supporting me the whole way. Also, Dear Art Department, I love all of my gorgeous covers.

Thank you to Amanda VanLaningham for answering all of my questions on adoptions. You were beyond patient and talked out every single scenario I threw at you…and there were a number of them.

To my friends, who lend a lot in the department of moral support and answer a plethora of random questions: Jessica Lemmon, Tara Wyatt, Katie Hotard, Amy Lipford, Katie Privett, Marina McCue, David McCue, and Michael Widener.

To everyone at My Favorite Books (which just so happens to be my favorite bookstore), especially Amanda Babcock. To all of the ladies over at Scandalicious Book Reviews, all of you are amazing. Lola, thank you for taking the time to give me tips and tricks with your mad graphics and design skills. Teena, thank you for being a loyal and dedicated reader. I always enjoy hearing your thoughts, and am so appreciative for your love of these books and my writing.

And back to Nikki Rushbrook, because there is more to be said. You are much more than a beta reader. You are a constant sounding board who has never let me down, never said you didn't have the time when I needed to talk something out, and has never led me (or my characters) astray. You dubbed Shep the Jackass Whisperer (which he totally is) and helped me push these books to where they should be. Thank you.

To all of my readers. Thank you for going on this journey with me in Mirabelle, Florida. I can't wait to start another one.

And, lastly, to my dog, Teddy. I adopted him in the middle of writing this book, and his puppy snuggles and sweet face are the best forms of stress relief a girl could ask for. Adopting him was one of the best decisions I've ever made.

About the Author

Shannon Richard grew up in the Florida Panhandle as the baby sister of two overly protective but loving brothers. She was raised by a more than somewhat eccentric mother, a self-proclaimed vocabularist who showed her how to get lost in a book, and a father who passed on his love for coffee and really loud music. She graduated from Florida State University with a BA in English literature and still lives in Tallahassee where she battles everyday life with writing, reading, and a rant every once in a while. OK, so the rants might happen on a regular basis. She's still waiting for her southern, scruffy, Mr. Darcy, and in the meantime writes love stories to indulge her overactive imagination. Oh, and she's a pretty big fan of the whimsy.

Learn more at:

http://shannonrichard.net/

Twitter: @shan_richard

Facebook: http://facebook.com/ShannonNRichard

CPSIA information can be obtained
at www.ICGtesting.com
Printed in the USA
LVOW12s0127090418
572752LV00001B/20/P